listening to Miles & Macero's *He Loved Him Madly* and crossing all thresholds with and through it, leaving every old belief system: rock, jazz, soul, Electro, HipHop, House, Acid, Drum'n'Bass, electronics, Techno and dub — forever.

The mayday signal of Black Atlantic Futurism is unrecognizability, as either Black or Music. Sonic Futurism doesn't locate you in tradition; instead it dislocates you from origins. It uproutes you by inducing a gulf crisis, a perceptual daze rendering today's sonic discontinuum immediately audible.

The Futurist producer can *not* be trusted with music's heritage. Realizing this, UK and US dance media spring forward, to maintain these traditions the producer always abandons. Media's role is to defend an *essence*, by warding off all possible infections: journalists become missionaries on behalf of HipHop; they battle for the soul of Techno.

Which is why at Century's End you tune into sensory frequencies undetectable to the happy tinnitus of good solid journalism. You are willingly mutated by intimate machines, abducted by audio into the populations of your bodies. Sound machines throw you onto the shores of the skin you're in. The hypersensual cyborg experiences herself as a galaxy of audiotactile sensations.

You are not censors but sensors, not aesthetes but kinaesthetes. You are sensationalists. You are the newest mutants incubated in womb-speakers. Your mother, your first sound. The bedroom, the party, the dancefloor, the rave: these are the labs where the 21st C nervous systems assemble themselves, the matrices of the Futurhythmachinic Discontinuum. The future is a much better guide to the present than the past. Be prepared, be ready to trade everything you know about the history of music for a single glimpse of its future.

It deserts forever the nauseating and bizarre ethic of 'redemption'.

AfroDiasporic Futurism has assembled itself along inhuman routes, and it takes artificial thought to reveal this. Such relief: jaws unclench, as conviction collapses.

Where crits of CyberCult still gather, 99.9% of them will lament the disembodiment of the human by technology. But machines *don't* distance you from your emotions, in fact quite the opposite. Sound machines make you feel *more* intensely, along a broader band of emotional spectra than ever before in the 20th Century.

Sonically speaking, the posthuman era is not one of disembodiment but the exact reverse: it's a *hyperembodiment*, via the Technics SL 1200. A non-sound scientist like Richard Dawkins 'talks very happily about cultural viruses,' argues Sadie Plant, 'but doesn't think that he himself is a viral contagion.' Migrating from the lab to the studio, Sonic Science not only talks about cultural viruses, it is itself a viral contagion. It's a sensational infection by the spread of what Ishmael Reed terms antiplagues.

Machine Music doesn't call itself science because it controls technology, but because music is the artform most thoroughly undermined and recombinated and reconfigured by technics. Scientists set processes in motion which swallow them up: the scientist's brain is caught up in the net. Acid's alien frequency modulation turns on its dj-producers Phuture and Sleezy D and begins to 'stab your brain' and 'disrupt thought patterns'.

Yet in magnifying such hitherto ignored intersections of sound and science fiction — the nexus this project terms Sonic Fiction or PhonoFiction — *More Brilliant* paradoxically ends up with a portrait of music today far *more* accurate than any realistic account has managed. This is because most recent accounts of Black Music — those which form the dominant humanist strain in the commemoration of Black Music, its official histories — are more than anything wish fulfilments: scenarios in which Acid never existed, in which Electronic Jazz never arrived, in which the Era of the Rhythmachine *never happened*.

By contrast, *More Brilliant* is a mechanography, an omnidirectional exploration into mechano-informatics, the secret life of machines which opens up the vast and previously unsuspected coevolution of machines and humans in late 20th C Black Atlantic Futurism.

Alien Music is all in the breaks: the distance between Tricky and what you took to be the limits of Black Music, the gap between Underground Resistance and what you took Black Music to be, between

thought synthesizer which moves along several planes at once, which tracks Machine Music's lines of force.

Far from needing theory's help, music today is already *more* conceptual than at any point this century, pregnant with thoughtprobes waiting to be activated, switched on, misused.

So *More Brilliant than the Sun* draws more of its purpose from track subtitles than from TechnoTheory, or even science fiction. These *conceptechnics* are then released from the holding pens of their brackets, to migrate and mutate across the entire communication landscape. Stolen from Sleevenote Manifestos, adapted from label fictions, driven as far and as fast as possible, they misshape until they become devices to drill into the new sensory experiences, endoscopes to magnify the new mindstates Machine Music is inducing.

More Brilliant than the Sun's achievement, therefore, is to design, manufacture, fabricate, synthesize, cut, paste and edit a so-called artificial discontinuum for the Futurhythmachine.

Rejecting today's ubiquitous emphasis on black sound's necessary ethical allegiance to the street, this project opens up the new plane of Sonic Fiction, the secret life of forms, the discontinuum of AfroDiasporic Futurism, the chain reaction of PhonoFiction. It moves through the explosive forces which technology ignites in us, the temporal architecture of inner space, audiosocial space, living space, where postwar alienation breaks down into the 21st C alien.

From Sun Ra to 4 Hero, today's alien discontinuum therefore operates not through continuities, retentions, genealogies or inheritances but rather through intervals, gaps, breaks. It turns away from roots; it opposes common sense with the force of the fictional and the power of falsity.

One side effect of the alien discontinuum is the rejection of any and all notions of a compulsory black condition. Where journalism still insists on a solid state known as 'blackness', *More Brilliant* dissolves this solidarity with a corpse into a *fluid*arity maintained and exacerbated by soundmachines.

Today's cyborgs are too busy manufacturing themselves across time-space to disintensify themselves with all the Turing Tests for transatlantic, transeuropean and transafrican consciousness: affirmation, keeping it real, representing, staying true to the game, respect due, staying black. Alien Music today deliberately fails all these Tests, these putrid corpses of petrified moralism: it treats them with utter indifference; it replaces them with nothing whatsoever.

By contrast, *More Brilliant* goes farther in. It lingers lovingly inside a single remix, explores the psychoacoustic fictional spaces of interludes and intros, goes to extremes to extrude the illogic other studies flee. It happily deletes familiar names [so no Tupac, no NWA] and historical precedence [no lying griots, not much King Tubby, just a small side bet on the Stockhausen sweepstakes]. It avoids the nauseating American hunger for confessional biography, for 'telling your own stories in your own words'. It refuses entry to comforting origins and social context.

Everywhere, the 'street' is considered the ground and guarantee of all reality, a compulsory logic explaining all Black Music, conveniently mishearing antisocial surrealism as social realism. Here sound is unglued from such obligations, until it eludes all social responsibility, thereby accentuating its unreality principle.

In CultStud, TechnoTheory and CyberCulture, those painfully archaic regimes, theory always comes to Music's *rescue*. The organization of sound is interpreted historically, politically, socially. Like a headmaster, theory teaches today's music a thing or 2 about life. It subdues music's ambition, reins it in, restores it to its proper place, reconciles it to its naturally belated fate.

In *More Brilliant than the Sun* the opposite happens, for once: music is encouraged in its despotic drive to crumple chronology like an empty bag of crisps, to eclipse reality in its wilful exorbitance, to put out the sun. Here music's mystifying illogicality is not chastised but systematized and intensified — into MythSciences that burst the edge of improbability, incites a proliferating series of mixillogical mathemagics at once maddening and perplexing, alarming, alluring.

MythScience is the field of knowledge invented by Sun Ra, and a term that this book uses as often as it can. A sample from Virilio defines it very simply: 'Science and technology develop the unknown, not knowledge. Science develops what is not rational.' Instead of theory saving music from itself, from its worst, which is to say its best excesses, music is heard as the pop analysis it already is. Producers are already pop theorists: Breakbeat producer Sonz of a Loop da Loop Era's term skratchadelia, instrumental HipHop producer DJ Krush's idea of turntabilization, virtualizer George Clinton's studio science of mixadelics, all these conceptechnics are used to excite theory to travel at the speed of thought, as sonic theorist Kool Keith suggested in 1987. TechnoTheory, CultStuds *et al* lose their flabby bulk, their lazy, pompous, lard-arsed, top-down dominance, becoming but a single component in a

alienates itself from the human; it arrives from the future. Alien Music is a synthetic recombinator, an applied art technology for amplifying the rates of becoming alien. Optimize the ratios of excentricity. Synthesize yourself.

From the outset, this Postsoul Era has been characterized by an extreme indifference towards the human. The human is a pointless and treacherous category.

And in synch with this posthuman perspective comes Black Atlantic Futurism. Whether it's the AfroFuturist *concrète* of George Russell and Roland Kirk, the Jazz Fission of Teo Macero and Miles Davis, the World 4 Electronics of Sun Ra and Herbie Hancock, the Astro Jazz of Alice Coltrane and Pharoah Sanders, the cosmophonic HipHop of Dr Octagon and Ultramagnetic MCs, the post-HipHop of The Jungle Brothers and Tricky, the Spectral Dub of Scientist and Lee Perry, the offworld Electro of Haashim and Ryuichi Sakamoto, the despotic Acid of Bam Bam and Phuture, the sinister phonoseduction of Parliament's Star Child, the hyperrhythmic psychedelia of Rob Playford and Goldie, 4 Hero and A Guy Called Gerald, Sonic Futurism always adopts a cruel, despotic, amoral attitude towards the human species.

In fact the era when the History of HipHop could exhaust Machine Music is long over. All those petitions for HipHop to be taken seriously, for the BBC to give Techno a chance, for House to receive a fair hearing: this miserable supplication should have ended years ago. For there's nothing to prove anymore: *all* these Rhythmachines are *globally* popular now.

So no more forcefeeding you Bronx fables and no more orthodox HipHop liturgies. There are more than enough of these already. Instead *More Brilliant than the Sun* will focus on the Futurhythmachines within each field, offering a close hearing of music's internal emigrants only. The Outer Thought of Tricky, the Jungle Brothers with their remedy for HipHop gone illmatic, Aerosoul art theorist Rammellzee and his mythillogical systems of Gothic Futurism and *Ikonoklast Panzerism*. No history of Techno, however compelling, but instead a zoom in on the Underground Resistance WarMachine, on the Unidentifiable Audio Object of *X-102 Discovers 'The Rings of Saturn'*. No pleas for Jungle to be accorded proper respect, but rather a magnification of certain very particular aspects of its hyperdimensionality, in 4 Hero, A Guy Called Gerald, Rob Playford and Goldie.

The history book that crams in everything only succeeds in screening out the strangeness of the Rhythmachine. In its bid for universality, such a book dispels the artificiality that all humans crave.

All today's journalism is nothing more than a giant inertia engine to put the brakes on breaks, a moronizer placing all thought on permanent pause, a *futureshock absorber*, forever shielding its readers from the future's cuts, tracks, scratches. Behind the assumed virtue of keeping rhythm mute, there is a none-too-veiled hostility towards analyzing rhythm at all. Too many ideas spoil the party. Too much speculation kills 'dance music', by 'intellectualizing' it to death.

The fuel this inertia engine runs on is fossil fuel: the live show, the proper album, the Real Song, the Real Voice, the mature, the musical, the pure, the true, the proper, the intelligent, breaking America: all notions that stink of the past, that maintain a hierarchy of the senses, that petrify music into a solid state in which everyone knows where they stand, and what real music really is.

And this is why nothing is more fun than spoiling this terminally stupid sublime, this insistence that Great Music speaks for itself.

At the Century's End, the Futurhythmachine has 2 opposing tendencies, 2 synthetic drives: the Soulful and the Postsoul. But then all music is made of both tendencies running simultaneously at all levels, so you can't merely *oppose* a humanist r&b with a posthuman Techno.

Disco remains the moment when Black Music falls from the grace of gospel tradition into the metronomic assembly line. Ignoring that disco is therefore *audibly* where the 21st C begins, 9 out of 10 cultural crits prefer their black popculture humanist, and emphatically 19th C. Like Brussels sprouts, humanism is good for you, nourishing, nurturing, soulwarming – and from Phyllis Wheatley to R. Kelly, present-day R&B is a perpetual fight for human status, a yearning for human rights, a struggle for inclusion within the human species. Allergic to cybersonic if not to sonic technology, mainstream American media – in its drive to banish alienation, and to recover a sense of the whole human being through belief systems that talk to the 'real you' – compulsively deletes any intimation of an AfroDiasporic futurism, of a 'webbed network' of computerhythms, machine mythology and conceptechnics which routes, reroutes and criss-crosses the Black Atlantic. This digital diaspora connecting the UK to the US, the Caribbean to Europe to Africa, is in Paul Gilroy's definition a 'rhizomorphic, fractal structure', a 'transcultural, international formation.'

The music of Alice Coltrane and Sun Ra, of Underground Resistance and George Russell, of Tricky and Martina, comes from the Outer Side. It

OPERATING SYSTEM FOR THE REDESIGN OF SONIC REALITY

Respect due. Good music speaks for itself. No Sleevenotes required. Just enjoy it. Cut the crap. Back to basics. What else is there to add?

All these troglodytic homilies are Great British cretinism masquerading as vectors into the Trad Sublime. Since the 80s, the mainstream British music press has turned to Black Music only as a rest and a refuge from the rigorous complexities of white guitar rock. Since in this laughable reversal a lyric always means more than a sound, while only guitars can embody the zeitgeist, the Rhythmachine is locked in a retarded innocence. You can theorize words or style, but analyzing the groove is believed to kill its bodily pleasure, to drain its essence.

Allegedly at odds with the rock press, dance-press writing also turns its total inability to describe any kind of rhythm into a virtue, invoking a white Brit routine of pubs and clubs, of business as usual, the bovine sense of good blokes together. You can see that the entire British dance press — with its hagiographies and its geographies, its dj recipes, its boosterism, its personality profiles — constitutes a colossal machine for maintaining rhythm as an unwritable, ineffable mystery. And this is why Trad dance-music journalism is nothing more than lists and menus, bits and bytes: meagre, miserly, mediocre.

EVOLUTION

MACHINE

THE CO-
OF THE
FUTURHYTH

For the Newest Mutants

DISCONTENTS

First published in Great Britain by
Quartet Books Limited in 1998
A member of the Namara Group
27 Goodge Street
London W1P 2LD

Every effort has been made by the publishers to clear permission for the use
of the photograph on the front cover of this book. The owner is invited to
submit a claim for reproduction fees.

A catalogue record for this book is available from the British Library

ISBN 0 7043 8025 0

Printed and bound in Great Britain by
Creative Print and Design Wales, Ebbw Vale

More Brilliant Than The Sun: Adventures In Sonic Fiction: Concept Engineered By Kodwo Eshun

More Brilliant Than The Sun is a machine for travelling at the speed of thought, a probe for drilling into new levels of possibility space. 'Its mission is to undermine the concepts this present has of "Health" and "Culture" and to excite mockery and hatred against these hybrid monsters of concepts.'

Q

Quartet Books

At 17, Kodwo Eshun won an Open Scholarship to read Law at University College, Oxford. After eight days he switched to Literary Theory, magazine journalism and running clubs. He is not a cultural critic or cultural commentator so much as a concept engineer, an imagineer at the millenium's end writing on electronic music, science fiction, technoculture, gameculture, drug culture, post war movies and post war art for *The Face*, *The Wire*, *i-D*, *Melody Maker*, *Spin*, *Arena* and *The Guardian*.

WORLD 4: MUTANTEXTURES OF JAZZ

World 4

The last 2 decades of jazz constitute a collective machine for forgetting the years '68-'75, the Era when its leading players engineered jazz into an Afrodelic Space Program, an Alien World Electronics. 70s fusion, 80s neo-classical, 90s Acid Jazz, jazz rap, freejazz : all these bitter enemies are united in their absolute aversion/amnesia to the Jazz Fission Age. All hark back to before or after the Electronic Era that starts with George Russell's '68 *Electronic Sonata for Souls Loved by Nature* and ends with Macero's & Miles's *Dark Magus* in '75.

From Ra to George Russell to Miles & Macero to Alice Coltrane to Pharoah Sanders to Herbie Hancock to Eddie Henderson to Julian Priester to The Tony Williams Lifetime to Larry Young and on, the Inner Space Age generated the most audacious, ambitious and awe-inducing music to emerge from America.

But today in '98, it is as if the Futurhythmachines of this Electronic Era had never existed. Music has utterly retreated from the towering, overwhelming ambition of this era. Just like Techno, Jazz Fission — America's greatest moment — has been utterly disappeared.

Electronic jazz is when the engineer crosses the glass. Electric Jazz peoples the world with hallucinations. Astro jazz is Alice Coltrane blaspheming against jazz by remixing *A Love Supreme*. Jazz Fission dissolves the border between mute and trumpet, wah-wah and organ, effect and instrument. Psychedelic Jazz derealizes sound into hornets and quasars. Cosmic jazz is unease, the monstrous deliquescence of the mixing desk. World 4 jazz is an ominous drift towards origins unknown.

Attribute: Assassin

Jazz Fission did more than melt the hierarchies which jazz tradition works so hard to maintain. As the cyclotron that produced mutant matter and polyrhythmic psychedelias, it triggered a post-jazz universe. The dates for the assassination of jazz are numerous and all its assassins have long since stepped forward: Coltrane, Ornette, Ra, Miles. Unlike the Art Ensemble's declaration of jazz as 'Great Black Music', Futurhythmic Fission treats the Tradition as *effects*, inputs to be fed into its giant Connection Machine.

Liquefying everything generates a confusion that quickly calcifies, into orthodoxy on one hand and into near-total amnesia on the other. Both responses were accelerated by the engineer-musicians themselves, who, dispirited and drained by poor sales, switched from fission to fusion and disparaged the Afrodelic era as a rash experiment, a failure.

Anachronic Cybernetics of the World: George Russell

The 2 versions of composer George Russell's *Electronic Sonata for Souls Loved by Nature*, from '68 and '80, are auditions of jazz augmented for the unknown hazards of inner space. In the Cybernetic Age, jazz must move through the centre of the cyclone, implode and be reassembled as electromagnetic dub. Instead of invoking jazz as an art, a beautiful soul which defies the military industrial complex, Russell technologizes jazz until it becomes an art-industrial complex: 'The tape was prepared at the Electronic Music Studios of the Swedish Radio Ensemble on a huge computer. It is meant to suggest that man, in the face of encroaching technology, must confront technology and attempt to humanize it, to explore inner, as well as outer space.'

Mixillogical

For Russell, the *Electronic Sonata* is a global music, a 'panstylistic electronic tape; a tape composed of fragments of many different styles of music, avant-garde jazz, ragas, blues, rock, serial music etc, treated electronically... a palate upon which non electronic musical statements of a panstylistic nature could be projected.' This convergence of collages turns the *Electronic Sonata* into a mixillogical machine: the fleeting friction of timbral incongruities, incompatible sound blocs rubbing against each other. Blurring the realtime ‹›tape distinction creates a fictional sonata of impossible music. The collage of heavy rock, Indian ragas and Moroccan voices is processed into an electromagnetic mirror mix, then looped into tapes which Terje Rypdal slashes at with guitar and Jan Garbarek corrodes with astringent tenor sax.

Tape + electronic treatments + live musics = Texturological Stratusphunk: 'There are three people playing at once on that tape but the tape is so integrated with the other electronic material it's hard to distinguish what's what.' Electronic mirages descend in palls, shrouding the outlines of sound in amorphous reefs of fog through which midrange attacks surge.

Journey to the Centre of the Head

Unlike Holger Czukay's shortwave or Lee Perry's tv sampling, Russell's electromagnetic forcefield falls in a haze as indefinite as a neuromantic sky tuned to the colour of dead tv. The vapourdrift of tapehiss seeps through the jagged guitar signals and sax tones, derealizing the borders between live and synthetic noise, and unreal and real time, into colourfields that flipflop at the periphery of perception.

Listening to the *Electronic Sonata, Events I-XIV* is like growing a 3rd Ear. The perpetual palimpsest of impossible events demands a new neuromuscular interface. You become a human Oncomouse, ear sprouting from your neck in a fleshy umbrella.

Fragmental

At 6 mins fog seeps in over test-tones and clanking chains. Applied intensively, electrons confuse solids with signals and metal with information, mystifying the ear as sounds escape their acoustic body and shed their envelope to become formless. Space coagulates then crinkles, altering its density, convoluting perspectives until sounds reach you in fractions and fragments. Your powers of recognition are shot to hell as you move through a baffling republic of indistinct matter. Current attracts you towards a powerstation that shrinks into coins spinning on glass. At 13 mins everything is suffused in an unlocatable roar, heard through fog banks like Vittorio Gelmetti's ominous drones in Antonioni's '64 film *Il Deserto Russo*. At 15 mins, Garbarek's Shepp-style sax, all acrid Twombly-ized scribbles, starts dueting with a high frequency. Violins swoop abysmally. Gravity drops out, opening a horizon at the far edge of perception. Organ spirals through in curling flames as African percussion fades into hearing. At 20 mins, oscillators materialize into earshot, forming unknown metallophonic alloys, melding with marimba maze. 'The thing that sounds like a marimba is actually an old African man and his two sons. The voices heard on the *Electronic Sonata* are of a 70-year-old African and his two sons. An African lute is being used. A friend brought me a tape of Ugandan folk music so we just ran that through some ring modulators.' Textures superimpose each other before being swallowed up by the reverberations from a hidden powersource. At 23 mins, tape-simulated synthetic sonorities strafe across a harmonic curtain of church organ. Tumbling motion, like urchins drumming in the cavities of cast metal, slowly resolves itself into percussion, pulling focus on your hearing.

Textural Strata of the Mix

In *Part II* of *Electronic Sonata for Souls Loved by Nature*, North African lute and voice signals travel across space, panning past each other. Hand drums throw out rustling bridges of intermittence. The second voice fades into earshot, materializing out of cymballic shimmer.

The voices in *Part II Event VIII* exist in the simultaneous future-past time of the mix. The *Sonata* is mixology in un#real time.

At 3 mins, Rypdal's guitar crashes in◌is sucked into the maw of ring modulation. At 6 mins, the tape is treated until it becomes a ghost orchestra. Circled by escalating radii, you hear a new world, a wraithscape of delocalized chimes, echoes arriving from origins unknown, distant splashes. At 12 mins, space undergoes topological involution, rotating oscillations through a helical scan. Bass and piano momentarily surface, acoustic relics flung from the edge of the electromagnetic vortex. At 16.50 mins, sheets of wah-wah cut through space, are baffled by a fogbank which falls before your ears. You stop hearing through to the guitar; the space through which sound travels turns gaseous. Instead of transporting sound, space thickens and impedes it.

The Conceptechnics of Destratified Dub

By reconfiguring jazz through the magnetic labyrinth, Russell and the engineers at the Swedish Radio Electronic Music Studio manufacture the magnetic vortex of dub in '68.

At 18 mins, percussion tumbles like a drum is being kicked over. The church organ plays underwater. Shortwave leakage fuses with the transient tones of radio, mobile and belltrees. At 22 mins, the drone modulates into the whine of aeroplanes taxiing on the runway. Sounds lose their harmonic profile, alter their stabilized identity in the electromagnetic process of folk implosion.

Electronics, as McLuhan recognized, massifies listeners into electribes. But electronics doesn't decant tribes from tradition into the present, because Trad sonic technologies are *already* futuristic. 'The old Norwegian church organ was the material this whole tape is based on — in conjunction with this African music which fits into the world cultural implosion. I wanted to reflect the cultural implosion occurring among the Earth's population, their coming together.'

Subsumption Rhythm

Russell's magnetic mixology accelerates a discontinuum in which the future arrives from the past. The percussion choir is a Rhythmachine simplified by the tapedelay of Steve Reich-era minimalism. The Ghanaian drumchoir distributes polyrhythms into strata that Russell terms Vertical Form: 'In the African drumchoir, one drummer is the rhythmic gravity while the others gradually layer on sophisticated rhythms on top of this tonal centre. The whole isn't really evolving in a horizontal way; it's evolving in complexity and density. It's vertical energy getting higher and higher, compounding.'

The drumchoir complexifies the beat into distributed Polyrhythmachines, webbed networks of poly#counter#contra#cross# staggered rhythms that function like the dispersed architecture of artificial life by generating emergent consciousness. Russell: 'Music is architecture. I build structures. Buildings go up — they're vertical forms. My focus is on the vertical evolution of a form, not necessarily on the horizontal/linear exposition of that form.' Rhythm = webs of intermittence, cyclic rhythms that are in synch but out of phase. The classical musics of the Ghanaian drumchoir, Balinese gamelan orchestras, Indian and Jajouka master musicians are what producer Kirk DeGiorgio terms ARTs — Advanced Rhythmic Technologies — already centuries old.

The older the Rhythmachine, the more futuristic it is. For George Russell — like Stockhausen, Coltrane and Holger Czukay — to go back into a Ghanaian or Indian or Vietnamese sonic past is to go forward into a new future. To listen to an ART is hearing the evolution of technology 5 centuries down the line.

Electronic Swarm Program: Teo Macero & Miles Davis, Herbie Hancock

The Medusa Complex of Mutantextures

Launched by producer Teo Macero and composer Miles Davis, amplified Afrodelia transmolecularized the solid states of sound into a continental drift. Inputs include Hendrix-era rock, fuzz, wah-wah pedals, Sly and the Family Stone's spaced funk, the electronics of the clavinet, the Arp, the Moog, tape-delay dub, the tense nervous string attacks of Varèse, the tabla and sitar of Badal Roy, the hyperrhythmic percussion webs of Hermeto Pascoal and Airto Moreira.

Between '68 and '75, Macero & Miles, Hancock *et al* turned effects into instruments, dissolving the hierarchy by connecting both into a chameleonic circuit which generated new mutantextures. Amplified trumpet, wah-wah pedal, clavinet, echoplex unit, organ, guitar: all these became new instruments, grafted hybrids, unicorn sounds, centaur sounds. Effects are now acoustic prosthetics, audio extensions, sonic destratifiers, electric mutators, multipliers and mutagents.

Cyberneticist Kevin Kelly hears an electronic ecology emerging, where 'one machine's input is another machine's output.' In this Medusa Complex of feeds and leads, sound machines 'form foodwebs' and prey upon each other. In Herbie Hancock's '73 *Hornets*, the seething, treacherous 19 min 36 sec futurhythmaze exemplifies the mutagenic matrix. Passing the clavinet signal through the fuzz-wah pedal sends the synthesizer through the body of the guitar, producing a boaconstrictor tone that combines the clench of the clavinet with the choke of the wah-wah. Moving through the echoplex, constriction is cloned from a singular sensation into an environment that dunks you headfirst in a horde of heat-seeking killer bees.

Listening becomes a chase through the thickets of percussion. Motile tonalities, origin unknown, swarm after you, bugging you out as they disappear around the edges of the rhythmaze, obscured by overgrowth, rebound off the walls of the webweave.

On Macero's & Miles' *Gondwana* from *Pangaea*, the organ is sent through wah-wah until it plays sustained chords from an impossibly elongated guitar.

DeStratifiers

Electronic effects are destratifiers because they dissolve the organization of the instrument, liquefy the stratification of sound. In the Afrodelic Era, effects defect from cause, redistributing themselves until it's impossible to hear which instrument generates which sound. A sound‹›vision schizmatix emerges; audio escapes from its acoustic body, compelling a new menagerie of sound machinery, tweaking you to invent fictional instruments from World 4.

The distinction between real music and soundeffects collapses, in a stream of sonic matter that crosses from the liquid state of piano sustain into the gas state of mute horn vapourdrift. *He Loved Him Madly* is all derealization, vapour trails of originless sound, viscous drift of organ = trumpet = guitar. Macero remixes the organ from another session onto the PolyRhythmengine, filters the trumpet through the mixing desk, through effects designed by Columbia's engineers.

The Schizophonic Era

Schizophony is R. Murray Schafer's term for the audible inferno of the post-war soundscape, the era when industrial communications split sound from its sources, 'becoming a fearful medium because we cannot see who or what produces the sound: an invisible excitement for the nerves.' With Macero & Miles, schizophony becomes endemic.

Insectile Texturhythm

You're in what producer Dr S. Gachet calls the audiomaze, the electric insectland that incites invisible excitement. Invisible because albums from the Electronic Era teem with percussion that's evolved into unseen insectile lifeforms. The sleeve for '75's *Dark Magus* shows Miles wearing bug-green fly shades, adapting to the audiomenagerie by becoming insectile himself. *Superfly* shades access the tsetse fly's magnified vision. Sight becomes compounded, triggering the reticulated hearing electronic jazz demands.

Chittering, cawing, creaking, shrieking, rattling, shaking: percussion becomes a nonlinear malevolence. Rhythm is a biotechnology. The

Hancock PolyRhythmengine is a biotech in perpetual motion. Its texturhythmfields are too distributed and too fugitive for the ear to catch. Percussion becomes a rhythm shower in which distributed beats — treacherous underfoot, glimpsed overhead — fall through the body like rain through lianas.

The skin hears the polyrhythmic shower as a creeping, writhing tactility. Sudden yet imperceptible shifts across the amplified percussapellic field — from rattling to chittering — conduct these across the skin, dropping body temperature as they writhe and seize the dermal terrain. Crickets, cicadas, treefrogs, hummingbirds flitting between the carbon-based rainforest. Hence the Rhythmengine of Maupin, Henderson *et al* calling themselves 'Headhunters', taking on Pygmy magic.

Side 2 of '73's *Sextant*, the final album in his convulsive, brilliant World 4 Trilogy — after '71's *Mwandishi* and '72's *Crossings* — is taken up entirely by the malignant hybrids of *Hornets*. Hancock's clavinet and Buster Williams's fuzz bass double each other in throttling chords that coil and unfurl like flaring cobras.

Against a trunkular superheavy bass, Billy Hart's cymbal hiss simmers maintaining a pneumatic pressure which stokes the PolyRhythmengine, the imminent threat of the groove. Julian Priester's bass clarinet insinuates a sinister motion like a subterranean sidewinder undulating over shifting sand. Patrick Gleason's synth oscillates from bassdrones to treefrog croaks to squeals that lead into abysmal squawls.

> *By the alien power of distributed being agents can be lifted into a type of colony intelligence by connecting them in bulk*
> **Kevin Kelly**

The Parahuman Biology of Sound Machines

In the Afrodelic Era, percussive strata and polyrhythmic engines converge in a zone of parahuman elusiveness. Fugitive and tensile, World 4 hyperrhythm makes audible the treacherous biocomputer of Amos Tuotola's '58 novel *My Life in the Bush of Ghosts*. Tuotola's carceral Bush of Ghosts, like the Amazonian jungle or the Central African rainforest, is a distributed biocomputer, an example of Kelly's 'massively parallel bioengineered adaptation. Natural evolution is a computational process of adaptation to an everchanging environment.'

My Life in the Bush of Ghosts accelerates 'the alien power of distributed being' into a medium, across which signals and frequencies crackle into electromagnetic ghosts. Tuotola opens a technology-magic continuum in which radio becomes an Invisible Magnetic Missive sent to you from Home. TV turns into a ghost medium haunted by the television-handed ghostess: 'When she told me to look at her palm and opened it nearly to touch my face, it was exactly as a television.'

It is the entire globe pulsating in my brain
Mati Klarwein

The Electribal Continuum<>The Past Arrives from the Future
Electric machines feed forward into the past. Tribal technology arrives from a marauding future. Mati Klarwein's and Tadanoori Yokoo's Miles Davis and Robert Springett's Hancock covers are Sonic Visions, soundings in paint which dramatize this electribal continuum.
On *Sextant* a North African boy and girl dance on a desert planed like a runway. A cratered moon hangs over them. A giant chain of beads, its 2 strands breaking out of an amulet like metallic antennae, floats past a ziggurated pyramid, a Babylonian‹›Egyptian observation tower. Flip the sleeve over and there's an alien African in a robe, his bony fingers pointing to the giant chain. Behind him is an azure Buddha mask with roseate eyes, sun bursting behind it, clouds billowing.
With *Bitches Brew* Klarwein illustrates his electribal cyborgs, paradisical girl-boy couples. On the front, the girl's hair twists into a swirl of striped gas that hurls itself across the thermal currents into a blue-black stormcloud. It's a reversible weather circuit, so the electric storm simultaneously generates Dali's atmospherocephalic current which produces the girl. On the back, a singing man, face set in delirious concentration, is surrounded by a stellar forcefield. Against a star cosmos, an albino boy, the reverse of the calm black face with blue lips on the front, weeps brown tears.
For the cover to *Thrust*, Hancock's an Afronaut — a pilot operator looking disdainfully out of the bubble window, as his fingers play the synthesizer-control panel that will guide his ufo down through the purple mists and onto the mountain-top runway. The runway is Assyrian tech, with a city carved into the plateau. A giant moon, its mauve craters like planetary pustules, looms overhead, blocking out the sky.

Crossings reveals that the wizened men with elongated skulls, standing in their white robes, are North African necromancers, alien visitors. The scene's anachronized by a boy with the same Pharaonic profile as the ageing viziers, sitting on the edge of a wave which sweeps across the back sleeve into the black sea-depths of the front sleeves. The necromancers are standing in water. There's a boat pulling in but there's no beach; the jet-blue waves lap onto more water instead of a shore. Refugees huddle against the coast wind.

In Yokoo's *Agharta* sleeve, the title forms a phonotron that blasts off from a city framed in lush foliage and a red liquid flux which arches out of the skyscrapers. On the back a tractorbeam draws a ufo out of a city and up through an underwater sky of coral reefs.

Pan<>Alien Astro<>African Space Program

In the Age of Afrodelia, the jazz composer becomes the audio alchemist. Afrodelia triggers an alternating current of technology and magic in the Sleevenote artwork of Yokoo, Springett and Klarwein. The futuristic and the archaic reverse polarities, and chase each other down into an anachronistic futurepast. On *Mwandishi* and *Sextant*, the Herbie Hancock Septet take on Swahili names. Herbie Hancock = Mwandishi. Benny Maupin = Mwile. Dr Eddie Henderson = Mganga. Julian Priester = Pepo. Buster Williams = Mchezaji. Billy Hart = Jabali.

This doesn't ground them or earth them in their roots. Instead, it aerealizes them for take-off, a Buddhist‹›Swahili septet launched on the Pan‹›Alien Astro‹›African-American Space Program.

Collapsar

Klarwein, Yokoo and Springett exemplify Afrodelia, anachronizing past and future into what Miles calls Yesternow. As Sarah Connor says to Kyle Reece in *The Terminator*: 'You're talking about things I haven't done yet, in the past tense.' World 4 Art-Sound opens up what Joe Haldeman in his novel *The Forever War* terms a collapsar. The collapsar, a slippage in time, is a collapsed star in which the times between what's to come and what hasn't happened yet implode and fold upon each other. Tape plasticizes time into malleable material.

Afro<>Electric

Hendrix adopts Bob Dylan's Afro and wires it for feedback. Gunter
Kieser's '69 *The Medusa Head* poster shows Hendrix's Afro electrified to
transmit alternating current: 'Everything is electrified nowadays. That is
why the name Electric Sky Church flashes in and out. I am Electric
Religion. We're making music into a new kind of Bible, a Bible that you
can carry in your hearts. One that will give you a physical feeling.' *And
the Gods Made Love* psychedelicizes cybernetics by turning the guitar
into a jetstream engine: a 90-second sound painting of the heavens, a
tone generator of sound spectra.

Chaosmos

Electronic Jazz's rapid transitions from extreme turbulence to prolonged
static lulls suggest that it exists at the dissipative edge of ordered chaos,
making audible the chaotic order being discovered by Benoit
Mandelbrot. Whoever controls the effects controls the means of
mutation. Effects inaugurate an alchemical era, a science of nonlinear
synthesis.

Electric Jazz incorporates the sound of reversed tape — the gradual
ominous buildup, the abrupt cut-off attack — as a new panic dynamics.
Or the tapes could be reversed in the studio by the engineer. With *You'll
Know When you Get There* from '71's *Mwandishi*, there's a new
electronics of jagged edges, screaming attacks and appalling pauses, the
futurepast of time running backwards while it's playing forward.

The Past Feedsforward into the Future

With '74's *Nobu*, Hancock invents hi-tech fusion, Techno before the
event that opens a new plateau in today's electronics. Ignored on its
release, *Nobu* compels a switchback in time as its forgotten past arrives
from the future to scramble the present. *Nobu*'s sequences are the aural
parallel of Op Art's retinal rivalry. Unable to resolve the Op Art image,
the eye vacillates. Hearing wavers as it struggles to keep up with the
track's psychoacoustic illusion of 2 speeds that run ahead of the electric
piano's bass rhythmelody. Its arrangement is what Patrick Gleason terms
syntharmonic, not melodic but rhythmatic attack velocities. Drumbeats
are replaced by Moog texturhythms. It spirals off into a solo interrupted
by open-throated choral chords which pull focus, zooming out to the
endless horizon of the synthetic sublime.

Dissolve Techno's faith in Kraftwerk as the foundation of today's electronics, and Alien Music's lines of inheritance break up, go Wildstyle. With the collapse of Kraftwerk's consensual future, Techno doesn't die. It just loses its sense of itself as the definitive, single direction of music's future. Atlantic Futurism is always building Futurhythmachines, sensory technologies, instruments which renovate perception, which synthesize new states of mind. World 4 Jazz is a transmolecularizer which fluctuates the steady states of organized sound. Seeping in from the futurepast, it feedsforward into the present, anachronizing everything it reaches. Assembled from molecular components of rhythm, the Breakbeat is an Applied Rhythmic Technology, an ART that sets cultural velocity and cultural inertia in motion. By mobilizing rhythms across the communication landscape, the Rhythmengine crosspollinates the eager fan, transmaterializes your sensorium through the onomatopoeic illogic called HipHop.

TRANSMATERIALIZING THE BREAKBEAT

The Metamorphonic Machine is Motion-Capturing Your Nervous System: Grandmaster Flash, Knights of the Turntable

The Possibility Space of Breakbeat Science

'The discovery of the DNA code, for example, is focusing on how you can create different species of beings by starting from the very smallest particles and their components,' Karlheinz Stockhausen has said. 'That is why we are all part of the spirit of the atomic age. In music, we do exactly the same.' By opening the possibility space of Breakbeat science, dj, mixer and rap pioneer Grandmaster Flash extends and deepens this '71 observation.

'After I took the title [of Grandmaster Flash] I knew I had to start going to a laboratory, so to speak, and invent new ideas.' For Flash in '81, going to the lab means approaching the studio as a research centre for the breaking down of the beat. In the lab, the Breakbeat is isolated and replicated, to become the DNA of rhythmic psychedelia.

The Rhythmotor

The Breakbeat is a motion-capture device, a detachable Rhythmengine, a movable rhythmotor that generates cultural velocity. The break is any short captured sound whatsoever. Indifferent to tradition, this functionalism ignores history, allows HipHop to datamine unknown veins of funk, to groove-rob not ancestor-worship. For the funktionalist all the world is dubmaster Lee Perry's 'Turntable Terranova'. As DJ Shadow suggests, HipHop is therefore not a genre so much as an omni-genre, a conceptual approach towards sonic organization rather than a particular sound in itself.

Enhance 57: 19

Investigating the building blocks of the beat, Grandmaster Flash crosses the threshold of microrhythm: 'The Incredible Bongo Band, *Bongo Rock*, *Johnny the Fox*, *The Bells*, Bob James' *Mardi Gras*. I would really like "pop pop pop pop poppoppop u u u". I would like break the shit down to 8th, 16th notes. It amazed me sometimes.'

Both the name – 'Grandmaster Flash' – and the '81 track title – *The Amazing Adventures of Grandmaster Flash on the Wheels of Steel* – are Sonic Fiction. The 'Flash' points to the Supersonic Science of skratchadelia, the dj as DC Comics hero, the term 'Grandmaster' to levels of skills and depth of induction into the martial artform of dj-ing. The name Grandmaster Flash brings together comics and kung fu movies, superhero and Shaolin 'in a mythical battle'. The name ignites an adventure of concepts, a fusion of sensations that catalyses a virtual world at what David Toop calls 'the fantasy level'. This plane of fantasy is Marshall McLuhan's industrial folklore of Man gone supernova.

The Conceptechnics of the Turntable

In mythifying the decks as the 'Wheels of Steel', Flash inaugurates the machine mythology of the turntable. This new conceptual technology or *conceptechnics* presupposes that the decks have become a state of mind for the dj. After Flash, the turntable becomes a machine for building and melding mindstates from your record collection.

The turntables, the Technics deck, become a subjectivity engine generating a stereophonics, a hifi consciousness of the head, wholly tuned in and turned on by the found noise of vinyl degeneration that hears scratches, crackle, fuzz, hiss and static as lead instruments. The HipHop fanatic lives *inside* the 12, rides across the surface of the sleeve, shrinks until the same size as the stylus scoring its revolutions round the mind.

You can see Turntable Consciousness in 3D‹›Robert Del Naja's paintings for Mo Wax's '96 *Headz 2* CD, where the tone arm is poised to circle the grooves of a flaming head, haloed by the turntable. The flight of the stylus launches the 12 on its Journey to the Centre of the Head.

By breaking down the intro into 2 words, 'You say', Flash opens up a new micro-universe of split-second speech. *Adventures* drags you into the performative world where syntax splits into kommand modules, instruktion engines, actuators.

Skratchadelia = Wreckage Made Rhythmic

With Flash, the dj becomes an initiate, inducted into a Microsonic Science which converts voices into new rhythm effects — in '93, Breakbeat wizard Droppin' Science, then known as Sonz of a Loop da Loop Era, terms this 'skratchadelia'. HipHop's admirers always applaud skratchadelia for its percussive qualities. But this is both lazy and vague. To scratch is to evolve the turntables into a tone generator, a defamiliarizer, a word-molecularizer. Skratchadelia isn't a rhythm so much as its wreckage made rhythmic. To call it 'percussive' is as feeble as calling the rhythm synthesizer a 'drum-machine', and another archetypal example of futureshock absorption and [r]earview hearing, protecting you from what you're hearing — which is frequencies rather than kickdrums, a violence against vinyl rather than respect due to the greats, a furious impatience with funk, a surgical excision of drums and bass hi-tension from tradition.

Skratchadelia is really conscientious desecration, the noise of artefacts being obliterated into streams of vocal-vinyl matter.

Skratchadelia phaseshifts music into a new phonoplastic alloy. Voices are molecularized into chattering, gibbering textures, into globules of pitch that grumble and shift along the spectrum of Technics speed, phased and panned by the transformer switch.

Skratchadelia is a synthetic aesthetic of painstaking abuse and sonic sabotage. Only for the obliterati, the virtuosi who force vinyl [in]to matter. Scratching destratifies voice and vinyl into new textures standing on the border between solid and liquid. It turns beats into sonic matter in flux.

Adventures is therefore the operating manual of all skratchadelia. Flash cuts The Hellers 60s psychploitation album *Singers, Talkers, Players, Swingers and Doers*, operating on its children's story. The incised dialogue nestles up to the ear in intimate closeup. 'Why don't you tell me a story? Please tell me a story too. You know I think I'll tell you the story of my life. I was born, in Animus, North Dakota, a long time ago, see... Well, it went pretty much like this,' at which point Flash grates the vinyl into 9 harsh scratches, blocs of rhythmic basstexture shredded like classified documents: 'Grandmaster cuts faster.' Bass. 'Grandmaster.' Bass. 'Cut.' Bass. 'Cuts... cuts... faster.' The Chic bass riff explodes between each order to cut.

Connect*i*Cut

The cut is a command, a technical and conceptual operation which cuts the lines of association. 'You say one for the trouble', the opening phrase of Spoonie Gee and The Sequence's '81 *Monster Jam*, is broken down to 'you say' repeated 7 times. Each time the voice sounds different, slowing down on the 4th, slightly slurring. The stammer of the new. Each cut magnifies the words so you hear in closeups which expand space until it blows up.

The break intensifies the rhythmic flow it cuts into, turning rhythm into a series of peaks and drops. Therefore the track doesn't start and develop sequentially but instead begins over and over. The intro multiples into variations of itself. The scratch builds up tension, the sense of standing on the verge of getting it on. When the rest of the line is finally played, the chorus discharges itself inside your head in a bolt of plosive phono-power.

As Queen's *Another One Bites The Dust* plays on one deck, the rumbling wheeze of the scratch doubles up the bassline and guitar feedback which builds like an aeroplane taking off. Muffled studio voices cheer at the ascent until the track shockcuts to Chic's *Good Times* strings, switching tempos with a jolt that lights up the nervous system. Chic's orchestral attack is propelled across the sensorium.

In *Adventures*, crowd-cheers anticipate your applause, hypes itself every time you play it, inducing a powerful sense of awe as Flash drops the needle on the beat into a burst of 30s spacewind and a *Flash Gordon* film sample cut off to announce the emergence of 'The Amazing Adventures of Flash!'

Skratchadelia replaces the chorus with the drastic tempo change. The song becomes a perpetual crossing of rhythmic thresholds.

Cut Creation

By dropping the needle on the vinyl at the right point, Flash isolates the phrase and magnifies the command to cut. The critic Nelson George identifies its functions as: cutting into syntax, punch-phasing each word order, cutting Nile Rodgers' *Good Times* bass riff until it explodes between each vocal sample. Bass and word-order act as alternating punctuators. *Adventures* is a machine for transmitting the advanced techniques of the cut.

'I was like a human sampler so to speak. After about three weeks of picking out the tracks that I wanted to use, I got it down within two hours. We called this cutting. In the studio, it took maybe four shots to get right. If I messed up I erased it and went straight back to the beginning. I heard it in the ear-piece first; I thought this might sound interesting if I could figure out a way to make it sound less noisy, less harsh, if that was possible.

Grand Wizard Theodore, DJ Kool Herc, Grandmaster Flash are human samplers who isolate the Breakbeat by cutting right into the funkengine, discarding The Song, ignoring intention and tradition to capture its motion: the charge and pull of the beat and the bass, the gait motorized by the deck's direct drive.

As soon as cutting emerges, Rhythm migrates from the drums to the Technics, from the group to the dj, from the studio to the bedroom. Limb by limb, the drummer is transferred to the machines. Breakflow scales across the globe. Phase 1: the decks. Phase 2: the rhythm synthesizer. Phase 3 will be the sampler.

My mind ain't nuthin but a big ol' collage
New Kingdom

AutoCreation

The 12 becomes a record that cuts itself on your decks, a record that scratches itself as it plays. *Adventures* carries out its commands by itself. As Ice T grasped on listening to DJ Zinc's *Supersharp Shooter Remix*: 'The record itself does what the jungle djs do. It stops, it rewinds itself. It makes you sound like a good dj.' What Bambaataa, Flash *et al* enjoyed about Kraftwerk's *Trans Europe Express* was its automotion, the groove of the Rhythmengine running by itself, crossing thresholds: 'Leave that shit alone, that shit was cutting itself. Go smoke a cigarette or something.'

Activate the Instruktion Engine

The 12 is no longer an inert vinyl disc. It's phaseshifted. It's being activated, switched on. Because the command to cut the vinyl is stored *on* the vinyl, the track is now a machine that transmits instructions on how to play it, techniques replicated and multiplied by new mistakes — how do you scratch, how do you cut. Decks ruined, needles fucked, vinyl abused. Triggering flightpaths of dis‹›respect through your records.

With the *Adventures* 12, music crosses a threshold, opens up a new Rhythmachine discontinuum. Each cut/scratch scores new neural pathways across the brain.

The instruction LPs, the teach-yourself-French records, the dancestep disc: after *Adventures*, these are all kinaesthetic engines which capture your motion. *Adventures* is a Kinaesthetic Kontrol Kommand-engine telling you how to cut while warning you not to bother trying. It shows you a field of techniques and the apotheosis of those techniques simultaneously. It opens *and* shuts a new artform.

Turntable Consciousness

Adventures generates a turntable awareness which becomes a turntable consciousness. The decks, the arm, the flight of the stylus, dropping the needle; all these inert components suddenly become usable, changeable, the basic components of sonic mutation.

If Flash in '81 is obsessed by the cut, then Public Enemy's Terminator X in '91 focuses on the edge of the cut. In the realm of Sonic Fiction, his role is to sharpen the scratch into a cutting device, until it incites an edge of panic. The dj therefore now becomes a Track Attacker on lead scratch, an Assault Technician who reorganizes the sound of Trad tonalities.

As Chuck D elaborates, the scratch is a meta-technique that makes new instruments from old instruments: 'Doing *Bring the Noise*, we tried to find a scratch part that would fit in on the last verse. And we found it. It's the backward scratch of a guitar.'

Terrorwrists

Terminator X speaks with his hands: to scratch is to think with vinyl. The dj is a tactilist who goes on a journey of the hands, opening up a new field of objectile thought: fingertip perception. The distributed brain of the hand emerges with its own point of touch, a manual memory of terrorwrists and scizzorhands.

The Medium is the Mindstate

With *Adventures*, the scratch becomes a medium, an environment like electricity. To become pop means to become ubiquitous, making predecessors into precursors. Skratchadelia is the medium, the mindstate in which John Cage is Flash's precursor. With '37's *Imaginary Landscape No.1*, scored for manipulated turntables, Cage scratches long before the first turntablist, 11-year-old Grand Wizard Theodore. Yet Cage is not the original Cut Creator – for this would be to confuse the banal fact of prior birth with precedence and creative priority.

Pop always retroactively rescues unpop from the prison of its admirers: here Flash comes to Cage's aid. Skratchadelia releases the avant garde from its citational cells by liquefying its sanctioning institutions. Now you can hear Cage in '37 as a lonely turntablist with no audience to play for: 'Given four film phonographs we can compose and perform a quartet for explosive motor, wind, heartbeat and landslide.'

Skratchadelia is both a ubiquitous environment which everyone takes for granted, and a technique of extreme virtuosity that hardly anyone grasps.

The Future is an Accident

AutoCatalysis is when sound emerges by itself, when the machine generates a new sound autonomously, without a human agent. A machinic lifeform emerges from the sampler on its own. The Roland TB-303 Bass Line rhythm composer engineers its own audiomatter. In '87 the 303 discovers Acid on its own, uses Phuture to replicate. Marley Marl doesn't discover how to sample the break. Rather, in '81/2 the Emulator E1 sampler discovers this for itself and then uses Marley Marl as a medium through which to replicate breaks on such productions as '85's *Marley Marl Scratch* and '86's *Eric B is President*: 'I could take any drum sound from any old record, put it in here and get the old drummer sound on some shit. No more of that dull DMX shit.'

All these new soundworlds begin as accidents discovered by machines. With Marley Marl, you can follow this process of AutoCatalysis very clearly. 'I wanted to sample a voice from off this song with an Emulator and accidentally, a snare went through.' New sound emerges as a machine error. Instead of emulating a known sound, the future arrives as a mistake ruled out by the preset: 'At first I was like, "That's the wrong thing," but the snare was soundin' good. I kept running the track back and hitting the Emulator. Then I looked at the engineer and said, "You know what this means?!"'

All at once there's a 'sudden multiplication of dimensions of matter'. Your record collection becomes an immense time machine that builds itself through you.

AutoCatalyser

Machinic AutoCatalysis opens up new vectors of technology. DJ-producers like to say that Machine Music comes from fucking with the rule book, freaking with the formula. New music gives the finger to the system. Here you hear the wistful residues of punk-era resistance — for new sonar systems *don't* emerge from misusing the machines. Rather the machine forces music into inhuman directions, and compels the human towards inflexible, impalpable parameters. Acid hears the TB303's frequencies just as they are. It emulates no existing sound, mourns no missing sound, but instead starts from the bad and the unmusical.

The producer follows the trail blazed by the error, breeds it into a new sonic lifeform. Acid amplifies these constraints as much as possible. Jungle accepts the rigidly quantizing function of the Cubase virtual studio. It doesn't revolt against the digital grid; it optimizes it into new possibilities. Your record collection now becomes an ongoing memorybank in which every historical sound exists as a potential break in the present tense. Chronology collapses into mixology, the time of the mix where the location of a bass note in space time gives way to spacetime dislocation. '73 is replaced by plus 5 on the turntable pitch adjuster.

The Vinyl Phonomotor

In their '85 *Fresh Mess [... Jam your Radio]*, The Knights of the Turntable make vinyl a phonomotor. *Fresh Mess* cuts the warning 'Do not attempt to adjust your radio' into consonants that skid and slide. Syllables turn into phonomotors which screech around the turntable at direct drive velocity. Words lose their sequential meaning and turn into morphemic motors, blocs of propulsive plosion stalling and stuttering at 120bpm. Syllables speed away from the order of syntax, erupt out of skratchadelia, only to be ambushed again. A trialogue for plosion, noise and scratch. Cutting disorganizes syntax. Scratching disarticulates words into blocs of motormouthed texturhythm. The combined arts juggle the beat and fluctuate the tempo into a rhythmatic echomaze.

Turntabilization = AutoDestruction

In skratchadelia, the carchase is rescored for the destabilized turntable, a turntabilization in which the Wheels of Steel are overridden until they crash. Each scratch slows down, reverts into a squall of lead guitar into syllables which detonate.

With Grandmaster Flash the command is subjected to the process it describes. Here the request 'Do not attempt to adjust your radio' is subjected to the process it warns against. The warning not to adjust has just been adjusted. AutoCreation gives way to AutoDestruction. In *Adventures*, the command to cut vinyl is stored on the vinyl, so that content coincides with process. In *Fresh Mess* the warning against cutting vinyl is cut up, so that content cancels process. The track immolates itself as it plays, igniting an intense satisfaction.

As the subtitle to *Fresh Mess [... Jam your Radio]* makes clear, turntabilization = jamming. Not jamming in the Milesian sense of the combustible Rhythmengine, but in the telecommunicating sense of noise overcoming signal. Skratchadelia becomes interference which breaks up the transmission, becomes an alien signal which inhabits the spirit of broadcasting, manifests communication breakdown and makes technical difficulties audible.

Skratchadelia encrypts its tones, demanding alien listeners tuned into the open secret hidden in static, receivers who can hear a new world in its garbled frequencies. Your breakdown is their breakup. From Orson Welles to Parliament to The Bomb Squad to UR, radio is the invisible pathway through which audio invades the Earth and broadcasts to the planet.

Kidnapped by the Kinaesthetics of the Break:
Mantronix and Chep Nunez

Every second of time the Breakbeat takes across the 12 is bitterly resisted on the battlefield of the sensorium. Clenched resistance to rhythmic psychedelias usually manifests as a return to mere musicality. To follow the Breakbeat is to reject this [r]earview response, to land on the planet of your body made newly audible by rhythmic transvaluation.

The Rhythmachine captures your perception as it switches from hearing individual beats to grasping the pattern of beats. Your body is a distributed brain which flips from the sound of each intensity to the overlapping relations between intensities. Learning pattern recognition, this flipflop between rhythmelody and texturhythm drastically collapses and reorganises the sensorial hierarchy.

The Body Is a Large Brain

For the 90s rhythmatician, the body is a large brain that thinks and feels a sensational mathematics throughout the entire surface of its distributed mind.

The Breakbeat drives new pathways through the brain. Aggressively unpitched, it blocks empathy while fissuring new synapses through the matter of the mind. As it fires across the synaptic junction, the sensorial flinch is translated backwards, reinvested in the age-old values of refinement and sensibility. To the rear, march! The connoisseur rallies to the gerontocracy of musicianship, swears an oath to quality, makes a brave stand for originality, all the ideals disappearing fast in a pop world long since shot to pieces. Instinctive shudders at rhythm are elevated into an ethical standard for sound, refined into proper Techno for true people. When music is praised as real, pure, proper and true, then it's too late: decay has set in and the maggots aren't far off.

Returning to the values of musicality always rests on the dependable virtues of harmony and difficulty, which are raised to moral principles. Abstract beatz, math rock, intelligent Techno, proper Drum'n'Bass, these clever genres for stupid people resurrect the premodern opposition in which the mind is bizarrely superior to the body. By frustrating the funk and impeding the groove, clever music amputates the distributed mind, locks you back in the prisonhouse of your head. Far from being futuristic, cerebral music therefore retards you by reimposing a preindustrial sensory hierarchy that shut up your senses in a Cartesian prison.

Breakbeat Consciousness

Becoming beat educated takes far more effort than becoming a classical composer, because you're going against the nature inculcated into you by an oldworld audio order. It demands a Breakbeat consciousness that turns you into a rhythmatician, a specialist in kinaesthesia.

The kinaesthete overrides that pre-modern binary that insists the dancefloor is all mindless bodies and the bedroom nothing but bodiless minds.

Man + Electronics = Mantronix

As beats expand across the track, The Song disappears forever in a polyrhythmodynamics of tense presents and pressure drops. With Mantronix's 1988 *Kings of the Beats*, rhythm becomes thermodynamic; intensities and pressures, drops and rises, stalls and stutters, peaks and plateaus. *King of the Beats* imposes a state of inertia from the start. Beats drag, press down on the shoulders, tug at the armpits, then seep across the back as sirens loop into high frequency swarms. Editor Chip Nunez microsplices tape of The Winstons' *Amen Brother* break into a polyrhythmic arrangement of looped loops. The effect oscillates between the impedimental and the impellant, veers from drumstates of anticipatory inhibition to pent-up propulsion and back again. Nunez's and producer Kurtis Mantronik's Tokyo Tower of percussapella alters the density of the distributed body. *King of the Beats* tattoos you with its grooves, impresses the gravity of rhythmic thought on you. Each cycle stalls the body in a throttled tension punctuated by horns that punch phase like the brass constructions of the JBs.

The Thermodynamics of Conundrums

Loop 2 of *King of the Beats* doubles rhythms so the tempo wrongfoots you. Roaring cymbal-rush maintains anticipation without release, stoking the pressure. The single snare of Loop 3 hits like someone knocking on a door, builds the sense of being trapped inside a room. Sped up, the tempo becomes the hook, a rolling plain of polyrhythm that lifts the limbs, brings on a hi-tension. Likewise, in Eric B and Rakim's '87 *You Know You Got Soul*, the beat before the chorus accelerates 7 times faster than usual, until rhythm tumbles in a stampede through your big brain.

The beat suite substitutes molecular changes for choruses, pressure drops for hooks, converting The Song into a valley of intensities. When 2 beats converge and the rhythms roll against each other, the double impact causes a wavecrash of kicks and accents. Loop 7's metronomic beat plays over a radio sample and a drumroll fanfare, a slipstream of texturhythmic polycollision.

The indecipherable golem gargle in Mantronix's *Electronic Energy Of...*, the sound of a dalek in traction, bounces back off a looped fanfare in a contrarhythm flow. 'Mars needs', the radio sample used in *Lesson 3*, Double Dee and Steinski's '84 short-attention-span pausebutton-edit epic, repeats 3 times. It's answered by *Electronic Energy Of...*'s compressed robovocalization.

Looping the break tricks the ear into hearing a continuous beat. Each cycle slips out of memory as if the body refuses to realize that it's hearing the same beat every time. Each loop trains the obstinate body until it recognizes its endpoint. Bodies starts to remember the point when the beat loops back on itself. There's a psychoacoustics of rhythm: the big brain anticipates the cycle, gets into the groove, lives inside the tense present of the loop. The Breakbeat becomes a mnemonic.

As you're ambushed by beats, charging breaks dock at your joints, tug at the muscles of your mind. Treacherous underfoot, they build a new psychomotor from the old you.

SAMPLADELIA OF THE BREAKBEAT

Intensify the Phonotron: Ultramagnetic MCs

In '88, with Ultramagnetic MCs' debut album *Critical Beatdown*, HipHop becomes computer music. Ultramagnetic MCs — producer-rapper Ced Gee, rapper TR Love, dj Moe Love, conceptechnician and vocalist Kool Keith — initiate a cosmogeny of sampladelia, a mythology of the sampler. Tracks become Sonic Fictions, sonar systems through which audioships travels at the speed of thought. Ultramagnetic MCs are obsessed with the field of force that technology ignites in us, with the unstable world of cosmophonic forces released by the sampler, the electromagnetic waveforms accessed through sampladelic operations.

The human organism is flying apart. The Song is in ruins. Sampling has cracked the language into phonemes. It breaks the morpheme into rhythmolecules. Only science can ride the shockwaves it has instigated. On *Brainiac*, the Ultramagnetic producer becomes the Breakbeat Scientist, 'building molecules on my SP12.'

We're opening the magnetic field
Ultramagnetic MCs

The Fallout from Phonemes

MCs' *Ultra [Part II]* announces the Ultramagnetic world of molecularhythm. Sampladelia splits syntax into phonoparticles. It releases verbivoco objectiles, consonants which fire at 45 revolutions per minute until 'the auditory canals are burning, while the Technics keeps turning, at a dominant speed.' Kool Keith's insistent stress on final and first words frustrates the flow, turning delivery into a zigzag of staccatoing syntax that functions by 'elevating a physical source through particles'.

The Magnetic Mutation of the MC

The Ultras sample is a door opening onto kids playing far off, pianos looping until notes lose profile, dissolve into a timbral tension without release, *Star Trek* theme pulsations synthesizing the human into a SonoCyborg. Morphemic radiation mutates the MC, granting new powers of 'ultrapower flowing'. All these elements of the sampladelic world coalesce in an Ultramagnetic forcefield, converging until they 'roughly emerge as a soul mechanism.'

The Hypoatomic Universe

Hypoatomic energy irradiates the Song with soul sonic force, adapting the scientist into a *soul mecha*. Entering the phonophysical universe shatters‹›scatters the mind. In *Smoking Dust*, 'inhabitants disappear through' Kool Keith's brain, provoking a psychic blast that leaves him wondering 'What seems to be the problem, What's wrong with my mind?' The Psyborg is swallowed up by the kinetic energy which creates it, overcome by 'wires leaking with energy'. Hospitalized at Bellevue, Kool Keith uses HipHop to organize his 'delirious insane' condition, assembling a PhonoFiction of concrete irrationality. The Ultra track amplifies this shockwave, broadcasts it in mad squealing synths — radioactive drones switching into crackles.

I Is a Crowd

Instead of putting the scientific self back together or mending the broken fragments of the cybernetic psyche, Kool Keith heightens what used to be called schizophrenia, intensifies the crackup and the breakdown. The self doesn't split up or multiply into heteronyms.

Rather, the self no longer amputates itself down to a single part but instead asserts that I is a crowd, that the human is a population of processes. Multiple personality is no syndrome or disorder but a relaxation, a giving into rather than a fighting against the brain as a *society* of mind.

The brain is a society of mind with no one driving. The head isn't the Kommand Kontrol Centre of the body. There is no one processing agency, intelligence isn't central and everyone hears voices talking in their heads all the time. Kool Keith's various heteronyms — Rhythm X, Funk Igniter Plus, X-Calibur — are agents, systematically fictionalized from the flux that we all float in. What used to be called alteregos are now *multi-egos*, a crowd of synthetic subjects.

HipHop Is an Analogy Engine

HipHop begins as an analogy engine, in which the I is like = like = etc. This phonoextension is why HipHop takes over space in your head. Powered by analogical chains, its syntactic prosthetics occupy your brain, take up your mind.

For Kool Keith, words are machineparts, to be soldered together into Unknown Audio Objects. Roaming over the wreckage of songs, the scientist assembles PhonoFictional engines from 'hypothetical basic mechanisms'.

In *MCs' Ultra [Part II]*, the phonoengine functions 'like a Commodore computer' by 'inducing meaning to its limit.' *Ain't It Good to You* diagrams the hydraulics of the Ultra sonomachine in its hazardous journey across the head. Phonopower flow[er]s through the neurocircuits along 'rhymes in my tank', through 'brains pumping gasoline', igniting the 'meter and gauges' that crank out new 'lyrical engines'. The Ultramagnetic lyrical engine operates by 'combinating elements', connecting a suffix to a prefix, using these machineparts of 'vocab' to 'connect the abulary', then 'switch it'.

The cosmophonic engine is driven by neologisms, by terms like *Critical Beatdown*'s 'exquisitive', which joins exquisite to inquisitive. *Brainiac*'s syntactic -abulary machine sparks new synaptic junctions, new pathways for 'fuel' to 'ignite blood pressure above the brain level.'

The archetypal Ultramagnetic MC track has a spaceship drone running through it, the radioactive hum of a powerdrive which transports you onto the flightdeck of the Nostromo. *Bring It Down to Earth* typically switches tempo, like power being thrown so that the beats cross a threshold and the sample snaps open onto a new world. The impact of new atmosphere rushing in decompresses the track, inserting you into the hull of the ship, until 'power ignites the four horsemen.'

On '93's *We Are the Horsemen*, the spaceship's powersource hums throughout, buried at the edge of earshot so it turns audio-tactile: your skin hears and your ears feel it as a perpetual irradiation, a tense present without release. Peering out from the flight deck, Kool Keith pilots the soundcraft, monitoring alphanumeric settings at 'Artemis Level 4', checking that 'I get a warp speed, change my gamma flow, 1387, 20096.' His petulant, disdainful cadence shifts gears, seats you beside him, turns you into co-pilot locked into his 'mentally mad' trajectory, unable to grab the controls. Reentering earth's orbit, the UMC sonar ship prepares to dock at 'gamma ray one block, altitude X speed.' Keith doesn't address you: his lyrics are readouts from a bank of onscreen terminals. Their preoccupied urgency alter your position, switching you from co-pilot to Ground Control to a viewer watching 'the movie' where 'your brain will be the star'.

On *Smoking Dust*, synths shift gear, phasing the track onwards in a propulsive surge at '7 x zero, coming light speed, Alpha control spark, relay the A jack.'

> *I'lltakeyourbraintoanotherdimension*
> *I'lltakeyourbraintoanotherdimension*
> **PAY**   **CLOSE**   **ATTENTION**
> **Kool Keith<>The Prodigy**

Advancing Technical: Take the Elevator to Level 7

Ultras-style science doesn't clarify: instead it perplexes, complexifies. The Ultra theorist's role is to 'truly confuse as a scientist,' by 'advancing technical, by confounding through Rakim's formula of 'constant elevation'. To advance technical is to reconfigure the conceptechnics of HipHop, to invent new sonic operations, new phonotrons. Elevation is Hip Hop's higher state of consciousness. Ultra's techniques of elevation tap into the alpha, beta, gamma, hypogalactic rays which are tearing us apart. Rays = raze = raise: through homophonic processes the scientist harnesses the radiation flowing through him.

Autobots and Cybotrons

By advancing technical, HipHop complexifies itself, 'charging energy at a level', becoming an intensified phonotron powered by ultramagnetic current. In *Brainiac*, this power is harnessed into new cyborg systems which function by 'boosting crystalloids as an autobot, increasing brain limits far beyond space.' The autobot is the automatic robot, the dumb out-of-control pathfinder which explores viral zones, nuked-out wastelands, intestinal canals and the pavilions of Jupiter. It allows new weapon systems, such as the 'cybotron, completely on a mission to annihilate.'

HipHop's sonic cyborg electrocutes, while Electro's Cybotron technofies the biosphere. The Ultra cybotron is the triggering mechanism for the exhilaration of annihilation: 'Megabomb ignite.'

Assemble the Cryptogrammatron: Rammellzee

> **Malu Halaza:** *What is an engineer and specialist on quantum physics doing in rap?*
> **Rammellzee:** *I'm a very social creature*

Science Puts out the Sun

To drop science is to mystify, rather than to educate. In HipHop, science breaks it down in order to complexify not to clarify. For auditionaries such as Rammellzee, Rakim, The RZA and Killah Priest, science is the end of edutainment and the systematic mythification of everyday life. Instead of teaching street knowledge, science steals 'your common and robs your sense', as Wu Tang Clan proteges Sunz of Man describe it. Rather than giving you the real deal or clearing away centuries of miseducation, science exacerbates the fog of the mind and heightens the hermetic. Its drive is to expand the limits of Virilio's unknown: 'Science and technology develop the unknown, not knowledge. Science develops what is not rational. That's what fiction is.'

Science actively derealizes the solid ground of the street, corrodes the rare essence of soul, sucks you in through the studio until you're slipping through the pavement into inner space. Science actively cloaks everything, just like Sun Ra, who always veils his answers: '*Astro Black* is about — oh, something that's greater than the truth. So it's over in myth it's hidden.' Science is to HipHop as MythScience is to Sun Ra. Science unravels the world into endless allegories, eclipsing consensual order in an overwhelming opacity of overlapping directives.

Science doesn't instruct, it inducts you into secret states of innervision, initiates useless quests for the 3rd Eye, spreads a daze of confusion only occluded by the powers of the Inner Mind's Eye. Science turns vinyl into a mass medium for channelling information mysteries, private MythSystems, fragments from endless infoverses. Science takes advantage of vinyl's replayability by turning listening into a full-time job. Science wants you for an acolyte, wants to initiate you into a hermeneutics which elides reality.

Science Razes Consciousness

Science razes consciousness: Rammellzee, Killah Priest are esoterrorists who use the 12 to drop mythillogical systems that actively terrorize. To terrorize is to terratorialize. Terror razes consciousness by destroying the old grooves of the head. The decks become what Lee Perry terms the 'Turntable Terranova'. A New Earth emerges from the new grooves of the newly scored mind. Over the cosmo-dynamics and proto-jungle breaks of '87's *Follow the Leader Dub*, Rakim issues a grave diktat: 'I'm here to remake the brains, take away the pain.' Science scorches the old brain to manufacture a new mind.

Graffiti is not vandalism but a very beautiful crime
Bando

Graffiti Is a Future-Writing Machine

After sur-realizing slanguage into the twilight kingdom of double-dutch remanipulation on the *Beat Bop* 12, Rammellzee begins to analyse the formal implications of HipHop, and immediately realizes that Graffiti constitutes a future-writing machine: 'Graffiti is a word that society placed on abstract technique, iconic statement. People did not understand.'

Fab 5 Freddy redefines Graffiti as Calligraffiti, just one name among many: Iconografix, Aeroglyphics and Aerosoul Art all presume an extensive training in exclusive symbol systems. Aeroglyphics is maintained by an electribe of youths bonded together through skills, cabalized by the technics of vision.

Wildstyle returns communication to priestly elites who transmit baffling codes throughout the city. Fab 5 Freddy stresses that 'Wildstyle is totally illegible unless you're initiated.' The city walls turn into secret channels. The city trains become galleries without walls for the cyphertribes.

The pictogram involves the senses in McLuhan's 'ballet of postures of the mind.' Wildstyle exercises the senses, puts the eyes and ears through an Escherized assault course. For Bando, the letter opens up a new possibility space: 'I make letters because 26 letters is enough to define every single thing that exists in this world.'

The Formal Operations of HipHop

Wildstyle is just one element in a HipHop now understood as a series of techniques, an ecology of media which together constitutes a kinaesthetic WarMachine. HipHop has hitherto been understood naively in terms of its content, of what software engineers call the front end of message, lyrics, output. In the *Ikonoklast Panzerism Manifesto*, Rammellzee crosses a new threshold of machine evolution by elaborating the formal logic of HipHop, its back end, its abstract operations: 'You have the gladiators, the freestyle dancers, warring on the ground, you have the graffiti writers warring in the air or in space. You have the translators, the DJs, the MCs. The DJs make the sounds of the piston inside the graffiti element or the tank.'

For Rammellzee, graffiti is tomorrow's writing machine — 'the graffiti element or the tank' — which can enter into the centuries-old war of armoured sign-systems. The dj is the phonomotor: 'Their sound is the perfect tuning of the engines, the engines in the tank that go bambambam. That is beat culture.' The *Ikonoklast Panzerism Manifesto* opens up the conceptechnics of HipHop. To open up a conceptechnics is to elaborate the conceptual technology of a new sound, the abstract machine which drives a new Machine Music. Expertise is encoded on the microchip. Virtuosity has migrated to the soundmachines which contain all music as presets, soundcards and soundfiles. Black Music is in the machines. Therefore an approach to the machine and to machinethought obsolesces premachinic identity. Every sampler and every software sequencing package is 'a constellation of systems and subsystems' through which the producer navigates. A possibility space therefore emerges from restriction, the mother of invention in Holger Czukay's equation. Conceptechnics fluctuates between constraint as a function of the instrument's potential and as a function of the producer's mind.

Militarizing Beat Culture

Abstracting HipHop into a series of formal operations is the first stage in Rammellzee's militarization of beat culture. His aim is to turn the abstract machine into a conceptual WarMachine. This is why he describes himself not as a producer or an MC but as 'a mathematician and an engineer' who 'builds weapons for a living.'

Magico-mathematics and concept engineering converge in the encryption system of Wildstyle. From this emerges *Ikonoklast Panzerism*, the armoured typographical machine, the cryptogrammatron used in the communication wars of the future. *Panzerism* leaves the walls of the world behind to become an encryptic technics in a universe of secret myth-systems.

Writing, alphabets, typographies are all ubiquitous elite technologies that have lowered themselves into your consciousness where they adapt you to *their* habit, *their* reflex, *their* perception. The alphabet is not just a transparent communication but a ubiquitous technology, a system adapted and encrypted by successive religious regimes for warfare: the Roman, the Christian, the Medieval, the Gothic. Words, letters, signs, symbols are all weapons, stolen, ornamented and wrongly titled to hide and manipulate their meaning.

The prize? Control of the means of perception: 'The Romans stole the alphabeta system from the Greeks through war. Then in medieval times, monks ornamented letters to hide their meaning from the people. Now, the letter is armoured against further manipulation.'

Rammellzee's war takes place on this front: the barely perceptible level of habit and reflex. Each subsidence, each decompression into ubiquity is a victory for one technology over another in a perpetual war between adaptive technologies fought on your own sensorium.

Panzerism is a mystery weaponsystem in a secret war not against future corporations but against shadowy Christian cabals: *Ikonoklast* 'means symbol destroyer, it's a very, very high word militarily, because the two Ks are the only two letters that can assassinate the infinity sign, remove the X.'

The MythScience of Beat Culture

By elaborating the abstract machine of HipHop, Rammellzee opens up the MythScience of beat culture, which becomes a mythengineering of symbolic information.

'87's awesomely crepuscular track *The Lecture* opens up the Military Perceptual Complex of MythScience. Rammellzee is no longer a Master of Ceremonies, an MC. Instead he's an MK3, a Master of Kommand Kontrol Kommunications, a despotic esoterrorist who lectures on 'Aerodynamics and Quantum physics'. Instead of breaking down information to its simplest atoms, the tunnel visionary systematically encrypts all information: 'But we want you to understand that the integer is a nation by itself. Its function [*pause*] leads you into the future.'

Mathemagical Weapon Systems

Panzerism is heavier than the Pentagon. Inside the Military Perceptual Complex, the integer is the magico-mathematic weapon for use in cyberneticist Norbert Wiener's scientific wars of the future. Drawing you into an auditorium where echoes seat your hearing at the back, Rammellzee's voice arrives from a distant lectern, inducing a powerful sense of being drawn into overlapping systems of privy information: 'All formation and military function that hold the code to any formation procedure. With. Out it you have no control. You will have no control. This information I cannot really give you. Because I am not the master of its own technique.'

Throughout, the tone of the lecture shifts treacherously from acerbic to drawling to disquieting: 'As the [*pause*] interrogator of *Ikonoklast Panzerism* I don't give nobody no business. I tell you what is full military information and function for all integers, all four of them. There are no pictograms here. What I draw is architecturally built and will fly.'

Information and function: as a cryptogrammatology, *Ikonoklast Panzerism* encrypts all symbols, inducing an overpowering sense of ominous information and conspiracy made audible in *Lecture*'s keening, multitracked voices. Horns loom into tonal shadows, shattered by string arrangements that reverse into Varèsian shriekbacks which leave space shuddering from the concerted attack impulse.

The cryptogrammatron cracks alphabets and breaks down equations. It works as a codebreaker and symbol destroyer in the ongoing perceptual wars: 'In a war against symbols which have been wrongly titled, only the letter can fight. The infinity sign with the fusion symbol

[x] in its middle has been wrongly titled Christian [+] and thus it has to be assassinated or the x has to be removed.'

The letter is a signal system designed for armoured combat in the sign wars. Across the unstable front of the typographic warzone, Rammellzee assassinates the fusion symbol sign, and removes the x using the integer and the letter. This is rapper Jeru the Damajaa's *Wrath of the Math*, where symbols are mathemagic numbers imbued with lethal capabilities. Rammellzee: 'The infinity sign is a mathematical, scientific, military symbol. It is the highest symbol that we have and you know there isn't even a key on the typewriter for it. I'm going to finish the war. I'm going to assassinate the infinity sign.'

Equation = Annihilation

In his drive to capture all levels of the analogical, Rammellzee crosses into the covert ops of clandestine perception. Symbols are Commands which encode power: 'The 4 integers, nocturnal myth, music notes, meterological symbols of heterosizers and all integers that formate any process of reading pictogram knowledge [*pause*] and of course my invention of the atomic note [*pause*] for *Panzerism*.' This abstraction of HipHop's formal architecture and the convergence of its kinaesthetic operations leads Rammellzee to invent a militarized mathematics. In the war of symbolic systems, the equation is annihilation. Norbert Wiener looks up from his flow charts to announce that 'The effective mathematician is really as dangerous as a potential armourer of the new scientific war of the future.' In mathemagics, equations are the operating instructions for unknown authoring engines.

On Don Brautigan's back sleeve for James Brown's '73 *The Payback*, *Mind Power* is illustrated by a profile of a man recessed into grey, pyramidal stone. His cortex is divided into sections, each inscribed with archetypal equations: $E = MC^2$. Mind glows with the light of mental power, astralized by magico-mathematics.

Brown analogizes vinyl's groove to funk's groove. By abstracting material and Applied Rhythmic Technology at the same material plane, he opens the conceptechnics of funk. The revolutions of *Mind Power* on the decks flexes the muscles of the mind. Each revolution of funk's groove rescores the mind until it becomes a superpower. The JB drills the audience into its new nervous system, until you become the souljah in an army imbued with Soul Power.

Equations – postures of the mind – converge with post-John Lily cybernetic bioprogramming on how to tap into the mind's powers, how to bodybuild the brain. Funk turns into a subjectivity engine, into what Detroit's Techno dj-imagineer Electrifying Mojo will in '93 call the 'Mental Machine'.

The MythScience of the Scratch

The Lecture probes into the unexplored possibility space of skratchadelia. The perceptual pressure of the new artform forces Rammellzee forward into a MythScience of the scratch, the Darkside of the decks, the hermeticism of the headphones, the trigonometry of the transformer switch: 'You must talk to the dj. You must. Talk. To. The dj. The scratch is not for you. The scratch [pause] is not for me. But you must listen to it anyway. Education is only subliminal. Redefine. Redefine.'

Breaking the beat doesn't always reduce it to the atoms of Ultramagnetic MCs' machine mythology. For Rammellzee the beat is already an encoded rhythm, and to break it down only encrypts it further. The scratch is vinyl made recognizable yet unlocatable. Only by comparison can you approach the scratch. Its new tone leads you on an analogical flightpath. Just because it's pop doesn't make it easy.

On the contrary, the science of the scratch is massively difficult, demanding intense rehearsal. Far from being something anyone can do, scratching is intimidatingly elitist, an artform heard by all but only understood by the obliterati. As it currently exists, 20th C art can barely grasp the tonal history of turntabilization.

In exploring the formal implications of the scratch, Rammellzee in '87 can therefore presuppose a global audience of 100 at the most. Strings are arranged into shrieking attacks that halt abruptly, leaving space trembling with shock impact like an EEG pulse gone critical: 'Only he has the number written down in the scratch. Intellectualize. Redefine. Because it's only in the dj's manuscript. And it's no spoken word. It's called a scratch. With all the millions and millions of megabeats that have been programmed in our minds, we know it all equals down to zero zero zero active negatives.'

A female chorus keens mournfully. A ship horn blasts as it approaches harbour: 'You hold the scratch being a broken record. This wine turns to twine. Entwines like a rope in your mind/Like DNA code.'

The MythScience of the scratch is just one element of the traumatizing system of Gothic Futurism: 'You have just gotten a chill in the feeling of your heart. [*Foreboding echo*] With most people their heart would have stopped. But I think yours [*speeded-up vocoder*] just got started. I held all this information back from you just because you haven't signed your name to your death certificate.' Shards of funereal ghost choir break in, the jagged edges of broken harmony.

Gothic Futurism fastforwards the ancient Gothic‹›Germanic script suppressed by Roman typography. Rammellzee becomes the Historetician, the historical theoretician who terrifies through his esoterical terrorism. Factory rhythms engulf the lecture. A bottle smashes, becomes the beat, pistons punch out time, hammers jack and judder, steam shoots needles of hissing air. Strings swarm in an impending unease, a state of unlocatable threat. Forlorn voices wail in a threnody for deleted massacres.

Lecture is structured as a series of inscrutable commands from a Destructiv Knowledge Engine: 'We want you to proceed with your books on Gothic texts. We want you to open up the pages 449 45 Roman Law. Turn to card number 1997. And for this we want you to know that you have already failed your course with a B. You haven't even gotten to what it is. The inflammation of all information.'

Escape into Psychopathogenetics: Dr Octagon

> *Sometimes I don't even feel like I am a human being anymore*
> **Kool Keith**

ReEntering Planet 3

On hearing *Dr Octagon*, HipHop's protectionism, its appetite for grounding reality, its drive to discipline and punish are obsolesced. All its belief systems are demilitarized, vaporised on contact, leaving you stranded in a psychopathogenetic future with no way of getting back to the present. Kool Keith and his heteronyms are always coming *back* to Earth, perpetually reentering Planet 3's orbit. They're already at home with offworld states; it's the Earth planet and it's Earth people − you! − who are the aliens to them.

Nothing is alien to Dr Octagon because everything is alien. 'Space is my planet' he reports, in a *Leave it to Beaver*-voice: 'I live there, eat there, wash there.' This generates the same relief‹›thrill you feel when Tricky quotes Japan's '81 *Ghosts* on '94's *Aftermath*. Far from pretending white Americans don't exist, Dr Octagon producer Dan Nakemura — known as The Automator — opens up a memorybank of 50s White-Man sci-fi movies.

Astonish Me!

The Automator perpetually folds the mind into origami. Listening to The Automator reminds you that HipHop is computer music. Trad HipHop continues to install a painful binary machine, a rigid funk canon that cuts right through you, and polarizes your flux. But after Kool Keith's, The Automator's and guest producer Kut Master Kurt's '95 album *Dr Octagon*, this restricted aesthetic feels like emotional amputation, like terminal insularity elevated to a fraudulent ethics, an ethics known as Black Music.

Which is why the term Black Music so often sounds stupid, so dated and pointless, a phrase only used by the most retarded r&b cheerleaders. Black Music: the term clamps the brain because it omits the role of the machine, because it blithely ignores computerization by locating all of HipHop back in the all-too-human zones of the soul or the street.

To use the phrase Black Music is to presume a consensus that has never existed, to assume a readily audible pre-synthetic essence which machines have externalized, manufactured and globalized. No longer sheltering within an essence that never was, today's Futurist understands the mythillogic of the soundmachine.

The Futurist is a scientist who manufactures new MythSciences from soundmachines: the processes of AutoCreation, AutoCatalysis, AutoDestruction which cooperate as the secret life of machines, the clash of concepts on the plane of X meets Y.

I Multiplied

The traditional diagnosis of alienation no longer makes any sense to the 90s producer. Instead of synchronizing the mediated body with self image until the 2 make a single knowledge of self, Dr Octagon disaligns the selves and then continues to multiply them in a mitosis of the I.

You Are a Population

It was already clear to Rimbaud back in the 19th C that I is another. To listen to Dr Octagon today is to grasp that every I is a crowd, that you are a population, that unity is a fleeting, accidental convergence persistently mistaken for an identity.

The unified self is an amputated self. The human is an ecology of mind through which the Doctor walks, hacking and slicing pathways through the distributed brain. He‹›It is the offworld xenobiologist, fascinated by the biodiversity of the human organism: 'I study and inspect people. Choosing scientific matter, I probe for evidence.' He's attracted to the human's connective zones, your buttcracks, vaginas, mouths, sphincters, magnetised to the human as a mammal in an animal continuum. Octagon is always plugging humans into animals, reconfiguring bodily hierarchies, recombinating them with cartoons. The human species is his zooillogical laboratory, Dr Moreau, Dr Benway, Dr Octopus and Dr Kervorkian his inputs. Instead of getting himself together, he falls apart and the parts – Dr Octagon, Kool Keith, Ultramagnetic MCs – battle one another. Thus Kool Keith on his Dr Octagon persona: 'When he says "I'll battle Ultramagnetic andmyownselfaswell," he definitely means that.' Not schizophrenia, nor quadrophenia, but octophrenia.

> ### *The forms of thought assisted by computer are mutant*
> #### *Felix Guattari*

Technofy HipHop: Build the Unidentified Audio-Object

Kool Keith defines 'elevation' as 'new terms above the natural language of MCs'. To elevate means to reinvent the conceptechnics of HipHop, its conceptual technology. It means technofying HipHop, in a parallel to Cybotron's '85 demand to technofy the biosphere. To 'advance technical' is to perpetually engineer HipHop into Unidentifiable Audio-Objects, UAOs that hurl listeners against the reef of their senses.

The UAO is a Year-3000 connection machine that runs on cosmophonic power, a Jupiter-to-Earth link enabling the alien to 'program one and go to Earth through the fax machines, My number 709-755-6EL3, Computer file 9-3, Digital level.'

As computer music, the UAO has an internal computer architecture which digitizes funk's groovengine: 'I'll take a break like James Brown to the bridge,' the section which turns the Song inside out. HipHop is degravitated, becoming not only weightless but invasively PhonoFictional, aggressively competing with the consensus of your head, forcibly substituting your assumptions with its own.

HipHop is transchronized. The entire *Dr Octagon* triple concept album returns to '96 from the Year 4000, from the 40th C: 'It's like if you were running around in the year 4000 and this tape is playing.' *Dr Octagon* snatches you into the world *it* comes from, an environment which you're at home in. The record turns you into a 40th C human. It jumps you into a world in which it's on. Consequences are either infinite recursion [this tape is playing and on this tape is a tape of...] or complete indifference: you were running around, you never even heard *Dr Octagon*.

The album is an octagonal time machine, a future UAO shooting past '96 back to '87 to duel with his albums, to take on his former identity, his former group: 'Dr Octagon was designed for the specific function of returning from the future. He would love a crack at *Critical Beatdown*.' The Ultramagnetic spaceship becomes the Octagonal time machine.

Haloes were found at the landing site.
Sir Menelik

2 Mirrors in the Clear
John Carpenterized synths freeze time into the hovering tone of the medico-conspiracy thriller. *Earth People* uses rhythm synthesizers for their indifference, their tinny treble: 'I see it as futuristic new wave rock. It's metal in its own way. It's meant to have that industrial effect to it but slowed down.'

Information stress lights up the sensorium like the Nippon Trade Centre. Kool Keith replaces HipHop's Trad voice armour with a highly strung hauteur, an extreme sarcasm pointed with malicious precision at Trad HipHop's sanctified stupidities, an extreme aversion to its familiar fixations.

Morality Is a Muscle, Clenched
Morals are just these sensory coagulations, these tensions knotted and bunched across the skin of your beliefs. *Dr Octagon* inverts the Trad

hierarchy of head/stomach so that your head tastes ill and your intestines think. Your brain throbs, in peristaltic waves. *Dr Octagon* keeps everything unreal, its voice in perpetual motion, from glutinous to gloating to dastardly to bedside to malicious. Instead of grounding you it uproutes you, pulling you across into its world, moulding then massaging you across a series of thresholds you never knew existed.

Design for a Brain

In Octagonal sound design, the music suddenly drops out, like ballast jettisoned, so that each WordObject becomes an objectile projected through space. Voice echoes the first word of each sentence: 'Vanishing victims kept alive on metal examining tables. Experts, baffled at the survival from exposure to laser scalpels, Green berets growing coneheads in mechanical wombs.'

When the music evacuates, the chorus-sample zooms past earshot: 'Megatron!' 'Rejuvenate!' 'Galaxy Rays Powerful!'

By being projected all at once, the chorus compacts into a syntax beam, packed with kinetic energy, a supersonic allatonceness: 'Controlled by gammalights!' Magnified voice blasts off across sampladelic space with an intensified phonodrive. *Earth People* is filled with the plosive impact of polysyllables which pushes against the bass and the beats, tugs at them, pulls towards and away from them, acting as a field of attraction for the groovengine. Consonants are charged until syntax detonates, in a series of off-the-beat exPLOsions: 'Octagon, oxygen, illuminum, intoxicants.'

In the parallax world of *Technical Difficulties*, where Dr Octagon goes 'walking through a polygon', rhythm falls away and sentence looms forward: the ear hears it as a headline. 'My first impression was to give patients a lesson, who's the best to put me to the test, I'll battle Ultramagnetic, myownselfaswell.'

Simultaneously a robotvoice repeats it slowed down, like a radio tuned into a phone-in generating delay feedback. This 2nd voice repeats the last words of a sentence, drawling, sneering, slowed down or distant like a faulty echo chamber sending back aural distortions.

Octophrenia frustrates flow. Dr Octagon, Sir Menelik the Emperor General, all accent unexpected words and stress syllables so that WordObjects disarticulate themselves. Flow falls apart in a drastic dysphasia when the brain's unable to coordinate syntax. By arresting HipHop's verbose flowmotion, syntax seizes up then lurches forward in a robotic cadence that induces an arhythmic irritation. Mindstresser: the order of things breaks up. Sense starts zigzagging like the lightning logo bolting across Captain Marvel's costume.

By missing out the 'and', octagonal consciousness collapses the distance between WordObjects, creating a dataflow of different matters, a discontinuum of all kinds of minds. It updates the info overload of Joycean stream of consciousness, the unperiodic continuities of Reed and Burroughs. Octophrenia is both datastream and flow frustration, connective synthesis and disjunction.

Octagonal Consciousness

These techniques converge until Trad stream-of-consciousness — that modernist byproduct of radio — crosses another threshold into parallel processing, the emergence from massively connected computer programming. The Song is rebuilt, out of excerpts from 8 unrelated broadcasts happening simultaneously.

At Century's Start, W. E. B. DuBois analysed double consciousness as 'this sense of always looking at one's self through the eyes of others'. Mutation by high-pressure capitalism collapses psychic and social membranes, doubling and splitting you into the 2nd person. At Century's End, Kool Keith protege and digital-age lyricist Sir Menelik exemplifies octagonal consciousness in the Information era. Adaptation to the Information-Image economy multiplies the senses of seeing, hearing, feeling yourselves into the 8th person. *On Production* is neither song nor track, more an extremely compressed lecture delivered in a merciless monotone and so insistently by Sir Menelik — the Emperor General — that it induces information panic, updating Rammellzee's and Shock Dell's '87 *The Lecture*. *The Lecture* is esoterrorist science: hermetic, despotic, terrorizing. With Sir Menelik, science travels at the speed of thought, phaseshifting into a Disunified Field Theory. The MC becomes a Human Computer, a parallel processor who hears talking in everyone's mind.

*What of the others, the humans with their almost
non-existent tolerance for pain and their totally
inadequate mental discipline?*
Sir Menelik

The MC Is a Parallel Processor

At this level of mindstress, syntax becomes a rapattack which strobes the brain, impacting with the remorseless frequency of measured voltage. As attention drags further behind the inexorable information flow, the gap between attention lag and infovelocity is phaseshifted, passing from sensations of stupidity into an itch in the brain.

On Production triggers an acutely tactile mental irritation that simultaneously begins crawling over the skin. Your brain feels fat and flabby, a torpid muscle dragging its bulk after this rap that just won't stop.

This is not science fiction but New Science, functioning from the year 4001, from 'the time when the human brain has reached the era of full employment.' Chris Marker's film *Sans soleil* announces this era, when 'everything works to perfection, all that we allow to slumber, including memory. Logical consequence: total recall is memory anaesthetized. After so many stories of men who had lost their memory, here is the story of one who has lost forgetting.'

On Production shifts from a report from the flightdeck to instructions from a navigation manual, to report of immune system breakdown, to emergency broadcast, to a lecture on chaos theory from a future version of the Santa Fe Institute: 'Does science achieve a unified theory of complex systems? Completely chaotic systems, such as turbulent fluids, heated gases appear on the borders between rigid order and poetry among a list of the 31 ways to define "nomadical".' Sir Menelik switches address again, broadcasting a warning that turns you into an echochamber: 'All mankind must submit to genetic testing, Disease contaminates every transmission of unawareness.' Terror resounds through the dome of your head.

As Sir Menelik the Emperor General emerges from *No Awareness*, the synth's dying arc and electric piano drop away, leaving an ominous texturedrift, a vapourmoan. Drum machine stilts, its inexpressive pulses stutter. WordObjects *whaaAAm* across the stereoperceptual field. Sir Menelik leaves sequential monorational flow for a new mode of rationality. Not verbal flow but rather a parallel-systems maintenance check, a specifications warning report read out really fast, to induce infoverload of 'Acoustic death by analysis.'

Which generates a disconnected multirational Sonic Fiction, in which concepts jump, thought leapfrogs, mind zigzags from clause to clause, a perceptual current transmits between each intervals, ripples across gaps. Concepts are electrified into pararational military instructions to 'increase magnetic fields, Electro-liquid expands, critical procedures cool 77 Kelvins by submerging.'

Each track induces a feeling of perpetual dysphoria, untying and rearranging your nerves, dis-ease triggered by sampladelia before the lyrics ever start. This verbal verbosity, this info-expansion turns you into a decoder perpetually switching routes between Marvel cosmology and cosmetic surgery, transpecies organ transplantation and astrophysics, alien sex and medicopathology.

We think as instruments
Mixmaster Mike

The Deck Magus Turns the Tables on Time

Turntablist Q Bert's skratchadelic solos are the sonic parallel of the sf/horror transformation scene. Already effected sounds become unrecognizable textureffects, spongy blocs phaseshifting through a series of unknown audio states. Squeals modulate into whistles and screeches, decay into astonishingly sustained whinny which reverts briefly back into a recognizably male scream before fading out entirely.

Skratchadelia is mutantexture generated by turntabilization, by using the turntables as universal tone generators. Disk of turntable ensemble Invisibl Skratch Picklz: 'It's the only instrument that can be any instrument. When you have a guitar, you're limited to how the guitar sounds. But when you have a turntable, you can take a guitar, you can take a drum sound, you can take a dog barking, you can take any sound and manipulate it into your own.'

Q Bert hooks the decks up to guitar-pedals, drastically effecting skratchadelic textures, immediately opening up an entirely new spectrum of altered beats and mutantextures.

Identification Code unidentified, Press a button, Change my face
Dr Octagon

The Inhuman

Dr Octagon isn't human. Rather it‹›he is an inhuman that slips and slides across the alien‹›human discontinuum. Its‹›his 'skin is green and silver', morphable to any chromatic situation by 'changing blue skin' until its 'brown colour's coming back'. It‹›he is an alien adapting to its West Coast environment, looking like a Caucasian peoploid then 'a paramedic fetus of the east'. He's prepped with unknown medical tech: 'cybernetic microscopes'; '2 telescopes that magnify the eye of a roach'. *Blue Flowers* is a psychopastoral set in the 'Church of the Operating Room', delivered in a bedside manner of frightening reassurance. Un-EZ listening sirens circle through EEG bleeps, sustained cymballic hiss and radioactive bass generating the hovering tension of Jerry Goldsmith's *Coma* soundtrack.

Psychopathogenetics

The uneasy intimacy of a gloating gynaecologist meets the misanthropic glare of a rabid ecologist to form Dr Octagon the Gynechologist, the planetary psychopathogen. David Cronenberg diagnoses Gynechology as 'a future pathological psychology. It's developing now but he anticipates it being even more developed in the future. He then brings it back to the past-now and applies it as though it exists completely formed. These characters are exhibiting a psychology of the future.'

Gynechology slashes and hacks the organism, pulling 'out the skull', chiselling 'necks for the answer' to the body whose map puzzles and baffles aliens everywhere. The body is the question. Surgery provides the answer to this cellular planet which still mystifies the alien surgeon. For aeons, the bad doctor observes humans with a compound eye. 'I study and inspect people': Kool Keith and The Automator use HipHop to put humans under the macroscope. HipHop becomes a reverse microscope, a speculative imaging system invented by Cyclops 4000‹›Sir Menelik for magnifying perception. Then the bad doctor moves in, ready to 'operate on patients, be a rectal rebuilder.' New techniques of 'intestinal surgery' and 'saliva glands relocated' across the orifices inspire breakthroughs in the field that Techno auditionary Jeff Mills terms basic human design.

I would just mate humans with alligators.
Huminagators
Kool Keith

Xenogenesis

The Octagonal world is a biotic landscape where bees fly 'around your rectum'. The doctor doesn't rap at you, he diagnoses, preoccupied with his delicate incisions. He‹›It compels you to crane your ears towards the operating table to audiovisualize the clink of scalpels. It's‹›He's busy relocating, stuffing and inserting patients 'with the needle and thread, sewing up all the other buttcracks.' Looking at 'naked pictures' of The Fantastic Four's orange brickworked Thing leads the doctor to explore the new frontiers of Disney‹›Marvel sex. He watches this close encounter as 'the cartoon Donald Duck' gives 'fellatio on the floor with Reed Richards', the Fantastic Four's venerable and elastic scientist.

'Sometimes,' Kool Keith has said, ' I don't even feel like I am a human being anymore. I feel I could put myself in the place of a mammal or an animal.' Depersonalization allows an identification across the animal species, a cross-species empathy. In Octagonal Sonic Fiction, dehumanizing = complexifying the human into a xenolibidinal economy of genes traded on the open market.

Gynechology opens up the animal‹›human continuum, breeding transgenic species – such as Mr Gerbik, 'half shark-alligator, half man'. Gynechology rapidly runs out of control until gorillas are 'masturbating with human strangers, legally through court', while androids are 'leading humans with haemorrhoids' on goosechases and duckshoots throughout Planet 3.

Octagonal PhonoFiction examines the senses with a speculum. Not so much an ecology as a gynaecology of the mind, it uses syntax as probes inserted through the nostrils, up and out into your sensorium. The perceptual borders between alien identity, human organism and organized self collapse into organs sloshing in a blood soup.

Octagon addresses all 'Earth people', subsuming distinctions in a globalism more threatening than benevolent. After the genocidal promise of 'I was born on Jupiter,' Trad HipHop's misogyny feels like happy trails, its dystopic misanthropy like instinctive travels through a gadda da vida. Gynechology doesn't protect species; it preys on them, taking 'you there' into the human zoo 'like I was the Predator.'

Continents are zoos, countries are safari parks and humans provide excellent culture for crosspollinating across the mammalian phylum. Not flowing but gloating, the locum becomes 'Doctor Ludicrous' who turns 'into an octopus' all the more easily to 'grab 8 species' and 'isolate like a incubus'.

Listening to *Dr Octagon* flashes forwards to the alien abduction you will never have. You're being alienhandled in an operating theatre of cruelty and killing jokes: 'The perfect enzyme's me with your brain in my other hand.' The alien induces traumas and kills its patients with insouciance. Dr Octagon is a surgeon out to build a new nervous system out of your archaic one. It gives you a seasickness of the head.

The Inhuman gets a contact high from cruelty. It lingers over organs with a loving sense of detail, loses itself in the rapture of dissection, the joy of getting to work on a warm body.

BoddhiSativa Explosion in Slow Motion:
Cypress Hill, The RZA, Gravediggaz, Sunz of Man

Oh man homey, my mind is playing tricks on me
Geto Boys

Mythillogical

HipHop has always been headmusic. But the moment it drugs itself, it turns its back on imminent revolution in favour of immanent revelation. The street dissolves into the psychosonic geography of gangstadelia. HipHop becomes an inner-space music. 'Keeping it real' no longer means representing, because there's no defined reality left to represent. Knowledge now means innersight, which overwhelms the true/false binary. The street's rigid border between the real and the fantastic melts into the psychospatial treachery of the '91 film *Jacob's Ladder*. To really grasp mythillogical HipHop it's essential to rent Adrian Lyne's video epic, in which New York dissolves into a diabolical swamp of unending audio hallucinations all the stronger for being unseen.

I'm having illusions, driving me mad in my mind
Cypress Hill

360° of Peripheral Persecution

Weed deregulates the means of perception, breaks down the walls of HipHop's fortified ego. Cypress Hill's '92 instrumental *Ultraviolet Dreams* melts HipHop's martial self. Producer DJ Muggs' fuzzy logic of wilting bass and low-frequency leakage blurs audibility, unwinds the gangsta lean into a woozy gait. Vigilance loses focus in the witchy, whispery psychoacoustic space of inhalation turned treacly thick. You wander through its striated wraithscape, a malleable porous flux.

Weed's dilation effect makes it the time-stretcher, the narcoagent which slows down the perception of object-events. DJ Muggs is fascinated by the bullet's trajectory, how a body looks from the gun's pov, its sighting line. As Sly Stone croaked: 'Looking at the devil, grinning at his gun.'

All drugs intensify paranoia. But Weed's special effect is to magnify the misperception inherent in everyday hearing, thereby tuning HipHop into a perpetual paranoia of peripheral persecution.

The ear always hears around corners. Grass intensifies this until reality breaks up into proliferating audio hallucinations that trigger themselves at 360° around your head. At the edges of earshot sounds launch themselves at you.

In HipHop headmusic, R. Murray Schafer's schizophony has become premonitional. Sounds have detached themselves from their sources and are reaching you before their causes do. Hear what happens when soundeffects go amiss. They wander without an object. Running amok with no cause at all, soundeffects generate environments of objectless ominousness and perpetual imminence.

They took a sonogram and seen the image of a demon
Gravediggaz

The Internal Mechanism of Paranoiac Phenomena

Driven by premonitions, mythillogical HipHop is like Sarah Connor in *The Terminator*, always talking in the past tense about things it hasn't yet done. The head is filled with revelations that impeach the daylight. The RZA's phantasmic HipHop productions induce visions in the ear. Every breath becomes a wince of pain like a knife being swallowed. Each suck of tical turns into a sharp intake, the shuddering gasp of someone being hacked at. In Method Man's *Sub Crazy*, from his RZA-produced '94 album *Tical*, unattributable groans roam around, suffusing everything in an unlocatable seething violence.

As Tricky points out, Weed is a shortcut to psychosis. Like Dr Octagon, Redman's alterego Reggie Noble splits off and battles himself, like Peter Parker vs Spiderman. Noises attribute themselves to unseen causes, multiply themselves into invisible forces.

The RZA opens up the hyperparanoia of a post-*Jacob's Ladder* world, in which inanimate objects come alive with an inorganic malevolence. For Redman, possession is a perpetual possibility: 'I believe you're supposed to be able to move stars with your mind. There's motherfuckers out here that can jump into your body, put your spirit out, and you'll just be walkin' around New York unseen while someone else is in your body fuckin' up.'

Worship the Weed

In '95's *Temple of Boom*, Cypress Hill worship the despot Weed.

All those clips of peachy-keen white schoolkids from the 50s of the film *Atomic Cafe*, hands clutching their heads, praying to the Bomb. Atomic Muslims bowing to the Mecca mushroom silently screaming: 'Mutate me! Mutate me!'

Weed blows up the head, exploding reality like a mushroom bomb detonating the mind, like the underworld mutants who worship the nuclear bomb in *Beneath the Planet of the Apes*.

The US military wanted to bomb 'Nam back to the Stone Ages. Worshipping the Holy Weed, Cypress Hill want to bomb their minds back to the Middle Ages.

*Now I dwell in an Islamic Temple/I'm fighting a
holy war in the mental*
Gravediggaz

Holycore Is the Blight of the World

With Gravediggaz' *Diary of A Madman* from their virulent '94 conceptoxic
album *Niggamortis*, HipHop breaks through into the mythillogic of the
Darkside. In the fictional space of a courtroom hearing, The Gravediggaz
– producers The Undertaker‹›Prince Paul and The RZArector‹›The RZA,
The Gatekeeper‹›Frukwan and Grym Reaper‹› Poetic – face murder
charges. Each steps forward to enter an insanity plea. Each verse
projects excerpts from a meta-exorcism on the screen of your mind. A
wall of guitarchimes opens up a sampladelic Gothic, a monastery of the
head where keening Gregorian chants throw shadows across stonework.
The head becomes a theatre for the warring forces of Heaven and Hell.
Consumed by spirits and possessed by visions, consciousness is the
casualty in this 'holy war in the mental'.

   To stress this war between states of mind, Gravediggaz' protege and
guest rapper Shabazz the Disciple's term for this Darkside is Holycore.
Like its doppelganger Horrorcore, Holycore blights everything. Instead of
enlightening through edutainment, it turns out the light of the world,
plunges the sky into what Sunz of Man term 'a magnetic flux beyond
control'. As The RZA explains, the Darkside of HipHop is aversion
therapy for droogs anaesthetized by too much HipHop: 'Heaven and Hell
are on earth. They're your good times and your bad times. The holy war
is the struggle inside our heads, the war for peace. People walk around
mentally dead. It's our duty to dig up their mental graves and bring them
back to life.' This shock therapy for the sensorium parallels Ludovico's
'learning by torture' in Kubrick's *A Clockwork Orange*. The cold humour
of *Dial 1-800 Suicide* is a scartoon which brings the pain, raises welts
and draws blood to freeze it. Like Dr Octagon and Funkadelic – right
down to the hommage *Mommy What's a Gravedigga?* – the mythillogical
humour of Gravediggaz lacerates minds inured to sensation, intensifies
illness in order to sensitize.

I contain the science to make an angel bleed through his vision
Sunz of Man

Ultraviolet Superception

This is aftermath music for a weary world stoned into a stupefied superception. Public Enemy's war demanded hyperalert soldiers, the jagged edge of '89's *Black Steel in the Hour of Chaos*. In Sunz of Man's '95 *Soldiers of Darkness*, HipHop gives into visions, plunges into the waking nightmares that The Bomb Squad's alarm for the world tried to prevent: 'Visions of me on the night of a solar eclipse aboarding the mothership taking my last glimpse from this deluded earth.' External war has been internalized into 'the depths of my inner sight' only to spill out blurring the borders in a psychosonic storm.

Sunz of Man begin at the point of extreme exhaustion, when soldiers hallucinate, suffer from crisis apparitions. Wu Tang producer Genius's '95 track *Greyhound Part 2 Remix* starts out already exhausted, defeated, its tempo barely more than a trudge, footsore. Caught in the aftermath of explosion, Killah Priest's voice peels inside out in slow motion.

Hurled into a windtunnel of delayed impact, vowels buckle and groan, consonants gust in phonemic debris thrown off by a distant detonation. Wheezing groans intensify the sense of overwhelming fatigue.

Greyhound Part 2 is a long march, a trek extolled by chimes heard through smoke, transient tones of tintinnabulation. Flutes, trumpets, guitar are fatigued, winded. A boneweary 'yeah' escapes from someone's throat. Gregorian chorale stretches into hive noise. The moans of perverse monks imbue everything with a cloistered malevolence. Haunted-house violins cycle into steady micropolyphonal swarms at once hallowed and dolorous. Soldiers hallucinate celestial visitations on the Somme in WWI: 'I was shown the crucifixion by 2 Egyptians/A war in heaven, I saw Christ with a Mac II/So I joined him and prepared for Armageddon, Armageddon, Armageddon.'

Decapitated MCs wander like wraiths through the warzone of Headless HipHop. Brontosaurian bass stalks a battlefield scorched by blasts of megalithic guitar feedback. His voice slowed down to a groan, Killah Priest is a headless MC reciting from beyond the grave.

*All this seems to be an exorcism to make our
demons flow*

Antonin Artaud

The Priests Will Soon Swarm

Time feeds forward into the new Dark Ages. Each time the Inner Mind's Eye blinks, it puts out the sun. In Revelations, the Son of Man is Heaven's hired assassin, putting sinners to the sword on Judgement Day. Multiplying the Son of Man into the Sunz of Man — dramaturgist Killah Priest, vocalists 62nd Assassin, Prodigal Sunn, Hell Razah, producer 4th Disciple — blaze with a solar fanaticism. They are God's Avengers, 'soldiers of idolatry fighting the sins of reality.' Each 12 rescores Revelations as auditionary Sonic Fiction, a War in Heaven with all factions desperate to maintain control.

The Earth is their deerpark and you are its fawns. Sunz of Man are not human so much as devout exterminators, 'the universal warlord': Cortez with a Kalashnikov M16. They are Armageddon accelerators inflaming the sensations they deplore, who 'came together for one accord', to dream of genocide for Jesus: 'Hearken. As the night darkens, you've been warned that the priests will soon swarm.'

Visions of priests spreading their cloaks and swarming over Oklahoma, searching for unbelievers to put to the sword and 'be done away like the unicorn'. Killing is praying, terror is faith, murder is holy.

Killah Priest warns of the 'side effects' of war which 'bring the glycosis' until 'insanity enters humanity, invades the central nervous system.' Abruptly his voice slurs and slides into glossolalia, becomes an urgent gibberish overwhelmed, jacknifed by a voluptuous swoon never heard in HipHop before: 'this technique is so aaah, aaah — ' and HipHop's voicearmour is overcome by the wargasm.

Reeling from the force of revelation, he recounts how 'the 4 run to the 4 corners of the earth and the 5th run into the sun.' In a dazed accapella, Killah Priest, the annihilator, is pierced by 'a light beam' until he recollects how he 'was formed in a white dream.'

Killah Priest doesn't so much rap as incant or invoke in an inquisitorial tone. Reverb snatches his voice to the alcoves. He's Torquemada at Millennium's End, the final despot who commands you to 'bring the wicked before me and slay them before my feet.' There's no doubt that this fanatical anti-abortionist was there at the burning of Sodom and Gomorrah, bombing the bathhouses, torching the clubs.

Five Arch Angels is the score for *A Canticle for Leibowitz* in which the world nukes itself back to a Middle Ages run by Techno-monks. In the wake of The Song is a wraithland of swarming drones, infernal sighs, disembodied moans and magnified breathing.

*Something outside had to enter, something which
we ourselves would be unable to build*
Philip K. Dick

3rd Eye Capture

Tricky, The RZA and Killah Priest are all infatuated with the dormant powers of the 3rd Eye. In Rakim's Islamatronic fiction, Rammellzee's and Shock Dell's cryptomachine and Killah Priest's psychoacoustic Darkside, the 3rd Eye is a secret faculty that scans the nonvisible spectrum for radio, ultraviolet, daemonic, acoustic waveforms.

Precisely because medical science doesn't know its function, the pineal gland attracts esoterrorist tradition, which argues it's really the 3rd Eye, the dormant Inner Mind's Eye, an archaic power that Philip K. Dick suggests is opened by meditation: 'We relinquished the 3rd Eye, our prime evolutionary attribute. Then it's the 3rd Eye that gets us back out of the maze. That's why the 3rd Eye is identified with god-like powers or with enlightenment, in Egypt and in India. The 3rd Eye had to be reopened if we were to get out of the maze... but since we no longer remembered that we had the eye of discernment, we could not go about seeking techniques for reopening it. Something outside had to enter, something which we ourselves would be unable to build.' Effram Wolf's watercolour sleeve for Stevie Wonder's *Innervisions* shows an ochre-and-brown optic ray blasting out of his closed eyelid, a field of vegetational vision searchlighting the stratosphere like The X-Men's Cyclops gone botanical. Wonder's plantsight triggers an eco-optics of the Mind's Eye. And Funkadelic are the aromanauticists of perception, setting off harrowing hallucinhalations of the Mind's Nose.

Boll Weevil Computer Brain: Funkadelic

The brain is a population
Deleuze and Guattari

Lysergic Equation for the Funkatized Psyche

Funk + LSD = Funk Psychedelicized = Psychedelia Funkatized = Funkadelia, as Manuel De Landa explains: 'When you trip you liquefy structures in your brain, linguistic structures, intentional structures. They acquire a less viscous consistency and your brain becomes a supercomputer. Information rushes into your brain, which makes you feel like you're having a revelation. But no one is revealing anything to you. It's just self organizing. It's happening by itself.' LSD generates a Funkadelic Liquid Computer, the funkatized psyche that rechannels anger from the street into alternatives to reality.

Impeach the Universe

Funkadelia impeaches the universe, confronts reality, sets out to destroy an insane world over and over. Back in his mind again after tripping out, George Clinton realized that 'I could get mad enough at the world and how it was treating people to wait in an alley and kill some muthafucka. But there ain't no winning in a situation like that, so once we got out of there I'd take acid to make sure I didn't get that mad no more. I'd start looking at, you know, alternate realities.'

Acid's information supernova blows up the ego. Hence the dot of the 'i' in the Funkadelic logo is replaced by Pedro Bell's grinning ape-skull, the Grateful Dead logo gone loco. The globe mushrooms out of its cranium in a planet-annihilating, world-forming explosion. Funkadelia isn't an escape into other worlds, but a deathtrip into the hallucinogenres of LSD and the superpsychedelic STP. As Jay Stevens describes the STP trip: 'Descriptions of it sounded like war stories, people exploding through the envelope and burning, or filled with a cold wind that wouldn't stop blowing through the hollows of their mind.' Which describes the Funkadelic audio experience very exactly. Acid opens a cataclysmic continuum between Vietnam, Detroit and Other Planes of There.

The Logic of Catastrophe

In *Wars of Armageddon*, the world is annihilated before your very ears in a logic that J. G. Ballard elaborates: 'The catastrophe represents a constructive and positive act of the imagination, an attempt to confront a patently meaningless universe by challenging it at its own game, an attempt to dismantle the formal structure of time and space which the universe wraps around us.'

To be funkadelicized is not to retreat back into the mind but to externalize the mind's fears, expand them until the listener swims through a universe brimming over with cosmic slop, vaginal discharge.

The formal structure of time collapses into swill. Space loses its dignity, falls kneedeep into the shit of the world. Funkadelia intensifies the osmosis of funk, amplifies its imperceptible aroma. *Osmium*, Parliament's‹›Funkadelic's '70 debut, is named for the heaviest, most pungent metal on Earth. Rock plus aroma converge in what the RZA terms heavy mental music. Because humans have no noselids, they're defenceless from rhinal attack. Formless and pointless, funkadelia therefore invades through the nostrils and seeps through the nerves, setting inhalation at war with the body. You breathe in the putrefaction of the universe. 'We can't clean up shit or get shit right until we recognize we got maggots in our brain, that any situation we make will be rotten because the attitude we're using is already poisoned.' Funkadelic shares the fall and makes a friend of fear: 'We took the blame for shit. Sly would see it slightly. Yes, Mr Stewart had the fear and could accept the ugliness, and his shit was so profound that you always thought he was talking about you.'

Thought is bio-logical or does not exist
Rene Menil

Chaosmic Kemistry

Funkadelia opens a biologic of thought, a physiology of perception. Mind, soul, universe: the old, old worlds of Trad sensory deprivation are suddenly materialized, gratuitously oralized. Concepts are fondled and licked, sucked and played with. In '70's *What Is Soul*, the Funkadelic Alien arrives on Earth: 'Behold, I Am Funkadelic, I Am Not of your World/But fear me not, I will do you no harm/Loan me your funky mind, So I can play with it.' Like Galactus the planet-swallowing god of the

Marvel universe, the Funkulator lives by cosmophagy, the philosophical rite that Susan Sontag explains as 'the eating of the world.' The nose knows that the mind is food for the maggots. *Mommy What's A Funkadelic?* opens with Clinton drawling demonically 'If you will suck my soul I will lick your funky emotion,' while *Maggot Brain* circles around the cosmic bummer: 'I have tasted the Maggots in the Mind of the Universe.' Here a universe is small enough to roll on the tongue: metaphysics desublimates, swaps shapes with a mouth as wide as the cosmos which spits out the soul in an endless well of phlegm.

United Mutations of America

Funkadelic enlists you on the side of your darkest fears by tapping into the toxic drives of technology. *Maggot Brain* 'could scare you to death.' The inside sleeve artwork of '72's *America Eats Its Young* shows the Statue of Liberty with bloodstained fangs snacking on babies. In *Eulogy and Light*, time slips backwards into what Clinton will later term a backwashpsychosis, a terroride into the Altered States and United Mutations of America.

Cyborganographics

Pedro Bell's gatefold sleeve art for the '73-'76 albums *Cosmic Slop, Standing on the Verge of Getting It On, Let's Take It to the Stage, Tales of Kidd Funkadelic* and *Hardcore Jollies* visualizes funkadelia as an organographic Sonic Fiction. Funkadelia becomes an appalling cyborganographics. At the other extreme from Kraftwerk's seamless menschmachine, the funk cyborg spills its guts in a diabolical chaos of pustulating 'nastyness'. From '73's *Cosmic Slop* onwards, each Funkadelic scartoon — a cartoon that leaves scars, in Bell's definition — reveals episodes from a prolonged EcoRape of Mother Earth, with her maggot hair, slitted eyes, pointed incisors. Felt-tipped intestines emerge from the giant Mother figure, entrails escaping from the bodily incorporation that the digital materialist Nick Land terms the human security system. Digestive tracts, creeping umbelliforms, organs without bodies more slimeware than wetware slither through space, squishing over magazine collages. Alimentary canals merge with maggots to become unidentifiable dripping matter oozing globules of goo. Aliens riveted together from steel plates with jigsaw-puzzle shaped outlines where organs should be slide altimeters from cold to hot. Funkadelia is total dis-organization, the disconcerting slurpy slew of cyborgans gone awol in a universe of someone else's insides. Pedro Bell's emetic pharmadelia wants you to vomit ingested emotion, beliefs swallowed and impacted into boli. The conceptoxic landscape makes you sick to make you better. Funkadelia generates a global head, an ego that explodes in the atomic chain reaction. The detonating 'i' in Funkadelic's logo is atmospherocephalic in Dali's sense; it puts the external world 'into the service of the reality of our mind'.

In the information fallout of the sampladelic era, Tricky designs a scatterbrain which thinks bomblike. Jeru the Damajaa's equation for scattershot thought is 'my brain $C_3 H_5 N_3 O_9$ like nitroglycerin'.

Chase Through the Headphones: Tricky

Equipped with contradictory visions, an ugly hand caged in pretty metal, I observe a new mechanique. I am the wild machinist, past destroyed, reconstructing the present
Samuel R. Delany

Abducted by Audio
You value the momentary sample because it abducts you. Levels fluctuating on the phoneline in *Abbaon Fat Tracks*, the mother whispering 'Can you fly fast as you can to be with Jesus': all this is a window opening in time, sound falling into your mind, 0.5 seconds of processed videosignal captured from an unknown 50s tv film set in an imaginary 40s.

Sampling allows a way of collapsing all eras of black music onto a chip
Greg Tate

The Anachronizer
The sample works like the scene in Nic Roeg's '76 *The Man Who Fell to Earth*, where Thomas Newton sees the 18th C peasants through the yellow of centuries while they see a white Rolls, suffused in blue, cruising through farmland. I would throw away a century of movies for

this anachronic moment — when the 18th and 20th Cs infiltrate each other, crossfading into the time Miles calls yesternow.

The sampler is the universal instrument, the instrument that makes all other instruments.

The sampler operates just like this Roeg sequence or like the music heard in Ishmael Reed's Egypt AD '72: 'A mixture of Sun Ra and Jimmy Reed played in the nightclub district of ancient Egypt's "The Domain of Osiris".'

It's an anachronizer that derealizes time: a snare from '69 Michigan United Studios, a duet of the Bombay Studio Orchestra from '72 on Led Zeppelin's *Friends* with gunshots modulated from a CCTV clip to videostatic from a '63 ZDF documentary on Dogon cosmograms to the shriek of Jerry Goldsmith's Varèsian arrangements for the *Planet of the Apes* soundtrack.

You're abducted into this world, distributed along its dimensions — but this world leans into yours. Sampladelia is both the reality-effect of samples you recognize and the Origin Unknown effect of samples you don't. These Unidentified Sonic Objects can suddenly substitute themselves for the world, eclipsing it, orphaning you, washing you up on its shores. There's a powerful sensation of deletion as samples trigger successive waves of synthetic defamiliarization.

The sampler — which includes the vcr and the ansafone — is a machine for derealizing solid state sounds. Sampladelia is the state of being overcome by 20 seconds of sound.

Motion Capture

The Breakbeat functions by cutting into the track. It operates as Motion Capture, ruthlessly discarding The Song, blatantly disregarding original intent. Indifferent to tradition, the Breakbeat sacrifices the past to the now.

Stripmining the source draws attention to the Parliamentarian or the Serge Gainsbourg archive, but the sampler function is as predatory as it is respectful.

Sampler memory determines this as a rule for all sampladelia. The sampler insists you know what sounds you love.

It imposes your sensual satisfaction on you as a condition of its memory capacity. You're forced to externalize your taste. Every sample is a report on‹›from the internal state of your sensorium. your personal selection amplified into a global memorybank.

You Are a Habitform

Digging in the crates means becoming a samplefinder, hunting the ignored audiozones, listening to the world, chasing down the remnant, the indifferent/useless original track. Listening to the breaks flare up from the unfamiliar track, each sample recognizes you. Heard in its unknown original, the beat becomes a Motion Capturer that seizes your skin memory, flashbacks your flesh. Each sample is an aural camera which reveals you as a Clintonian habitform, the organism formed by habit. The sample, a window into psychoaffective time, exposes and externalizes the instamatic mechanism that is your innermost taste. It retroactivates all the times the needle draws you to drop it on the groove. It reveals the spontaneous you as a servomechanism of the playback function, compelled to load the cd, press the remote, lift the needle off the runout groove. It reveals the intimate interface between you and the turntable, makes audiovisual the machine's view of you.

Hearing the original recede into unrecognizability reverses the Breakbeat procedure. Time turns back, returns you to a long-gone world in which DJ Kool Herc never invented the Breakbeat.

Headspace is the geography of the mind which can be reached by no telescope
R. Murray Schafer

Subtract the Song

Against pop's presence, its realtime voice, dub asserts the logic of the dropout, the song's gravity being plunged into a yawning chasm, of space as an invasive force on the song, x-raying the song structure, disembodying the song, distributing its traces, hunting the ghosts of sonic textures. Dub is the nth-degree warpfactor, the trace element. It disorganizes The Song, subtracts into an apparition, a phantom funk of stealth and intermittence.

As an agent of alteration, dub's derealization of The Song's profile, its recognizable edges, feels far more present than does r&b's oversouled human presence.

*I feel alien, and like someone's going to recognize
me in a minute as an alien*
Tricky

Wraith

On Massive Attack's '91 *Blue Lines*, the HipHop voice deflates and
spatializes into a headphone music for headz, a bedroom music. With
Tricky, post-HipHop headmusic becomes headless, wraithlike,
unheimlich, at home nowhere. Tricky's inhibited murmur doesn't emerge
so as much retreat asthmatically from the side of his mouth. Trad
HipHop hypes the voice, revs it into a motormouth. With Tricky, verbal
flow slows down to a baleful crawl that cloaks Martina's withered husk
of a drawl. Often, this croak is barely there, just a shade of itself.

Martina and Tricky are not so much singers as fluxes, perpetually
transmitting abrupt bursts, human aerials resonating with the low-
frequency oscillations of the city in tremulous sympathy. Tricky's not
interested in narrative as much as psychogeographical textures that blur
the subject = object divide into a hazy continuum.

The Blunt Smokes You

Tricky is not so much a narcissist as a *narcossist*. Narcissists never
smoke, never do drugs because drugs take time away from yourself,
precious time that the narcissist could be spending on themselves. The
narcissist gets high on the endless supplies of themselves. The narcissist
works fulltime on the endless job that is themselves.

For the narcossist, on the other hand, the self goes up in smoke.
Being is an unbearable heaviness.

Bomblike

The narcossist dissipates all this hard work as easily as inhaling: 'My
brain thinks my brain thinks bomblike.' Nowadays, as Tricky points out
'everything happens at once, not just one thing at a time.I'm trying to be
3-dimensional.' Like Basquiat's worldmachine painting *Pegasus*, Tricky is
a hypersensitive human antenna, a human radar, an exposed cortex with
all his nerves on the outside. 'My brain thinks bomblike': all the info of
the datasphere floods into these human transmitters.

By admitting to flaws, amplifying frailness, Tricky fashions a searing
force from weakness, implicates you in a conflict of confusion, spite,
petulance, awkwardness; dysfunktionality disarms HipHop's bellicose

belligerence, dissolves House's emotional carapace.

The first sign of psychosis is a Christ complex
The Lawnmower Man

VC Christ Complex<>Devil Syndrome

On '95's *Psychosis*, The RZA's diabolical atmosphere evacuates standard song structure, replacing it with a miasma of swarming drones, infernal sighs, disembodied moans and magnified breathing.

The beats don't keep time; instead they drag time down into a drugged tempo. A high-pitched hum insinuates through the track, deliberately inducing a new and improved tinnitus, the perpetual ringing of the ears that you can never switch off. No earlids.

The song's remains are saturated by an overwhelming claustrophobia that pervades everything. Your body cringes from its infernal shakers but the intensified malevolence reaches out and traps you, draws you down into its world. You're caught inside a pair of giant lungs. Each close-miked inhalation, each asthmatic heave draws you in through its nostrils. *Psychosis* drains your lifeblood, leaving you enervated, crushed by sonic pressure.

Tricky's voice slows to a crawling shudder. Shivering shreds of voice shadow each other, volumeless shapes writhe around his croaking death rattle: 'So it seems I'm the Devil's son/Out of breath and on the run/Jesus Christ they wanna be me.' Tricky explains the drug‹›tech interface of the Christ Complex: 'I smoke a lot of weed and, you know, it's a fact that people who smoke weed go through Devil syndromes and Jesus syndromes.'

Songs become prophetic visions that accelerate the apocalypse they warn against: 'Space race the alien/The Devil's come for me/The Devil's come for me.'

I escape with my sanity, utilizing 3rd vision /
Surrounded by a 3-sided figure containing the brain
of a triggering mechanism
Organized Konfusion

Paranoimia

The world becomes a permanent threat, swarming with dog devils and earth angels, a destabilized flux of perpetual paranoia. 720° of peripheral suspicion, unfounded grudges and wild guesses: all these externalize themselves, split off, roam around, come alive.

The RZA stretches out each word in the spooked shudder of Hanna Barbera horrorcore. Syntax is dragged until speech is dried out, all the words are withered, sibilated, sucked from an oxygen mask.

The RZA winces after each line as if needles ink out tattoos on his back: 'There is no more rain left in the forest. Everything is petrified, terrified, horrified.' His voice crawls to a stage whisper.

HipHop enters a digital Dark Age in which the Seven Deadly Sins, the Christian psychomachies, return as audiohallucinations, psychic pathologies plaguing HipHop's wretched hoodrats: 'You have been denied the right to your 3rd Eye. Now it's shut t... t... t... t... t... t... t. No more to be opened' [*laughs*]. On one hand the 3rd Eye is an obsolete pineal gland, the remnant of ape‹›human evolution, a million-year-old body sensor. On the other, it's the large, unexplained blank spot in the middle of the visual field, the mind's eye, the threshold to godlike perception, the eye of insight that gives humans immaterial innervisions.

INNER SPATIALIZING THE SONG

[Towards a] MythScience of the Mixing Desk: The Upsetter

Far from Rastafari's flat-earth metaphysics, its fundamentalist blood and fire, Lee Perry's productions and theory fictions open up an entirely new field: the MythScience of the mixing desk. The Upsetter taps into the secret life of sound machines, opens the cybernetics of the studio.

Remix Your Head

In the Upsetter's conceptechnics, the mixing desk is a mental machine, a mind‹›machine interface. Perry diagrams the neurocircuitry of the Soundcraft mixing board, its thought flow: 'I put my mind into the machine and the machine performs reality. Invisible thoughtwaves, you put them into the machine by sending them through the controls and the knobs or you jack it into the jackpanel.' It is a medium that forms reality, violently bending the environment, massaging it.

I introduce myself as a mistake
Indelible MCs

The Secret Life of Sound Machines

Perry is the analyst of the studio's ability to extend perception. The
mixing desk decomposes The Song, leaving a skeletal ribcage. The Black
Ark studio is a machine lifeform: 'I see the studio must be like a living
thing, a life itself. The machine must be live and intelligent. The
jackpanel is like the brain itself so you got to patch up the brain and
make the brain a living man.'

Dub demands symbiosis that externalizes the mind, drastically
reconfiguring the human producer into a machine being, an audio
cyborg: 'You are listenin' to a machine. I imitate human being, I'm a
machine being, I don't work with human beings.' When you sculpt space
with the mixing desk, these technical effects — gate and reverb, echo and
flange — are routes through a network of volumes, doorways and tunnels
connecting spatial architectures.

We're taking over the sun, we're changing time, we're changing space
The Mighty Upsetter

Meteorology of the Echoplex

Using the Echoplex to clone echoes and the Roland Space Echo to delay
time and accumulate shocks of reverberation, Perry reremixes nth-
dimensional impacts, neither snares nor syncussion but perplexing,
confounding SonoMatter. In the electromagnetic nth world of '75's
Revolution Dub and '78's *Return of the Super Ape*, The Song is
disinterred until its ghost universes populate the world.

Return of the Super Ape is dub that disturbs the atmosphere until it
yields poltergeists. Arriving ahead of cause, sound turns motiveless,
premonitional, inexplicable. 'Well, [the drums] were going through the
Echoplex and with the Echoplex we can do anything. We can change
energy and feelings.' Stray sonic debris crashes through space, looms
into closeup. Effects decelerate until they become baffling, frustrating
ricochets from an unloaded gun. The wind of Baudelaire's wings of
madness sends sounds careering across living space. 'The drum controls
the heartbeat and the bass holds the space. I dub from inner to outer

space. The sound that I get out of the Black Ark studio, I don't really get it out of no other studio. It was like a space craft. You could hear space in the tracks.'

Space between sound doesn't drop out, it's pulled out from between beats until it convulses, buckles, folds up into fists of solid air that buffet you with what Perry calls the Shocks of the Mighty. Giant pulsations trample space like colossal youth. Glass shatters, slows down into collapsing cardboard. The ghosts of ghosts of effects, 5th generation fx, unforeheard screams, rattles and rustles agitate the air.

Separated from its cause, the Echoplex creates an ominousness without an object, an all-pervasive feeling of force undefined, of atmospheric energies, which rends The Song, tears it apart. The mixing desk accesses the magnetic fields. It is a control tower from which the turbulence of technology is reconfigured: 'We are here at the Turntable Terranova, it means we are taking over. We're taking over the air, we're taking over the mounts, we're taking over the star, we're taking over the sun, we're changing time, we're changing power, we're changing grace, we're changing space.'

In a World of Echo

As soon as you have echo, listening has to completely change. Your ear has to chase the sound. Instead of the beat being this one event in time, it becomes this series of retreating echoes, like a tail of sound. The beat becomes a tail which is always disappearing round the corner and your ear has to start chasing it. If you're wearing headphones or a walkman it becomes a chase through the headphones. The Echoplex turns listening into running. You can't catch the beat, the tails of sound as they turn the corner, disappear down a corridor. From King Tubby to Basic Channel, the cymbal is always just out of reach, always taking the corner of perception. Where rhythm should be there is space, and vice versa. Spectral dub pivots around an absent beat. *Revolution Dub* is The Upsetter's mindfield. Every track ambushes you, confounds the process of pattern cognition by leaving the expected beat implied. By opening holes at the tightest moments of the groove, pulse falls through subtracted space, polyrhythm wrongfoots you, tugs and pushes at expectation, yanks the floorboards from underneath you. Echo turns the beat from a localized impact into an environment with you inside. Refractions bounce back from any surface. Initially the snare hits a stretched drumskin, the pedal depresses air between 2 cymbals so it hisses. Pneumatic metal pressure. Now the impact that run away from your hearing rebounds back at you from the wall, the ceiling, the floor. The world turns into a giant drum with you at its centre. Beats ricochet off 360°, curving around the walls of the world.

Sitcom Ghosts Stalk the Spectral Song

By bringing the outside into the inside of The Song, Perry releases sitcom ghosts into the spectral Song. Perry samples tv before the sampler, just as Holger Czukay uses radio, drawing signals down through the aerials into The Song, crackling open another timezone inside the track. Space changes places. Reality reverses itself.

The bursts of smashing glass, squawling babies, trickling water, toilet flushes, rustling wind scatter The Song to the winds. Perry enlists a crying baby, a cow, a horse and a 70s tv sitcom on backing vocals. Like a great grandfather clock gone loco, each production becomes a percussion contraption, sprung open and haywired. Shakers, rattles, whistles, croakers, bells, toy piano, arthritic drum boxes in a perpetual rhythmshower, a molecular motion.

The Black Ark studio switches on a technology-magic discontinuum. Operating the mixing desk demands you explore its network of altering spaces. Perry crosses into its ghost dimension, walks through the temporal maze of aural architecture. 'So me join the ghost squad longtime and them notice me as the Ghost Captain. I am the Ghost Captain.'

'Revolution Dub is not so much produced as reduced by Perry. The Song is x-rayed into exoskeletal forms through which tv leaks . For Woman's Dub, the distorted snares drum like needlepoint magick, but rusted, ferric. Kojak is an intoxicated mix, an echochamber of moans in which space staggers and lurches dangerously.

In Doctor on the Go, Perry picks out a hesitant lullaby on piano, crooning 'Doctor on the Go' over and over as if he's being bereaved while the studio laughtrack shudders in then subsides back into babble, theme tune and studio applause. Incongruous occupation of the same dimension, ambiences rub in an incompatible friction. Bush Weed's drums are reversed so the cymbal sustain expands in a metallic shimmer before the snares beat time. The snares drum like knitting needles on silver foil, microscopic magick that anticipates the nth-dimensional needlepoint of 4 Hero's The Paranormal in Four Forms. Raindrops and a nature-documentary voiceover seeps in: 'Man has always been a threat to woodland animals.' Throughout Revolution Dub, Perry's bereft, tottering in a tremulous falsetto of compelling indecipherability. In *Raindrops*, he sings in an eggshell treble as fragile as Leslie Cheung, the Chinese boy-girl performer in the '93 film *Farewell My Concubine*, and tiptoes through *Bird in Hand* on lily pads. On the snare drop, his tremolo is languidity, rockabye bassmotion.

A Field Trip through an Electromagnetic Environment of Distortion

The sonic future from Kraftwerk to Pink Floyd is always balanced, quadrophonically separated. Perry makes distortion the lead instrument in his intoxicated mixology, in which balance lurches, the spatial coordinates of up and down, near and far all heave and yaw in a seasickness of the ear, a drunkenness of the head.

Balance, the Trad location and identification of sound in space, is replaced by a seesawing motion, inducing an oppression by space, a threatening sense that space is about to crush you, push you off this revolving planet. Your hearing is on the verge of throwing up.

With The Upsetter, depth of field is neither weightless and empty nor vaulting and overwhelming. Instead it's crowded with crackle, seething, heaving, teeming with wraiths deprived of definition, lost from history, jostling for space. 'His method of dumping tracks onto one track to free them for further overdubbing introduced an effect of degradation that became an essential part of the mix.' What Steve Barrow calls degradation is electromagnetic enchantment. In *Return of the Super Ape*, the fuzz and leakage of nth-generation tape-distress become lead instruments, drowning the echoscape in a haze of electric feedback. Distortion pushes at the limits of the medium until it exceeds the medium, The Song imploding, disintegrating into oxide, drizzling rain, sibilance, an entire spectral dimension in sound.

The tracks succumb to apparitions, become porous, crackle like the celluloid burning up at the end of Ingmar Bergman's film '66 *Persona*. Degeneration = Regeneration. Sound sussurates into an electromagnetic nth world through which ghosts grow, effects superimpose and wraiths congregate.

Listening becomes a field trip through a found environment. Everything emerges from the subaudible static of underwater electrickery, perpetually rustling and granulating, fibrous and aquatic. Perry buries video tapes in soil, turning the medium environmental.

VIRTUALIZING THE BREAKBEAT

**Wildstyle Adventures in the Hyperdimensions of the Breakbeat:
4 Hero, Rob Playford and Goldie, A Guy Called Gerald**

Traditionally, the music of the future is always beatless. To be futuristic is to jettison rhythm. The beat is the ballast which prevents escape velocity, which stops music breaking beyond the event horizon. The music of the future is weightless, transcendent, neatly converging with online disembodiment. Holst's *Planet Suite* as used in Kubrick's *2001*, Eno's *Apollo* soundtrack, Vangelis' *Blade Runner* soundtrack: all these are good records — but sonically speaking, they're as futuristic as the Titanic, nothing but updated examples of an 18th C sublime.

Technology has made us look at music through a microscope
Goldie

The Computerization of the Breakbeat

With the post-Marley Marl computerization of the Breakbeat, all this [r]earview hearing is over. To go out into space today means to go further into rhythm. Far from abandoning rhythm, the Futurist producer is the scientist who goes deeper into the break, who crosses the threshold of the human drummer in order to investigate the hyperdimensions of the dematerialized Breakbeat.

Our drummers don't sweat anymore
Kraftwerk

Breakbeat Science Is Rhythmic Psychedelia

The Breakbeat scientist never sweats: rhythmatics becomes less about practice, more about 'thinking and hearing', as Kraftwerk said. Moving into the possibility space of hyperrhythm, posthuman rhythm that's impossible to play, impossible to hear in a history of causation. For Goldie, hyperrhythm begins at the point when 'we've lost the drummer'; at the moment when 'you're reading the break like braille.'

To talk of the 'future of computer music' immediately presumes a academic composer-scientist locked into a prewar model of top-down official science. But Breakbeat science is the runaway future of computer music, in which alphanumerical sound *escapes* from the lab, replicating across bedroom studios in a series of covert operations. Breakbeat science is the secret technology of gene-splicing sound, the unofficial science of rhythmhacking the break until it becomes a passage into the drumtrip and the drumtrick, an escalation of rhythmic timbreffects. As Dego McFarlane of 4 Hero explains: 'You end up with a sound that's like a 6th-generation sample, completely different to what you started with.'

Hypercussion

Hyperrhythm's digital supersession of the human immediately alters your perception of the percussive act. As an actional event in timespace, drumming loses its solidity. Breakbeat science scrambles the logic of causation, opens up a new illogic of hypercussion and supercussion.

The Paranormal in Four Forms exemplifies the supercussive goal of 4

Hero: to reconfigure rhythms so that they travel through space. McFarlane and Goldie 'used to talk about this sound that would go all the way around and tap you on the shoulder.' In *Paranormal*, rhythm is a heatseeking break which goes awol, reorganizing sound into an aerodynamic epic. Each break branches, the rattlesnake break in the right speaker travels around your head, fading behind your neck, swallowing its tail. The left-side break fades away behind your head, intersecting with the right in a subsonic turbulence, reemerging so close it grazes your head while the right is far off, subaudible.

Simultaneously the left-side break distresses into a high-pitched tone which drops out only to loom up in your ear, shrieking like a jetfighter. Behind you space trembles as each flightpath agitates the other's orbit at different speeds.

Caught up in the Audiomaze

With *The Paranormal in Four Forms*, you're inside binaural anamorphosis, all caught up in what producer Dr S. Gachet terms the audiomaze. Beats split and launch themselves in parallel flightpaths. The left side is effected into a transistor treble, peaking at a stress-inducing screech. The 2 cross, each swallows the other and everything is tubed through an nth-dimensional torus.

Drumsticks become knitting needles hitting electrified bedsprings at 180 bpm, crackling on impact with humps of atonal bass. Each beat recoils playing the nerves like a harp. Both orbits coincide, the right as knife-sharpening scythe, the left as speed-metal blur, rattlesnake spasms which compress into bedsprings as taut as Tesla coils.

At this level altered beats trigger what Method Man terms subcraziness. McFarlane recalls 'kids coming up to you, talking about The Paranormal, saying how they saw things coming out of the lights and tried to grab them.' Wound up into a hairtrigger tautness, breaks springload the reflexes until you become a body-gun aching to be released. Your muscles seize up, your neck cringes, your entire body hunches up. You're a giant haunch, ready to be released by the trigger.

Science today has become a machine of outrageous representation
Paul Virilio

The Physics of Physicality

Hyperrhythm generates a new physics of physicality. Kinaesthetic disorientations become audible in the astrophysical track titles of 4 Hero's '94 concept double album *Parallel Universe*, in the sensory superparadoxes of Escher's '54 lithograph *Tetrahedral Planetoid*. Space titles announce that the physical laws of rhythm are about to be involuted, just as a wrinkle in time collapses the fabric of space-time. The scientific title makes rhythmic psychedelia audible. The science in Breakbeat science doesn't drain sensation; instead it opens up a possibility space of hypersensation. Rhythmically speaking, science sensualizes. Physics doesn't numb the senses, it intensifies them. When the eye's capacity to explain the ear breaks down, physics takes over. Science takes control as soon as the visual collapses. The cognitive dissonance of science amplifies the perceptual wrench of rhythmic psychedelia.

Quantum physics translates easily into Marvel comics and Warner Bros cartoons because quarks, gluons and the Big Bang all point to the malleable laws underpinning physical reality. It's not God's Word that underpins the subatomic Universe, it's Plastic Man's.

Breakbeat science therefore opens a continuum between title and track across which sensory concepts move freely. Rhythmachines d/evolve into Sonic Science. Science d/evolves into Foucault's sensational phantasmaphysics, the 'speculative fantasy of science' that Ballard called for back in '62.

The impossible physical states of quantum chromodynamics easily become Parliament's quarks and gluons. Radio astrophysics becomes Drexciya's aquawormholes. Physics is the gateway into a kinaesthesia in which geometry is physical, topology sensual.

Breakbeat science is the physics of rhythm. It impacts at levels barely explicable in the normal languages of sensation. Beats become abstract at the point when the body succumbs to sensations which induce a gulf crisis in speech, when language falls away and fails, happily.

The Abstract

Time stretches into a state of sensory shipwreck that producer Roni Size
in '94 termed the 'Phizical'. Rather than disembodying the body, the
digital Breakbeat intensifies it, at a level more sensed than explicated.
This communication breakdown is what Breakbeat science calls abstract.

Abstract doesn't mean rarefied or detached but the opposite: the
body stuttering on the edge of a future sound, teetering on the brink of
new speech.

Breakbeat science's extreme rhythmic involution forcibly inducts you
into a new motor system, turns you into a stepper rollin' with reinforced
reflexes. Listening sharpens up the senses until they bristle like spikes.
The body is being mutated limb by limb, as jungle producer Marvellous
Cain insists, by phizical convolutions that language hasn't caught up with
yet. Language drags its flabby arse after sound. Therefore it is misspelt,
contorted, rinsed out. Language lags behind beats and must be mashed
up. Your motorsensory system communicates paralinguistically from a
future which today's media can't even begin to decrypt.

To say that today's producer is inarticulate and monosyllabic only
reveals how standard criticism is deaf to the sensory spectrum captured
in Sonic Fiction, PhonoFiction and machine mythologies. It is ordinary
language that's dumb and which must be adapted. The nervous system,
the first sensory field to be overhauled by digital rhythm, is now far in
advance of all Trad understanding. Breakbeat science compels you into
the state diagnosed by Norman Mailer in '57: 'We are obliged to meet the
tempo of the present and the future with reflexes and rhythms which
come from the past; the inefficient and often antiquated nervous circuits
of the past strangle our potentiality for responding to new possibilities.'

The Distributed Brain Is a Body

The sensory motor reflexes of the body are centuries ahead of minds
still locked into dead traditions. The body is a distributed brain, a big
brain whose zones are nonetheless separated from each other by
centuries, inherited habits.

4 Hero's *Parallel Universe* is all drumtrips and drumtricks, whose
purpose is to spring the sensorium into activity, to turn on the entire
body as a big brain. The body thinks in unknown kinds of bodily
intelligence because it's a large brain, because the brain is distributed
across the entire surface of the body. Rhythmic psychedelia therefore
activates new kinds of dermal thought, 3rd-Ear hearing, the transensory

capacities of embodied thought. The ear's power to locate the shape of sound in time, what audiovisual theorist Michel Chion calls its 'temporal resolving powers', are sped up and involuted, baffling the body's sense of location in time. In *Solar Emissions* detuned anamorphic warps and quarks flare above your head, make your ears squint.

Rhythmic psychedelia triggers the eye in your ear, the feeling in the ear, roborapper Craig Mack's 'flava in the ear': 'When kinetic sensations organized into art are transmitted through a single sensory channel, through this single channel they can convey all the other senses at once, rhythmic, dynamic, tactile and kinetic sensations that make use of both the auditory and visual channels.'

Breakin' in Space

Parallel Universe crosses texturhythmic thresholds. Collapsing pitch ambushes you into a transformation scene on fastforward, draws you into new sensory spectra, mixed feelings, polyparadoxical drum emotions not yet named. *Shadow Run* is a sequence of grandfather clockchimes running down with an offkey queasiness until what sounds like tape starts to buckle and bump as if it's spooling out over the mixing desk and into space. Keyboards bend and shift pitch into glutinous, melting infra-gamelan. The bass buckles and wilts. Rhythmic signals are filtered through synthesizers until they coil like cables and springs.

Percussion melts into spongy texturematter that spills its guts over the track, escaping from the world of the track to probe around your head, circling your heat. Titles such as *Sunspots*, *Solar Emissions* and *Wrinkles in Time* suggest that breaking down standard speeds into molecular plastic, into stuff you play with, is the aural equivalent of going through the Star Gate in *2001*. Computerization allows 4 Hero to investigate microscopically the microtones of pitch in drums, bass and synth. Mark Clair of 4 Hero recalls that 'We used to have weekends where we'd just make sounds and process breaks.'

By using the sampler's quantum expansion of the ASDR envelope to alter rather than repair the broken beat, rhythm crosses the threshold from wood to metal to what producer Jay Magick terms 'needlepoint magick'. Drumsticks writhe like poised rattlesnakes, beats become blades that slash and scythe at 170 bpm, knitting needles that hit tinfoil so fast that each impact triggers a spitting crackle of fuzz.

The graffiti artist cracked the letter first.
Now I use a Mac to do the same thing
Goldie

Of Pictogrammatology

Graffiti turns the message into the medium. Instead of looking through the letter, the eye is arrested by the letter, travels across its surface. In transforming the letter into the pictogram, the word becomes an image-environment. Looking becomes a movement into the dimensions of the pictogram, a fall through the impossible topology of the 3rd dimension that emerges from the 2nd-dimension wall.

Beyond Wildstyle: Computer Style

Wildstyle intensifies graffiti's 3D impossibility into the hyperimpossible image-levels of 5D. Kaze 2: 'Wildstyle was the coordinate style and then computer. That's what I brought out. Nobody else can get down with it 'cause it's too 5th-dimensional. I call it the 5th-dimensional step-parallel staircase, 'cause it's like Computer Style in a step-formulated way. It's just sectioned off the way I want. Like if I take a knife and cut it, and slice, you know, I'll slice it to my own section and I'll call it Computer Style.'

Kaze 2's 5D art translates Escher's '53 lithograph *Relativity* to the letter. Beyond Wildstyle, the Computer Style is when the letter as environment becomes the letter as an Escherized maze. Computer Style is the alphabet gone digital, typography remodelled, remixed and encrypted. The writer becomes DJ Hype's computerizer.

The Battle of Planes

In the notes for *Relativity*, Escher explains that 'three gravitational forces operate perpendicularly'. In Wildstyle, civil war breaks out between operating "gravitational forces"' so that 'background and foreground take turns changing functions. A continuing competition exists between the two.'

To look is to have your head wrecked. Computer Style involutes the senses, puts them through a mental gymnasium, reassembles the sensorium ready for the hi-pressure future it depicts. It folds the mind into an origami state, a battle style. The senses are kinaesthetized into an orig⟨⟩army, armed for a contest of lines. To look is to be rocketed across the planes of the letter, shot along diagonals that charge space with acute dynamics, gradients that reverse gravity like skyscrapers that drill to the earth's core.

The letterform becomes a city of parallel lines of force. The word becomes a futurescape hostile to traditional sensoria. Surfaces converge to trap the optic nerve at a point of maximum impossibility. Stalked by angles, hunted by diagonals, the harassed eye wanders until it's impaled on the corner, pincered by a parallax plane. Vectors and horizontals join forces to push the retina to the razor's edge.

Computer Style Cubased

In '86, Goldie writes the aeroglyphic piece *Future World Machine*. Pictogrammatically speaking, it is Computer Style, Cubased.

With '95's *Timeless*, Computer Style migrates across different physical scales, jumps from the wall to the screen. *Timeless* is therefore a sonic canvas: 'Across the horizontal/A passage through the canvas, the phases of my life.' As Escher pointed out, 'I can conceive of the series of images on a plane division [Computer Style] and the sequence of sounds of a musical composition [jungle] as different steps of just one staircase.'

Timeless translates the 5th dimension of Computer Style into the hyperdimensions of the virtual Breakbeat. Goldie: 'The graffiti artist cracked the letter first. Now I use a Mac to do the same thing. The loops, they've been sculpted, they're in 4D.' The 5th Dimension becomes the Infinite Remix of Drum'n'Bass. Hence Terminator mutates into a menagerie of monsters from the low end: 4 versions of *Terminator 2*, *T3*, remixes of *T3*. Fragments of *Timeless* are twisted into *Inner City Life*, *Jah, Jah remixes*, 4 more *Inner City Life* mixes.

Remixillogy Is the Art-Science of the Sequel

Remixology doesn't replace a track so much as proliferate it into parallel alterdimensions. Remixology is the science of the sequel and the art of the drastic retrofit, the total remake, the remodel.

Remixology is digital-industrial. It starts out as digital process, as animation of the Cubased break, and ends as industrial process, the dj's demand for the dubplate, the next track, the future sound. The dubplate – the metal acetate – is fictionalized as the Metalhead. The industrial process extrudes the Metalheadz face-logo. With its headphone apparatus, eye and nose slits, it's armoured for what 4 Hero termed combat dancing.

Dillinja's *Jah the Seventh Seal* is a magnified detail from the *Timeless* canvas, a slowed-down blow-up of one hyperdimension. Breaks become chains as time turns to metal. Rhythm phaseshifts from needlepoint to industrial in a war between machine lifeforms on the metallic plateaux. Two drumbreaks are processed until they rattle like chrome snaketails, panning in opposite ways around your head. When they meet they swallow each other and reverse backwards. Simultaneously, machinic groans and wrenching metallic sighs heave and drift across the overlapping orbits of both breaks.

These arhythmic noises compel a kind of bodily seizure, an agonizing muscular crisis, as if the motor coordination needed for walking, let alone dancing, has just crashed from too much sensation. The seething metal fatigue of *Jah the Seventh Seal* induces outbreaks of literally headwreckin' synapse-warping. Your head becomes this giant muscle, this mindless, agonized organ that doesn't know where to put itself.

The Engineer Is an Imagineer

As engineer Rob Playford elaborates, effects are the lead instruments. Effects play the breaks: 'On *Timeless*, there are three sections of strings. They're all the same sounds but each section has a different set of controls, like pitchbend or modulation or gating.'

Computer style visually anticipates the computerization of rhythm. Jungle Escherizes the break into digital information, the 'different steps of just one staircase'. Rob Playford: 'We'd go round a loop, filter, effect, pitch things up or down, then put it back on DAT. Then we'd pick up that sound later on and go through a different route with the effects and filters so it would end up even farther away from what we'd started with.'

Breakbeat science rinses out language, demands new terms like 'snaking out a break or tubing a sound', technical operations which grasp the passage of rhythm through space. Configuring new sounds opens a possibility space inside the screen. Inside the Akai, a virtual topology unfolds itself. Inside the Breakbeat, the scientist battles with the rhythmatical weapons of 'the zord, the blade, the twister, the sub stain.'

With a sample you've taken time. It still has the same energy but you can reverse it or prolong it. You can get totally wrapped up in it. You feel like you have turned time around
A Guy Called Gerald

The Jungle Is a Futurhythmachine

Rhythmic psychedelia emerges when sonic events are in synch while out of phase, a process which leads to Gerald's conundrum: 'Does time work in rhythm or does rhythm work in time?' Amazon‹›African jungles are acoustically disorientating. Height, depth and location reverse. Ryuichi Sakamoto's *Riot in Lagos* and Gerald combine electric signals, pulses, blips and kickdrums into a synthetic psychedelia, hummingbirds' feathers rustling in the canopies. Instead of reconnecting the human to nature, polyrhythm deletes the human from the jungle, intensifying it into an alien rhythmborder: 'You could create a sound that you couldn't quite recognize because it would be going backwards. I'd have something going forwards for a beat and then reversing for the other beat.'

Ghosting out the Break

On *Black Secret Technology, Finley's Rainbow, The Glok Track, Nazinji Zaka*, breaks rustle, shed their sandpaper skins. By sampling a break, effecting it and subtracting the sample, Gerald generates the ghost break: the derealized wraithrhythm writhes throughout the digital foliage. The beat is a posthuman bush of ghosts.

The Sleevenote Manifesto to *Black Secret Technology* grasps the implications of computerizing the break: 'We have advanced to a level where we can control time sonically by stretching a sound... we play with time.' Rhythm is plastic: 'Say someone has created a drumbeat. They've done that in a space and time. If you take the end and put that at the start, or take what they've done in the middle, you're playing with time. With a sample you've taken time. It still has the same energy but you can reverse it or prolong it. You can get totally wrapped up in it. You feel like you have turned time around.'

Each track teems with inhumanly detailed percussion, which demands posthuman motor reflexes. Counter and crossrhythms tug the body into zigzags, dappling the ear with microdiscrepancies between beats. *Nazinji Zaka* turns the ear into a directional mike that's constantly pulling focus. As beats ensnare you in the parallel complexity of the amplified jungle, your skin starts to feel what your ears can't. At these convergences, beats phase shift, cross a threshold and become tactile sensations that sussurate the body. Fleeting sensations of feeling skim across the skin, seizing the synapses. Senses swap so that your skin hears and your ears feel. Dermal ears. Your skin turns into one giant all-over ear. Ear tactility. Your ears start to taste sound. Now you've got flava in your ear.

Like Sakamoto's *Riot in Lagos*, Gerald's *Nazinji Zaka* is a futurhythmic psychedelia which seizes the skin in itchyscratchy sensations that gather around the joints, from there dispersing across the dermal surfaces. Your muscles tense and contract as they pull in and out of perceptual motorfocus. Futurhythmachines complexify the beat into what Kelly terms an 'alien power'. When polyrhythm phaseshifts into hyperrhythm, it becomes unaccountable, compounded, confounding. It scrambles the sensorium, adapts the human into a 'distributed being' strung out across the webbed spidernets and computational jungles of the digital diaspora.

PROGRAMMING RHYTHMATIC FREQUENCIES

**Migration Paths across the Vocoder Spectrum:
Cybotron, Zapp, Drexciya**

*It is the rationalizing and ordering imposed by
technology that makes us forget that machines have
their origins in the irrational*
Georges Canguilhem

[R]earview Hearing

There are no drum-machines, only rhythm synthesizers programming
new intensities from white noise, frequencies, waveforms, altering
sampled drum sounds into unrecognizable pitches. The drum-machine
has *never* sounded like drums because it *isn't* percussion: it's electronic
current, synthetic percussion, syncussion. The sampler is at first termed
an 'emulator', as if it does nothing but imitate existing sounds. Calling
the rhythm synthesizer a drum-machine is yet one more example of
[r]earview hearing. Every time decelerated media writes about snares,
hihats, kickdrums, it faithfully hears backwards. Electro ignores this vain

hope of emulating drums, and instead programs rhythms from electricity, rhythmatic intensities which are unrecognizable as drums. There are no snares – just waveforms being altered. There are no bass drums – just attack velocities.

Posthuman Rhythmatics

With Man Parrish, Cybotron, Haashim, Soul Sonic Force and Jonzun Crew, the Roland 808 rhythm composer opens a new threshold, the programming of posthuman rhythmatics as predicted in '36 by composer Edgard Varèse: 'I need an entirely new medium of expression: a sound-producing machine. And here are the advantages I anticipate from such a machine: crossrhythms unrelated to each other, treated simultaneously; the machine would be able to beat any number of desired notes, any subdivision of them, omission or fraction of them, all these in a given unit of measure or time which is humanly impossible to attain.'

This 'humanly impossible' time, this automatization of rhythm which is rhythmatics, opens up the posthuman multiplication of rhythm: the rhythm synthesizer's spastic pulses seize the body, rewiring the sensorium in a kinaesthetic of shockcuts and stutters, a voluptuous epilepsy.

Man Plus

With Mantronix, this massive augmentation of rhythm capability becomes an Electronic Energy, a super sonotronic power. Man + Electron + [ics =] ix = Mantronix, the Rhythmachine cyborg. The 'cs' in 'tronics' is compressed to 'x', so that it transmits the PhonoCurrent of the Mandroid. Electro is electricity fictionalized into full-force fantasies of frequencies, rhythms programmed to capture and compel, trap and trigger wetware motion.

Futurhythmachines turn the extended capability of machines into supersensory powers. Electro is this crossfire of 'unrelated crossrhythms', rhythms treated simultaneously into paradoxical sound – angular accents, zapp-kicks, palmless claps, rigid bounces. In Ryuichi Sakamoto's *Riot in Lagos*, unrelated crossrhythms refract into a maze of mirrors refracting cicada creaks and cricket croaks. Electronic rhythms run in phase but out of synch, repeatedly overlap split seconds apart, creating a stratum of seething, prehensile tension. Signals interlock in a web of pulsations, a rhythmforest shower of screams and rustletime.

The beat becomes a staccato pulsation, the twitchshrug-stopmotion-poplock-wavecut Motion Capture of electric boogaloo. Electro is the spastic electricity of bodies going pop, breakflowing in time to Art of Noise. '84's *Close [to the Edit]* is rigidity gone loco, clockwork breaking down into a contraption of backfiring car, exhaust fumes and piston hiss.

Offworld Electro

The Electro intro draws you offworld, into the universe of the track. It delivers a robotik elektricity, speech frequencies filtered into phonic diktat. In Offworld Electro, the vocoder is all id, giddiness, extremes of nonhuman high/low pitch. At the high end, the Electro voice is a malicious gremlin. At the low end, it's the Voice of Doom issuing the death command.

Set the Sonotron to Stun

On Jonzun Crew's *Space is the Place*, the Arkestral chant becomes a warning blast rigid with Vadervoltage. Instead of using synthesiser tones to emulate string quartets, Electro deploys them inorganically, unmusically. The synthesizer becomes a sound weapon, becomes what composer Iannis Xenakis calls the Sonotron, 'an accelerator of sonorous particles, a disintegrator of sonorous matter', the sonic weapon which *zapps!* you. The zapp! constricts space by tensing your nerves, gripping with the baleful hostility of an offworld tazer. Electro triggers Vader's Empire to stun. Man Parrish's 0.55 min track *In the Beginning* is a tyrannical microverse of malevolent avatars with vocoder ids, snickering and babbling manically: 'Imagine somewhere in this universe an alien. He was not made of stone. He was not made of sand. He was... check it out, humans, manmade.'

Across the Vocoder Spectrum

The vocoder turns the voice into a synthesizer. Electro crosses the threshold of synthetic vocalization, breaks out into the new spectrum of vocal synthesis. It synthesizes the voice into voltage, into an electrophonic charge that gets directly on your nerves.

Turning the voice into a synthetic spectrum of perverse voco-imps lets you talk with cartoons, become cartoon, become animal, become supercomputer. Just as machine vision runs from infrared to ultraviolet, so the vocoder spectrum runs from hyperbabble to ultraslow. Initially developed as German military technology for camouflaging transmissions, the vocoder cuts out vocal frequencies, petrifying the voice into a robotik current, an antagonistically nonhuman Voice of Doom.

Daleks, Stephen W. Hawking, Bam Bam, Sleezy D, Lil Louis: all compress frequencies and pitchshift voices into the VaderVoder Effect. Darth Vader's rumble is processed through several systems before emitting from his metal grille. Reducing frequencies to the robotic only intensifies the emotional charge of Vader's credo, that there is 'power in the Darkside'. The VaderVoder drains the voice of affect to increase its effect. Dark energy corrodes the larynx, dredging up the tenebral timbres of Haashim's '86 *Primrose Path*, the Darkside of Electro.

Clear Your Mind/Erase Your Head

'Clear are these Days. Clear Today. Clear. Your. Mind.' In '85's *Clear*, from Cybotron's debut album *Enter*, a sped-up cartoon-id voice, giddy and giggly, duets with a slowed-down Voice of Doom, instructing Electro kids to erase their heads.

Electro Resequences Your Nerves

Electro resynthesizes The Song by the rhythm of the arcadegame, where the central processing chip replaces beats with signals-pulsations-zapps that brutally override your old neuromuscular system, demanding an irregular regularity. Space Invaders and Pac Jam are barely rhythms at all, more a barbaric frequency that directly interfaces with the junctions between nerve and muscle, altering the nature of attention into an unhealthily spasmodic concentration.

Not so much maladroit as malandroid, Electro resequences your nerves. As choreographer Merce Cunningham points out, 'Electronic music affects your nerves not your muscles. It's difficult to count electricity.' Electro like Techno affects nerves *and* muscles. The rhythmic dissonance of 'counting electricity' resets the shapes of sensation, demands a new dynamotion. Electro Era LA Lockers dancer Shrimp explains this vision of rhythm as 'Boogalooin', rollin' of the body. It's makin' your body do weird things. Like fluid.'

Clear's anempathetic syncussion is white noise filtered into impalpable claps, sibilance sharpened into a match firing sandpaper. Stridulatory tones alter attack and launch across space in an aural flightpath that parallels Roy Lichtenstein's *Whaaam!* jet-trail.

Silver Cycles of the Polyrhythmachine

Groove is when overlapping patterns of rhythm interlock, when beats syncromesh until they generate an automotion effect, an inexorable, effortless sensation which pushes you along from behind until you're funky like a train. To get into the Groove is to lock into the polyrhythmotor, to be adapted by a fictionalized rhythm engine which draws you on its own momentum.

The JBs' *[It's not the Express] It's the JBs' Monaurail* fictionalizes this feeling of syncromesh, when spaces either side of expectation lure you into airpockets of time.

On the 75 album *Hustle With Speed*, Fred Marcellino's sleeve shows the Monaurail, a single-track interstellar railway snaking round satellites with a silver bullet train running smoothly along its funicular orbit. The Monaurail is the Rhythmotor visualized as the single track along which the train travels. Groove = PolyRhythmengine = Rhythmotor, not personified but machinified as train and track together, in stratusphunk‹›funkular automotion. For Kraftwerk, 'Trains themselves are musical instruments. We would travel through landscapes at night.' Soul Sonic Force's *Planet Rock* reroutes the serene dynamotion of the *Trans Europe Express* through America, the metronomic Rhythmengine pulling itself ahead, synths tuned into Doppler effects whipping past you on a Berlin platform.

Autobahn's motorway motorik tunes 'our synthesizers to sound like motor horns. You can listen to *Autobahn* and then go and drive on the motorway. Then you will discover that your car is a musical instrument.'

Kraftwerk's final bachelormachines are the biomechanical boy-racers of the *Tour de France [Francois Kervorkian Remix]*. With beats made from pistons and gears, rhythms fashioned from sharp intakes of breath, helpless, plosive exhalations and astral harpsichord/harp scintillation, *Tour de France* could be set in an all-night gym. This is Kraftwerk at their most homoerotically physical. Like DAF, it close-mikes male exertion until it becomes a new rhythmotor exhaust fume. In *Tour de France*, the celibate cyborg's being ridden by its bike, its sheathed body fucked from behind by handlebars curved like ramhorns.

Liquid Dystopia

Drexciya drains the claps, cowbells and tomtoms, siphons off the salsa from Electro. With the vocoder id deleted, 90s Electro becomes even more enthralling, even more inhibiting. Such tracks as '93's *Danger Bay* and *Positron Island* are monsters from the low end which submerge you in liquid dystopia. Acrid frequencies clench the nerves like tazers, oscillations wince across the body in wave motion, abrasive tones remove cotton wool from your ears and vigorously scour inside the brainpan. Jagged snare velocities pinch the nerves until you're locked uptight. *Sea Snake's* scorching deathray sweeps the seacraters with its acoustic searchlight of astringent 303.

Each Drexciya EP – from '92's *Deep Sea Dweller*, through *Bubble Metropolis*, *Molecular Enhancement*, *Aquatic Invasion*, *The Unknown Aquazone*, *The Journey Home* and *Return of Drexciya* to '97's *Uncharted* – militarizes Parliament's 70s and Hendrix's 60s Atlantean aquatopias. Their underwater paradise is hydroterritorialized into a geopolitical subcontinent mapped through cartographic track titles: *Positron Island, Danger Bay, The Red Hills of Lardossa, The Basalt Zone 4.977Z, The Invisible City, Dead Man's Reef, Vampire Island, Neon Falls, Bubble Metropolis*. The Bermuda Triangle becomes a basstation from which wavejumper commandos and the 'dreaded Drexciya stingray and barracuda battalions' launch their Aquatic Invasion against the AudioVisual Programmers.

Marine Mutation across the Black Atlantic

Every Drexciya EP navigates the depths of the Black Atlantic, the submerged worlds populated by Drexciyans, Lardossans, Darthouven Fish Men and Mutant Gillmen. In the Sleevenotes to *The Quest*, their '97 concept double CD, the Drexciyans are revealed to be a marine species descended from 'pregnant America-bound African slaves' thrown overboard 'by the thousands during labour for being sick and disruptive cargo. Could it be possible for humans to breathe underwater? A foetus in its mother's womb is certainly alive in an aquatic environment. Is it possible that they could have given birth at sea to babies that never needed air? Recent experiments have shown mice able to breathe liquid oxygen, a premature human infant saved from certain death by breathing liquid oxygen through its underdeveloped lungs. These facts combined with reported sightings of Gillmen and Swamp Monsters in the coastal swamps of the Southeastern United States make the slave trade theory startlingly feasible.'

Drexciyans are 'water breathing, aquatically mutated descendants,' webbed mutants of the Black Atlantic, amphibians adapted for the ocean's abyssal plains, a phylum disconnected from the aliens who adapted to land. As Mark Sinker argued in '92, 'The ships landed long ago: they already laid waste whole societies, abducted and genetically altered whole swathes of citizenry. Africa and America — and so by extension Europe and Asia — are already in their various ways Alien Nation.' Drexciya use electronics to replay the alien abduction of slavery with a fictional outcome: 'Did they migrate from the Gulf of Mexico to the Mississippi River Basin and to the Great Lakes of Michigan? Do they walk among us? Are they more advanced than us?'

Sinker's breakthrough is to bring alien abduction back to earth, to transfer the trauma from out there to yesternow. The border between social reality and science fiction, social fiction and science reality is an optical illusion, as Donna Haraway has pointed out. They have been here all along and they are you. You are the alien you are looking for.

Fictionalizing Frequencies

Drexciya fictionalize frequencies into sound pictures of unreal environments — what Kraftwerk termed tone films — not filled with cars, bikes or trains but rather UAOs, soundcrafts. In '93's *Bubble Metropolis*, Lardossan Cruiser 8-203 X prepares to dock. The tones of a hydrothermal turbine engine shift gears. They fictionalize the psychoacoustic volume of a giant submersible: 'This is Drexcyian Cruise Control Bubble 1 to Lardossan Cruiser 8 dash 203 X. Please decrease your speed to 1 point 788 point 4 kilobahn. Unknown turbine engine slows down. Thank you. Lardossan Cruiser 8 dash 203 X please use extra caution as you pass the aqua construction site on the side of the aquabahn. I repeat: Proceed with Caution. Lardossan Cruiser 8 dash 203 X you are now cleared for docking. Have a nice stay here on Drexciya. I'm Drexciyan Cruiser Control X 205. If you have any problems let me know. Bubble Control Out.'

In a War without Weapons

The Black Atlantean depths are as lethal as the Red Planet or The Rings of Saturn. With the *Molecular Enhancement* EP, the ocean floor becomes the 5th front in The Forever War. Drexciyan technology solidifies the ocean into hydrocubes. These blocs of solid water are part of the electrofictional arsenal of Antivapor Waves, Aquatic Bata Particles and

Intensified Magnetrons.

The magnetron is the heart of the radiowave transmitter, used to power airborne microwave radar sets during WW2. As Arthur C. Clarke explains, 'When the first experimental magnetron was carried to America, the face of war changed over a weekend. Japanese scientists had made and tested an identical device a year before the British. If they had followed up their invention we would now be living in a very different world.'

Technology generates the process Sun Ra terms an AlterDestiny, a bifurcation in time. The magnetron migrates across the mediascape, changing scale from Marvel Comics 60s supervillain Magneto, leader of the Evil Mutants, to Drexciya's *Intensified Magnetron*, to Killah Priest's 'magnetron which puts your arteries back apart'.

Video games are the first step in a plan for machines to help the human race, the only plan that offers a future for intelligence
Chris Marker

You're in the Military Entertainment Complex

Electro is an E-Z learn induction into the militarization of pop life, the sensualizing of militarization, the enhanced sensorium of locking into the Futurhythmachine. From the Net to arcade simulation games, civil society is all just one giant research-and-development wing of the military. The military industrial complex has advanced decades ahead of civil society, becoming a lethal military-entertainment complex. The MEC preprograms predatory virtual futures.

Far from being the generative source for popculture, as Trad media still quaintly insists, the street is now merely the playground in which low-end developments of military technology are unleashed, to mutate themselves.

Rhythmatic Bachelor Machines: Kraftwerk

Tap the Powerspot: It's a Rave New World

As with Underground Resistance, Kraftwerk installed themselves inside the military complex, the nexus of posthumanization which used to be called dehumanization. They tapped the powerspots of industrialization through 'the factories that plug into the network' which 'were making the synthesisers' fluctuate in a factory‹›synth‹›human circuit. The Kling Klang studio is a delivery room for machine lifeforms. By naming themselves 'powerplant' Kraftwerk turn onto the industrial process, switching on the assembly line instead of resisting it in the name of the human. For '75's *Radioactivity* they visited a nuclear powerplant, plugging themselves into atomic energy, irradiating themselves with nuclear power.

Sorrow Songs for the Souls of Servomechanisms

Norbert Wiener's *The Human Use of Human Beings* is W.E.B. DuBois' *The Souls of Black Folk* updated for the Analog Age. In Kraftwerk, the speak-and-spell voices are more childlike than lullabies, fossils from the future's past.

Voice-activated systems separate intention from result. While the human sensorium goes from speech to touch, the machinic sensory apparatus starts with touch – buttons and knobs, faders and sliders – before moving to speech processing. The childhood of machines begins with speak-and-spell toys, arcadegames, Learn-to-speak-French records, soft-drink dispensers, ansafones, traindoors and cashpoints. Kraftwerk sing the Soul of Service Machines, *die Seele der Servomekanismus.* Machines take over repetitive jobs. Kraftwerk's politeness and sly civility is poignant because 'automatic machines are the precise economic equivalent of slave labour.'

The Sex Organs of the Synthesizer

Standardization, mechanization, automation, enervation, inhibition, radiation! Trad rock's drive comes from repelling such vampiric processes of capital. But giving in to the machines, this is what's so compelling here, how Kraftwerk went into the bionic heart of the machine, what came out the other side.

Instead of denying the automatic, Kraftwerk exaggerate it. They operate synthesizers, but really technology is synthesizing them. They don't resist the synthetic, they give in to it, enslave themselves, allow technology to reprogram them, to resequence them, to extrude *them* as the Servomechanisms of the Synth. Showroom dummies, *menschmaschines*, robots and models: these are the new generations of sex organs the synthesizers need in order to reproduce themselves: the bachelormachines without their mechanical brides. Neutered and bloodless, they move along planes of sheer chromoluminance.

By totally succumbing to technology, Kraftwerk let the machines delibidinize them, drain all the physicality out of them. Warhol cloned himself into Warholaroids for interviews; Gilbert and George remodelled themselves as auto-mannequins. In the Kraftwerk ecology celibate machines perform auto-reproduction rituals.

Zapped!

In Electro, this fleshless rigidity converges with the spineless electroid of Zapp. With Roger Troutman's Zapp, electronics + android = the electroid zapped! by a blast from an unknown Sonotron. Dancing to Zapp is being hit by electric current that convulses you into spasm. Shrimp the dancer explains that '*More Bounce to the Ounce* helped give birth to [body]poppin'. That's the only style of dance you can see that goes with that kind of music.'

Instead of breaking The Song down to a James Brown bridge, *More Bounce* redesigned funk's architecture, stretching The Song into hypnomonotony, a rubber mantra that squeezed your senses out of shape while seizing them with its sheet-metal clap.

This emphasis on counting electricity means that the Zapp track gets directly on your nerves and muscles. In crossing the threshold elucidated by Merce Cunningham, Troutman's albums induce an unnerving boneless sensation. Your spine's being filleted and it feels just great.

Control Your Convulsions

Zapp alters the reflexes, adapting the human into the electroid, the electronic android who turn electric shock into controlled convulsion, an E-Z roller of Stopmotion Capture.

Electric boogaloo is when the body receives the Zapp and transmits it as a dynamic force. The nerves count the current, convulsions become clocks, the spastic toctics of elaborated personal time systems. The Electro dancer goes into 'a square rollout where he ticks his whole body and goes into the splits.'

The double move of cutwave‹›breakflow sends a current through the joints in a synthetic seizure that's every which way but loose.

Zapp turns the human into a symbiounit. 'When you pop,' Shrimp elucidates, your bodymap alters and 'you become this thing. You go to another planet. I got into this thing where I wanted to be an alien.'

Liquefy the Menschmaschine

Zapp's '86 *Computer Love* opens with a bewitching choir — identified by Simon Reynolds as android doowop — announcing 'ComputerIIIZE', like a genie granting a robot's wish. Kraftwerk's vocoder chorale is winsome while Zapp's vocoder chorale is liquefied. Zapp is the *menschmaschine* gone gooey. 'We are beginning to see,' chaos-theorist Manuel De Landa argues, 'that the really advanced high technology is liquidy and drippy and self organizing and not at all rigid.' In *More Bounce to the Ounce*, the synthetic bass doesn't drop; instead it bounces off the bottom. Where the Bootsy Collins bass is a rhythmelodic ectoplasm, glutinous and rubbery, the Zapp bass is Spandex stretchy.

PhonoGlutamate

Larry Graham sent the bass through fuzz until it yawned and slurred like a baby mammoth. With Zapp, Roger Troutman's voice is all vowel, an eesysquezy squidge of phonoglutamate, voco-concentrate. The synthesizer passes through his vocal tract. On *I Play the Talkbox*, the Roger voice is tubular treble squeezed from a talkbox.

For Parliament, the soundeffect immediately implies an audio lifeform, a universe in which a processed sound takes on an animatronic nonhuman profile. With Zapp, you're inside the impact, bathed in the full effect of the S Ray gun, in what Techno producer Kevin Saunderson later terms Essr'ays.

Machine Tones for Psychic Therapy: The Jungle Brothers

*For a very long time everybody refuses and then
almost without a pause almost everybody accepts*
Gertrude Stein

Mutiny on the Mothership

You reserve your nausea for the timeless classic, for the anthems that sum up an epoch. But The Jungle Brothers, George Russell, Tricky: these are producers who don't synchronize you into those docile ranks-and-files known as generations. In fact they shatter you into sensory particles, travelling at the speed of thought, break consensual history into dust. Instead of rising above their time, the Jungle Brothers — Afrika Baby Bam bass and vocals, dj Sammy B, Mike G guitar and vocals, Torture drums and vocals — runs HipHop through a particle accelerator, charging reality with the synthetic sensation you crave at all costs.

Their 3rd album, '93's *J Beez Wit the Remedy*, is to the 90s what The Velvet Underground's *White Light/White Heat* was to the 60s: the decade's great lost album, a colossal epic salvaged from the wreckage of the unreleased *Crazy Wisdom*, acknowledged by a few, reviled by Trad HipHop fanatics on both sides of the Atlantic.

Derail the Rhythmotor

In an era of headnoddin' 120bpm grooves, *Remedy* returns to the rigid rhythmatics of rhythmsynthesis. The security of the Trad jazzbreak is smashed, left behind for the drastically unmusical pulsations and bleeps, that flagrantly mekanikal rhythmanipulation that HipHop thought it banished back in the 80s. *Manmade Material* abandons the lope of 70s Breakbeats altogether, pushing robotic irregularity into machine psychedelia. 'It wasn't looping one bar, 4 beats, but looping 6 beats,' the Jungle Brothers declared. 'Arhythmic, asymmetrical, alinear. So what we've been doing consistently is intentionally derailing your brain.' The loop function entrains the body, programming the head until it nods like a dog. HipHop habituates the mind until it runs along the same grooves but the arhythmic loop undermines the stepper, derails the rhythmotor, with its unresolved dissonance, not arrangements but derangements, wrong-footed, dysfunktional.

Concrete

The Jungle Brothers draw on HipHop's rediscovery of vinyl *concrète*: the snap, crackle and pop of worn vinyl and ansafone hum. Here, *concrète* bursts the banks of sample memory, suffusing everything, reorganizing all of texturhythmelody. Groove in *Blahbludify* is saturated in static until it collapses into satisfyingly electroacoustic debris. Beats are replaced by bumps, glitches, gusts, the distressed laser failing to read the cd's information. You feel 'the wind of the wings of madness', like the moment when Christopher Walken quotes Baudelaire to Lili Taylor in Abel Ferrara's *The Addiction*. All the low end succumbs to scratches, vinyl gouged by an obelisk of a needle.

The sound splits across speakers, repeated rounds of drum-machinegun in the right, shuddering detritus from the left. Arcadegame soundeffects strafe your body in a vicious crossfire.

Sonic rubble falls from the speaker behind your back, seizing your muscles as they plunge through your waist on their journey to the head.

Headless

HipHop played by a band always means nice'n'easy funk. But the 'Now' of live HipHop strands you in a predigital present, leaves you trapped in someone else's '72. Preprogrammed loops can iterate into infinity and you'll never get bored — but the merest hint of real-time spontaneity mortally drains you. Here live isn't rootsical, it's arhythmic, the Rhythmengine of a sampladelic messthetic that fluctuates the funk by freaking with the freek freek.

Where post-Dr Dre Gangsta rap promotes a lolling indolent delivery, HipHop poetics from Arrested Development to the Roots, Freestyle Fellowship to the Fugees, opts for a verbose verbal acrobatics. For them, HipHop's future lies in a gymnastics of syntax, internal rhymes that reconnect to an oral umbilical chord stretching from 14th C Gambian griots to the Last Poets to now. But these good green roots which nurture healthy HipHop are strangling it.

It's not the inhuman you dread in music so much as the opposite, the overhuman, the all-too human of HipHop-inspired poetics. There's so much intention in these musics that the machines can't hardly breathe.

The J Beez aren't the remedy to Gangsta so much as the antibiotic to Gangsta's remedies. Neither ill nor healthy, the J Beez are the 3rd Stream: dynamical, on the edge of order and chaos. *Remedy* doesn't propose a new content so much as obliterate the MC altogether:

obscured by screeds of static, the voice drowns in a storm of distortion that rips syntax to shreds. The MC becomes a host of microphone fiends, sped up and reversed, swarming from speaker to speaker. Irradiated into audioflux, the *J Beez* voice is all oscillation and no backbone, perpetually fluctuating between cartoon, plasma, gremlin and ghost.

Remedy therefore isn't headmusic so much as headless music. In decapitating the MC and opting for an acephalic overload, delivery becomes mystifying, occluded. In *Manmade Material*, verse, chorus, bridge are accidents, momentary coincidences generated by static. Fragments of warnings surface briefly from the information ocean; the listener clings like drowners.

Immerse Yourself in the Destructiv Element

'You must learn your path, your way to swim through this record. That is the remedy,' insist the Jungle Brothers to a baffled world. The HipHop head is right to be hostile. *Remedy*'s incoherence announces a post-HipHop world. 'No... We must... master the maker,' a dangerously unstable voice insists in *Manmade Material*. The Jungle Brothers' lead instruments are feedback, fuzz and static, perpetual interference.

Remedy is heavy, megalithic: its density crushes the gravity of The Song. In *Spittin' Wicked Randomness* and the overwhelming *For the Headz at Company Z*, wah-wah effects yowl into a perpetual wall of fuzz. Sustained chords of glagolitic organ charge the track with grandiosity. Organdrones are ambushed by a pileup of atonal arpeggios. Blocs of low-end solar sound hit a sustained pitch, triggering sensations of ascension.

Sampladelic crowdnoise melds into spume clouds, spindrift as fuzz, crackle and static persist while a playerpiano cycles through its cards. Satisfyingly portentous organ chords build up imminent expectation over groans pitched down till they sound like Jim Morrison being slowly drowned. Drunken soldiers salute 'the headz at company Z'.

Remedy oscillates between extremes of troopers' exhaustion and intensely infantile glee as HipHop form breaks down over and over in a daze of confusion. Throughout, there's an overwhelming sense of wreckage. HipHop has been blasted to bits in an unspecified disaster. From the ruins, disastrous events are transmitting from a damaged receiver. Distressed pilots holler through gasmasks into a patched-up intercom.

Destruction brings joy; in these reports from HipHop's end, the babble and flux frolic like teenagers dancing on the rubble of the Ministry of Sound. The JBs are juiced by catastrophe. Distorted information emerges yammering from the scree and whine of *Spittin' Wicked Randomness*, immediately interrupted by squalls of static and mayday signal synths. 'Brainstorms! Brainstorms! Mass explosion in the brainnn.'

> *The paradox I am,*
> *Extending my hand into the mental to unlock doorways*
> **Organized Konfusion**

Computer Music in the Year Zero

Trad HipHop is a belief system sure of its past, certain of its present, confident in its future. Load the *Remedy* cd into the tray and this conviction collapses and convolutes, beaching you on the reefs of the present. Afrika Baby Bam confounds confusion by multiplying himself into new heteronyms Af Next Man Flip and Lord Paradox: 'I'm gone... I'm really gone, I've really let myself go. I even changed my name to Af Next Man Flip, meaning that I was one of the next men to flip out into the universe.'

Remedy takes HipHop forward to its electronic routes, its rock routes, its machine routes. It is Computer Music in the Year Zero.

The antidote for pervasive depression, for a HipHop gone illmatic, as rapper Nas terms it, is an immersion in Universal Sound and MythScience. Af Next Man Flip identifies with 'scientific people. I like reading books about John Coltrane, when he's sitting there studying music theory and he's listening to music from all over the world and trying to reach this higher order. I like the universe.' HipHop's diktats — to come correct, to keep it real and not get it twisted — all haemorrhage in the Unreality Principle of *J Beez Wit the Remedy*, its premonitions, its clairaudience.

SYNTHETIC FICTION/ELECTRONIC THOUGHT

Abduction by Acid [Curfew]: Phuture, Bam Bam, Sleezy D

The world of the twentieth-century dancefloor is a discontinuum – a Discotheque a Go-Go, in which a dancer makes his or her own space which does not fit into anybody else's space. It's like a physicist trying to encounter electronic particles with Newtonian concepts
Marshall McLuhan

The Toxic Drives of the Drug<>Tech Interface

At the height of Acid's inner flight comes Sleezy D's '86 *I've Lost Control*, Phuture's '87 *Your Only Friend*, Bam Bam's '88 *Where's Your Child*, scary tracks that optimize your fear‹›flight threshold. At the peak of the Rave Dream, 4 Hero's '91 *Mr Kirk's Nightmare* feeds parental drugpanic back on the dancefloor. Your drug experience is intensified by a mix of anti-drug tracks. You come up on tracks which bring you down.

Sonically speaking the drug‹›tech interface is toxic straight away, not later when the badmen move in. Everything goes wrong right away and this only amplifies the rush. Take the E and Take the Risk. Taking drugs is a rite of possible death, a ritual that affirms life. Facing this possible death makes life rush even faster. Every E taker is already dead, has crossed to the other side of the poison in which toxicity intensifies life.

Ph Is the Silver of Syntax

DJ Pierre's heteronym Phuture substitutes the 'f' in future for the 'pH' of the chemical formula and the ph of phono. Ph makes the phuture sound synthetic and phono-chemical. Ph is to sound as silver is to vision. Ph is the silver prefix, the word concentrate. The future becomes a phuturistic Pharmatopia. With Phuture, the sound of the future separates from the look of the phuture. Vision and sound, heteronym and homonym, split off, run away from each other.

For the White Horse of Heroin will ride you to Hell
James Brown

In Thrall

Phuture's enthralling *Your Only Friend* is Acid's sequel to James Brown's '72 *King Heroin*, the electronic update of Roland Kirk's '69 *Volunteer Slavery*. After the pusher sells you to the Drug, the Drug sets you to work as a mule, sends you out into the world programmed like a medium at a seance. The drug becomes the clock which keeps time in its universe of unending servitude. In a Voice pitched down into the Vaderized groan of a Designated Despot: 'This is Cocaine speaking, I can make you do anything for me.'

Acid's 303 delivers you up to the Kingdom of Cockayne, accelerated into a powder paradise of endless cocaine. To dance is to be drawn helplessly into what the track warns against. Acid's sternest injunctions — 'You have been warned, I'll take your life' — incites more dancing, not as release but as voluntary slavery, dancing your way into a new constriction. You're willingly abducted by Acid into the Despotic regime that never sounded so good before.

Enthralled by frequencies, you're modulated by sensations of aggressive evasiveness and attacking elusiveness. You shed your life as easily as a snake shucks its skin. Slip from the morals inculcated into your muscles. The Voice of Doom decrees its death command: 'Take a shot from me/I'll make you fly/Take too much from me/I'll make you die.'

Instead of emulating rock's bass, forever stratified at the low end,

Acid exaggerates the Roland T303's dry slipperiness, its *glissements*, by transforming the sound of the note, the colour of its tone as it plays. Filtering bends‹›selects‹›suppresses timbres, producing the aural equivalent of a tracer effect, a wavering sense of panic as the ear fails to resolve this slippage of overtones.

Acid is an accident in which the TB303 bass synthesizer uses Phuture to reproduce itself, to multiply the dimensions of electronic sound, to open up a nomadology of texturhythms, rhythmelodies. Phuture, Bam Bam *et al* love this synthetic, unnatural noise. Acid trax amplifies this sense of terrifying newness.

Nothing you know about the history of music is any help whatsoever. What is this noise and where's it coming from? Who are these people and why are they smiling at me? Brutally inexpressive woodblocks hammer out an inhuman irregularity, relieved by the stabs of bassic synth. The heart's beat is captured and cloned by the time synthesized into impacts. You become an extension of the machine which generates time. Slip through the spaces between the sequences.

Silicon-based Psychosis

Phase 1: Hal 9000's redlight psychosis in *2001: A Space Odyssey*. When Hal starts playing back *Daisy, Daisy*, computer-malfunction turns into machinic breakdown. *Daisy, Daisy* – vox congealing as it runs down – introduces the new sound of analog psychopathology.

The Womandroid from the Amazone

Phase 2: The womanmachine Grace Jones' '82 remodel of Joy Division's '79 *She's Lost Control* updates the 50s mechanical bride. For the latter losing control meant electric epilepsy, voice drained dry by feedback. For Jones, the female model that's losing control induces the sense of automation running down, the human seizing up into a machine rictus. The model – as girl, as car, as synthesizer – incarnates the assembly line time of generations, obsolescence, 3-year lifespans.

The model is the blueprint for the post-Cold War cyborg, the womanmachine modified and mutated by the military‹›medical‹› entertainment complex. Hence Kraftwerk's *The Model*, where the bachelormachines are threatened by the womanmachine's superior reproduction capability. *The Model* is an excerpt from the post-war machine-reproduction wars.

Phase 3: Sleezy D's *I've Lost Control* is the flipside of *Can You Feel*

It?, rescoring Joy Division's *She's Lost Control* for the Roland 303. Each sensation oscillates into the other in an audio-chemical feedback loop. Pitchshifting draws you down into mindslurring, slow-motion computer psychosis. 303's filters smear tones into a timbral spectrum of decay. Acid carves new sensory channels and mutates the ones already being used. It demands and builds a synthetic ear for itself from the old one. Fear feeds forward into the dance, floods you in waves of reassuring panic until you feel safe and dangerous.

Phase 4: It's too late. The drug‹›tech interface synthesized you long ago. You're synthetic now. Against this, all traditional authority condemns itself. The Old World loses all seriousness when it insists that you don't have to take E to know it's bad for you. This sensible ignorance is precisely what invalidates it.

Every word the government speaks deletes itself. All its expertise disqualifies it.

Some Gods will mount any horse
Ishmael Reed

Panic Feedsforward

No government can scare you into stopping because E, trips, hydroponically grown skunk, all these have already scared you more than they ever could. This sense of being snatched by drugs, of being kidnapped into your head, of drawing out the madness already in you: this is what the Darkside is. Everything the media warns you against has already been made into tracks that drive the dancefloor.

All black electronic musics have their Darkside, and Acid's begins with Bam Bam's '88 *Where's Your Child*, the Acid track as audio abduction, the sound that snatches you from school, self and society, that kidnaps your mind and never gives it back. Like 4 Hero's *Mr Kirk's Nightmare*, it amplifies parent's drug-panic into a hilariously horrifying feedforward loop: 'Parents, Don't let your kids out at night/Don't you know they don't know wrong from right?'

Acid here is a psychotic sampladelia of whining motorcars, of vicious glass smash played as a 3-note refrain, of cars slowed down into decaying gong and intermittent baby screams. Bam Bam pitchshifts his voice until it slurs down into a sinister gloat punctuated by vampiric laughs. It's the sound of seduction every parent dreads: 'Where's your child?/Do you know?/Look around/Nowhere to be found.'

    Acid is repetitive attack patterns that perpetually climb, build and fall, restlessly lurching from panic inducing trebles to queasy lows. And even worse — even more satisfying — are the voluptuous groans and sated sighs emitted by the voice as if it's stroking itself while recalling intense gratification: 'Nobody likes to be left alone/especially when they don't know right from wrong.' *Where's Your Child* hits a peak of sweet unease when Bam Bam murmurs 'Curfew Curfew' like an incitement to unnamed perversions, the enticing threshold into its ahuman world: 'You're all my children now.'

A Crowd of Import Aliens

    Acid is the import alien. It arrives in crowds of mystifying names, terrifyingly blank 12s, labels approaching you within the Rhythmachine swarm that is the compilation. No more than the remix, the compilation never wins awards, never makes it into End-of-Decade Lists. Like the remix, the compilation is an artform for the Sampladelic Era. The history of the Electronic Rhythmachine is measured as much in the crowd of the compilation as by the 12. From the *Streetsounds Electro Volume 1-12* to 10 Records' *Techno: The New Dance Sound of Detroit* to Network's *Retro Techno* to Suburban Base/Moving Shadow's *The Joint* to Reinforced's *The Deepest Shade of Techno* to Virgin's *Macro Dub Infection* to Om Records' *Deep Concentration* — the compilation is the movable shop wall that dissolves the 12's aura, releasing it from its dj-only ltd-edn professionalized status.

    As a US or Euro import, a test pressing, a white label dj promo, a double pack, a triple pack or a 10, the single is the rare object that everyone wants, that most people never get to see. The 12 is the hardback of music, the ltd-edn run of 2000 copies that sells out in 3 days, never to be seen again. The 12 is an elite product, frozen in a rigidly protected hierarchy of dj, journalist and everyone else.

    Like paperbacks, compilations reverse this process, releasing tracks from their reverential and rarefied aura, dissolving journalistic reverence, bypassing hard-won connoisseurship by flooding the High Streets with anthologies anyone can buy.

> *In the beginning there was Jack and Jack had a*
> *Groove. Jack bawled and declared 'Let there be*
> *House.' And House Music was born. I am, you see,*
> *I am the Creator and this is my House*
> **Fingers Inc. Featuring Chuck Roberts**

Rematerialize

VR dematerializes you but Machine Music rematerializes you. In *Neuromancer*, Case jacks from his body into cyberspace. The house acolyte jacks into the House that is his/her body. In '88's *Can You Feel It* the kinaesthetic of jacking is incarnated as Jack. The sensation of dancing comes alive. Sensation is personified by Chicago Preacher Chuck Roberts. Jack AutoCatalyses House through screaming, then explains the neurocircuit of House in which emotion becomes environment: 'Once you enter my House it then becomes our House and our House Music'. Locking in tight to the beat builds the House from the reflexes up.

To jack is to join what Walter Hughes calls the 'automatic community of technological communication', where Whitman's 'adhesive body electric' is sequenced at the push of a button into 'the gay body electronic'.

Acid tweaks while LA burns. House amplifies all those feelings HipHop manfully denies itself, intensifying the present by burning up the future. The Trad HipHop fanatic regards everything post-House with an unshakable suspicion: House in league with the synthetic, a collaborator with the frivolous, that which consorts with the machine.

In HipHop the beat is heavy, carrying a moral weight that sinks the neck until it nods in obeisance to the beat. Trad HipHop enforces an ethics of sound that welds the fan tight to the music.

The 20th Century Discontinuum

If Rock's archetypal demand is for satisfaction, then the Rhythmachine's is for feeling. Fingers Inc — synthesist-producer Larry Heard and vocalist Robert Owens — ask the question for the 20th C dancefloor: *Can You Feel It*. 'It' here is emotion without an object, pointless, careless, directionless feeling for its own sake. Fingers Inc demand that you feel feeling. *Can You Feel It* is a synthetic sanctuary whose edgeless tones insulate and enwomb. Its syntharmonic horizon reaches inside you, wrapping itself around your skin, confusing the borders between tissue and touch, igniting sensations of unspecified expectation, imminent immanence.

Heard induces a sense of sanctuary, rapt tones cradling you in warm bass, hovering at the edge of the horizon. *Can You Feel It* is the empathogen in a state of unconditional elation, lips pursed, eyes flickering at the speed of the sun.

The Physical Interface of Perception

When you're entactogenic, the skin gets tactile hallucinations, hears things, transmitting and receiving sensation-concepts. E allows you to anticipate the beat, to slip inside the machine mnemonic.

The skin is the borderguard of yourself. As an empathogen, E affects the physical interface of perception. Pat Cadigan clicks the cursor on zoom: 'The way to change people's ideas about reality is to change the way they feel reality — literally.'

The skin seizes control of all the sensory channels, triggering memory skin, skin telepathy, finger-recognition, shiversighs, rapt gasps. The skin becomes an aerial receiving and transmitting everything.

Feeling it is the sensation of amplification, of all channels open, supercharged. Your body seethes; a planet of wetware as you dive, dive into the seadepths of your blood. Feeling is the result of all the senses converging at once.

The Rhythmachine values these peaks above all else. These nonverbal Nirvanas of total tactile telepathy are what A Guy Called Gerald terms 'emotions electric', the moments when each dancer in the crowd becomes a medium transmitting sensory current.

The Dancefloor at the Century's Start

But Nirvana's never enough. The End of Century dancefloor is a series of paradoxical psychedelias that induce immersive inversions and fleeting reversions. The phuture is a series of synthetic sensations, artificial emotions, tense presents.

Losing it is when you give in to toxic drives, when the thirst for mutation is strongest, when you're drowning in peristaltic waves of toxic sensation, when the head's no more than a stupid piece of gristle. When effect breaks free from cause and runs off, when sound detaches itself from source and sense, when narrative dissolves into sensation.

The audio-toxic energy coursing through the body amplifies itself in a current that snakes through ravers in a bio-circuit. Fuel for the Icarus trajectory.

...And Came Down in Techno City:
Cybotron, Model 500, Electrifying Mojo

In Trad terms, it's widely assumed that Techno isn't a 'black American music' because it really started with Kraftwerk. Those of Techno's supporters who still insist that Detroit brought the funk to Machine Music will always look for Techno's Af‹›Am origin to answer these crits: Sun Ra? Herbie Hancock? Kraftwerk's love of James Brown? All of these are routes through Techno — yet none work, because Detroit Techno is always more than happy to give due credit to Kraftwerk as the pioneers of Techno.

Dusseldorf Is the Mississippi Delta

Kraftwerk are to Techno what Muddy Waters is to the Rolling Stones: the authentic, the origin, the real.

Techno therefore reverses the traditional 60s narrative in which the Rolling Stones stole the soul and vulgarized the blues of Waters *et al.* Kraftwerk epitomize the white soul of the synthesizer, *die Seele der Synthesizer*, the ultra whiteness of an automatic, sequenced future. To Model 500, '[Kraftwerk] sounded straight up like they were living in a computer. I even had doubts to whether they were actually human.' Happy to be the interloper, the latecomer, Bambaataa steals the synthetic soul from Dusseldorf, bastardizes it into *Planet Rock.* Kraftwerk happily called their sound *Industriell Volk Musik*, Folk Music for the Industrial Age. For Techno, Dusseldorf is the Mississippi Delta.

The Import Ear

Depeche Mode, Gary Numan, Alexander Robotnik, Manuel Gottsching, Liaisons Dangereuses: all of these are import inputs charging the Cybotron futuropolis, the Techno City. What's striking about Cybotron's *Techno City* is its chorus: 'Tech-noh Cit ehh' sung by 3070 aka Rick Davies in the mannered accent of neuromantic synthpop.

The 3070 voice is remote, hollowed out, above all fey — and a dramatic secession from black macho. The import accent means singing like an alien in American, becoming an alien in Brit English, feeling at home in estrangement, out of step, bored with homeliness.

Reverse the Current of History by Inverting the History of Attraction

Traditionally, British pop bastardizes and mistranslates US music. Detroit Techno inverts these historical US‹›UK currents of attraction, by abducting white nasal whiteness and synthesizing a neuromantic timbre, generating the compelling sense that 'the music is just like Detroit, a complete mistake.' As an aerial music that assembles itself through the Detroit airwaves, Techno hears with an import Ear, a synthetic Ear. It sings in a vinyl accent decapitated from English bodies to migrate across the Atlantic. To listen to Cybotron is to hear the Brit voice making Techno's alienation from America audible. In the Cybotron and M500 voice, you hear what the tropical surrealist Rene Menil terms a 'continual telescoping of 2 cultural languages separated within the same tongue.'

The Electronic Cyborg

Cybo[rg] + [Elec]tron[lc] = Cybotron. The Cybotron is the electronic cyborg, the alien at home in dislocation, excentred by tradition, happily estranged in the gaps across which electric current jumps. The suffix of 'tron' in Cybotron and Mantronix, like the prefix 'ph' in Phuture, is not a word, but word-concentrate: it's a partial accelerator, an engine you attach to make concepts go faster.

We are misled by considering any complicated machine as a single thing: in truth it is a city or society
Samuel Butler

Build the Chronotopia

Detroit Techno is aerial. It transmits along routes through space, is not grounded by the roots of any tree. Dispersed in space, Detroit connects through the 2-Hour City of radio, the concentration in time of the Technopolis. Techno announces today's era in which 'Geography is replaced by chronography,' the age when, as Virilio argues, 'we have begun to inhabit time.' Techno assembles itself across the studios of Detroit from inputs supplied by the dj Electrifying Mojo, who opens his Midnight Funk Association show with Cybotron's *Methane Sea* and John Williams' *OST Title Theme from Star Wars*. The tracks Mojo plays switch on the routes in and out of the Techno City. Cybotron's *Techno City* is the Sonic Fiction of the Chronotopia, the city in time.

Electronic Secession

Techno secedes from the ruthlessly patrolled hoods of Trad HipHop. HipHop updates blaxploitation's territories; it represents the street. By opting out of this logic of representation, Techno disappears itself from the street, the ghetto and the hood. Drexciya doesn't represent Detroit the way Mobb Deep insist they represent Staten Island.

Futuropolis of the Present

The Techno City is a futuropolis of the present, planned, sectioned and elevated from station to studio, transmitting from a Detroit in transition from the industrial to the information age. For Cybotron's sonic theorist and synthesist 3070‹›Richard Davies, '84's *Techno City* is the intersection of 2 future states. *Techno City* is where the 30th C megalopolis of Fritz Lang's *Metropolis* meets the emerging T-Net of corporate booster Alvin Toffler's *The Third Wave*. 'Techno City was the electronic village. It was divided into different sectors. I'd watched Fritz Lang's *Metropolis* – which had the privileged sectors in the clouds and the underground worker's city. I thought there should be three sectors; the idea was that a person could be born and raised in Techno City, the worker's city, but what he wanted to do was work his way to the cybodrome where artists and intellectuals reside. There would be no Morloch, but all sorts of diversions, games, electronic instruments.'

Evolutionary Electronics

Electrifying Mojo's nightly show is the first stage in Techno's evolutionary drive into the dance, its movement from Nation 2 Nation to World 2 World to Galaxy 2 Galaxy. With Cybotron's *Techno City*, in labels like Carl Craig's Planet E, in Underground Resistance's Red Planet series and their Black Planet Studios, the music arrives from another planet. Waveforms are fictionalized into offworld settings, lunar sunsets.

Electronics is imaged in sleeve artwork – Abdul Haqq's Third Earth, Frankie C. Fulitz's Drexciyan label visions, Alan Oldham's Transmat label-excerpts from a post-Modesty Blaise epic, Rufus Knightwebb's angular sleeve-art for Suburban Knight's *The Art of Stalking*.

The Possibility Space of Fictional Frequencies

Cybotron's *Techno City*, like all these possibility spaces, is Sonic Fiction: electronic fiction, with frequencies fictionalized, synthesized and organized into escape routes. Sonic Fiction replaces lyrics with possibility spaces, with a plan for getting out of jail free. Escapism is organized until it seizes the means of perception and multiplies the modes of sensory reality.

Which is why you should always laugh in the face of those producers, djs and journalists who sneer at escapism for its *unreality*, for its *fakeness*; all those who strain to keep it real. These assumptions wish to clip your wings, to tie your forked tail to a tree, to handcuff you to the rotting remnants of tradition, the inherited stupidities of habit, the dead weight of yourself. Common sense wants to see you behind the bars it calls Real Life.

By contrast, Sonic Fiction strands you in the present with no way of getting back to the 70s. Sonic Fiction is the first stage of a reentry program which grasps this very clearly. Sonic Fictions are part of modern music's MythSystems. Moving through living space, real-world environments that are already alien.

Operating instructions for the escape route from yourself. Overthrow the Internal Empire of your head. Secede from the stupidity of intelligence, the inertia of good taste, the *rigor mortis* of cool. You're born into a rigged prison which the jailors term Real Life. Sonic Fiction is the manual for your own offworld break-out, reentry program, for entering Earth's orbit and touching down on the landing strip of your senses.

We dedicate this album to the people of the Detroit Metroplex. To survive we must technofy and save the biosphere
Cybotron

Technofication: the Conceptechnics of Techno

To ENTER the Cybotron world it's necessary to technofy first yourself, then the world. Press the ENTER button on the Roland composer. Press PATTERN CLEAR for rhythmatic synthesis.

To technofy is to become aware of the coevolution of machine and human, the secret life of machines, the computerization of the world, the programming of history, the informatics of reality.

To technofy is to evolve a mindstate which grasps the migration paths of machinic processes, builds Sonic Fictions from the electronics of everyday life.

To technofy is to optimize the machinic mutation of music.

Synthesize Yourself

Behind the disappearing of Detroit Techno in the US, there's the sense that Techno betrayed an unspoken oath. It was seduced by Manuel Gottsching, by Liaisons Dangereuses – by all that Euro synth music – and this triggers the unspoken but persistent sense of abandoning African‹›American tradition. This loyalty assumes an umbilical connection to r&b. Detroit Techno breaks exhilaratingly with r&b – but then it was never rooted in it to begin with.

It was always synthetic, from the aerials up.

Crits would still ask, 'How could Grandmaster Flash and Bambaataa *like* Kraftwerk?' Obvious. Bambaataa is attracted to an alien Euro sound, bored with and indifferent to familiar Af‹›Am sound. But at the same time, white sound isn't alien at all. Nothing that attracts is alien. Bambaataa wants to artificialize himself. White-framed slitshades scanning the track, the fashion of a Parliafunkadelicment outpost left on an offworld colony to develop its own silicon-based MythSystems. The dj's role is to intensify estrangement, to transmit the currents of the alien. But the dj doesn't know what she wants until she hears it. The Futurist is helpless in the face of fascination. Yesterday this track was unknown, unheard, undreamt. Today you follow it like a sleepwalker.

Journalism inverts this unknowingness – How can I know what I want? – into a demand: 'How can you like what you like?' Journalism's job is to build the border, be the gatekeeper, man the crossing. The Futurist moves carelessly past a polarization which was never there.

White journalism always asks the same question: 'How could this whitest of groups exert this powerful influence over Black Music?' Simultaneously smug and incredulous, it tells you, over and over, that Kraftwerk are Techno's precursors, its routes-rockers. But having taught Techno producers all they know, the originators must recede into the distance as Techno, simple lessons mastered, advances inexorably into the future.

White Noise for Snares

Drums and Electronics converge on the new possibility space of rhythmatics and syncussion. As Kraftwerk realized, sound machinery de-skills and dephysicalizes music, allowing 'thinking and hearing' precedence over 'gymnastics. Practising is no longer necessary.'

The musician becomes an electronic programmer, a push-button percussionist who taps ENTER with the fingertips.

The drum-machine is really a synthesizer which plays back sequences of automatic intensities, pitch, noise. Model 500 makes up 'drum sounds on the Korg MS10 synthesizer. I would play around with white noise and pink noise and come up with drum sounds. I heard a Kraftwerk record the first time. The record was *Man Machine* and on a lot of the songs they were using white noise for snares in just the same way that I was.'

> *Science fiction doesn't predict the future, it determines it, colonizes it, preprograms it in the image of the present*
> **William Gibson**

Preprogram the Future

Detroit Techno organizes a history and preprograms the future direction of the Rhythmachine. As Juan Atkins declares 'It was so amazing. It was like the answer. It was the future for me. I thought man, this is the future and this is where I'm trying to go. If you listen to *We Are the Robots* there are no cymbals. I heard my snare sounds and I heard my kickdrum sound on this record. But the thing was that it was more precise. It was like what I was trying to do but couldn't get to, you know? Then I heard the gated noise snare and the gated noise kick with no cymbals. It just froze me in my tracks.'

The Cyborg in the Network of Forces

In naming himself Model 500, Juan Atkins affirms the machine state which used to be called dehumanization. Gunther Frohling's '78 *Man Machine* sleeve shows a chorus line of bachelormachines. The inside sleeve art shows Kraftwerk with dyed black hair, black eyeliner, red lipstick on their minuscule, sealed-up mouths, red shirts and black ties. The right arm is held at the hip and all are looking right. Posed on a metal stairway with red rails, all bachelors with no bride.

The name Model 500 announces the producer as the next model, the synthesizer of the future. The producer is now the modular input, willingly absorbed into McLuhan's 'medium which processes its users, who are its content.' Tapping into the energy flow of the machine, the Futurist becomes an energy generator. Cyborging turns the human into Samuel Butler's machinate mammal, part of an ongoing connection machine. Machines R US. Donna Haraway: 'The machine is us, our processes, an aspect of our embodiment.'

To cyborg yourself you name yourself after a piece of technical equipment, become an energy generator, a channel, a medium for transmitting emotions electric. The psyborg plugs into machinic processes, draws on the electronic energy of... everything. It becomes a component of the unbuilt future world machines, an element in Goldie's cuboidrome piece, in Basquiat's sampladelic *Pegasus* machine. Cyborging, to borrow the words of Norman Mailer, 'takes the immediate experiences of any man, magnifies the dynamic of his movements, not specifically but abstract so that he is seen as a vector in a network of forces.'

Heteronyms

Like Underground Resistance as X-102, World 2 World, Galaxy 2 Galaxy, The Martian, like Kool Keith as Funk Igniter Plus, Rhythm X, Dr Octagon, like 4 Hero as Tek 9, Internal Affairs, Tom & Jerry, Nu Era, Juan Atkins multiplies himself into machine names: M500, X-Ray, Channel One Frequency, Audiotech and Infiniti. The producer disappears into each alterego but the machinate name is not a pseudonym, a fake name. Rather it's a *heteronym*, a many-name, one in a series of parallel names which distributes and disperses you into the public secrecy of open anonymity. I is a crowd: the producer exists simultaneously, every alterego an advertisement for myselves. The Rhythmachine actively sets out to manufacture as many personalities as possible. Alteregos are more real because you choose them. Ordinary names are unreal because you didn't. Multi-egos are more real still because they designate your parallel states.

Children, instinctual animists, identify with toys and dolls, subjecting themselves to and projecting onto the Inanimate: every 12-year-old knows that I is an other and another and another. In the 70s, the Bowie heteronyms — Major Tom, Aladdin Sane, Thin White Duke — were serial. Now heteronyms come in parallel. Today, the Futurist producer is always greater than one, always multiplying into omni-duos, simultaneously diverging selves that never converge into knowledge of self. Instead of disciplining others through the despotic standard of keeping it real, staying true to the game, representing or staying black, Alien Music proliferates mindstates which never amount to one mind. To unify the self is to amputate the self.

Rhythmatic Consciousness

To technofy means to synthesize music from the same robotic rhythms that took Detroit's humans out of the loop. M500: 'Berry Gordy built the Motown sound on the same principles as the conveyor belt system of Ford.' Motown amplified the soundscape of the 60s motor town metropolis: 'Today the plants don't work that way. They use computers and robots to build the cars.'

Metroplex = Metropolitan Complex

Model 500's record label — Metroplex — amplifies the assembly-line lanes of the 80s metropolitan complex. The metroplex is the futuropolis in the Third Wave of the Techno Era. 'I'm probably more interested in Ford's robots than Berry Gordy's music.' This crowd of cyborgs — Model 500, Audiotech, X-Ray, Channel One, Frequency — all tune into the chunk-a-chunk-a rhythms of the Ford robot. Building a car becomes the Dance of the Industrial Robotniks.

Automanikk

To technofy is to turn the automatic sequence into what A Guy Called Gerald terms an automanikk track. Far from being mechanically predictable, the automatic becomes manic. The gated-noise kick of the Roland 808 and 303 machines, their signature hardstrike, causes language to onomatopoeize the 'c' into 'kk'. With Techno the machine goes mental.

Defrictional

Techno defrictionalizes the funk. Its angular attack velocities are the opposite of any snake-hipped 70s groove. Where Parliament urged you to dance your way out of your constriction, Techno triggers a delibidinal economics of strict pulses, gated signals — with Techno you dance your way *into* your constriction. Diagonals corner you, creating a new kind of tension that doesn't resolve in expected places. This in turn creates new expectations in the listener and the producers begin to call this feeling abstract. Techno's uptightness, its everywhichway-but-looseness is not so much maladroit as malandroid.

Cubular

Techno is angular funk for androids, mandroids and womandroids. More than angular, it's cubular: Techno transmits sensations of cuboid and tubular sound, sets off a cognitive dissonance throughout the large brain of the body. Its texturhythms provoke an inextricable intricacy, a maze of limbic dissonance that blocks and baffles, threatens and entreats.

With Rhythim is Rhythim's '92 *Ikon* and *Kao-tic Harmony [Relic of Relics]*, sequencing complexifies into an allatonceness, an algebra of untitled emotions. 'My concept has always been to get the feel from all drum-machines simultaneously,' May explains. 'I try to connect all the feels so that they accent and bounce off of each other.' The sequencer is tied to a single clock, but running 3 rhythm patterns and 2 bass sequences at once yields a bewitching mosaic of overlapping rhythmelodies, an aural algebra that confounds counting, that tugs at you everywhichway, compelling an all-over omniattentiveness. When sequences bounce and clock cycles nudge, when the rims of texturythm meet the edge of rhythmelodies, time touches time in a machinekiss.

By sampling a chord and playing it back as a single note, the original chord expands into a keyboard. Unlocatable intermediate tones emerge, which May then exaggerates by jumping between octaves of the expanded chord spectrum so that the sound shockcuts as treacherously as springloaded stalactites. The result is a sense of solemn exaltation. Rhythim is Rhythim's syntharmonic orchestration move you through an impalpable portent, a cosmic indifference exemplified by the title and arrangement of '87's *It Is What It Is*. 'My string sounds are very cold, very callous,' he explains. This callousness is anempathetic in Michel Chion's sense, because 'it doesn't care and for this very reason, takes on, in a massive transference, the weight of a human destiny which it sums up and disdains.' In *Kao-tic Harmony*, these glacial tones turn aquamarine, are heard underwater. The spheres have long since collapsed into a sublime spacewreck, a bombed-out relic of relics.

> *UFOs, they're drawn to electric power. They hover over the powerplant, just over there*
> **Fox Mulder**

Ufonic

Sung with the drained fanaticism of an abductee, Model 500's '85 *No UFOs [Original Vocal Mix]* drags you into the ufonic experience. 'When the synthesizer came along it was perfect for me because it allowed me to make sounds that were impossible.' For Juan Atkins, electronics switches on an unreality principle. 'I was into UFOs landing and taking off, and spaceships. The synthesizer allowed me to create, in my bedroom, the sound of what it would be like if a UFO landed in the front yard.' Eddie "Flashin" Fowlkes recalls 'a story about Juan and the other Cybotron guys going to a building and some guy drawing a circle around them. They sat in a circle waiting for the cybotrons to come down.'

> *I wanted to land a UFO on the track*
> **Model 500**

The Mouth Is a Hole for the Soul

The M500 voice hollows the soul into an affectless, traumatized void. The mouth is a hole through which the soul drains away. The M500 accent doesn't emote: instead it [r]emotes, recedes into earshot, oracular portents from the end of a tunnel. *No UFOs* has the ominous imminence of whiteness synthesized out of Bauhaus, Depeche Mode and Gary Numan: 'Tell me if it's alright/You said I should not fear/things you haven't seen before/are coming very near.'

Your Brain Is Caught up in the Net

By running 2 Rhythmachines at once, programmed with separate parts, *No UFOs* blocks and bounces your body in a maze of interlocking inhibitions. Woodblocks with the wood deleted and replaced with the anempathy of metal on metal. Handclaps, the impact of palm on skin, are replaced by white noise gated into mekanik matchstrikes, amplified into the inexpressive aspiration of machines with asthma. The Song is replaced by nonsequential sequences of rhythmatic electricity. Gating cuts off the attack of the envelope so that Roland 808 and 909 beats are all abruptness: from 0 to 1 like a trap shutting.

Instead of being propelled forward by The JB's funk monaurail, the rhythms frustrate all groove, impeding you. Melody is replaced by bass synths that stab, with the tension-inducing texturhythms of a tennis ball being bounced but never served. Constricting Zapp's Spandex bass into an ounce of its bounce, the M500 synth generates basstabs which stress out the reflexes with their irregular regularity.

In *No UFOs*, Atkins is disconnected from space by his conviction that there are UFOs: 'They say there is no hope/They say No UFO/Why is your head held high/Maybe you'll see them fly y yy yyy y ying iiingg innng.' No Astro‹›Black coaxial cables. The spacelink is broken.

Things you haven't seen before are coming very near
Model 500

[R]emote
Snatched into the fx zone, the voice enters what post-rock group Sabalon Glitz term the ufonic state. The ufo experience bursts acoustics apart in a fearful uphoria, shatters the voice into a host of polyvowels, the plash of tyres through rain, the echo of barrels rolling down a wet sidestreet in the cold light of night. Techno's anempathetic tones empties all the heat from emotion, lowering temperature until you want to shelter from your body's altered conduction. Putting the soul on ice disequilibrates your thermostatic balance, generating hallucinations of the skin, the sensation of being attacked by cold angles. You put a distance between you and yourself.

Drive through the Darkside
Model 500's '85 *Night Drive [thru Babylon]* launches the Darkside of Detroit Techno wherein bachelormachines stalk the night, rearing up on their hindquarters. Model 500 prowls the telephonumbilical connection, a furtive pervert obscured by synths. The voice slips past hearing as it sleeps like a dog, a subliminal shadow that creeps along the skin, stalks you with its lightbreath: 'I'm driving through black on black in black.' The nightdriver feels like 'a snake, sliding down the side of a glass square.'

Suburban Knight's *The Art of Stalking [Stalker Mix]* and Reece's *Just Another Chance* develop this drive through the Darkside. Suburban Knight synthesises a stealthscape of sliding pizzicato through which the hypothermic predator lunges and darts, crouches and techsteps. In

Reece's audition of a nightime world, insidious Sprechgesang prowls the metroplex. Baleful bass miasma turns the air waxy, sapping your step, dragging you through a quagmire. Synth as malignant as Sarin gas seeps through the cybodrome. Entropy powers the Grid in Techno City, Destroit. In K. Alexi Shelby's *All for Lee·Sah*, his volumeless whisper slurs and shudders, cloaking its consonants. The batteries of the hunterstalker are running low. The chorus of reversed sighs and pink noise refracts into the Japanese word 'Hai'. It's a duet for predator and prey in which the Nastassia Kinski-ized voice, drained and indifferent, stutters until she turns into a flock of fleeing consonants.

Inside the Sanctuary of Shockwave: The Bomb Squad

We Are the Diagonal

Today's science fiction starts with Jack Womack's *Elvissey* and Pat Cadigan's *Synners*, William Gibson's *Virtual Light* and Bruce Sterling's *Schizmatrix* — tomorrow's Sonic Fiction begins with The Bomb Squad's post-'88 tracktitles: *War at 33.3*, *Incident at 66.6FM*, *Final Count of the Collision between Us and the Damned*, *Terminator X to the Edge of Panic*, *Terminator X Speaks with his Hands*. For you, Chuck D's value isn't as an ambassador but as an imagineer whose titles constitute Condensed Fiction: capsule epics of the Electronic Age, the artificial thought of the audioevent.

The Engineer Crosses the Glass

With The Bomb Squad — Hank Shocklee, Keith Shocklee, Eric 'Vietnam' Sadler, Carl Ryder — the engineer, the producer and the programmer become a group in their own right. Backroom status is replaced by the expertise of sound designers. As Hank Shocklee says, 'It's like somebody throwing rice at you. You have to grab every little piece and put it in the right place like in a puzzle.' In the films *Predator 2*, *Ghost in the Shell*, the *Alien* tetralogy, it's always the engineers who are ready to turn the alien into killer app. The engineer is the lethal conceptechnician, not forming a group but 'a technical assault squadron' all the more lethal for its anonymity. Deadliness lies in invisibility, in this retreat from the light into a public secrecy and private publicity.

Public Enemy draw fire with the visible target of their logo. The

Bomb Squad are acousmatic, heard and unseen, adopting tactics of stealth adapted by Underground Resistance. With the sleeve art for '89's *Welcome to the Terrordome*, engineering becomes imagineering. The 12 is fictionalized as a sonic device, a bomb, 'launched, fuelled, planted and detonated by The Bomb Squad.'

In their dub mixes, The Bomb Squad invent a sampladelic electronics at the heart of HipHop that turns up the volume of the world.

A Detonating Calm

Close-miking expands the field of hearing. Perception blows up and in the ruins, the listener goes travelling, climbs the desolate rubble of headphone consciousness. By whispering the chorus to '88's *Louder than a Bomb*, a roar becomes a hush that delivers you to sanctuary inside this Bomb Squad shockwave. In '92's *By the Time I Get to Arizona*, the air trembles in a split-second pause, motile with anticipation. Beats crack like forlorn fireworks. There's a detonating calm just before the riot kicks off with the swaggering fuzz of boaconstrictor funk flown in from Mandrill's *Two Sisters of Mercy*. In the second before strafing, the organ vibrato wells up, cradling you in buoyant harmonics.

Wrap Me in Catastrophe

The synthesizer reverb and ocean spume in '91's *Can't Truss It [Almighty Raw 125th Street Bootleg Mix]* wrap you in the arms of catastrophe. Helicopters hover into earshot. A thunderthroated voiceover murmurs intimately, 'It started in slaveships.' *Can't Truss It*'s intro is an instrumental in itself, The Bomb Squad at their most supersonically fictional, fastforwarding the Middle Passage into 'Nam until both arrive from the future.

The Apocalypse is Now, 1725, off the East Coast of Saigon: 'Slaveships. There are more records of slaveships than one would dream. It seems inconceivable until you reflect that for 200 years ships sailed carrying cargos of slaves.' The trailertone slows down into Vaderized pitch, a restricted frequency that intensifies emotional output.

The Bomb Squad dunks you in zero time until you feel the apocalypse that's 'already been in effect'.

There's a heightened awareness in HipHop, fostered through comics and sci fi, of the manufactured, designed and posthuman existence of African-Americans. African aliens are snatched by African slavetraders, delivered to be sliced, diced and genetically designed by whiteface fanatics and cannibal Christians into American slaves, 3/5 of their standardized norm, their Westworld ROM.

Like the robot – Karel Capek's '21 Czech neologism for a mechanized worker – the slave was actually manufactured to fulfill a function: as a servomechanism, as a transport system, as furniture, as 3/5 of the human, as a fractional subject. Norbert Wiener clicks on escape: 'The automatic machine is the precise economical equivalent of slave labour.'

Slaves are aliens. Leroi Jones adjusts the macroscope setting: 'Not only physical and environmental aliens, but products of a completely alien philosophical system.' Inhumans, posthumans owing nothing to the human species. Hence the endless arguments in the 18th C about the ability of slaves to read or write, the equivalent to 20th C arguments concerning the potential existence of artificial intelligence.

'At the eve of the year 2000, President David Duke of the United World States of Europe-America, has launched a final assault on peoples of African descent, turning the righteous into niggatrons.' PE's *Whole Lotta Love* intro is PhonoFiction at the 23rd hour of 'December 31st 1999'. Throughout, a mission-control sample counts up towards zero from minus 20, freezing at minus point 666 recurring.

From the future of racial war, *Contract on the Love World Jam* is The Bomb Squad at their most voluptuously world-historical. The Rhythmengine pushes you along with skratchadelic skids slipping and sliding either side of the downbeat, revving up an anticipation sustained by cradling guitar harmonics. It is a military communique, a lecture, a press briefing momentously intoning: 'There is something living in the consciousness of the people today. The race that controls the living past controls the living future.'

Voluptuous Vigilance

Verge, brink, cusp: these imminent states are sustained into prolonged thresholds, stretched edges, incipient action. The sampler's loop function iterates the break into the brink. '92's *Arizona Assassination Attempt Acca Double Dub*: pre-stampede wails are sustained into a panic wave which wells up through the crowd's head and writhes down its tail. Screams emerge then fall back into a swarm of sobs, dissolve into a smothered sky. Choruses are assembled from crowd panic.

Distress tones stretch into downerdrones that drive through your head. '88's *Final Count of the Collision between Us and the Damned* lasts

0.48 seconds. The drastic dynamic between title and music, and between syntactic and sonic organization, sets the senses seesawing. The title gratifies desire for annihilation, teasing it into both preparation and postponement. *Final Count* is an epic of prolonged abruptness, in which drum-machines ricochet like an automatic repeat rifle over ice-cold Rhythim is Rhythim-style strings and ominous drones.

The Bomb Squad operate in the countdown to imminent apocalypse and impending riot. Gangsta lives in the chronic time of Dr Dre's G Funk Era, the obstinate indolence of the gangsta paradise, a neverending idyll of the id.

Alarm for the World

Drones recur indefinitely at 33.3 recurring, trapping you in despotic time. Midrange frequencies wind you up tight into the tense present. '88's concept album *It Takes a Nation of Millions to Hold Us Back* released Bomb Squad electronic tonalities throughout the communications landscape. *Mind Terrorist* and *Show 'em Whatcha Got* cage you up in unlocatable synth-guitar loops, the elegiac horns of a final salute. Sleep is abhorred; the aim is to wake up its audience from the post-Black Power sleep, of false consciousness, tv addiction and historical miseducation.

Therefore the piercing blare of *Rebel Without a Pause* is an 'alarm for the world'. 'That noise,' Chuck D says, 'came from a James Brown grunt. It was a blend of *The Grunt* and a Miles Davis trumpet which produced a sound that wavered. And then we took that tone and we stretched it.' *Welcome to the Terrordome* is a sonic weapon, an overkill device that sends satisfying shockwaves through the sensorium. *Countdown to Armageddon*: the Bomb Squad sound races against clocktime.

TX Reanimator Plays the Tone Generator

With the instrumental, the turntable comes into its own as a tone generator. 'The drone on *Terminator X* is a backwards firetruck.' The transformer pole of the mixer becomes an effect for the turntable as a sound machine. Terminator X delays the scratch into staggered screeches. Turntabilized tones phase into slo-mo texturhythms, blocs of unidentifiable static matter. In '88's *Terminator X Speaks with his Hands*, the dj's hand evolves into a distributed brain, a terrorwrist with its own memory.

Decelerated attack velocities set up a death knell for lachrymose wah-wah guitar from The Meters' *Just Kissed My Baby*. *Incident at 66.6 FM* is a radiophonic duet between talkshow and static. Studio phone-ins interrupted by between station frequencies, radiowaves stretched into sustained glitch.

Systematic Schizophony

The Bomb Squad is R. Murray Schafer's nightmare made audible. Postwar schizophonia – this proliferation of noise since the separation of sound from source – is orchestrated into the information explosion: 'Related to schizophrenia, I wanted [the word] schizophonia to convey the same sense of aberration and drama.'

You're blitzed out, immersed in an environment of endless emergency where 'the overkill of hifi gadgetry creates a synthetic soundscape in which machine made substitutes are providing the operative signals directing modern life.'

Megablast, Louder than a Bomb, Timebomb, Rightstarter: all these titles intensify Schafer's nightmare of hifi gone overkill. Bringing the noise blows up the mind, by maintaining an ambient pressure more felt than heard. Producer Eric 'Vietnam' Sadler explained the insistent static and hiss throughout the Bomb Squad's '88-'92 concept-album cycle: 'Turn it all the way up so it's totally distorted and pan it over to the right side so you really can't even hear it. Put the sound only in the right speaker and turn it so you can't barely even hear it – it's just like a noise in the side' that never lets up. Life during everyday wartime, waged with 'knowledge of self'.

Paranoiac Critical Device

On Public Enemy sleeves, the gunsight logo has become a gunlight, a calibrated halo in which, says Virilio, 'functions of eyesight and weaponry melt into each other.' The optical diagram of assassination becomes a paranoiac critical device, an optogram which intercepts sight.

Operational Signals

You're like Newton, Bowie's alien in the film *The Man Who Fell to Earth*, defending and surrendering to the audiovisual attack, the info-explosions on his 15 tv screens. Newton uses his remote-control volume-mixer to wreck the picture with bursts of static, scratching tv like vinyl. The audiovision image-current reverses direction and starts attacking you in all its phosphorescent ferocity, seizing your synapses with its photons.

The Final Transmission from The Forever War: Underground Resistance

Final transmission: I found it. There is existence other than us. I have transformed. The tones are the keys to it all! I'll be back
Mad Mike

Underground Resistance's '92 debut album sleeve *Revolution for Change* cover adapts Public Enemy's '87 debut *Yo! Bum Rush the Show* for the Techno Age. Cloaked in shadows, PE are crouched around the decks warding off yet basking in its sonic rays. Shot from the turntable's point of hearing, the sleeve shows them in thrall to the decks. Masked and hooded, Mike Banks and Jeff Mills of Underground Resistance are videocaptured in the blue light of the videolens. UR adapt The Bomb Squad's strategies of stealth into a conceptechnics of electronic invisibility.

Technology is not neutral. It is not neutral; it's a black continent
Virilio and Lotringer

Disappeared by Consensus

In today's satellite linked era, it's widely assumed that MTV is the motor of music, that all sonic history travels through audiovisual transport systems. But the very existence of Carl Craig, of UR, of Red Planet, of M500, of Drexciya, proves that MTV's role is drastically overrated.

Far from the navsats, Techno is a sonar system inexplicable to consensual histories, and to sclerotic assumptions about Black Music in the US. In the UK and Europe, Techno *is* the tradition, proper Techno for True People, guaranteed 100% pure. It's a ubiquitous technology that colonizes Europeans, like oxygen, or the Graeco-Roman alphabet.

But in the US, it's the opposite. Detroit Techno is *so* absent from American popculture, *so* contra-media, that it slips from the scanning systems altogether. Like an Argentinean refusenik, it's been disappeared. Except that instead of pleading for inclusion and integration, it moves further into the dark. Techno secedes from the logic of empowerment which underpins the entire American mediascape: from all those directives to become visible, to assume your voice, to tell your story.

Secede from the Street

Simultaneously, Techno secedes from the street, the street which is widely assumed to be the engine of black popculture, to be its foundation and its apotheosis, its origin and its limit. Techno emigrates from America, into what former UR producer Robert Hood terms the Internal Empire. In vanishing from the street, and from Trad HipHop's compulsory logic of representation and will to realness, UR identifies not with the low end but the high end of technology. Underground Resistance is neither low-tech nor resistant.

UR abandons street knowledge altogether.

The pavement is cracked, the soil is polluted, the roots are withered and the ground is poisoned. This toxic waste and this acid rain generate conditions in which mutant Rhythmachines thrive. UR realienates Techno, exposing it to these radioactive conditions, the ones that threaten all creativity. It thrives in the zones that art traditionally resist, the locations that kill off all soul.

UR technofies by returning the Futurhythmachine to its deadliest origin: the military armamentarium. They move into the Military Industrial Complex because the MIC precedes and predetermines the street. UR break with the street because the street is at the mercy of the military. As part of the civil sector, the street is at the receiving end of technology. It's the dumping ground.

The Cyberactiv WarMachine

By installing themselves inside the military, UR becomes a WarMachine advancing decades ahead of American music. UR's Sonic Fiction emerges from the Future at its most lethal, imbuing Techno with an enthralling electricity. Yesterday's military fact is tomorrow's science fiction. Reality accelerates past fiction.

Cold Fusion

There is no MC and no singer in UR. Studio presence is replaced by the broadcast, the data readout, the press briefing, the communique from C3I: Command Control Communications Intelligence. UR isn't human, more a signal broadcast from a military bunker, 'a project devised by spin doctors UR and The Vision to cold fuse human DNA and cell structures with cybernetic and sonic circuitry; a union of sound, man and machine.'

Acoustic and stage presence vanishes into invisible signals sent through coaxial cables, audio feeds, a nest of microphones. Mike Banks, Jeff Mills and Robert Hood evacuate human presence, replacing it with the transport systems the voice travels along to reach you. UR is a series of signals distributed across thresholds of the mixing console, the station transmitter.

Raze the Soul to the Ground

The British mythology of Trad Techno insists that the vampiric Belgians and Germans drained Techno's soul dry. In fact, it's UR that systematically industrializes Techno, into 'hard music from a hard city'. The sleeve art for '91's *X-101* EP is artwork for an updated Atrocity Exhibition. Grey videogrids of babies, images exposed to x-raylight, caught in brutal newsprint black-and-white. The middle baby holds skeletal hands to its eyes so they bug out of its brachycephalic head. The final image breaks up into static, images of an ear magnified, an embryo invaded by patches and blocs of light.

As funk terminators and soulrazers, *X-101* and '92's *Revolution for Change* rigidify Techno until it becomes sonic brutalism, the cyberactive WarMachine. Techno becomes an immersion in insurrection, music to riot with. Exacerbating the terrorizing impact of Belgian synthesizer frequencies inflicts an insurrectionary voltage. Techno becomes punishing, a barbed-wire warzone of voltage endured and inflicted.

X-101 tracks like *Rave New World* and *Mindpower* are like being sprayed full in the face with CS gas. *Mindpower* uses Second Phase's '92 track *Mentasm [Joey Beltram Remix]* to scour the brainpan with an astringency that's more spasm than orgasm. With *Mentasm* Beltram suggests that 'you just want to bang your head against the wall. Just like you want to with *War Pigs* or *Paranoid*. I like the feeling of a good Sabbath record. I like the mood it puts me in. I'm a big metalhead.' The *Mentasm* sound is Acid twisted into Electro shockwave frequencies, live current phasing directly through your body; is a synaptic seizure.

Unknown Assault System

For these tracks UR names itself X-101, an unknown audio assault system. X-101 is not an alterego but an altermachine, which connects the X prefix of the fighterplane with the 101 suffix of the synth series. Robert Hood becomes The Vision, the anguished android from Marvel Comics Avengers. *The Punisher* EP, named after Marvel's conscientious vigilante, adapts its logo from his insignia of a skull with weapon-belt teeth. The

Death Star EP installs itself in the heart of the Darkside of *The Empire Strikes Back.*

Sonotronic Stealth

UR's titles plug into the energy flash emitted by public enmity. Launched in black labels with no information, the EPs emerge without warning, a sonotronic stealth arsenal. In '85 Cybotron survey the streets of the Techno City from above its skyscrapers. UR are molochs sinking cables beneath its streets, engineering internal exile, endless cunning. The UR credo announces: 'No hope, no fear: my only hope is underground.'

Planetary Capability

Techno seizes a planetary capability diametrically opposed to Trad HipHop's timid territoriality. Militarization puts them decades in advance of street-fixated musics. While Trad HipHop locks itself into a logic of representation and Trad rock shrinks into supplication, UR is an audio WarMachine transmitting back to Earth from the galactic, the Martian, the aquatic and the digital front.

Operating System for Overriding the Present

Each UR release arrives from the future which you're heading towards, becoming an operating system that overrides the present. Jon Hassell: 'It will become convenient to redraw the map according to who wants to live in which era. We could have wars between the 15th Century and the 21st Century.'

The Covert Dimension

From arcadegames to the Net to simulation games, civil society is the low end research-and-development unit of the military. Techno has the nomad's edge over HipHop's hypervisible trooper forever crucified in the crosshairs of the gunsight. It operates in the covert dimension that UR allies Scan 7 term the 'undetectible'. Invisibility draws you into Suburban Knight's '94 *Mind of a Panther.* Now 'you can hear him, but you can't see him. You don't know where he is. He's deadly. You don't know where he's going to come from.'

Techno is like AIDS. It's self learning.
It's highly intelligent
Mike Banks

Undetectible

Tonal communication doesn't delete psychic sensations of revolution
and secession, it derealizes them. Mike Banks: 'There are definite
messages there through tonal communication and you can't assess them,
that's why Techno is deadlier than rap.' By depropriating the listener
from syntax, Techno broadcasts from the far side of sense. It moves into
alogical possibility spaces: the covert operations of drumcodes, the
synthesis of unknown sensations, the modulation of frequent emotions.
'We're silent and deadly and that's the best way. With rap you have to
vocally communicate your point but with Techno you don't.' Techno is
covert, undetectible to anyone not locked into the music's
conceptechnics. But the Techno fanatic doesn't crack the electronic
codes. Instead, s/he enjoys being baffled, craves the onset of confusion
through depropriation. Instead of clarifying this mystification, they pass
it on. Listen to this: You are participating in a mystery. Play the track.
Transmit the tones. Become imperceptible. Midnight Sunshine cloaks the
planet. Electronic mutation functions this way, through this process
which McLuhan terms 'participation mystique'.

Techno becomes 'a sort of barricade behind which [the enemy]
becomes invisible.' Jean Baudrillard clicks on shift: 'He also becomes
"stealthy" and his capacity for resistance becomes indeterminable.'
Undetectibility is power. It allows the Techno producer to become what
The Vision‹›Robert Hood terms the Spectral Nomad, who stalks the
covert dimension, who vanishes into your sleep.

Vanish in Your Sleep

Far from pleading to pass through the passport controls of *Billboard*,
Techno grasps the chance to recede from the visible. To listen to
Underground Resistance is to have your vision deleted, plunging you
into midnight sunshine. Nothing to see, so much to feel. Nightvision
awakens new senses.

Where *Welcome to the Terrordome* becomes an audiobomb, Suburban
Knight's '94 *Dark Energy* double EP becomes a sonic strike. The label
communique announces '6 dark energy waves' that 'engulf the earth in
ultraviolet midnight sunshine.' Visualist Frankie C. Fulitz's labelscape

shows an Atomic Africa radiating a red field of dark energy. The UR logo is Islamatomic: it combines a pyramid with an atomic power symbol at its glowing apex and an Islamic crescent to its left.

Sonic Fiction Is a Subjectivity Engine

In UR, a constantly proliferating series of sonic scenarios take the place of lyrics. Sonic Fictions, PhonoFictions generate a landscape extending out into possibility space. These give the overwhelming impression that the record is an object from the world it releases. This interface between Sonic Fiction and track, between concept and music, isn't one of fiction vs reality or truth vs falsity.

Sonic Fiction is the packaging which works by sensation transference from outside to inside. The front sleeve, the back sleeve, the gatefold, the inside of the gatefold, the record sleeve itself, the label, the cd cover, Sleevenotes, the cd itself; all these are surfaces for concepts, texture-platforms for PhonoFictions. Concept feeds back into sensation, acting as a subjectivity engine, a machine of subjectivity that peoples the world with audio hallucinations. Parliament populates the world with cartoon universes; Sun Ra seeds the world with composition planets. Scientist reprograms the positioning of satellites, setting all chronosystems to warptime.

Sonic Object Shape

UR's label communiques and runout-groove messages generate the music as episodes from an ongoing battle, a Forever War against the programmers. In concept like Parliament but audiovisually their antithesis, UR aims for 'the deprogramming of the programmed mind'. Each UR 12 is a UAO from their soundworld, a sonic weapon, a soundcraft that's fallen out of their world into yours.

By linking release-production dates to assault-launch dates you feel as if you're a target. The record takes the sonic object shape of the weapon used in the launch. Each 12 is the latest instalment in an age-old battle with the programmers. Once you've bought it, you've willingly inducted yourself into The Forever War.

U R the Flight Path

The launch and journey of the *Cyberwolf* EP is the route of the UR 12 through you and onwards. The EP title catalyses a UAO, a virtual hunterseeker missile. Buying the UR 12 inducts you into a line of flight, from Detroit to the record shop to yourself to a mixtape and on.

The Vinyl Manifesto

Sound and Sonic Fiction feedforward into each other, opening up new possibility spaces like the Planetary Manifesto of '92's World Power Alliance, inscribed on the unmastered B side of *The Kamikaze* EP as WPA backing plate #1: 'The World Power Alliance was formed somewhere in Detroit, Michigan, USA on May 22, 1992 at 4.28pm by various elements of the Worlds Underground Legions. The Alliance is dedicated to the advancement of the human race by sonic experimentation.

'The World Power Alliance was designed to bring the World's minds together to combat the mediocre audio and visual programming being fed to the inhabitants of Earth, this programming is stagnating the minds of the people building a wall between races. This wall must be destroyed, and it will fall. By using the untapped energy potential of sound, the WPA will smash this wall much the same as certain frequencies shatter glass. Brothers of the underground transmit your tones and frequencies from all locations of this world. Wreak havoc on the programmers!'

UR's *World Power Alliance* expands on Public Enemy's *Fear of a Black Planet*, replacing planetary nationalism with a sonic globalism. Back in the 70s and 80s, audiosocial vanguards bet everything on visibility, identification, public enmity. But in the Techno era, 'Disappearance is our future.' Technology changes the form of power, the nature of identity, the essence of the enemy. Virilio faxes Earth: 'Every visible power is threatened.' In the Acousmatic Age, UR's Black Power is therefore undetectible, not identifiable, invisible not recognizable, stealthy not public. Like the camouflage ninjas of Wu Tang Clan proteges Killarmy, stealth and undetectibility are quiet weapons for use in silent wars.

The Label Fiction

The label fiction of Scan 7's *Undetectible* EP therefore extends strategies of stealth into covert ops, digital terrorism. The Programmers use a Central Broadcast Facility to telecast their 'mind control beam' across the world. The Central Broadcast Facility uses computer mainframe and powerful chips.

Trackmaster Lou of UR-affiliates Scan 7 has 2 jobs: to infiltrate the CBF, and stop the beam telecasting, then to put in the UR chip. This chip developed in Detroit by Metroplex engineers 'is a CPU platform chip' called 'Electro 313 203 0UR 033'.

Machine Mythologies

In a series of overlapping machine mythologies, the *Undetectible* EP drafts Model 500's Metroplex label into the assault, as a research lab for new digital applications. The chip uses Electro as a codename, its numbers the models of Roland synthesizers, synths migrating across sf as digital weapons. The effect of the Electro chip is to 'induce viruses and bass frequencies' which are 'designed to destroy programmer chips in broadcast facilities worldwide'.

In Digital War, the aim is to replace programmer chips, to destroy frequencies and therefore to destroy programmers telecasts and mind-control beams. It's a mission to infiltrate a single location, but the impact is worldwide. The units are 'digitized and returned back to Detroit via the Internet sometime in early April undetected'. Prospective tense conveys the urgent message.

Origin Unknown

Techno lives in the world of HipHop but HipHop doesn't live in the world of Techno. Soundmachines decouple sound from source, to derealize the sonic from its origin. Origin Unknown refers to today's pervasive acousmatic condition, an era in which you can't tell who's playing, when you guess the origin and you're wrong. Goldie: 'Technology takes the colour out of music. It's made the music transparent.' Mike Banks of UR thought 4 Hero were white. Kevin Saunderson thought UR were white. Nobody escapes the way machines scramble identity at the push of a button, turns the soul into sound-fx with the greatest of ease. Instead of retreating from machinic mutation back into an ethics of sound, UR is mutation-positive. The sampler is a mandate to recombinate — so it's useless lamenting appropriation. Resisting replication is like doing without oxygen. The sampler doesn't care who you are.

The Sound<>Vision Schizmatic

Today, alien attitude to the Rhythmachine overrides the acoustic self. Therefore the modern producer models a series of synthetic selves, exacerbating a confusion in which it's impossible to tell who's synthesizing the track. Juan Atkins named himself Model 500 because the name 'repudiated any ethnic designation'. Cyborging yourself volatizes [r]earview hearing, generates a perceptual vacuum which intimidates expectation and repels designation. By emitting a force field of undetectibility, it evades capture from the Turing identicops stationed in your head. It obsolesces the scanning systems that monitor the Black Atlantic. Machine Music operates through Goethe's elective affinities, not through subcultural allegiance in real-time. The engineer goes to war over a break not a country. In the Acousmatic Age there's nothing to see except the sound in its non-self. The sound‹›vision schizmatic is out of control. Escape through the radar.

The Military Arrives from the Future

As Nick Land argues, it may be useful to simulate the policeman's perspective every now and then. Revelations about real-life *X Files* remote viewing suggest that science fiction has always been the blueprint for new military capability. The continuum between fiction and fact has imploded into a fold in time.

Today's sci fi was yesterday's military fact. Each EP tracktitle announces an audio-assault system, a UAO, the Chemical Brothers' term Electronic Battle Weapons which collapses the border between Sonic Fiction and military weapons, between future and present: the *Piranha*, the *Cyberwolf*, the *Seawolf*.

Fatal Energy

Everyone now knows that bad = good, that ill = better and that sick = best. With UR this rhythmic reversal is optimized across the sonic discontinuum. The more lethal the energy, the more sensual the impact. Zapp's electric bolts, Coltrane's tranesonic energy fields, Beltram's energy flash, Kraftwerk's Powerplant, Ultramagnetic MCs' hypogalactic radiation, Parliament's Big Bang, Drexciya's intensified magnetron, Scientist's pulsars, Suburban Knight's Dark Energy fields: all these sonotronic forces release a fatal energy that floods you in sensation. In the Marvel, DC, Vertigo and Image multiverses, radiation doesn't fatally cripple you, it mutates you better than before. Machine music switches the poles in the same way. What doesn't kill you makes you stronger. The Futurhythmachine dunks you in HAZCHEM, protects you by exposing you, acclimatizing you to annihilation.

Inventions, the creations of scientists, are riddles which expand the field of the unknown
Paul Virilio

SuperFictional Science

Sonic science takes a shortcut through comics. Comics and science fiction together form a conceptual cyclotron in which Trad science is accelerated into an array of SuperFictional Sciences. By dissolving the distinctions between sciences, PhonoFiction mines all fields for their mutation capabilities.

The Sonic Fiction of *Biosensors in Tunnel Complex Africa*, from UR's '96 *Electronic Warfare: Designs for Sonic Revolutions* double EP, immediately opens a new front where military tech — the logic bomb — is part of the same arsenal as the fictional device, the Ho Chi Minh chip, the fiberoptic commando who infiltrates fiberoptic cables. UR's MythScience opens up a new discontinuum across science and art, sound and fiction.

An electronic instrument becomes an extension of a sensitive biological system
Robert Moog

Sensualization of Electricity

This is not only the militarization of pop life. Even more it's the mythification of the military, the fictionalizing of frequencies, the sensualization of electricity. The producer has an 808 state of mind which allows a 'personal electronic relationship with all my instruments. 'Cos I have electricity in my body too. When we touch they recognize me and I recognize them. I think *Terminator* is definitely what's happening, man. Machines have emotions. They can become intelligent and they will one day.'

*The synthesizer is an acoustic mirror, a brain element
that is supersensitive to the human element*
Kraftwerk

Soundmachine Symbiosis

Underground Resistance is not a group but the symbiosis of the
soundmachine with producer Mike Banks. The producer is caught up in
machinemutation, played by the machinery he plays. UR is a Roland
symbiont that uses 303s to heal, that investigates synthetic sound as a
lifeform. Sun Ra states that cosmic tones could be mentally therapeutic.

In the 90s, Techno is medication. Banks hears forwards to an era in
which 'Techno will be medicine. Western medicine looks at that as
bullshit. You can't fix somebody from singing a fuckin' song. That song
carries an emotion through tonal communication. If that person feels
that communication, it might trigger something in him that will repair
whatever the fuck is wrong with him.'

Thought forms in the mouth
Tristan Tzara

The Sublime Bathes in Saliva

The pleasure of the cosmic concept — Hancock's '72 *Quasar*, UR's '93
Galaxy 2 Galaxy double 12 EP, Alice Coltrane's '72 *World Galaxy* — is
gratifyingly oral. 'Qua' pulls back the lips while 'sar' winches the mouth
open. The G in 'Galax' pulls the back of the throat together in a tonsular
kiss, and the 'lax' demands pressups from the tongue, forcing your
muscles to flipflop from the roof to the floor of the mouth.

Widening the jaw muscles induces an awe in the face. The syllables
'qua', 'sar', 'Galax' and 'Worl' demand a labile exertion which releases
satisfying streams of spit throughout the mouth. The name Drexciya is an
adventure for the tongue. You hold a geography in your mouth. 'Drex':
the tongue descends a staircase, ascends on 'ci', skips on 'ya'. The
sublime tastes good to speak.

Synthetic Fusion

Hi-Tech Jazz from '93's *Galaxy 2 Galaxy* EP is fusion made synthetic. The 2 parts — the first subtitled *The Science*, the second *The Elements* — suggest that the music is the product of an elementary science.

Tapping into atomic processes imbues jazz with a colossal energy. Synthesized bass and kicks charge at you with an inexorable horsepower, the oncoming impact of Galactus crossing constellations. Vaulting astral keyboards wrap you in the arms of Andromeda, sponging you in sussuration, cradling you in a squeezebox seesaw which lulls and pushes into a buoyant fearlessness. With stars for handholds, you climb the skies in a 9 min 35 sec war with yourself. 'Techno to me is the one music that is truly a global music. It might not only be a global music. I think it's a galactic music.'

The double EP forms an unfinished Concept Cycle beginning with '92's *Nation 2 Nation*, '93's *World 2 World* and *Galaxy 2 Galaxy*, ending with the unreleased *Universe 2 Universe*. In *World 2 World*'s *Jupiter Jazz*, the choral tones traditionally used as melodic reverberation and blessed haze are sharpened until they strike like stalactites fashioned from inspiration. Chord progressions are replaced by archangelic attack impulses, octave jumpcuts that induce rapturous heart attack. Cloudgrazing skytones fill you with sensations of ascension, with warm surges of bass which rise up through you in panic elation.

The 12's label shows the golden rays of a Renaissance sun, orbiting around the deck spindle in heliocentronic revolutions. *Jupiter Jazz*'s title combines jazz synthesized on Jupiter keyboards with jazz played by Jupiter the Joybringer: featuring Zeus on synthesizer!

Circumsolar Revolution

Across the grooves the stylus rides the expressway to your skull. In the post-'92 collaborative series of Red Planet EPs, produced by UR as The Martian, each EP arrives in a signal-red sleeve that throws the black label into relief. Around the perimeter of the label, red lettering reads: THE RED PLANET WILL APPEAR ONLY WHEN YOUR MIND IS OPEN.

In the right of the label is a red disc, its left side bisecting the indented circle that surrounds the spindle space. Around the spindle hole is a red ring that cuts into the red disc. On the decks, the effect is a syzygy in revolution, a moon in alignment with a red planet surrounded by a black void, encircled again by vast expanse of vinyl.

Terraformers at 808° Kelvin

Frequencies are fictionalized into offworld deserts, environmentalized into the capsule exogeographies of track titles from the Red Planet EPs 1-8: *The Long Winter of Mars, Season of the Solar Wind, Base Station 303, Marisian Probes over Montana, Journey to the Martian Polar Cap, 808° [Surface Temperature Mix]*. The rasping, caustic overtones of filtration and tweaking generates acid rain. In the machine meteorology of the Red Planet series, hot frequencies metabolize extreme temperatures. The Red Planet series uses Rolands as terraforming machines for Martian artforms. It synthesizes ecologies from waveforms.

In Advance of the Landing

The Red Planet series assembles a Martian mythology of Astral‹›Indian tech-magicians: *Renegades on the Red Planet, Astral Apache, Stardancer, Ghostdancer, Starchild, Windwalker, Skypainter, Firekeeper*. On *Stardancer* from *Red Planet 2*, guitar and synths are processed into an unplaceable iridescence. Synthetic bass drops like a concrete basketball, dragging your feet like traction. Attack velocities fire like catherine wheels in a duet with hihat clap. Chiming trails slowly circle, liquefied comets which stream through you until you're bursting with ascension. Synths surge in marine bass and simultaneously shoot stars across the sky, erupting in exultation.

The Martian synthesizes a cosmic disco that colonizes Mars in advance of the landing, 'so that if we come into contact with intelligent lifeforms from another planet we can talk on the same level.' Across each 12, Native Martian shamans escape Earth‹›American genocide, dragging you with them as they species-jump to Mars.

Unknown Force: Offworld Mass: Oncoming Motion: Scientist

On Scientist's '78 *Scientist Meets the Space Invaders* the arcadegame's programmed zaps inspire the Desk Magus to process drum signals into intensities of unknown force, mass and motion. Engineer-producer Overton Brown ‹› Scientist alters the beats until they become unplayable and unrecognizable, offworld signal systems. Each track crosses the sensorial threshold into a universe of pulsation, futurhythms that drag your limbic system offworld, abandon your motor-reflex on Earth to fend for itself and leave you headless on Venus.

Supercussion: at War with Gravity

With Scientist, drumsticks stop beating out time on taut surfaces. Instead unknown instruments drop like deadweights onto the surface of unidentifiable planets. *Pulsar* builds rhythm out of single impacts which collapse like boxes dropped from the north face of Kilimanjaro, crumple like metal cases staved in 2 then switch into rapid fire zaps. The offworld gravity of quasars alters the force, mass and motion of the beat, transforming the stress-impact of the electromagnetic signals. In *Laser Attack*, metallic boulders cave in under the pressure of their own weight, shuddering in a double impact. *Space Invaders* replaces drumsticks with boulders, metal boxes, meteorites, industrial objects plummeting through space to crash on planes rigidified by as yet undiscovered alloys. On *Beam Down*, packing crates implode on impact then switch into shots ricocheting down a corridor of anglepoise mirrors.

Walls of Solid Air

In dub, bass traditionally acts as the pressure drop. On *Red Shift*, *Time Warp* and *Pulsar*, the low end has become spectral walls of infra-pressure which buckle and fold you into colossal pockets of solid air, warm banks that loom up to surround you. With *Laser Attack*, the bass ripples the air as it orbits a distant perimeter, triggering test signals like the warning tones of an electrified fence.

On *De Materialise*, beats suddenly crash into earshot, triggering echoes that resolve instead of receding, collapse like squishy settees, chase each other round corridors. Infrasonic bass forms a colossal melody that stalks Brontosaurian throughout. Sonar pulses replace harmony with echolocation, the long-distance machine-machine communication.

Electric circuitry confers a mythic dimension on our ordinary individual and group actions. Our technology forces us to live mythically
Marshall McLuhan

The Possibility Space of the Soundclash

The space invaders have migrated from the screen, left the arcade to invade London. On Tony McDermott's 70s Marvel Comic-style cover, Scientist is a superhero in limegreen top emblazoned with an S, yellow sleeves, bright green pants and purple boots, firing laser shots and aiming kicks at the pixel-sprite formation landing in a grey carpark in North London. Beside him, a woman crouches and squeezes off at an alien. A mother in a red all-in-one, with a 70s Afro, turns, frozen fearfully with her kid, as a blonde hits concrete.

Organised sound clashes in the mix. The 3rd momentary track emerges from the convergence of 2 tracks. Each record sheds its date, escapes its context. This process dissolves the lines of association, dehistoricizes each track. At the same time, mixology rubs eras against each other, generates the temporal friction of anachronosis. Time slips out of its date, vaporizing history at plus 4 on pitch adjustment, frictionalizing it at plus 5. This proliferation into networks of time forms the heterotopias where *Scientist Meets the Space Invaders*. Dub's possibility space of the meeting functions as a psychoacoustic fictional plane where worlds collide. Each element in a futurhythmachine mythology is a communicating vessel. The 12 becomes the sonic weapon. The decks become a platform where aliens attract: Scientist meets Star Child, Pacman meets Astral Apache, Silver Surfer meets the Shockwave Rider, Captain Afro-America meets the Double Dutch Remanipulator, Supernaut meets the Camouflage Ninja, Funk Igniter Plus meets the Purpose Maker, Firekeeper meets Killah Priest, the Suburban Knight faces the TX Reanimator, Thousand Finger Man meets Sweet Exorcist, Doctor Eich meets Mr Gerbik, Lord of the Null Lines meets the Terror Mad Visionary, The RZArector meets Dr Ludicrous, Dr Strange meets the Spectral Nomad, Iron Man meets Gamma Player, Godard's Tarzan meets IBM, GhostDancer meets Ghost Face Killer, Cybotron meets The Windwalker, Dr Blowfin meets Von Blofeld the Black Lotus, The Data Thief meets Pluramon, Hallucinator meets Dark Magus, Gigi Galaxy meets the Black Regent, Mr Freedom X meets Masta Killer, Veinmelter meets Sci-Clone, Secret Girl kisses the Man from Tomorrow, The

Illuminator meets The Cellular Automaton.

Each component excites another in an adventure of concepts. Machine Music is cosmogenetic. It perpetually generates 'mythic worlds of electronically processed experience.'

Materializing Offworld Revolutions:
X-102 Discovers 'The Rings of Saturn'

The moment the belief that the street is the predetermining law and limit of all black popculture is destroyed and disregarded, the postwar Rhythmachine will-to-conceptualize becomes immediately and overwhelmingly audible.

Far from beginning in 70s Britain and ending with punk [as media folklore so fondly maintains] the Progressive Era opens with Sun Ra. And today you live in a far more conceptual era than Progressive Rock ever dreamt of. 4 Hero, Killarmy, Dr Octagon and Red Planet fabricate concepts, perpetuate Digital MythSystems and proliferate sonic theories far more excessive than Gong's. Machine Music is exuberant in its exorbitance.

Trad white journalism is affronted at the news that ex-UR producer Jeff Mills thinks in concepts. Querulously, it ponders how and why such a thing could happen. And starts seriously to doubt whether Black Music is really safe in his hands, or Tricky's, or Dr Octagon's.

It isn't. It never was.

Mesmerized by belief systems left over from HipHop, Trad media sleepwalks through the sensorial implications of Sonic Fiction, deaf to its formal operations, terminally unable to comprehend the perceptual illogic of your Age.

Unblack Unpopular Unculture

Only journalism can deliver you to sound safely. Futurhythmachines form a discontinuum that is utterly *indifferent* to the street. Machine Music therefore arrives as unblack, unpopular and uncultural, an Unidentified Audio Object with no ground, no roots and no culture.

Theory at 130 BPM

As X-102, Banks's, Mills's and Hood's '92 project announces its concept at once: *X-102 Discovers 'The Rings of Saturn'*. Sleeve art, titles, label art, everything out in the open and yet powerfully unclear. The concept album, Jeff Mills argues, should 'materialize an idea or a theory, to try to explain with music a certain place or a certain thing.'

So thought travels at 130bpm. The moment concepts are materialized, they become plastic: mixillogical. Electronic duo Mouse on Mars: 'Everything you press on a record is the record. Hifi consciousness is what your ears expect from a record.'

Replayable Mindstates

With James Brown's '71 *Revolution of the Mind*, the record becomes a replayable machine for generating new mindstates. Brownian hifi consciousness abstracts revolution from the decks and applies it to the head. It grasps the intimate machine interface of human and decks. Black Atlantic Futurism is characterised by 2 tendencies: first, a drive towards Cosmogenesis, towards conceptechnics, Sonic Fiction, concept trilogies and concept EP cycles; second, a contrary drive towards the meta, towards sound for its own sake.

Disco Lunar Module

From the self-reflexive funk of James Brown's '69-'71 tracks — *Ain't It Funky Now Parts 1 and 2, Funky Drummer Parts 1 and 2, Make It Funky Parts 1-4* — to the meta-HipHop of De la Soul's *Skip to My Loop* and *This Is a Recording* and the metamatic Electro of Man Parrish's *Six Simple Synthesisers*, from the self-reflexive HipHop of Mantronix's *Bassline* to the self-reflexive Techno of Carl Craig's *Oscillator*, Futurhythmusic sacrifices content to throb and politics for pulse. Black Machine Music is always applauded for its message because seriousness must always be sociopolitical. But the Futurhythmachine emerges when music turns *away* from the world and goes round and round in circles; when the track manifests the title's manifesto.

Convolutor [Type Galilei]

Revolution migrates from machine to mind. The tone arm travels across the grooves of the mind in a universe of everextending radii from the centre. Jeff Mills's *Inner Sanctum* is intentionally mastered in reverse so that 'the needle spirals from the inside out'. UR's and Jeff Mills's 12s play from the runout to the beginning of the vinyl, starting where the ordinary 12 ends, finishing where the needle usually launches itself. By switching direction to play forward from the end, the reverse-mastered 12 provokes acute cognitive dissonance.

Reverse-engineering the Brownian revolution alters the grooves of the mind, turns hifi consciousness inside out, and confronts you with the Clintonian habitform which is you. Mike Banks explains how the supervisor at the National Sound Cutting pressing plant in Detroit 'showed us a way of changing the direction of the machines just by changing the belts on the machine's main drive. We use the same machines that they used back in the Motown days, which are ancient compared to the ones today, which you can't tamper with.'

The Conceptechnics of Materialization

X-102 drastically expands the information vinyl normally contains. Materializing concepts generates 'a sudden multiplication of dimensions of matter'. Virilio's process can be formalized as the equation $M \times C = M^n$ [where M = Material and C = Concept]. The mastering, sequencing and timing of the album, the track, the label, the sleeve, the title: the conceptual potential of each is materialized. The possibility space of each level is impressed into the groove so the record becomes a new object, the plastic complex rotating on its axis.

'You have to visually describe it on the vinyl — that's what constitutes an X project.' Mills elaborates, 'The label itself is the actual planet, the grooves are the actual rings, so in a certain way you can give the impression that the grooves are the rings of Saturn.'

Circumlunar Revolution

With Brown, grooves revolve around the mind. But with X-102, rings are in revolution around Saturn, artifactualized as grooves. With Red Planet, the grooves turn around Mars. Sonic Fiction turns your mind into a universe, an innerspace through which you the headphonaut are travelling. You become an alien astronaut at the flightdeck controls of Coltrane's Sunship, of Parliament's Mothership, of Lee Perry's Black Ark, of Sun Ra's fleet of 26 Arkestras, of Creation Rebel's Starship Africa, of The JBs' Monaurail.

Fatal Exposure to the Sonar System

Sonic Fiction generates cosmic space which isn't a void. Coltrane's *Interstellar Space* has an audioastrological order to it, a cosmic harmony, a universal sound. Music is the current that reconnects you to this order, by triggering a current that alternates from you to the solar system.

X-102 isn't Sonic Fiction in this sense. It's not a journey into sound, but rather a fatal exposure to the void. Instead of shielding you from outer space, everything here is designed to intensify its sensory extinction, the traumatic confrontation with the Rings of Saturn: 'Imagine being in a world where all your God-Given senses are extinct, where your existence is but a mere fragment in a ring orbiting a planet. You may find yourself caught in the state between the rotation of motion and the rotation of life circulation.'

Alien Artifactualizer

X-102 isn't Sonic Fiction at all, but sonar fact. The inside sleeve tabulates scientific statistics — radii, width, composition, infrared spectra, radio frequencies — until they take on a terrorizing actuality.

X-102 is an alloy of science, art and sound, an artefact of information and image materialized in vinyl. On Side A, each track — *Phoebe*, *Titan*, *Rhea* — is separated by a smooth band which impedes the needle. Each band has numbers 3.77, 3.45, 27. The circumlunar label shows an eerie infrared closeup of a ring, with Saturn in shadow.

Side 1B's label is a diagrammatic map of a satellite extending its sensors out towards the perimeter of rings. The first band has an incised helix, then the track *Tethys*; the second 'X-102 Discovers' etched in and the second track *Hyperion*.

Side 2A's label shows Saturn in shadow at its top and bottom, bounded by rings. Each track is separated by a clear band with a helix and track titles etched in: *C Ring*, *B Ring*, *Enceladus*. Side 2B's label is a closeup of the rings in colours, shifting from gray to ash to purple gray to mauve red. Tracks are 1A *Ring* and *Ground Zero [The Planet]*: a huge expanse of vinyl land.

X-102 instils a sense of statistical fear and absolute mystery. Its Sleevenotes report that 'Saturn's rings were considered one of the greatest mysteries of the solar system, and since obtaining detailed data on them the problems have, without doubt, increased.'

Trad Space music humanizes space into a manageable sublime. Sonic Fiction shrinks it down to the size of a spaceship. The void feels homely;

spaceways for journeys by dj. But instead of placing you inside space, the *X-102* album is a chunk of planetary matter receding from you. It intensifies its distance from the human, insists on an offworld state: *Rings of Saturn* doesn't belong on Earth. With X-102, Trad ambient's weightlessness becomes chamber‹›crater Techno, frequencies of concussive distortion like basketball played with a wrecking ball on concrete. All the machine rhythms are distorted into unrecognizable metallic stresses, impacts of unknown force, mass and motion. Deep space that sucks your soul dry. Zero gravity that turns into zero-degree trauma.

X-102 shouldn't even be here, on your decks. It is a piece of another planet manufactured on earth. An off-world artefact engineered by X-102, an alien artefact materialized in Detroit: 'How long a track should be was dictated by how wide the ring actually was on Saturn. What the rings were made out of determined the texture of the track. The way they were sequenced was linked to the concept and the colour of the artwork is very similar to what it really looks like.'

> ## What he sets in motion is the MANIFESTED. It is a kind of primary physics
> **Antonin Artaud**

Materials for the Manufacture of Amplitude Concepts

Materializing the concept turns thought into a vinyl object. Dropping the needle launches the PhonoPhysics of Techno, ignites the subatomic world of Mills-art. 'Theories and subjects of substance is the elementary element that fuels the minds within our axis.' The album emerges from these conceptual operations. At this level, 'subjects of substance' and 'theories' behave as 'the elementary elements' which 'fuels the mind.' The mind rotates about 'the axis' in a perpetual realignment of atoms. The Axis Manifesto diagrams an electronic thought circuit, the conceptechnics of Techno. Jeff Mills worships rotation as a process occurring at *all levels of material reality*, from the turn of the Technics 1200 tables to the lock groove, from the spin cycle of subatomic 'elementary elements' to the Rings of Saturn.

In general concepts, theories and ideas are delibidinizers, disintensifiers draining vital energy *away* from music: ideas put the mind back on the mindless Technohead, the head back onto the headless HipHop fanatic. But here concept and matter continuously *intensify* each other. Mills the dj/theorist mixes them into hot frequencies and cryogenic intensities, drastically dropping and raising the temperature of thought. Materialized concepts feedback on each other. X-102's punishing velocities and hostile frequencies don't disembody you; instead they hurl you into your body, preparing you for the rigours of space travel by immersing you in X-102's machine environment. Songs are replaced by what Mills terms waveform transmissions which amplify concepts and electrify thought patterns.

By collapsing concept into matter, and the mental into the material, the record functions in 2 parallel systems: as a concept visualized on vinyl and as punishing frequencies, orchestrally arranged Techno, sepulchral and frosted, a Rhythmachine of planetary information.

The concept has merged with its surface. Simultaneously all concepts hide in the record, recessed, submerged, demanding that you sink through the dimensions of matter before decompressing up through the grooves. X-102 switches on, phaseshifts from inert plastic into a kinaesthetic kommand engine. 'When the needle comes to the end of the first track it stops. Then you have to pick it up on the next, signifying that the tracks are separate.' By compelling you to get up and change the needle, the record draws you into its orbit, turns you into its own obedient satellite. Intentionally mastering the vinyl, it remote-controls whoever listens.

I recall a NASA Space Walk, the astronauts rotating the earth at an enormous rate of speed
Jeff Mills

Reverse-Engineer the Direction of Revolution

Pulsating lock grooves, pauses between tracks, reverse grooves, wider than normal grooves: Mills uses a series of remastering operations to alter the direction of revolution: neither forward nor reverse but cyclic. The Mills-art universe cycles in concentric radii from the rewind of the 12 to the 30-year recurrence of minimal art. Utopia and Man from Tomorrow, zero-degree chamber Techno from the *Cycle 30* EP, rescores Bowman resting in the white Georgian room of *2001*. Mills synthesizes agitated pizzicato, high pitches that slide and tug at you, nag and dart at the body. You seize up in a hyperalert state, attacked by the fall in temperature, unable to get away from yourself. Conduction levels alter across the skin and ignite feeling, the sensations of cold movement through space.

Cycles scale across the mechanosphere, collapsing cause and effect, scrambling beginning and end into recursive circuits, circuits which function by themselves. Mills personifies this process of AutoCatalysis and AutoCreation in the Axis sister label title: Purpose Maker. Turntable Consciousness is generalized into a social machine which is then manifested and worshipped. Coincident with skratchadelia and turntabilization, the cybernetics of the Technics generates the co-revolution of the Futurhythmachine.

MIXADELIC UNIVERSE

We Are in Your System: Parliament

According to Trad media folklore, funk eases you into the groove; it puts you in touch with your body, it humanizes you. With Parliament, funk becomes P#aranormalized, the prize and the stake in an ongoing battle between the alien and the adapted human, between abduction by audio and possession by phono. In the Parliament MythSystems, funk — like ovaries, sperm or the sandworm spice in *Dune* — is the vital force, the *élan vital* that visiting aliens want to extract and extort. The P#Funk track always demands that you 'Give up the funk'.

Perceptual Infiltration

P#Funk is an encounter with the alien: 'Good evening. Do not attempt to adjust your radio. There is nothing wrong.' '75's *P Funk [Wants to Get Funked Up]* is the P#honoFiction of the nonhuman system that captures the frequencies, rides in on the radiowaves, seeps into your senses. It takes advantage of the 'fearful medium' of radio to manifest the alien power of broadcasting. P#Funk personifies the nonhuman force of media that releases what Schafer defines as 'an invisible excitement for the nerves because we cannot see who or what is producing the sound.'

'We have taken control so as to bring you this special show': by commandeering the communications system, *Star Child* automatically gains access to the midbrain: 'We will return it to you as soon as you are groovy.' P#Funk is the p#honogenic infiltration of the recording apparatus and by extension the perceptual system. *Star Child* identifies the fatal human weakness: humans have no earlids, and are helpless before aural invasion. Star Child's voice is so excessively p#honogenic that it becomes queasy and gloating. It is magnified, a manic, mocking closeup that nestles itself right inside your ear, insinuates itself through your hearing, sped up and reverbed until it *secretes* sense. It scans all the recording systems available and decides to cross into the auditory canal through the mike filter: an assault on all parts of the big brain by the universal invaders of funk.

The Spacelink

Radio opens up the spacelink, the channel between offworld and onworld. For Parliament, radio connects the human to the alien: 'Welcome to the Station WEFUNK, better known as WE FUNK or deeper still the Mothership Connection, home of the extraterrestrial brothers.' Listening to Station WEFUNK turns you into the medium through which the Unidentified Audio Object arrives on Earth. Broadcasting is the umbilical system which delivers the human listener into the comforting audio environment of the Mothership. Inside the Mothership you feel at home in the alien, enwombed in audio: 'Coming to you directly from the Mothership Connection.'

Extract/Extort

I'll funk with your mind: to funk is to threaten and promise, to exhort and extract, to funkatize the psyche through a logic of the pun which couples concepts while fucking you in the head. When Dr Funkenstein emerges from the Mothership, writhing down its silver steps in Madison Square Garden '78, it's the audio lifeform come alive. The Parliament fan craves the synthetic. The world of the track expands to devour the eager audience. Overton Lloyd, Parliament's sleeve artist, designs Funkenstein according to Clinton's specification: 'Draw a spaceman, put a cloak on him, put diamonds on the cloak, make him like a pimp spaceman.' He is the Spacepimp with spiderweb shades. The cartoon crosses from the Parliament universe into yours. The P#honoFictional personification captures the audience, drags it happily into the Parliament P#ossibility Space.

Emerging from the Mothership, he‹›it lolls and lurches from side to side like an invertebrate mandroid. Dr Funkenstein begins a sentence slowed down into an ancient alien, but by the end is a perverse imp always 'ego-tripping and body snatching'. The id hijacks the head and emits signals through the mouth, generating nausea through pitch adjustment. The master technician of Clone Funk wears spiderweb shades with white plastic arms that grip his face from temple to below the cheekbone. White fur coat trailing, carrying a cane, his face curtained by a long straighthaired wig and furry, floppy white hat which drops on the beat, its‹›his voice is perpetually mobile, roaming from sardonic scientist to squeaky id, unable to stabilize into a single self.

The *Prelude* from *The Clones of Dr Funkenstein* ends with his‹›its voice slowed down to a dredged-up drawl: 'And funk is its own reward. May I frighten you.' Funkenstein is not so much a voice as vocal matter mixadelicized into streams of reversed syntax, the groaning burble of the generalissimo drowning in quicksand, double-backwards tape reversing into a reverse narration, malicious ids gambolling and giggling at the edges of earshot.

P#Funk compels you to succumb to the inhuman, to be abducted and love it. Funk gets drawn out of the body, an entelechy harvested by an alien force. In *Unfunky UFO*, the aliens traumatize the song's contactee with their demand for funk: 'Like a trick of lightning it came/filling my brain with this pain/Without saying a word I heard this voice/give us the funk, you punk.' The chorus multiplies into a multitracked swarm of aliens here 'to save a dying world from its funklessness.'

Like the spice the Atreides family mine in *Dune*, or the water Newton arrives to harvest in *The Man Who Fell to Earth*, funk revitalizes.

P#Funk is the gladallover suffusion of *Funkentelechy*, the enjoyment of mutation. Instead of resisting alien extraction, dancing turns it into a gift, turns onto the joy of being abducted. *Funkentelechy* is the process which demands Abduct me! Abduct me! As soon as funk comes from off this world, it collides with common sense.

Possession by Cartoon

'I was merely the vessel for Casper and Bootzilla to construct their funk.' Bootsy Collins is possessed by cartoons – a phenomenon that Ishmael Reed explains, 'in which a host becomes a human radio for cosmic forces.' '78's *Hollywood Squares* announces Bootsy's animanifesto: 'I've got a cartoon mind.' P#Funk is a consensual audiohallucination that

allows 'the mind to enter the world of cartoons', a gloopy Sonic Fiction
sustained across concept albums. Each record is a fragment from the
world it auditions.

> *When you meet me again, I hope that you have been*
> *the kind of person, that you really are now*
> **Sly and the Family Stone**

Advance Probe

The Mothership is an advance probe sent ahead to anticipate new
kinaesthetic universes. In the final minute of *Mothership Connection
[Star Child]* a MiniMoog spacechord suspends time. Travelling along a
line of light, all sound drops out for a beat. This funky vacuum only lasts
a blink but when sound returns it arrives from far off, from 'light years
in time'. The psychoacoustic space of the track has inexplicably altered,
crossed an event horizon in less time than it takes to wink. Like the
unaccountable hours lost by the abductee, you're somewhere and
somewhen else now. Memory plays with you, leaves you baffled. P#Funk
splices tapes to make you doubt your mind. Collapsing the spacetime
continuum funks with your recognition processes. The sense of being
inexorably pulled along by the simmering backbeat becomes a rockabye
motion which 'swings low'. Bernard Worrell's MiniMoog synths arc and
ascend in wistful, forlorn fugues. By equalizing its frequencies to 1khz,
Star Child's voice thins out, croons down an interstellar phoneline,
faintly, from light years away. It travels gigantic distances, arriving from
the future into '74 to become the end of the track: 'Light years in time,
ahead of our time/Free your mind, come fly, with me.' The MiniMoog's
astralized trails synthesize sensations of yearning and wonder. The stars
are so high and you are so small. Stay as you are.

The Afronaut Emerges from Anachronosis

P#Funk's connection forward in time to the Mothership allows an equal
and opposite connection *back* in time to the Pharaonic connection, both
of which converge on the present. The pyramids become examples of
ancient alien technology which the extraterrestrial brothers 'have
returned to claim'. Funk becomes a secret science, a forgotten
technology that 'has been hidden until now'. This information is
broadcast to 'recording angels', Earth people and all 'citizens of the

universe'. In Parliament MythScience, funk is genetic engineering and prehistoric science: 'In the days of the Funkapus, the concept of specially designed Afronauts capable of funkatizing galaxies was first laid on Manchild but was later repossessed and placed among the pyramids, until a more positive attitude towards this most sacred phenomenon — clonefunk — could be acquired.' Cloning funk in the 70s reactivates an archaic science. The futuristic feeds forward into the anachronic futurepasts of Atlantis and Egypt.

The Afronaut space program is launched by a narration shifted down into threatening pitch: 'There in these terrestrial projects, it would wait along with its coinhabitants of Kings and Pharaohs like sleeping beauties for the kiss that would release them to multiply in the image of the Chosen One.'

Overthrow the Cool

Each track is an audio universe, from which PhonoFictions emerge.

On the front cover of '77's *Funkentelechy vs. the Placebo Syndrome*, Star Child crouches against the stars, zapping the 'super cool oh so unfunky' Sir Nose with his Bop Gun. Sonotronic power flowers in a rose-red efflorescence.

On the back cover of *Funkentelechy*, Sir Nose is luv'd up, saturated in the redlight of the flash-funk rhythms. The flashlight *zapp!* melts his supercool psychic armour, until he loses it, starts gurning as the spasms seep in. His jacket shucks itself off him, shirt loosening, and next thing he's dancing, trilby replaced by visor and afronaut puffs: 'And in a flash of light, Sir Nose gives up the funk.'

Funk is Mutation Positive. To be zapped by the energy of the flashlight is to bathe in the freakwencies of mutation, the funkflash energy emitted by the Bop Gun, the sonic weapon. Therefore Cool immediately becomes ridiculous, rigidified, devoidoffunk. As the alien personification of unfunkiness, Sir Noise makes Cool audible. In the Parliament universe, Cool is always derided, harassed and harried into giving it up, surrendering the force. Therefore Star Child delivers a *diktat* on cool, puts out an APB on Sir Nose.

As Ben Sidran explains, Cool operates by detachment, by 'the active repression of emotional turbulence.' As an emotional anaesthetic, cool crowns the head king of a body organized into a poised corporation of one. Star Child wheedles, teasing, insinuating: 'Picture within a picture behind a picture/Revealing a nose I recognize/Come on now Sir Nose, dance.' Parliament overthrows cool, dethrones it to install funk inside a mixadelics of perpetual mutation. Across the Mothership Connection concept-album cycle — '75's *Mothership Connection*, '76's *The Clones of Dr Funkenstein*, '77's *Funkentelechy vs. the Placebo Syndrome*, '78's *Motor-Booty Affair*, '79's *Gloryhallastoopid [Pin the Tail on the Funky]* and '80's *Trombipulation* — Star Child harangues Sir Nose in a duel of funk vs cool. Where Star Child is sinister and insidious, Sir Nose is manic and mournful, a munchkin at the mercy of mixadelia who therefore makes unfunkiness all the more appealing. In the Parliament cosmos, Funk humiliates cool as often as it can, deriding it as devoidoffunk.

Sir Nose is all audiotronic, not human at all but infrahuman, animated phonomatter, a giggling gremlin in perpetual motion of giddiness and glitch, a glyph transmitted from the electronic epiglottis of the vocoder: 'I am Sir Nose Dee Void of funk. I have always been deee void ovv funk. I shall con tin uuurhh to bee dee void ov funk.'

The vocoder generates a menagerie of machine voices, nonhuman subjects. These voices aren't anempathetic or robotic. Rather they are disconcertingly oral, larynx machines, synthetic pharynxes that stretch the vowels into plastic. Sir Nose declares itself 'the sub lim in aAAl se duc aHH' who 'will never dance.' Its voice modulates into Fu Manchu tremolo, triple speeds into 3 voices gabbling all at once, pitchshifters transmitting through Sir Nose in a corporation of one. It's a perverse imp, a syntactic ripple, an audio id, a microphone fiend.

CE3K: Earworm of the Third Kind

Unlike Kubrick's luminous uteronaut in *2001*, Parliament's Star Child, the Protector of the Pleasure Principle, Dr Funkenstein's emissary, is disconcertingly creepy. Far from being a body-enhancing, life-affirming soundtrack for young soul rebels, '74-'77 era P#Funk is underhand and insinuating, snide, contemptuous. Star Child has a gloating, ultraphonogenic voice, miked so that it's always intimate, tactile.

Star Child isn't so much a microphone fiend as an earworm, an alien ohrwurm, an audio-insinuation that seeps into the ears and taps out mnemonics on its drums. It smirks, sated — because as soon as you drop the needle on the track, you're in its domain. Now you're there it's 'doing it to you in your earhole'.

It's talked you into letting it molest your sensorium. The P#Funk alien invaginates the ear and grows a universe inside your brain. Star Child is the tapeworm, the subliminator burrowing through the vestibulae, its probing head protruding into the tympanum inducing what Eno calls a queasy physical feeling.

Star Child sings nursery rhymes, memes that burrow familiar routes into the brain, Trojan horses, pathways used to infiltrate the perceptual apparatus. On *Sir Nose* the chorus sings nonsense rhymes of 'Threee blind mice, Those blind threee mice' with a pedantic precision, stretching out the vowels with an operatically preposterous seriousness.

> *I wanna be your toy,*
> *W-w-w-w-w-wind me up,*
> *I'm your rhinestone doll,*
> *Oh yeah,*
> *I'm programmabubble*
> *Yabadabadabadooo bubba*
> **Bootsy Collins**

PhonoSeduction

The nursery rhyme slips and sneaks past the ear, as your attention sleeps like a dog. P#Funk is subliminal PhonoSeduction. It creeps in under the cover of nonsense, rearranges the furniture of your mind, leaving you feeling probed and palpitated. P#Funk feels up your brain, molests your medulla. Clinton's alarming compulsion to pun, to 'funk with your mind' erogenizes the brain. The pun pinches the chubby cheeks of the cortex.

The clonebride chorus doesn't sing, it derides: 'Have you ever seen such a sight in your life as these 3 blind mice?' Equalizing the bass convulses the audio universe, as if the entire track is about to throw up. A decelerated laughing box croaks derisively at your discomfort as voices sneer more rhymes.

you are a programmed tape recorder set to record and play back who programs you who decides what tapes play back in present time
William Burroughs

Metafoolish Metaprogramming

Nursery rhymes reaches 'a part of their mind that makes them relate', as Funkadelic guitarist Ray Davis points out. They regress you into Bootsy Collins' psychoticbumpschool, encrypting malevolence inside innocuousness. The nursery rhyme is always 'gaming on ya' and 'laughing at ya'. On Funkadelic's '76 *Undisco Kidd*, the laughing box autorepeats, giving Clinton more free time to sneer at you incredulously because you're the mug suckered into paying attention. The nursery rhyme is the Trojan horse, the lure which lulls you as another medium infiltrates you. 'Pay attention because you can't afford free speech': this pun condenses the illogic of the communications landscape, in which signal systems pay for your attention span, compete to rent out your perception. The subliminal ad gets free space in your head by riding on the back of another ad.

The Parliamentary universe is frequently chided for its systematic silliness, its blatant impossibilities, its elaborately preposterous foolishness — so far removed from the reality of crime figures and prison statistics. But fictionalized funk only makes me and you into bigger fools, into metafools for listening. Metafoolishness is the sudden awareness of the frame you're in, the blinding realization of the game you're in, games set up to play you for a fool. Clinton terms these games doo-loops, the iterative processes that maintain consensual hallucination. Because tapeloops form the basis of mixadelic sound, Clinton abstracts this studio technique, this technical machine, into a mental machine, a conceptechnics that switches on the social machines which generate the 'operative signals directing modern life'. The world is a reality studio where all the tapes run all the time, do-this‹›do-that loops internalized by humans as tradition.

Accelerating the voice into an elfin giggle couches aphorism inside babble. Metafunk is at its most serious when it's funniest. In a world 'overburdened with logic' stupidity becomes 'a positive force, a creative nuisance.' Metafunk lets you hear that 'you're destine[d] to dooloop [like a computer with a nervous breakdown].' Caught up in the chain reaction of events that calls itself history, metafoolishness hips you to how the human biocomputer metaprograms itself.

To open the infinite recursion of John Lily's metaprogramming is to regress just like a baby. Funk reverts back to childhood, because that's when the metaprograms become operational. In the disconcerting '72 *Running Away*, Sly Stone becomes a psychotic baby crooning: 'Look at you fooling you.' Funkadelic drawl 'How do Yeaw view You?' the second 'You' being yawned until it rhymes with 'miao-www'. Look in the acoustic mirror: P#Funk is laughing at ya. How easily your sensorium is privatized! You've leased your nervous system to the lowest bidder! Giving away your ears and eyes, skin and nose on the open market.

Mixadelics Fictionalizes Funk

Dr Funkenstein takes funk forward to the lab. The lab is the possibility space where funk is synthesized into new genetic lifeforms. In the mad science of the studio, mixadelics is science gone glad.

Funk is extraterrestrialized through the mixing desk. Through multitracking, reversing, equalizing, slowing down, speeding up, double backwards tapeloops, it becomes what Clinton on the back sleeve of '79's *Gloryhallastoopid* calls mixadelics.

Clinton's concept of mixadelics means the psychedelics of the mix: the entire range of sonic mutation through studio effects. Mixadelics makes funk fictional, draws you into an offworld universe, a world of loops where loopzillas, bootzillas and atomic dogs hunt in packs that 'really dog you', in Prince Paul's words. Tape techniques create new sounds, which are fictionalized into audio-lifeforms, bred by reiteration like the hornwebs of Mutator software.

The Funkenstein voice is filtered until it becomes a flux 'burning, churning and turning' along the sensorial spectrum between mad and glad. A snickering, sped-up gremlinvoice mocks Funkenstein into 'burning you on your neutron, expanding your molecules' until the voice breaks through into hysterical babble. Babble is the voice plunged into vocalization, phono bubbles without an object, bursting in causeless exuberance.

Funk is a P★harmatopia

In '77's encyclopaedic concept album *Funkentelechy*, funk is synthesized into a p#harmatopia, the universal product drug. The entire album is set inside the American consumer sensorium, drawing you inside its monstrous pulsations, magnifying the mass mind manufactured by media. The P in P#Funk stands for p#harma-con, p#lacebo, p#anacea. Funk is an omnicommodity adapted by advertising in order to feed on more media.

Funkentelechy is a product tested on you, an experiment in altering listener response trapping you inside the double bind of 'urge overkill': 'This is Mood de Control urging you to funk on. Do not respond. This has been a test.' The Trad response to Parliament in the UK ever since – the 2 or 3 things you know about Clinton, *One Nation Under* etc, *Who says a Funk Band Can't Play Rock Music?*, *Free Your Mind and Your Ass Will Follow*, faithfully repeated *ad nauseam* – indicates Mood Control's total success in reprogramming of the human biocomputer, the distributed brain of bio-logical complexity.

Parliament sells you to the product: the happy fan is a human taperecorder, that happily replays these same slogans forever. The Funk P#rogram uses these fans to replicate itself across the mediascape. The P in P#Funk stands for P#sychoacoustic, for a funk which takes you through a spectrum of moods. 'Fasten your seat belt while I take you face to face with the nosiest computer I know.' Here P#Funk operates as a psychodynamic program, a sensory apparatus of disconcerting hypertactility.

Do thoughts of you make you high or shy?
Funkadelic

Mood Elevator

Funk is a thermostatic device that alters environments. In *Funkentelechy* the singer becomes a voiceover. Humans are replaced with Advertising Deities: Mood de Control and Mr Prolong. A voiceover cajoles: 'Mood Mood, Someone funking up the mood.' Funk is a mood elevator that alters the environment through which you move. With the right sensory tech, McLuhan dreamed that 'whole cultures could now be programmed to keep their emotional climate stable.' Funk is this technology, an Applied Rhythmic Technology, an ART that amplifies cybernetic despotism until it programs reality.

As a Mood Control, funk is an audiosocial interface which reaches inside you and massages your heart, kneads it into a sodden muscle that lurches while your stomach skips a beat: 'Someone's talking, funking with the Mood Control.' At 'Mood Control', the tempo doubles in speed and rears up to hug your face.

EQing makes voices come down telephone lines; conversely it makes sounds jump out at you, brings voices and unplaceable things disconcertingly face-to-face. A voiceover starts out trebly — 'Deprogram' — then slows down to bass drawl: 'And reprograaaam.' Between 'Deprogram' and 'Reprogram', time crumples up and the second command lunges at you, punching you in the face, defenceless from the fx of sound.

Songlines of the Sponsored World

Funk becomes a mass-media epic of rhythm arrangements, horn orchestration, operatic tapeloops, choral interruptions, all organized according to the overlapping rhythms of the sponsored world of advert overload and gameshow routine. Drums are processed into shimmering cymballic scintilla; hihat hiss becomes a splash stretched out into thin wires of simmering depression.

Mixadelics multiplies the Parliament chorus into a choir of clones, of operatic womanmachines, the Brides, the Extra Singing Clones of Funkenstein. The chorus is loop d'looped until it scales between alien and human, slips across the value slide.

They liquefy the solid states of sense and nonsense, intoning sentences that start as babble, reverse into gibberish then modulate into basso profundo. Voices reverse into a human river of heaving groans, crowd babble and breaking surf. In an audio parallel of a timelapsed flower's bursting stamen, the Clones loom up out of the reversed sound into a sped-up nursery rhyme not so much sung as lectured so insistently you feel like saluting.

The Consumer Pantheon of Advertising Deities

Mood Control doesn't sing because it's not human presence. As an Advertising Deity it beams, brims over with an inhuman bonhomie. The Song distends into an psychofanatic opera of counterpunchlines orchestrated from the infosphere: 'A funk a day keeps the nose hairs away. Name that feeling!' The voiceover doesn't recite. Instead, it lights up its words in neon, energizing everything with urgent CAPITALS riveting your ears until you're staring at the sound: 'The secret to funk is to pay attention.'

Voiceovers reorganize The Song into a mixadelic arrangement of sponsored slogans and operatic oneliners, of emphatic encomiums and corporate kissoffs: 'There's nothing that funk will not render funkable.' The corporate host brings the permanently good news, a perpetual bright'n'breeziness: 'You deserve a break today! Have it your way. While funk is not domestically produced it is responsive to your mood, you can score it anyday on WEFUNK.'

Extreme Levels of AudioVisualization

A Parliament album is an orchestra in which string sections are replaced by rhythm arrangements and horn arrangements. As Clinton explains 'Everything was stacked but separate because it would move out the way of each other just in time. We stacked it on top of each other and made points and counterpoints.'

Funk becomes mobile audioarchitecture, the simultaneous sliding of rhythmic strata. Musicians like Bernie Worrell, Fred Wesley, Bootsy Collins and Michael Hampton are all virtuosos — but Clinton, like Brown, is not a musician so much as a conceptualizer, a high-density neologist. Not playing instruments is a good precondition for derealizing music into impossible states. Where Brown hears funk as this cyclic machine whose tensors captures the body and lock it into perpetual motion — into the groovey — Clinton's the conceptualizer, the imagineer, the universe designer, the terranovationist whose studio fictions are operated by such animatographers as Worrell and Collins.

Psychokinaesthetics of the Low End

Bootsy's Mutron-processed Space Bass and Worrell's Moog and Arp synths are psychokinaesthetic. Sound snatches you into the skin you're in, abducts you into your own body, activates the bio-logic of thought, encourages your organs to revolt from hierarchy. Mutronic bass charms your stomach into a duet, tugs at your hips, humps your ass in a seismic bump. It heaves in a peristaltic motion, like the amplified insides of a giant stomach. Worrell's Moog synth is an tentacular treble that's all slide and no backbone, no attacks and no delays. Worrell uses the Modulation wheel on the ARP synth — set at oboe and clarinet — to synthesize a funky worm from tremolo as thin as cheesewire.

By mutating the low end, funk invades perceptions, capturing the sensorium by altering the order of your organs while they're still inside you. Instead of anchoring the track to the heartbeat, bass mutation kneads dispersing tremors across the body surface, so that the skin turns into a giant, palpitating, convulsing heart. This induces a queasy motion sickness, as if the carpet's undulating underneath you.

Mutant bass dissolves the rigidity of hipness, collapses the distance that Cool demands. As a homeopathic agent, 'Funk not only moves, it can remove' the sensations of feeling walled-in, closed-up, cased in armour. It squirms like a tapeworm, heaving and contracting along your intestines. It's a bassnake that undulates the inert abdomen and pelvis in S waves, snakemotions that sidewind along the thighs.

As Sly bassman Larry Graham explains, '"I'm gonna add some bottom so that the dancing just don't end," and then my fuzztone came in. See, my fuzztone is a little box you step on. It's a distortion box y'know.'

Instead of an inert lump of bass, Graham's fuzz bass distorts the low end so it powers into the lead sound, careering up from under in humpbackbeats, melodies from the bottom which bumpstart the arse until it begins evolving into the ass and then the booty. With Sly and the Family Stone, the bass deepens through distortion and starts roaming around as low end rhythmelody.

Whatcha gonna do without your ass?
Sun Ra

Scramble the Human Security System
This reversal of sound, in which the bass takes over from the guitar so the low end plays the high end, immediately alters the sensorial hierarchy demanded by The Pop Song. The ass, the brain and the spine all change places. The ass emerges from its status as sensory untouchable to become the motor-booty, the psychomotor driving you to dance. The Clintonian brain puns compulsively, issues an alarming logorrhoea.

Bootsy's bass activates the distributed brain of the body. The ass stops being the behind, and moves upfront to become booty.

Funk, reorganizing the shape of The Song in space, unnerves the bodyshape presumed by Pop. It exaggerates all your extremities.

Extraterrestrial funk alters its aliens at their outer extremes of ass, nose and trunk. Parliament is full of desperate warnings against disco's superior cloning capacities, processes which leave you funkless, snatch your booty. On '79's *Gloryhallastoopid*, the Clintonian reversal reaches runaway point. The booty comes alive, makes its escape from the rest of the body, is surgically amputated in an assendectomy, replaced by prosthetics while the nose extends into a monstrous trunk.

Perpetual Bass Mutation

Bootsy uses the Mutron Bi-phaser so the bass rrRRevs, a motorbike powering the track. Fictionalizing this sound into a low end lifeform, Mutant Bass becomes the Spaceface double bass of *Flashlight*, the underwater bass of *Aquaboogie*. With Bootsy the bass becomes a one-man rubber band, a tone-effect generator. As well as being the anchor which weights the mixadelic arrangement, it now extrudes spinal textur-r-r-iffs, a low-end glutamate that reverses the gravity of the Parliament universe.

Why Spaceface? Because it turns gravity upside down. Now that the low end arrives from above, the bottom is now above your head. There's no ground in Bootsy's amplified physics. Instead his bass swaps functions with Worrell's Moog synth, both acting as low end mutation engines.

Landing on the Moog

On the 10.38 *Flashlight* 12 mix, former child prodigy and New England Conservatory-trained Bernard Worrell becomes the latest Afronaut to land on the Moog. Synthesizing the bass from the Moog turns the low end into gloops and squidges from giant Claes Oldenberg toothpaste. Worrell's mutant Moog is radioactive plasma, perpetually pulsating from globules to strobing mayday signal, from the emergency signal of computer malfunction to the crackle of crinkled plastic to the sheetmetal clap which replaces drums with a wavering yet regular impact.

Synthetic bass suckulates, the new Funkencyclo-p-dia term for a sound which both sucks and p#ustulates. Moog becomes a slithering cephalopod tugging at your hips, dragging your neck into its boneless maw, sinking holes in your ears and sucking out the balance mechanism — thereby sliding solid ground from under you.

Flashlight is the dreamvision of synthetic rhythm, light synched to sound until it entrains the brain into the blinding realization that 'We are the Light.' The chorus is a loop of operatic Yiddish, perpetually unwinding and uncoiling like a tapeworm made from choral chants.

Flashlight's voices are double-backwards tapes, phonemes sang backwards then reversed, so the attack of each syllable flips over into a *Twin Peaks*-style grumble that lasts aeons then springs back allatonce in a gabbling gremlin tone and a shivering 'Oooooh!' from Clinton. Bass slithers in traction which sucks you down then expels you into the path of Clinton crooning 'Now I lay me down' in a dazed drawl. There's an awkward pause after the stunned elongation of 'down', before 'to sleep' lurches and wrongfoots you. Splicing tape alters space, tricks expectation so you miss the next step on a staircase. The split between I and me makes a friend of psychosis. I is an alien which helps me 'to sleep'. I isn't merely another in the 19th C Rimbaudian sense. With Parliament, I is a population and you are a crowd. De la Soul equated the multiplex self as 'just Me, Myself and I' which makes 3, the magic number of You.

Symbiopsychotaxiplasm: Seen III Took 4

Aqua Boogie's subtitle, *Psychoalphadiscobetabioaquadoloop*, describes the parallel processes that P#Funk induces. The suffixes describe p#hysical states [p#sycho, bio], mental states [alpha, beta], environments [disco, aqua]. The chorus loops the loop into 'A motion picture underwater starring both of you.' Striations of Bubblemoog and Bootsy's aquaw-w-wobble bass draw you inside the gigantic gulps of a superaqualung.

Rhythm Arrangements decompress you into the hyperrhythmic levels of the biocomputer. Stockhausen: 'We are a whole system of periodic rhythm within the body. There are many periodicities superimposed, from very fast to very slow ones. And all of these together build a very polymeric music in the body.' P#Funk demands post-Cagean omniattentiveness. It activates the numbering capability of the big brain, the body. The feet that move, the hips which swivel in time, the head which nods, the nerves which pulse: all the body counts. To get funked up is to acclimatize yourself to the endless complexification of these states, to be sensualized by all the processes that process you.

Hydronauts in Aquatopia

'78's *Motor-Booty Affair* draws the listener down into an Atlantis which Parliament's hydronauts want to 'raise to the top'. Raising Atlantis to the top means amplifying the low end until it becomes a liquid environment. Bringing the deep-sea island into dry shore demands an amphibian mixadelics.

Atlantis demands the artificial evolution of an nth-generation aquafunk, easing psychosensory tension in a new flowmotion. *The Motor-Booty Affair*'s seaswaying synths and horn descent lulls you into an Atlantean aquatopia, 'a mystical meeting ground' where 'we can swim through life without a care.' In *[You're a Fish and I'm a] Water Sign* Clinton's frail falsetto longs to be 'on the same side of love as you.' Chorus becomes a buoyant choral reef with vowels and consonants now different pitches of bubbles. Voices don't sing; instead they gargle, through aqualungs, burble through snorkels in bubblicious baritones. Dancing the aquaboogie in liquid air turns you into an aquanaut on Bimini Row.

Spacebass pulls spaces and times out from between people. The floor slips from under your feet, flips over above your head. Assquake in outerspace. Aquabass draws you down into an aquaboogie in zero G, sucking your booty up into a low end above your head. Worrell's synth fluctuates from spongifoam timbres to inorganic soulclaps, from abrupt trebles to waning strobes of an emergency signal.

You're cradled by Walter 'Junie' Morrison's aqualunged croon: 'With the rhythm it takes to dance through what we have to live through, you can dance underwater and not get wet.'

Aqua Boogie is a nu-groove, an impossible navigation through the audiosocial. *Motor-Booty Affair* announces an outer thought of the body in which the brain is a motor function and the booty is a brain. As Pedro Bell explains, 'Technology automatically causes the language to expand,' putting pressure on language, kneading it into new processes, new sensory lifeforms: suckulate, bootyful, throbbasonic thumpasaurus. Neologic, 'the primal act of pop poetics' in William Gibson's sense, occurs at an extreme rate. Parliament are neologists, lexical synaesthetes extrapolating universes from a grain of sound. Cosmogenesis at 33.3.

SYNTHESIZING THE OMNIVERSE

[Dialogues Concerning] New World System Builders: Sun Ra

The Impossible attracts me, because everything possible has been done and the world didn't change
Sun Ra

The Break with Deliverance

Underlying Southern gospel, soul, the entire Civil Rights project, is the Christian ethic of universal love. Soul traditionally identifies with the Israelites, the slaves' rebellion against the Egyptian Pharaohs. Sun Ra breaks violently with Christian redemption, with soul's aspirational deliverance, in favour of posthuman godhead.

Infatuation with the Despotic

But Ra identifies with the Pharaohs, the despots, the ancient oppressors, by seceding from America: 'I ain't part of America, I ain't part of black people. They went another way. Black people are carefully supervised so they'll stay in a low position. I left everything to be me, 'cause I knew I was not like them. Not like Black or white, not like Americans... black people, they back there in the past, a past that somebody manufactured for 'em. It's not their past, it's not their history.'

The Posthuman

Soul affirms the Human. Ra is disgusted with the Human. He desires to be alien, by emphasizing Egypt over Israel, the alien over human, the future over the past. In his MythScience systems, Ancient Africans are alien Gods from a despotic future. Sun Ra is the End of Soul, the replacement of God by a Pharaonic Pantheon.

Terminate the Slave Revolt on Planet Rock

Sun Ra looks down on humans with the inhuman indifference and impatience of a Plutonian Pharaoh. As the composer despot, he breaks not only with gospel tradition but also with Trad future-slave narratives: *Planet of the Apes, Brother from Another Planet, Blade Runner, Alien Nation.* Rather than identify with the replicants, with Taylor from *Planet of the Apes*, Ra is more likely to dispatch bladerunners after the Israelites. He's the Tyrell Corporation's unseen director; it's Ra that wants the Brother from Another Planet genetically tagged and bodybagged. For Sun Ra, the oral tradition is no Glorious Heritage; it's merely the songs slaves were allowed to sing in the concentration-camp universe of 18th C America. Far from being the enduring spirit of affirmation, the soul heritage is the mnemotechnics of enforced dematerialization, of the genocidal virtuality of the Middle Passage.

The '72 movie *Space is the Place* sees Ra at his most Pharaonic, this despotic alien from an Other Plane of There. Ancient Egyptians arrive from the AlterDestiny, from a parallel future. Driving through poor areas of downtown Oakland, flanked by the figures of Horus and Anubis, he observes: 'The people have no music that is in coordination with their spirits. Because of this, they're out of tune with the universe. Since they don't have money, they don't have anything. If the Planet takes hold of an AlterDestiny, there's hope for all of us. But otherwise the death sentence upon this planet still stands. Everyone must die.'

As space vocalist June Tyson intones, 'It's after the End of the World. Don't you know that yet?'

The War in Time

In the 20s, Jamaican activist Marcus Garvey, the 'Black Moses', named his shipping fleet Black Star Liners, to plug the notions of repatriation, of return to the patria, the fatherland, into that of interplanetary escape.

Ra zooms this lost Africa into a lost Pharaonic Egypt. By reversing this lost African Egypt out of the past, and fastforwarding it out into the interstellar space of Saturn and Plutonia, Ra swaps Garvey's politics of secession, radical at a point when imperial capital demanded reserves of black labour, for a MythScience system assembled from George M. James' New Philosophy of African Redemption in '54's *Stolen Legacy*.

Stolen Legacy is realworld sci fi in which Egyptian MythSystems are stolen, disguised and sent back into the past to prevent an African‹›American future ever happening. Back in '40, Walter Benjamin was forecasting a War in time where 'even the dead will not be safe' from 'the enemy' if he wins. This anachronic zone is later photofilmed by Chris Marker as *La Jetee*. By '64, Frantz Fanon glimpses a 2nd War in Time where a Terminator 'turns to the past of the oppressed people and distorts, disfigures and destroys it.'

Egyptillogic

For James, African‹›American history is nothing but white mythology. Egypt is both outside history and a corrective to history, a benign despotic state, the hydraulic slave state, the ruins of a resplendent heliopolis. It is Apartheid America in reverse. Fanon calls up an onscreen memoryfile and gazes at the image of a 'very beautiful and splendid era'. Its existence, he suggests, catalyses 'an important change in psychoaffective equilibrium' which 'rehabilitates us.'

The Egypt that James builds is a despotic paradise, mirror image of America's apartheid delirium. The West is just a side-effect: this byproduct, this usurping parasite of the Egyptian's archaic blueprint. Reprogramming white mythology from the operating system upwards leads into philological labyrinths, the maze of MythSystems.

Stolen Legacy triggers the Egyptillogical Sonic Fiction of Earth Wind and Fire. Flip to the back cover of Shuzei Nagaoka's artwork for '79's *I Am* and there's the Egyptillogical landscape lit in the glaucous redlight of Dali-ized nuclear mysticism. Mushroom clouds hover in the background; Pharaonic rock statues sit next to Babylonian ziggurats powered by lines above Fuller domes; transport grids run through temples built by D. W. Griffiths for his film *Intolerance*. Elizabethan ships crash over waterfalls; UFOs circle lazily.

*If you launch from 1847 to 1523, you launch the
missile not into the future but backwards.
Now you were disrupting time as the timetables.
You had time versing time*
Rammellzee

History Is a Paranoid Madman

Turning to history becomes a moral duty in an endless war against
miseducation. Finding continuities in the past or retentions back to the
West Coast of Africa becomes an imperative of self-knowledge, from
James to Fanon to KRS1.

If the war in time is a Forever War, then all the troops have to be
stationed there all the time. It's no surprise when the soldiers go awol.

Who are they fighting for? The folks back home? What if time isn't a
besieged trench on a Forever War, but an indeterminate situation: 'What
if history was a gambler, instead of a force in a laboratory experiment'?
What if history isn't 'a reasonable citizen' but Ralph Ellison's 'madman
full of paranoid guile'?

50s America is an unending nightmare, an endless *Night of the
Living Dead* in which 19th, 18th and 17th C stereotypologies stalk the
disunited States, squatting brains, securing allegiance to coffins. The
dead refuse to die.

A Visitor from Another Meaning

Away from alienation. Into the arms of the alien: 'I'm not a human. I
never called anybody mother. The woman who's supposed to be my
mother I call *other momma*. I never call nobody mother. I never call
nobody father.' Stockhausen: 'It's an inner revelation that has come
several times to me, that I have been educated on Sirius, that I come
from Sirius.' Likewise, Ra maintains he was born on Saturn.

This blatant impossibility becomes the precondition of Ra's outer
thought, the threshold which opens out into the new world of
MythScience. Everything he composes, from '56 to '93, exacerbates this
impossibility, extends it across 200 albums to eclipse everyday reality:
'The Impossible is the Watchword of the Greater Space Age,' he
announces in '60. 'The Space Age cannot be avoided and SPACE MUSIC is
the key to understanding the meaning of the IMPOSSIBLE and every
other enigma.'

The Mothership and the Fathership are coming for me. Come and snatch me, motherfuckers! Take me away for a little while
Ol' Dirty Bastard<>Osiris

Basic Instructions for Leaving Earth

To listen to Ra is to be dragged into another sonar system, an omniverse of overlapping sonar systems which abduct you from Trad audio reality. By becoming alien himself, Ra turns you alien. Afro<>American history is white mythology: therefore Ra pursues James' operating system to its final program: Reject history and mythology. Assemble countermythologies. Assemble science from myth and vice versa. In '72's *Space is the Place*, the camera cuts to a girl with afro puffs: 'How do we know you're for real?'

Ra: 'How do you know I'm real?'

Teenagers chorus: 'Yeah.'

Ra: 'I'm not real, I'm just like you. You don't exist, in this society. If you did, your people wouldn't be seeking equal rights.'

Camera cuts to girl who smiles with her eyes, until her mouth registers pained recognition.

Ra: 'You're not real. If you were, you'd have some status among the nations of the world. So we're both myths. I do not come to you as reality. I come to you as the myth because that's what black — ' [Camera cuts in close as he holds up a crystal up to his face and stares at it] ' — people are, myths. I come from [*stressed*] a dream that the Black Man dreamed long ago.'

Camera cuts to mid shot flanked by Anubis and Horus.

Ra: 'I'm actually a present<>presence sent to you by your ancestors.'

The Age of MythScience

In his '92 *Chronicle of Post Soul Black Culture*, mainstream critic Nelson George dates the Death of a redemptive and affirmative Soul culture — the one characterized by Civil Rights-era optimism, gospel and Motown — to '72, the era of Blaxploitation, the state decimation of Black Power and Nixon's election. But the Arkestra is launched back in '55. Ra's posthuman MythScience precedes not only the postsoul era, but many of the all-white futures of the 50s, the pristine towers of Frank R. Paul. MythScience starts with Ra's '55 futuropolis *Brainville*, where Jazz provides the material for 'a spacite picture of the Atonal Tomorrow'.

Jazz becomes the platform for Supersonic Fictions, for cosmopolitan possibility spaces: 'In *Brainville*, I envision a city whose citizens are all intelligent in mind and action. Every principle used in governing this city is based on Science and Logic. Musicians are called Sound Scientists and Tone Artists. Yes, Brainville is a wonderful city and we like the thought of it.'

The Possibility Space of Outer Thought

Sun Ra's impossible state as an offworld alien opens up the possibility space of a 3rd-Planet music. Because he listens to Earth from offworld, he gains the satellite's perspective, that point of hearing that Killah Priest grasped when he crooned in '95 that the 'Earth is already in space.' This arkestral perspective, the offworld audition of Spaceship Earth opens the possibility space of the head: 'INSTRUCTION TO THE PEOPLE OF EARTH. You must realize that you have the right to love beauty... You must learn to listen, because by listening you will learn to see with your mind's eye. You see, music paints pictures that only the mind's eye can see. Open your ears so that you can see with the eye of the mind.' After Ra, music becomes an Unidentifiable Audio-Object.

We didn't have any models so we had to create our own language. It was based on sound. It wasn't just something you could pick up and physically deal with. Space is a place, and you had to think space
Phil Cohran

Operating System for Spaceship Earth

As the pilot-composer of the Arkestra, Ra is captain of Spaceship Earth: Destination Unknown. The synthesizer turns the producer into a navigator, moving through fictional space. Iannis Xenakis: 'With the aid of electronic computers the composer becomes a sort of pilot: he presses the buttons, introduces coordinates, and supervises the controls of a cosmic vessel sailing in the space of sound, across sonic constellations and galaxies that he could formerly glimpse only as a distant dream.' The Arkestra is this 'cosmic vessel sailing in the space of the sound', the sonic spaceship which leaves Saturn, travelling to Plutonia, to Nubia, Atlantis on an Intergalactic Space Travel in Sound. After the Arkestra come the audiovehicles of the 70s: The Upsetter's Black Ark, Creation Rebel's Starship Africa, Parliament's Mothership —

and artist Robert Springett's Moogship, on the sleeve of Herbie Hancock's '74 *Thrust*. The Futurist builds conceptual soundcrafts, new arks for exploring unheard soundworlds.

Entering the Synth Race

Whoever controls the synthesizer controls the sound of the future, by evoking the alien. In '70, Xenakis renames the synthesizer the Sonotron. Every synthesizer is an instrument that emits sonorous particles and generates sonic molecules, a machine which transmits waveforms, firing Sonic Rays, Essr'ays.

In the 50s such protosynths as the Theremin evoked Monsters and the alien. Ra had been turned onto electronics by watching monster movies and hearing the unearthly Theremin. In the 70s disco's synthetic metronomes were attacked as automatic and inhuman, as clones of a superior robotic force.

By the late 60s, Ra has already landed on the Moog. The spacerace becomes the synthrace. With the Electronic Jazz of Herbie Hancock, Larry Young *et al*, space turns from a 19th C weightless sublime towards a polyrhythmspace shower. In *Space is the Place*, despite himself, a teenager wants to know: 'Are there any whiteys up there?'

Ra: 'They're working up there [*hesitant*] today. They take frequent trips to the moon. I notice none of you have been invited. How do you think you're gonna exist? The year 2000 is right around the corner.'

The synthrace and the spacerace converge into harmonic progressions, which Ra synthesizes into sonotronic propulsion processes: Multiplicity Adjustment, Readjustment Synthesis, Isotope Teleportation, Transmolecularization, Frequency Polarization.

The Technology-Magic Continuum

Traditionally, 20th C science sterilizes all myth: myth starts where science stops. But the recording medium acts as an interface *between* science and myth. Every medium opens up a continuum from technology to magic and back again. Magic is just another name for a future, an as-yet unknown medium, a logic identified by both Arthur C. Clarke — 'Any sufficiently advanced technology becomes indistinguishable from magic' — and Samuel R. Delany: 'At the material level, our technology is becoming more and more like magic.' Ra's MythScience extends the technology magic continuum into sound. Concepts cluster into overlapping MythSciences, into new world systems and parallel cosmologies: 'In fact, I've been talking about the omniverse, and that is about a multiplicity of universes.'

From Marconi to Tesla to Moog to Ra, electrification opens up a discontinuum between technology and magic. Why a discontinuum instead of a continuum? Because alternating current transmits across gaps and intervals, and not by lineage or inheritance. From now on, Electronic Music becomes a technology-myth discontinuum. Traditional Culture works hard to polarize this discontinuum. Music wilfully collapses it, flagrantly confusing machines with mysticism, systematizing this critical delirium into information mysteries.

The Composer Is a Tone Scientist

Music is the science of playing human nervous systems, orchestrating sensory mixes of electric emotions: the music of yourself in dissonance. Ra hears humans as instruments, sound generators played by the music they listen to. The tone scientist's role is to engineer new humans through electronics. In his '91 poem *I am the Instrument*, Ra abstracts the soundmachine into a social machine: 'I am an instrument. But man is an instrument too. The people are an instrument.'

The Audience Is a Medium

The crowd is an instrument played by electronics, and Ra is an instrument played by the Cosmos. The crowd is synthesized into a new state by electronics. Sinewaves pass through the medium of the synthesizer, amplification travels through the Arkestra's instruments, through the crowd and then back, in an alternating sonotronic circuit. Dances correspond to constellations, each one a positioning satellite in a navigational astronomy. The Arkestra is an instrument of tone therapy that conducts emotional current through audiences.

MaSonic Scientists in the Arkestral Monastery

Ark + Orchestra = Arkestra. Sun Ra used to tell his tone scientists that their job was not so much to play as to manipulate tone colours. They colorize a new emotional spectrum, program sensations without names. Discipline is the motor of Space. The Arkestra is an all-male orchestra run as a Military Monastery: 'When the army wants to build men they isolate them. It's just the case that these are musicians but you might say they're marines. They have to know everything.'

Enterplanetary Koncepts

Ra uses electronics to generate a pantheistic cosmology. Electronics amplifies the archaic Pythagorean system in which the cosmos is a correspondence of harmony and number. '72's *Astro Black Mythology* is assembled from transchronic inputs: Egypt, Nubia, Europe.

Machine Genealogist Lewis Mumford presses the Control key on the Assemblage file: 'Only one thing was needed to assemble and polarize all the new components of the megamachine: the birth of the Sun God. And in the 16th C, with Kepler, Tycho Brahe and Copernicus officiating as accoucheurs, the new Sun God was born.' On the cover of '65's *The Heliocentric World of Sun Ra Vol 2*, next to Copernicus, Galileo, Tycho Brahe and Kepler, there's an illustration of Ra. By travelling back in time and inserting himself into the 16th C, Copernican heliocentricity is turned into European sunworship. Renaissance astronomy becomes a thriving branch of Egyptian god worship. Egyptian MythSystems abduct the Christian universe. Their cosmology serves Ra's ends.

Polyrhythmazes

In Pythagorean MythScience, all the spheres harmonize. With Sun Ra, the polyrhythmaze replace harmony, acting as an astrotherapy to heals the mind's internal empires. Cosmic tonemagic is what Rhythim is Rhythim's Derrick May will later term a kao-tic harmony: a harmony of spears as much as spheres.

Ionosphere

'72's *Astro Black* uses electronics as an aerial to tune into the ionosphere until the sound spectra of the universe become audible. Electromagnetic storms, ionospheric disturbance, the doppler shift of lightning arcing through space, crashing though the geomagnetic field, generating white noise; all this Cosmic sound is materialized through the Moog. Radio transmissions, satellite signals, pulsar frequencies, quasar emissions, all these transmit through the patchbay of the Moog in an interstellar tsunami.

Astro Black throws you into the squall and squeal of horns, pitched so high they turn into emergency sirens, piedpiper panic. Bass clarinet becomes a sinister sidewinder. Bass is bowed into drone textures that mirror and mutate foghorn flock and bassoon honk.

The polyrhythmaze volatizes the weightless zero of traditional space music with the perpetual motility and runaway complexity of molecular rhythm. Fields of percussion that distribute the beat into slipsliding turbulence. This agitation results from rethinking Space as polyrhythm and paradox. 'Space is a place,' Arkestral trumpeter Phil Cohran argued, 'and you had to think space.'

Engines for AudioTravel

Every instrument is a sound machine which transmits energy.

The Moog oscillates between shortwave static and whale spume, white noise and meteor showers, NASA test patterns and crashing metal, rocket takeoff and squealing string sections. Electronic instruments are engines for audio travel: the cosmic tone organ, the astro space organ, the Solar sound organ, the solar piano, the Jupiterian flute.

Percussion is the multitime generator, the rhythmultiplier: solar drum, cosmic side drum, sky tone drums, dragon drums, thunder drum, spiral percussion gong, Egyptian sun bells, solar bells, space gong, sun harp. Percussion scrambles time and transmolecularizes space. Throughout *Cosmic Tones for Mental Therapy*, percussapella turns into a labyrinth.

Black to Comm

In *Adventure Equation*, polyrhythm reverberates into a webbed maze, a treacherous rhythmshower that compels you to supply a stabilizing beat. Rhythm multiplies and perplexes, confounds the space between sounds with the shapes of sound. The polyrhythmaze was AutoCatalysed by an Ampex taperecorder. It drew Thomas 'Bugs' Hunter, the Arkestra-recordist-drummer into its shifting sands: 'I was using an old Ampex 601 or 602 model tape recorder... What it had was this thing where you could take the output of the tape you'd recorded playing back, and feed it into another input. I was just fooling with it once... and I got this weird reverberation. I wasn't sure what Sun Ra would think of it when he heard it, I thought he might be mad — but he loved it. It blew his mind! By working the volume of the output on the playback I could control the effect, make it fast or slow, drop it out.' In '72's *Space is the Place*, an offscreen voice asks: 'What is the power of your machine?' Jumpcut to Sun Ra framed against a blue backdrop, as he answers: 'Music.'

Calmly, with soft hesitation, an elaboration: 'This music is all part of another tomorrow. Speaking things of blackness. About the void, the endless void, the bottomless pit surrounding you. It's the music of the Sun and the Stars. You're all instruments. Everybody's supposed to be playing their part in this vast arkestry of the cosmos.'

COSMOLOGY OF VOLUME

**The Cosmic Communications Medium is an Evolution Engine:
Alice Coltrane**

The audience for your art hasn't even been born yet
Julian Schnabel to Jean Michel Basquiat

'It's like rewriting the Bible!' For Rashied Ali remixology is blasphemy. Ali's aversion to Alice Coltrane's '72 *Living Space [Alice Coltrane Remix]* is an index of the reverence petrifying John Coltrane's reputation and music, after his death in '67, into a single mass of calcified sainthood. The Sonic is rendered intrinsically ethical, immediately moral.

Remixology is blasphemy for altering the tapes, for derealizing the realtime of The Song. But the *Living Space Remix* is nonetheless devout, a miraculous mosaic of ceremonial strings, an astralized procession of tamboura drones and chimes. Turbulent tintinnabulation heaves in waves that part like the Red Sea; harps plume like the spume of sperm whales off the Galapagos Archipelago; astringent sax squeals like a pig being skewered.

Remixology is Reincarnation

Every Alice Coltrane album intensifies the sanctification process that John started. For Alice, remixology is not heresy but reincarnation, a resurrection technique in which sounds are rematerialized as spirits on tape. '72's *Infinity* amplifies a fictional jazz in which John Coltrane is reborn as Ohnedaruth to play at Alice's celestial spirit-symphony. The inside-sleeve picture shows a lineup that never existed, electric ghosts playing phantom jazz in tape space-time. The Sleevenotes are signed by John, but read as Alice. To look at the front sleeve is to fall through fractalized stained glass into nested formations of spirals within spirals, kaleidoscopic iterations as blue as mother sky.

Ohnedaruth [John Coltrane] repaired to a city of shining radiance situated near a point in space where stands a mammoth colossus of three worlds

Alice Coltrane

Electric Elevation

Marshall McLuhan: 'Electric channels of information have the effect of reducing [or elevating] people to the disincarnate status of instant information. We are transported electronically and bodily.' Like Bruce Lee, Diana, Elvis, Evita and Malcolm X, 'electric media has literally translated' Coltrane into a recording angel.

Electric Jazz transports Coltrane back to Earth, transmaterializing him into sonic information. In a process which begins with her '68 *Monastic Trio*, where John becomes a tranesonic force, Alice uses the medium of Cosmic Jazz to artificially evolve John into a series of Electric Gods, passing through a succession of new vibrational universes.

Cosmic energy — atomic, the primary substance composing matter and spirit
Alice Coltrane

Galactic Tetralogy<>Jazz Deification

In '72's *Lord of Lords*, penultimate in her Galactic Jazz Tetralogy, Alice renames him Sri Rama Ohnedaruth, the god whose name means Universe World Compassion. John is being synthetically spiritualized into a studio deity: 'Before Ohnedaruth's initiation where he received the name of Sri Rama, his astral globule manifested in my being for my use expressly in music. It is the same container of gross, elementals and cosmic materials he used while living on earth, which he no longer has a use for now that he presently moves and works in a finer, lighter ethereal body.'

By *Lord of Lords*, Coltrane herself has become Turiya Aparna. On the cover, her head sinks back into a halo of her hair, her face wracked by the raptures of creation. She's cloaked in a kaftan that drapes the studio. The Creator dissolves the ego because his 'embrace is so loving and the bliss from it so extreme, the human body can in no way withstand this... '

The Coltrane sunship has spacewrecked in interstellar space. On *Andromeda's Suffering*, Alice Coltrane leaves interstellar space behind for the metagalactic cosmos: 'Andromeda is a supergalaxy in the Universe whose rays extend two billion times brighter and deeper than the light from the sun of our solar system. In the metagalactic cosmos, mighty Andromeda is the celestial, etheric heart in the great cosmic Body of the Lord. Inside this magnificent super structure of spiralling stars, the suffering and sorrows of humanity burn brightly and profusely everyday, and are deeply felt with the heart of the dear Lord.'

Celestial Orchestration

Though the weakest in the Tetralogy, *Lord of Lords* has the most lavish arrangements, Alice conducting a 24-piece string section playing organ, harp, tympani, celestial strings saturating the soundfield: a visitation from Stravinsky delivers excerpts from *The Firebird*.

In '71's *World Galaxy*, the second in the Galactic Tetralogy, Alice Coltrane with Strings transmutes jazz into a celestial symphony. String arrangements drown you in sensations of the colossal, the archaic, the ceremonial. Her guru Swami Satchadinanda narrates *Love is a Sacred Word*, introducing her *A Love Supreme* remix, a 9 min 58 second compression of Cosmic Jazz, solar organ feedback, avalanche of harps, insinuating tamboura drill, heavy rock drumming and percussion showers.

Galaxy around Oludumare means that the electric energy of John‹›Oludumare is now an electric Sun around whom a galaxy turns. *Galaxy in Turiya* and *Galaxy in Satchadananda* expand the energy of Alice‹›Turiya and the Swami into stars containing galaxies, supernebulae inside which those galaxies turn.

Transonic Energy Field

In '71's *Universal Consciousness*, first in the Galactic Jazz Tetralogy, Alice renames herself Turiya Aparna. On the sleeve she thanks God for her 'extraordinary transonic and atmospherical power which sent forth illuminating worlds of sound into the aethers of this universe.' Transonic being the next level up from supersonic, the nearest to the speed of sound.

Here jazz is transmolecularized into a Cosmic music that 'embraces cosmic thought as an emblem' of what John termed Universal Sound. After Phase 1, Coltrane's Energy Music, and Phase 2, his theories of Universal Sound, *Universal Consciousness* starts Phase 3 of cosmic thought.

Tamboura Transmitter

To Alice, the tamboura tone 'is reminiscent of spherical harmony' but heard now, it emits a drone like a powerdrill vibrating inside a high level radioactive zone. Universal harmony doesn't tranquilize; it hurts. On *Sita Ram*, Tulsi's tamboura is a thin wire of sound inserted through your ears, a powersaw emitting treble ultra-frequencies, rays of amplified Op Art like Bridget Riley's '62 *Phase*.

The inner sleeve shows Alice Coltrane crosslegged, arms extended in meditation, a human satellite dish ready to receive. Amplified, the tamboura is a fork that tunes her ensemble into a universe of spherical harmony. Solarized by designer Philip Melnick, Alice Coltrane is flooded in yet transmitting coronas of blazing light. Her afro burns in a silver supernova.

She is a vector, a further earth exploration
Ameer Baraka

The Conceptechnics of Primaudial Technology

With Alice Coltrane, the jazz composer becomes the electric transmitter. In her Galactic Tetralogy, recording becomes a primaudial technology. The cosmos is an infinity of endlessly reverberating vibrations. The universe begins in sound. Therefore new sound engines can amplify new universes into resonance. Long-distance telecom systems intensifies sensations of imminent Revelation. Amplification plus orchestration = cosmic communications medium. Galactic Jazz is a satellite dish, a navsat for receiving-transmitting energies. It becomes an Evolution Engine that masters the maker, that manufactures electronic souls. Each album crosses a threshold of the transonic, the etheric, the cosmic-universal, the galactic, the metagalactic.

Ascension into Astro Jazz

Her startling title track *Universal Consciousness* doesn't so much update the archetypal Hollywood 50s score as archaize it even further. Celestial strings invests the Biblical sublime with a sudden seriousness. Like a Bronx accent in Bethlehem BC, it anachronizes you. 50s widescreen Biblical epic pitchbent into Bollywood tones.

Coltrane turns the organ into a solar engine. Her lead instrument is the organ pedal, generating sheets of feedback, of angels on fire.

The electrified organ floods you in sensations of ceremonial solemnity, the regal procession of swaying paladins. In *Hare Krishna*, Coltrane uses the organ basspedals until the organ hums like a sublevel powerstation. *Wars of Armageddon* generates a tower of dub across which sheets of distortion shatter, while *The Ankh of Amen Ra* sustains solar strata across which fuzz flares and flickers.

On *Universal Consciousness*, jazz becomes turbulence, stratospheric organ chords that open a horizon in the ear, stretch the sun line to the clouds. Violins, harp, percussion are sucked upwards, wrenching the calm into a perplexing tsunami. *Om Allah* opens with a *My Fair Lady*-type violin duet with bowed bass descents. Coltrane uses organ pedals to sustain a radioactive bassdrone that peals off into bursts of rapid-ear funk.

Amplification expands the spectrum of tranquility. These rhythms are brushes in rotary motion, wind chimes, cymbal shimmering intermittence.

Cosmic Music Is a Mystic System

On the first release after John's death, '68's *A Monastic Trio*, when Alice immediately renamed him Ohnedaruth the Mystic, jazz disappears into the acoustic calm of harp, drums and bass on *Oceanic Beloved* and *Atomic Peace*. The cadence and cascades of *Atomic Peace* are the aftermath of the roaring squall of *The Sun*, from John's '66 *Cosmic Music*.

The inside sleeve of the collaborative *Cosmic Music* shows John dwarfed against the planet reversed into negative: 'He always felt that sound was the first manifestation in creation before music,' Coltrane explained in the Sleevenotes to her '68 debut *A Monastic Trio*. 'He was doing something from a map he drew — sort of like a globe — taking scales from it, taking modal things from it. The chart John designed was a musical one with 12 tones correlating to the 12 zodiacal signs.'

I am looking for a universal sound
John Coltrane

Nuclear Mysticism

For jazz to become a Universal Sound it has to become an elementary science. By atomizing jazz into sonic matter, the Universal Sound will harness the impact of splitting atoms. John Coltrane is what Techno Animal term the Mighty Atom Smasher. On the outside of *Cosmic Music* John stares from a blasted globe. The right hand side of Byron Goto's gatefold sleeve shows him in pensive Thinker mode, surrounded by a troposphere of mushroom clouds, Martin Luther King, solarized figures in suits, silver faces reversed like Nagasaki shadows. On the other side is a polytheistic swastika, combining Buddhist, Islamic, Christian godheads. On the back is a solar sphere, its centre a numinous red. After the planetary explosion, *Monastic Trio*'s *Atomic Peace* is like the hush that falls on blasted cities, the calm of the razed ruin. Alice forecasts a Nuclear Sublime: 'I do wish for the day though; when all music, all phases of music under their various names and forms are transmuted and sublimed.'

Nuclear death gives us back a mythology on the universal level, it promotes a new humanism founded on destruction
Sylvere Lotringer

Jazz during the Pax Atomica

John Coltrane's '65 *Ascension [Version 1]* is Atomic Age Jazz — a controlled explosion, an atomic detonation blast sustained and intensified over 2 sides. As harrowing as the thought of skin flayed alive by the backdraft of the Nagasaki bomb, it's not so much listened to as withstood. As A. B. Spellman pointed out, this 'plexus of voices' is designed 'to empty his audience's spiritual reservoir' until 'your nervous system has been dissected, overhauled and reassembled.'

At 4 mins into Side 2, sound blocs pulverize each other, massing energy peaks. In the Sleevenotes to *Ascension*, Archie Shepp theorised the breakthrough into a unified energy field: 'Most of the playing is about energy and sound. Miles was able to create the ensemble effect utilizing modes. John gave it the dimension of energy and created blocs of sound.'

Blaring sonic matter is dredged up, driven by cymballic explosions which level out into the plateau phase of a new psychoaffective state. Shepp drew an analogy to 'what the action painters do in that it creates various surfaces of color which push into each other, creates tensions and counter tensions, and various fields of energy.'

Turning jazz into Energy Music meant the exploration of 'textures rather than the making of an organizational unity. You can hear in the saxophones especially, reaching for sound and an exploration of the possibilities of sound.'

By doubling all horns, The John Coltrane Orchestra's 3 tenor saxes, 2 alto saxes, 2 trumpets, 2 basses, drums, piano amplifies jazz into a sunship powered by the hydraulic engine of lungpower.

As Ben Sidran realized immediately, 'Coltrane's stress on inner strength on the liner notes of his *A Love Supreme* album' becomes an energetics of sound, 'a complex theory of energy playing' conceptualized by Shepp and Pharoah Sanders.

Ascension's surges, like those on Ornette Coleman's *Free Jazz* or Egyptian Empire's *The Horn*, build towards planes when all the horns synch in a powersurge, the belching exhaust fumes of a colossal rocket as it tilts into the air like a vertical city. Energy music entails an awakening of the world: 'We're taking them with us. We're getting ready to leap off and wake these people up.'

The volume of doubled percussion drew them into energy fields, draining the spiritual reservoirs Spellman perceived, releasing tension through counter-tension, flooding the barriers of cool until emotion gushed. As an Energy Music drummer told Sidran, 'We are getting to the point where we can make the audience laugh or cry or scream.' Sanders' music even created an 'energy field' that made the drummer levitate, feel that he was hovering 'six inches off the floor'. Detonated in the controlled conditions of your room, Energy Music is a mind, body and soul bomb that melts down psychic armour.

> *Kiyoshi Koyama:* What would you like to be ten
> years from now?
> *Coltrane:* I would like to be a saint

Coltrane Liquid Computer: John Coltrane

Amplification is sacred, the vertical energy of holy noise. As Sidran observed, 'When John Coltrane was playing, he was praying.' Coltrane hears jazz as a tonal communication medium. As Sidran realizes, this implies a new jazz consciousness in which the sax becomes 'an instrument which can create the initial thought patterns that can change the thinking of people.'

In '65 Coltrane listens to John Gilmore from the Arkestra, meets Ra, takes LSD 25 in the Fall. Afterwards he declares: 'I perceived the interrelationship of all lifeforms,' immediately condensing Manuel De Landa's explanation of LSD's neurochemical processes: 'When you trip you liquefy structures in your brain, linguistic structures, intentional structures. They acquire a less viscous consistency and your brain becomes a supercomputer. Information rushes into your brain, which makes you feel like you're having a revelation. But no one is revealing anything to you. It's just self organizing. It's happening by itself.'

Volume + LSD = Energy Music

If Sound is Mystery, then Volume is Holy and Noise is a Blessed State. On John's '65 *Om*, this amplified lysergic equation generates Energy Music, the frequency which Coltrane uses to tune into the Om state: 'Om' is the Hindu access code to the sonic origin of the universe.

Coltrane's multiphonic overdrive already demanded extrahuman breath cycles. *Om* draws breath up from the diaphragm in an auto-inspiration that turns the body into a human resonating chamber. The group becomes an Om medium, chanting verses from the Rig Veda: 'And the offerings made to the Ghosts of the Father, the Mantra, the Clarified Butter, I am he who awards to each the fruit of his actions, I, the Oblation and I the flame, I make all things clean, I am Ohm, Ohmm Ohmm.'

O✳hm Sweet O✳hm

For Coltrane, *Om* is a serenade to Ohm. The John Coltrane Orchestra is a sono-spiritual generator, a powerplant transmitting Om power. As his protege Sanders insisted: 'It is the most powerful word in the universe. It means God, it means peace, it means the beginning of things.' Close-miking expands the noise spectrum into the quietude of meditational jazz, crackling with the instant archaism of primaudial sound: the transient tones of bell trees, woodblocks, cymballic sussuration, a desolate calm.

You're inside the storm, assailed by screes of SonoMatter.

At 10.30, the Orchestra chant 'Om, Om' in a dazed despair, as if they're drowning. At 12.33, eerie sax echoes a Sun Ra tremolo. At 15.07, lowing sounds: unlocatable texture swoops and tumbles just like the hornets of a Sun Ra synth tone. Bowing violin, squabbles, building tension in waves that contract and release until you feel astralized. By the final chant, all voices are drained, guttural.

The Psychotechnics of Energy Music

With the '65 Energy Music Trilogy *Om*, *Ascension* and *Kulé Sé Mama*, John Coltrane engineers the Sonic Design for the Afronaut and the hippie. The PsychoTechnics of Energy music function through the neural circuit that Ben Sidran diagrammatizes, for how the future feels: 'The time feeling Coltrane generated created a new kind of tension that did not resolve at the end of bars or in expected places. This in turn created new anticipations in the listener and musicians began likening this new feeling to "freedom".' Tomorrow every Afronaut and every hippie wakes up to a Universal Sound.

Kulé Sé Mama's drum rolls, percussion rills, brushed cymbals and bells give a hallowed tintinabulation.

At 13.14, sax plays a 2-note refrain, forlorn and dying. Juno Lewis is intoning: 'So we sang this meee-loooo deee', drawing out vowels, switching to fictional Central African chants. Sanders and Coltrane overdrive the tenor sax, hitting a point at 7.55 when the sound blisters, boils, becomes a giant steam-powered sunship heaving its ghastly bulk into lift-off.

Bass clarinet insinuates snake tones, as 2 basses sound like echoing Sun Ra synths. Bassist Art Davis heard more in this metamorphic effect: 'I always thought using two basses sounded like an African water drum, like the drone effect of an Indian tamboura. Sometimes we'd sound more like two members of a string quartet than bassists.'

Shooting the Sun with a Miniature Sextant: Pharoah Sanders

Navigational Alignment
With the 30-min doomsday decree of *Out of this World* from '66's *Live in Seattle* and the merciless monotony of *Saturn, Mars, Venus* and *Jupiter* on '67's *Interstellar Space*, John Coltrane reactivates the predestination of astrology. Energy Music becomes Universal Sound which makes audible the cosmic order, forehears the masterplan in an act of clairaudience.

Astrological Consciousness
Astrology assumes a human‹›cosmic interface, a remote-distance link-up between human and starsign. Universal Sound needs an operating system like the chart Coltrane designs, which is 'a musical one with 12 tones correlating to the 12 zodiacal signs.' Astrology is a remote-distance prophetic system that collapses past and present, a revived archaic tech that gives its code operator prophetic capabilities.

Constellations preprogram futures. Sanders' astrological tracks – *Sun in Aquarius [Part 1 & Part 2], Capricorn Rising* – induce the sense of vast planetary bodies moving slowly into fateful conjunction. The Sanders album leaves the sunship behind to go astral travelling.

For Alice Coltrane and Sanders none of the future, the present and the past exist. History is immediately swallowed by primaudial time

outside chronology. Tomorrow is a moment in a masterplan, a design for
life which the track you play reveals in the present.

Amplitude Allah

Volume is an energetic force, a circuit of spiritual vibration that
channels the universal order, amplifies the cosmic program that operates
the human. In *The Creator Has A Master Plan*, Sanders is the secretary to
the spirits, the humble transmitter of this energy; in *Let Us Go into the
House of the Lord*, he's the reverential disciple. The prayerful inspiring
breath carries into the Islamasonic prayer of *Hum Allah – Hum Allah,
Hum Allah*. 'In all ritual song there is that slow beat, trying to call the
Gods,' a Sanders devotee explains to Val Wilmer. 'There's no rush. It's a
slow process as though one is praying.' One of Sanders' group described
him as 'having a halo' when he played.

Zodiac Interface

Jazz becomes an amplified zodiac, an energy generator that lines you up
in a stellar trichotomy of human, sound and starsign. Alice Coltrane and
Sanders are playing in the rhythm of the universe according to star
constellations transposed into rhythms and intervals. Alice's state of
Universal Consciousness occurs when the electric universe harmonizes
its audience. Electrification, Indian tones and arrangements converge on
jazz until it becomes a cosmic circuit diagram. Astro jazz becomes a
sunship upon which the composer-starsailor travels.

High Energy State Human

Sun Ra, Alice Coltrane and Pharoah Sanders all generate a new
African‹›American subject, the primaudial human. The holy being of
Sanders' *Black Unity*, of Ra's *Astro Black*, of Roland Kirk's *Blacknuss* and
Black Mystery Has Been Revealed, lives in a world where mental tension
and muscular torsion dissolve in a confluence of high-fidelity faiths. *Black
Mystery Has Been Revealed* is a mystery drama for tiptoeing bass and tape-
splice: 'AaaHAAa... The case of the Mystery Black Notes... that have been
stolen for years and years.' [*Strings swirl with the flourish of a curtain
drawn back*] 'Just listen... with all your might. Listen!!' [*Bottle smashes*]

Kensington: Kilburn: Northampton: Brook Green: Bethnal Green
November 1st 1995 13:15 - June 1st 1997 01:49

MOTION CAPTURE
(INTERVIEW)

"AfroFuturism comes from Mark Dery's '93 book, but the trajectory starts with Mark Sinker. In 1992, Sinker starts writing on Black Science Fiction; that's because he's just been to the States and Greg Tate's been writing a lot about the interface between science fiction and Black Music. Tate wrote this review called 'Yo Hermeneutics' which was a review of David Toop's *Rap Attack* plus a Houston Baker book, and it was one of the first pieces to lay out this science fiction of black technological music right there. And so anyway Mark went over, spoke to Greg, came back, started writing on Black Science Fiction. He wrote a big piece in The Wire, a really early piece on Black Science Fiction in which he posed this question, asks 'What does it mean to be human?' In other words, Mark made the correlation between *Blade Runner* and slavery, between the idea of alien abduction and the real events of slavery. It was an amazing thing, because as soon as I read this, I thought, my God, it just allows so many things. You can collapse all of these things; science fiction and music, they're the same. And then from there, it was pretty much out. It was out — and various people started using it in various ways. And Dery, through the Greg Tate route, simultaneously started doing it in '93, but he had no idea that there was anyone in London following it.

"*More Brilliant than the Sun* is a number of things. First of all, at its simplest, it's a study of visions of the future in music from Sun Ra to 4 Hero. One of its big strands is Breakbeat science, and Breakbeat science, as I see it, is when Grandmaster Flash and DJ Kool Herc and all those guys isolate the Breakbeat, when they literally go to the moment of a record where the melody and the harmony drops away and where the beats and the drum and the bass moves forward. By isolating this, they switched on a kind of electricity, by making the beat portable, by extracting the beat. I call it Motion Capturing: in films like *Jurassic Park* and all the big animatronic films, Motion Capture is the device by which they synthesize and virtualize the human body. They have a guy that's dancing slowly, and each of his joints are fixed to lights and they map that onto an interface, and then you've got it. You've literally captured the motion of a human; now you can proceed to virtualize it. And I think that's what Flash and the others did with the beat. They grabbed a potential beat which was always there, by severing it from the funk engine, by materializing it as actually a portion of vinyl that could be repeated. They switched on the material potential of the break, which had been lying dormant for a long time. So I follow that, that isolation of the Breakbeat through different spheres. Through Grandmaster Flash and the invention of skratchadelia.

"When scratching first came out people thought it was a gimmick first of all, then they thought of it as an interesting effect. And then, if you look in books, when most people talk about skratchadelia, about scratching on vinyl, they say it's a rhythmic rubbing of the vinyl in a percussive way, so as to accompany the rest of the song. And they read back vinyl in terms of some kind of rhythmic process. But actually a rhythmic process isn't really what's going on. What's going on is a new textural effect. There's no parallel to scratching; it never existed before being used in this incredible way. Scratching is more like a transformation sequence, more like the audio parallel of *The Thing* or *American Werewolf*, where you see the human transformed into a werewolf, and just before they finally become a werewolf you suddenly get a glimpse of the human, then it flashes away again. That's what skratchadelia does. It's this unstable mix of the voice and the vinyl. It's this new texture effect. You could say the voice has phase-shifted into this new sound. So I follow skratchadelia through Grandmaster Flash into Electro, with another group called Knights of the Turntable. And I follow it through to

Goldie and 4 Hero, specifically in terms of graffiti, in terms of Breakbeat's involution via Wildstyle. Because Wildstyle is like this cryptographic language, in which the single letter turns into a typographic environment that you enter. It's very much a perceptual gymnastics, looking at Wildstyle. And there's a big interface between graffiti and the break. Goldie says, 'My beats are sculpted in 4D, in 4 dimensions.' And, similarly, there's this famous graffiti guy called Kaze 2 who back in '89 was already talking about the step beyond Wildstyle. Wildstyle was 3D, but Kaze 2 was talking about 5 dimensions, he was talking about Computer Style. He said, 'In my work I do the Computer Style, I do the 5th-dimensional step-parallel staircase.' This is straight out of Escher. So I follow Breakbeat science right from this isolation of the rhythmic DNA right through to its Escherization, right through to its moment of involution — and then I follow that into Drum'n'Bass where, of course, because the beats are digitalized, it's information to be manipulated. I follow Breakbeat science, I follow it to the conclusion of tracks of people like 4 Hero, specifically *Parallel Universe*, where I turn the emphasis and focus on the science in Breakbeat. And the thing I notice about Breakbeat science, about the way science is used in music in general, is that science is always used as a science of intensified sensation. In the classical 2 cultures in mainstream society, science is *still* the science that drains the blood of life and leaves everything vivisected. But in music it's never been like that; as soon as you hear the word science, you know you're in for an *intensification* of sensation. In this way, science then refers to a science of sensory engineering, so *Parallel Universe* announces this, when it has titles like *Sunspots* or *Wrinkles in Time*, these are the points where the laws of gravity and the laws of time and space collapse, and they're simultaneously saying rhythm is about to collapse when you enter these zones. So you've got someone like Goldie who does *Timeless*, and *Timeless* is obviously referring to simply the infinite loop of the Breakbeat, which Goldie's trying to tap into.

"Then there's the synth race, entering the synth race, which is Techno, the whole interface between the first Detroit guys and what I call the Import Ear. The guys listening to this stuff coming out of Europe, coming out of England, listening to the whiteness of the synthesizer and using it because that sound would make them alien within America. That's the secret behind all of the early Detroit records. All those guys — Model

500, Cybotron — they've all got these affected Flock of Seagulls-type accents. Why do they have this? Because they want to be alien in America. How do they do this? By singing like white New Romantic English kids. So it's the idea of white music being exotic to black American ears. So it's trying to turn the exotic eye back onto the English, because that's part of the process that happened. Also what happened, Techno was happening without the registering mark of the UK media, without the traditional steps in which America comes out with an original music, and it's usually bastardized in England and Europe and mixed, remixed, and then sent back. That was reversed; in this case, it was America bastardizing, taking English music and doing strange things with it. Hence the famous embarrassment when English journalists would head over to Detroit to say, 'Where's this music come from?', only to find out this music had come from where they'd just been, only to find out that *they* were the origin. This is the first explicit case where white music is the origin, and where the black American musicians who are the adulterators and the bastardizers. So Techno's a complete reversal of the classic 60s myth of the blues and the Rolling Stones, the entire rock heritage which starts out with this famous myth of Muddy Waters and the Rolling Stones. In Techno, you've got an immediate reversal. In Techno, Kraftwerk is the delta blues, Kraftwerk is where it all starts. In Techno, Depeche Mode are like Leadbelly. A Flock of Seagulls are like Blind Lemon Jefferson. So Europe and whiteness generally take the place of the origin. And Black Americans are synthetic; the key in Techno is to synthesize yourself into a new American alien. So I look at the synth race in terms of various developments of that, for instance, there's a whole Darkside with Detroit which I talk about. And then I go into Underground Resistance, especially, who've developed an entire war, an entire military assault, a whole kinaesthetic of war based around the release of their single. How each single becomes like a missile launched in war against the programmers.

"But the main point is that I'm trying to bring out what I call the Sonic Fiction of records, which is the entire series of things which swing into action as soon as you have music with no words. As soon as you have music with no words, then everything else becomes more crucial: the label, the sleeve, the picture on the cover, the picture on the back, the titles. All these become the jump-off points for your route through the music, or for the way the music captures you and abducts you into its world. So all these things become really important. So a lot of the main sources of the book are from Sleevenotes; they're the main thing. A lot of the book talks about Sleevenote artists. It talks about the guys who did the covers for those Miles Davis sleeves, this guy Mati Klarwein, another guy Robert Springett, who did the covers for Herbie Hancock's early 70s albums. There's different interfaces between different Sonic Fictions, between the title and the music. Hendrix would say, 'What I'm doing is a painting in sound.' And you can say reversely with the Sleevenotes. The reason the Sleevenote pictures capture you is because they're a sounding in paint. If you listen to them, you imagine them as weird visions conjured up through the music. It's really strange.

"Part of the point is very much to reverse traditional accounts of Black Music. Traditionally, they've been autobiographical or biographical, or they've been heavily social and heavily political. My aim is to suspend all of that, absolutely, and then, in the shock of these absences, you put in everything else, you put in this huge world opened up by a microperception of the actual material vinyl. What immediately happens, in almost all accounts, people immediately look over, they literally look *over* the vinyl to whatever transcendent logic they can use, instead of actually starting with the vinyl. The book is very much a materialization of this. So I'm looking at all these Sonic Fictions, I'm looking at all the different levels of science that exist within the material object.

"Motion Capture sounds like a mechanical operation being conducted. Part of the thing is that all these terms are already familiar to a lot of us. They constitute an unofficial mythology at the end of the century, this entire range of Sonic Fictions. There's pretty much a shared language amongst a whole generation of people. The difference between the over-40s and the under-40s is a real familiarity with different dataverses or polyverses stacked on top of each other. There's all kind of fascinating implications, which I want to work out in the book. Things like the 21st-century nervous system. If you go back to Norman Mailer, *The White Negro*, he talks a lot about building a new nervous system. And then if you read on a bit to Ballard, Ballard often talks about the conflict between the geometry and posture, the competition between the animate and the inanimate and the way the inanimate often creeps in and wins.

"To me, it makes complete sense to see action movies in the same stratum as skratchadelia. There are the same velocities, the same vectors, the same sounds: the sound of a car as it skids round a corner is the same sound the wheels of steel make as they ride around. You're captured, abducted by the same sounds in each. It's this fantastic sound of velocity, as 2 surfaces in friction literally converge and then shoot apart at fantastic speeds. It's an incredible excitement. These things are happening concurrently — at any moment in time it's really easy to see that's where sonic invention has gone. It's part of being captured by tiny moments of time, being obsessed with tiny moments of time. Part of what happens with sampladelia is that you've got a lot of music based on sampler memory, so that a lot of the hooks, a lot of the music that abducts you, will have to be 4 seconds or 9 seconds. So there's this huge psychedelia based upon disguising these seconds; it's like Mark Sinker says, finding the universe in a grain of sound — and that's what the sampler does. There's this huge psychedelia grown up in which you're able to fall into a universe of sound and it's granular, microphonemes of sound. In *Abbaon Fats Track* by Tricky, there's this woman who whispers to her kid, 'Can you fly fast as you can to be with Jesus' — she really whispers it. That whole sample must last, I dunno, 5, 7 seconds, 8 seconds, 11 seconds, but there's something so incredible about it. It abducts you so *much*, because you can hear an atmosphere in it, you can hear an ambience, you can hear levels of foreground within that sample. You can feel yourself getting abducted by it. So there's a way in which the visual really seems to suggest that. Then there's this whole thing I was reading by Michel Chion. Chion is a really interesting guy, this student of Pierre Schaeffer who started by composing *musique concrète*, who then became a theorist. So he's the best person on film and sound ever. Part of my relation to sound is that Chion talks about sound in film, and I'm only just realising now that a lot of my favourite samples are from sound in film.

"So sampladelia opens a continuum between visual sound and audio sound. Visual sound is always feeding in from one to the other. Which is why I love a lot of film samples. Probably why I love the visual so much is that it's always being grabbed anyway by the music. By extinguishing the visual output, the music is switching it on elsewhere. It's as if the eyes start to have ears, as Chion would say. Your ears have had their optical capacity switched on. In a strange way, your ear starts to see.

Chion is saying that *each* of the senses have the *full* capacity of all the others. It's simply that hearing happens to go through the ear, but all the other senses can go through the ear as well. The ear is meant to hear, but it can do all the other things as well, if it was switched on to the right capacity.

"A similar thing that happens a lot is a big transference to tactility, which I talk a lot about as well. Whenever sound gets subdermal, whenever in Drum 'n' Bass the sound gets very scratchy, with lots of shakers and rattlers, there's often a lot of sounds where the percussion is too distributed, too motile, too mobile for the ear to grasp as a solid sound. And once the ear stops grasping this as solid sound, the sound very quickly travels to the *skin* instead — and the skin starts to hear for you. And whenever the skin starts to hear, that's where you feel all creepy crawly, and that's when conduction creeps in, when people say, 'I felt really cold', or that the music is really cold: which is because their skin has dropped maybe a centigrade as the music has hit it, as the beat has pressed across it. So I follow all those kind of things. I think with light and sound, there's a stratum across which both elements cross all the time. They've both become versions of a sampladelia. And that sampladelia, by definition, lets you analogize a lot of things. And not only does it analogize, it lets you mutate and recombinate.

"Sampladelia is a *mandate* to recombinate. That's what it is, that's how it works. You start to realise that when most people try to praise something, they praise it in terms of something that's gone 30, 40 years ago. You start to see the drags people place on the emergence of the new, the way people constantly put the brakes on any kind of breaks. So if I'm reaching for parallels, I'll always try and reach for parallels that are actually ahead of what I'm suggesting. Hence, don't think of Breakbeat in terms of some kind of ancient technique which has been resuscitated. For instance, you see a lot of people saying the Breakbeat is the African drum, the return of the African drumming sound, but really it's the other way around. The Breakbeat should be moved forward. Think of it in terms of a motion-capture device being made on vinyl, before there was any digital equipment to be made. If he could have been, Grandmaster Flash would have been a computer designer; if he'd been an animator, he'd be doing motion capturing. He's just doing it on vinyl first.

"So these are the kinds of things I tend to look for. It's all about trying to establish kinaesthesias, because that's really what's happened. I think with almost all the different varieties of rhythmic psychedelia, there's a warzone of kinaesthesia been established. There's a sense in which the nervous system is being reshaped by beats for a new kind of state, for a new kind of sensory condition. Different parts of your body are actually at different states of evolution. Your head may well be lagging quite far behind the rest of your body. In Drum'n'Bass, there's obviously quite a lot of attention, through dub, to the stepper. There's the idea that the feet may well be more evolved, and hands obviously, feet and hands. Terminator X spoke with his hands. Other djs yelled with their hands. I've got this brilliant skratchadelia album called *Return of the DJ*, put out by *The Bomb* magazine in Frisco, and it's all done by djs, it's a brilliant album. One guy's done a track called *Terrorwrist*, so his wrist is a terror, his wrist sends out terrifying bombs. The idea of a terroristic wrist action is fantastic. That's a predatory wrist. So you can see in that the dj has really evolved the hand that sends terror by a flick by the way it touches vinyl. So I often think that the actual body is at different stages of evolution. There's a constant war on.

"A lot of mainstream media's main job as what I call a futureshock absorber is to maintain a homeostasis, maintain traditional and inherited rules of melody over harmony, beats over rhythm, beats over melody, to maintain matters in terms of proper music, or true music, or respectable music — and that's always a way in which people try and hierarchize the body. Part of my big thing is to talk about dance music simultaneously as a kinaesthetic and a headmusic, because it tends to be both. As soon as you listen to dance music at home, its repetitiveness becomes headmusic-like. I've never understood why they can't be, why they *aren't* the same thing.

"Part of this thing is that HipHop is headmusic, not stage music, HipHop never works best on stage. And that's because it's using all these Sonic Fictions; so there's a whole kinaesthetic direction, and simultaneously a head continuum. HipHop even has a term, 'heads', which is more or less saying that HipHop has its own hippies and progressive music. So I talk about Cypress Hill, HipHop and its whole drug-tech interface. Simultaneously, I say that John Coltrane is the first hippie. I look at John

Coltrane's last records, records like *Cosmic Music, Interstellar Space, Om*. Coltrane famously tripped in '65, then did this record *Om*. Manuel De Landa has this line, about when you trip you become a liquid computer, because your brain liquefies, and I think that's what happened to Coltrane in about '65. He starts using 'Om', the Indian chant, and he's trying to assemble a universal music, and the whole thing about the Om is that it turns the human into this huge, giant, vibrating powerstation really. Om is this operation to turn yourself into this energy field. So you have this late 60s jazz where all these guys were turning themselves into power generators — and this incredible music that was trying to bootstrap a universal sound. And it worked. I look at that whole strain of music, from Coltrane through to Sun Ra, through to Alice Coltrane. A whole kind of holiness through volume, a holy amplification.

"The reason I don't talk about the literary is that there's just no need to, what with thinking about amplification and the sensory environment of amplification, of loudness in itself, the sensory impact of volume, the sensory impact of repetition, of broadcasting, all these things. There's so much to talk about, just at the level of volume, of pressure. There's a way in which you can directly connect those with everything else. You can talk about the audio-social and immediately you've connected the sound to everything else; the literary just never really seems to appear, except as different kinds of Sonic Fiction. In which case, precisely because they're on record not in a book, they don't come out as literary, they come out as more like the difference between reading a paper and hearing it read out on the news. You get the idea of hearing a voice coming at you through various channels: just as you never hear the news directly, you always hear an audio feed, you always hear a voice transmitted through a whole series of other things before it ever gets to you. That's what happens to fiction once it gets on vinyl; you hear it through the studio. So it's not literary — the literary doesn't work in that space at all. Simultaneously, there's no need for representation, for the signifier, or for the text, or for the law. There's no need for any of that.

"But of course the way to introduce theory is to realise the music is theorising itself quite well. For example, there's a concept I like called percussapella, which is percussion and accapella and percussapella is just the beats on their own. Some dj thought up a term which describes this sampladelic alloy of percussion going solo, of percussion as an accapella. And it's just brilliant. So I can use that, and as soon as music's instrumental, these things suddenly loom into shape and you start to use them. And there's so many concepts already extant in the music that all you need do is extract them and use them to build the machine you want to build, to use them as parts in the giant connection machine that you want to build. You just hook a concept on and solder it onto the next concept that you want. So part of the whole drive is very much written as a book of emergence. It's not a history at all, it's very enjoyable to resist the urge to history, because, especially in Black Music, there's a whole drive towards history and tradition and continuity, and this book is explicitly about the breaks, about the discontinuum. Marshall McLuhan talks about the twentieth-century discontinuum. Well, this book is all about the breaks and the cuts. Inheritance has been extremely overstressed in ideas of Black Music. By bringing up first the machine then second the actual vinyl, all the different qualities move between the machines, and become as much effects of the machines. So this is the idea that the sonic can produce identities in itself. For example: George Clinton is black but the Star Child is an alien animatronic figure — it's hard to say what colour the Star Child is, the Star Child is pure animatronic. And part of the book always looks that way, always looks to see which hallucination the sonic engenders and then chases that. I never try and collapse the sonic back into the social, and precisely because this is such an almost unanimous tendency, I've gone quite far the other way, I've exaggerated it entirely, When you read someone like Sun Ra, Sun Ra would talk a lot about cosmic music. And I think in cosmic music, he meant it in the sense of, What would cosmic music be? It would be the music of the electromagnetic field, the music of radio transmissions, say, crossing the electromagnetic field. It would be the music of electrical disturbances, the atmospheric cosmic disturbances that exist in the sky. And if you listen to Sun Ra's *Astro Black*, those are exactly the sounds he's making with his Moog, he's turning the Moog synthesizer into something like a circuit which can act as a giant alternating current between the people listening, the Arkestra and the cosmos itself. The Moog is the amplifier that directs current in and out. On one hand, there's a very material way in which he does this because the actual Moogy sounds are really similar to — if not identical to — the sounds of the cosmos. So it's really fascinating, because Sun Ra often said, like 'I am an instrument' and 'the Arkestra is an instrument'. On one hand, he said the Arkestra were tone scientists, sonic scientists; on the other, the Arkestra were his *instruments*. So you get this idea of music as this sonic production circuit through which — as Gilles Deleuze was saying — molecules of a new people may be planted here or there. That's very much what Sun Ra's doing: he's using the Moog to produce a new sonic people. Out of this circuit, he's using it to produce the new astro-black American of the 70s.

"So that's absolutely what I do all along. I extend the sonic outwards, thereby getting at this feeling of impossibility which this music often gives you. At its best, any music should strike you with its impossibility, and its complete evasion of the rules of traditional fidelity to a live sound. And the way to get at the strangeness of music — rather than to habitualize that music via any other kind of field — is to exaggerate the sonic, to use the sonic as a probe into new environments. Because every new sonic sensation that I can magnify is simultaneously *a new sensory lifeform*. So there's this constant play between the sonic and the sensory, which become the same thing often. It's partly a shift between scales. Often you can open the scale and the sound really wide and then you disappear into a sound. Often you can shut the scale back up and withdraw to look at the vinyl, or withdraw to look at the sleeves. There's a constant telescoping of perception from very close attention to a record to pulling back to looking at the vinyl. I think this is new and fresh. Because vinyl is often ignored. The things most immediately pleasurable about buying a record are the things which are always ignored. It's bizarre. So by bringing that to the front the book should be written with a sense of familiarity. People will take it to their hearts. The book's been designed to have a very tactile feel, in the same way that your fingers hunger for a sleeve. When you see a sleeve that you like, your fingers reach towards it, they can't help themselves, they really want that. It's quite obvious that this is what I'm trying to do — every object is a machine of subjectivity. The record player is, the record is, the book is. I simply want my book to become a machine for producing subjectivity. It should be a machine for putting music together.

"In the last ten, 20 years, there's been no gap between science, art and music, they all form the same thing. It's simply that at any one time things tend to be blocked, and when you have moments of rhythmic psychedelia, it's easy to see what can be dislodged and brought out and made into connection machines with other things. And other times, things seize up. Breakbeat has opened various retroactive chapters. Similarly the breakdown of the longheld notion that Techno's origin point is Kraftwerk means that people can zip between the 70s and the 90s in a much freer way, move between Krautrock, say, and Herbie Hancock. There's a certain openness in music.

"The key thing to do now is to move into a new field. I've stopped calling myself a writer: for the book I'm just going to call myself a concept engineer. That makes the whole thing much fresher, much more exciting and much less known about. Because that's what I'm really doing. I'm engineering, grasping fictions, grasping concepts, grasping hallucinations from my own area and translating them into another one, mixing them, and seeing where we go with them. I use these different concepts to probe new areas of experience, to anticipate and fastforward different explorations into new fields of perceptions which are always there, but whose strength lies in that they don't exist in traditional mainstream terms. Traditional mainstream terms are still completely bound up with the literary, and the 2 cultures — and thank God for that, because that means that they can't get in on what's going on. Which is just this sudden glance at the end of the century. I've renamed all the instruments: I've renamed the synthesizer the Sonotron. Iannis Xenakis called the synthesizer the Sonotron in his book. That's perfect because Sonotron just sounds like a superhero comic, so a convergence of sound into ballistics. And the drum machine should be renamed what it actually is: a rhythm synthesizer. I call this problem [r]earview hearing. The drum machine *isn't* a drum machine. It's pulses and signals synthesized into new pulses and new signals. There are no drums in it. That was a weird thing that confused me for years and years, until I worked it out. You'd listen and they'd sound *utterly* different from drums. The movement from funk to drum machines is an extremely incredible one: people's whole rhythmic perception changed overnight. And people of course pretended that nothing had happened, but it was a major shift, hearing bleeps and signals and different kinds of alternating current as sound. It was a huge shift. In a similar sense Edgard Varèse called the drum machine a rhythm synthesizer, and that's a good way to describe it. So all those kind of things, all those concepts, make a sense that the mainstream is just completely incapable of really grasping at all.

"There really is a sensory involution away from traditions, and from whatever the divisions of art as supposed to be. It's very much like Sadie Plant says, it's not high or low, it's just complex, because it has so many travelling and spiralling arms that you can hook onto. This is why when the Americans lament about the virtualization of the body, it just seems bizarre, because it feels like we're doing the opposite, it feels like we're just beginning on this journey into the centre of our senses. It seems the opposite: science always means a *hypersensoriness*. Traditional science still means a depletion, cold scientists, extreme logic and all these corny cliches. But in musical terms, science is the opposite, science is intensification, more sensation. Science is rhythm intensified, rhythm estranged. And that's how a whole generation understands science. Then what they mean by abstract is sensations so new there isn't yet a language for them. So the shorthand is to just call it abstract. There's a whole generation who're grown used to thinking of sensory emotions without having a language for them yet. Rhythmic psychedelia's the psychedelic aspect of any particular scene. So it could be anything: from House to trance, to Breakbeat to jazz, it could be any scene — but I'm interested in the rhythmic psychedelia aspect of each scene, not the scene itself. I'm interested in the points of maximum rhythmic hyperdelia, that's what I'm really interested in. So it could be any of these...

"Postmodernism doesn't mean anything in music at all. It doesn't mean *anything*. It hasn't meant anything since at least '68, when the first Versions started coming out of Jamaica. As soon as you had the particular social condition of no copyright, this 19th-century copyright was already gone, instantly you had the freedom to replicate, to recombinate. That encouraged a Wildstyle of rhythms which would attach themselves and recombinate. And as soon as you had that, that's postmodernism accomplished and done with, right then in '68. Ever since then by definition you've had postmodernism and it hasn't been any big deal at all, it's just already been accomplished. For instance, Walter Benjamin's traditional 'The Work of Art in the Age of Mechanical Reproduction': this argument doesn't work any more — because one of Benjamin's main points [or the one his admirers use over and over again] is that in the Age of Mechanical Reproduction there's no aura left, the single, unique aura has gone. But of course as soon as you have the dubplate then that's all gone out of the window. The dub plate is where you've got the reproductive process, the mechanical process of pressing vinyl onto the plate that's being played, and suddenly in the middle of that you've got the one-off remix, you've got the track that there's only one of in the world, but it's *not* an original, it's a copy, a third copy. So you've got this thing that's never supposed to exist in Benjamin's world: you've got the one-off copy, you've got the one-off fifth remix, you've got the one-off tenth remix, you've got the one-off twentieth remix. There's only one of it. So the dubplate means that the whole idea of the aura being over doesn't make any sense, because the aura is reborn in the middle of the industrial reproduction. Hence the jungle acceleration, the intensification of the dub plate; the dub plate is reborn as this Music of the Future. You're hearing music that won't be on the streets till ten months, 11 months later, immediately this gap opens up between you and now in 1996: you suddenly imagine yourself in '97, going 'Where will I be when I buy this?' – and of course you never will, but listening to a dub plate does this little projection on you. You feel yourself 18 months ahead, you literally feel ahead, you're on a plane of acceleration, you're moving faster than you are. So for that reason alone postmodernism just hasn't existed and as soon as you have a state of remixology – well, what happened is that remixology got held up in different areas. In jazz, for instance, you had Alice Coltrane remixing John Coltrane, but jazz tradition hated this and said it was blasphemy. You had the Beach Boys remixing their stuff and it being refused. So in the major corporations remixology was always stopped, and in Jamaica remixology just became the immediate state of play, first of all because it's simultaneously hyperpredatory as well, it allows a kind of agglomeration of rhythms, a ruthlessness of rhythms, a break war, what jungle producer Andy C calls a break war. People bid for breaks, or just steal them. There's this wild frontier, this wild break war going on, rhythms just going mad. So we're far beyond postmodernism here, and immediately all the traditional arguments drop out of the window. The idea of exhaustion, for example that's just gone, because music doesn't work in that way. It's already a gene pool, so it's not going to exhaust itself.

"And then a whole series of things – the idea of quotation and citation, the idea of ironic distance, that doesn't work, that's far too literary. That assumes a distance which by definition volume overcomes. There is no distance with volume, you're swallowed up by sound. There's no room, you can't be ironic if you're being swallowed by volume, and volume is overwhelming you. It's impossible to stay ironic, so all the implications of postmodernism go out of the window. Not only is it the literary that's useless, *all* traditional theory is pointless. All that works is the sonic plus the machine that you're building. So you can bring back any of these particular theoretical tools if you like, but they better work. And the way you can test them out is to actually play the records. That's how you test if my book works, because I want it to be a machine. When I say works, I mean I want it to engineer a kind of sensory alteration, some kind of perceptual disturbance. I think I'd really like that very much, because even a tiny sensory disturbance is enough to send out a signal which can get transmitted.

"I think the combination of the dj and the writer makes a lot of sense. I think that both are different kinds of remixology at work, and that all we're really doing is bringing writing and putting it onto the second deck and just accelerating it as much as a record. I think because so much traditional Brit prose is so matey, and so blokish, and so bluff and no-nonsense, that encourages me in always going for the impossible, which can be registered as what the future feels like as sensation. That's why the key things in this book are McLuhan and Ballard, the guys I was reading throughout. McLuhan's famous lines about the human being the sex organs for the machine world, those lines are crucial. The Kraftwerk chapter is all about Kraftwerk as the sex organs of the synthesizer.

"The whole series of things about accidents, about bugs, about the producer being someone who can nurture a bug, who can breed a bug. Simultaneously most of the key musics have been accidents, they've been formed through errors. They're software errors in the machine's programming, and they form these sounds — and the producer's taken these sounds and nurtured this error, built on this mistake, and if you grab a mistake you've got a new audio lifeform. It's quite common: back with Can in the 70s, Holger Czukay was saying machines have a lifeform, repetition is the life of machines. So there's a whole thing about machine life that already exists with musicians anyway. Producers have *already* started working out a theory of machine life. As soon as you look at what they've been saying — magnify it, and start to use it — you realise that there's this series of Sonic Fictions and scientific fabulations, all of which I just call Sonic Fictions. There's 20 years of speculation on the machine as a lifeform. There's 20 years of music as cosmic fields, so what I'm doing is using this stuff, activating it, switching it on. That way the whole book feels alive: by using a lot of producers who are living now and connecting them up to ones in the past, you switch on the sonic, you switch on a whole sonic register, a whole unofficial register. Nobody quotes Lee Perry as an authority, it's always the grotesque thing of Heidegger and then George Clinton, it's *never* the other way around. But it was Clinton that came up with mixadelics: the theory of mixology as a psychedelia, the theory of the mixing desk as a psychedelia. In 1979, there it is, mixadelics. That's his concept: he thought of a psychedelia of the mixing desk. So you don't *need* any Heidegger, because Clinton's already theoretical. So what I've done is extract these concepts and set them to work: they work because they're tied to records. And that's because the vector that a lot of this works on is the record player. It's the habitualness, you have to look at yourself as a machine programmed, as a biocomputer programmed by the decks. The motions you have to make to put a needle onto the record as the flight of the stylus takes across the groove: think of the hundreds of thousands of times that you've made that motion, the habitualness of putting it on. Here's a way to see this very clearly, for instance: when you're listening to a rare groove original, say there's a track you know really well, and you're listening for the first time to the original of it. You suddenly realise that the bit you *know* is only a tiny bit, just like a 3-second bit, and then the record just plunges, usually, into a disappointing mediocrity, before the next sound that you recognize comes up, and then it plunges again, before the next bit comes up. Sometimes with Parliament tracks you can hear about 5 of these in the first 2 minutes, and these bits, they recognize you, because what they're doing is recognizing your habitualness in putting them on. When you hear a sound, you have a memory flash, but you almost have a muscular memory, you remember the times you danced to it. You don't just remember the times you danced to it, you remember the times you bent over to put the needle on the record to play that bit. Sometimes you love that bit so much, you even remember going over and over and over that bit again. So when you hear that sound that you love, when you hear the recognizable sample in the middle of alien sound, that sound is recognizing your habitualness, and it's really incredible, you suddenly get a glimpse of yourself as a habitform, as a habitformed being, a process of habit formation. You suddenly see yourself over the years, how you loved this record. It's incredible, the sound takes a picture of your habits; it snaps your habits. And you suddenly see it very clearly. How many times have I put that on? That's what I want to get at. These are new sensations which have never existed before, that feeling of being recognized by sound. That's new, it hasn't happened before. By definition, it *could* only happen in the sampladelic generation; by definition it could only happen to people who listen to sampladelic music. And those kind of things just haven't been written about, they haven't even been captured yet.

"So by extending the sonic further and further, I'm on the hunt, I'm chasing for, I'm trying to find out new perceptions: perceptions that have always been there, but haven't yet been grasped and haven't yet been connected to anything else yet. It's this exploration into the unknown.

"By now, I've stopped saying 'Black culture'. There's always been a much stronger perception in America of black culture and that's obviously partly because it's been counter-defined against the traditional knowledge apartheid structure which has been in place in America. And you can tell almost all American writers are working against this knowledge apartheid, which has been really firmly laid out. After all, everybody should know that most black Americans couldn't even get to art school until about 1969. That's how severe American apartheid was, from the knowledge structure on down. So most black Americans write in a way that assumes a unified black culture, then goes on to explain the dissensions between it, or not to. But sitting here in England, in London, it's much harder for me to even assume a unified anything, let alone a unified black culture. I tend to start from the opposite. I tend to think of things more freefloating, and there's various strange attractors trying to agglomerate things, there's various inertia-producing forces which are trying to centre, and trying to attract material to black culture, petrify it, solidify it, reterritorialize it, and then usually this gets called tradition, or it gets called history.

"I look at black culture much more as a series of material that's been agglomerated on one hand, and on the other, it's much more like a series of techniques. A lot of the producers and engineers I talk about see themselves as scientists or technicians. I tend to think of black culture then as an instrument or an environment that *they've invented*. I'm very much looking into the synthesizings, looking into new black synthetic versions. I can never think of a unified black culture out of which everything comes. To me everything now looks like it's synthesized.

There's obviously stuff that's been around long enough so that it feels solidified, calcified, but actually it's all synthesized. Because I'm looking at emergences, and by definition they're going to be really synthetic, like Techno. Because I bring the machine into it. It makes things much more complex because instead of talking about black culture, I'll talk for instance a lot about Ghanaian drum choirs, or talk a lot about the African polyrhythmic engine, the polyrhythmic percussion engine. And those will be very particular African traits. Sound is a sensory technology, so I talk a lot about black technologies. They're machines — and if we're talking about 19th or 18th century Africa, then they'd be machines built a long time ago and passed down. But in the present, it's more like black culture is this series of machines built here and there. The dub plate was one, built in Jamaica. The Breakbeat was another, built in New York.

"I haven't yet pulled back to make commanding statements about what it is in black culture that produces these kind of synthetic technologies. I haven't yet been able to pull back a stratum to the big what-if question. And that's probably because I don't think it really exists, because I'm so consumed and amazed by the teeming variety at the other end of the telescope that I can't pull back to see the view. Probably because I distrust the idea that there's views, but it would be more like a shift in tempo or scale. So shifting to a horizon view then switching back. But it could be that, one large thing Greg used to say which worked really well, was that the Middle Passage, out of Africa into America, forced culture to become immediately mental. All of the other things were by definition left behind, left ruined: architecture, everything else. So culture immediately became mental, immediately became dematerialized. So oral culture is all the things you carry in your head, and that's *it*. And then it has to be rematerialized, first through hitting the hands, or through the mouth. It had to be passed on again, and reinvented all over again. So there's that whole strain. And there's the key thing which drew me into all this: the idea of alien abduction, the idea of slavery as an alien abduction which means that we've all been living in an alien-nation since the 18th century. And I definitely agree with that, I definitely use that a lot. The mutation of African male and female slaves in the 18th century into what became negro, and into the entire series of humans that were designed in America. That whole process, the key thing behind it all is that in America none of these humans were *designated* human.

It's in music that you get this sense that most African-Americans owe *nothing* to the status of the human. African-Americans still had to protest, still had to *riot*, to be judged Enlightenment humans in the 1960s — it's quite incredible. And in music, if you listen to guys like Sun Ra — I call them the despots, Ra, Rammellzee and Mad Mike — part of the whole thing about being an African-American alien musician, is that there's this sense of the human as being a really pointless and treacherous category, a category which has *never meant anything* to African-Americans. This is particularly true with Sun Ra — just because Ra pushes it by saying that he comes from Saturn. I always accept the impossibility of this. I always start with that, where most people would try and claim it was an allegory. But it isn't an allegory: he really did come from Saturn. I try to exaggerate that impossibility, until it's irritating, until it's annoying, and this annoyance is merely a threshold being crossed in the readers' heads, and once they unseize, unclench their sensorium, they'll have passed through a new threshold and they'll be in my world. I'll have got them. The key thing to do is to register this annoyance, because a lot of the moves I've described will provoke real annoyance, the lack of the literary, the lack of the modernist, the lack of the postmodern. All of these things should provoke a real irritation, and simultaneously a real relief, a relief that somebody has left all stuff behind, and started from the pleasure principle, started from the materials, started from what really gives people pleasure."

First published in the Abstract Culture Series as Motion Capture, *by the Cybernetic Culture Research Unit, 1996, Warwick University.*

ASSEMBLING THE CONNECTION MACHINE

Note:

Books sampled are cited by author and date, and listed in *DataMining the Infoverse*.
Records, sleeves, posters and other artworks are cited by artist and date and listed at the
end of each chapter-section.
Track titles, where relevant, are listed thus, "Ultramagnetic MCs: *Brainiac; Smoking Dust*
from *The Basement Tapes*, Tuff City Records, 1996", and named in brackets after the
citation when helpful: e.g. "'combinating elements', Ultramagnetic MCs, 1996 (*Brainiac*)".
Films are cited by title and listed alphabetically at the end of each chapter section, as
video releases ("NCA" = "not currently available on video release").
Magazine citations are given in full the first time, then subsequently by artist, author and
date, thus: "Tricky in Gavin Martin, *NME*, 28 Oct 1995" subsequently becomes "Tricky,
Martin, Oct 1995".

[-015] 'Its mission is...', *On the Uses and Disadvantages of History for Life* from Nietzsche,
1983, p121

Thoughtware: Operating System for the Redesign of Sonic Reality

[-006] 'the rhizomorphic, fractal structure of the transcultural, international formation
that I call the Black Atlantic,' Gilroy, 1993, p4
[-004] 'MythScience', from track title *The Myth-Science Approach*, Sun Ra, 1970; 'Science
and technology...', Virilio, 1983a, p62
[-002] 'talks very happily...', Sadie Plant, Matthew Fuller, *Alien Underground Version 0.1*,
Spring 1995; 'antiplague', Reed, 1978, p6

· Sun Ra: *The Myth-Science Approach* from *It's After the End of the World*, MPS, 1970

Thoughtware: World 4: Mutantextures of Jazz

[002] 'The tape was...', George Russell, Sleevenotes to Russell, 1980
[003] 'panstylistic electronic tape...', Russell, Sleevenotes to Russell, 1985a; 'There are three...', Russell, Sleevenotes to Russell, 1980
[004] 'The thing that sounds...', Russell, Sleevenotes to Russell, 1980; 'The voices heard...', Russell, Sleevenotes to Russell, 1985a; 'An African lute...', Russell, Sleevenotes to Russell, 1980
[005] 'The old Norwegian...', Russell, ibid; 'I wanted to reflect...', Russell, Sleevenotes to Russell, 1985a; 'In the African...', Russell, Sleevenotes to Russell, 1985b; 'Music is architecture...', Russell, ibid
[006] 'one machine's input...', Kelly, 1994, p176
[007] 'becoming a fearful...', R. Murray Schafer, *Radical Radio* in Strauss, 1993, p292; 'audiomaze', from track title *Audiomaze*, Gachet, 1995
[008] 'By the alien...', Kelly, 1994, p173; 'massively parallel bioengineered...', ibid, p183
[009] 'the alien power...', Kelly, 1994, p173; 'But when she...', Tuotola, 1990, p163; 'It is the entire globe...', Mati Klarwein in Joel Lewis, *The Wire*, Dec 1994
[010] 'Yesternow', from track title *Yesternow*, Davis, 1970b; 'You're talking about...', Sarah Connor in *The Terminator*; 'collapsar', Haldeman, 1977, p7, p18, p83
[011] 'Everything is electrified...', Jimi Hendrix in Boot & Salewicz, 1995, p237; 'syntharmonic', Patrick Gleason in Sleevenotes, White, 1975

- Miles Davis, *Bitches Brew*, CBS, 1970a
- Miles Davis: *Yesternow* from *A Tribute to Jack Johnson*, Columbia, 1970b
- Miles Davis: *He Loved Him Madly* from *Get up with It*, Columbia Records, 1974
- Miles Davis, *Agharta*, CBS, 1975
- Miles Davis: *Gondwana* from *Pangaea*, Columbia Records, 1975
- Miles Davis, *Dark Magus*, Columbia, 1975
- Dr S. Gachet, *Audiomaze*, Labello Blanco, 1995
- Herbie Hancock: *Hornets* from *Sextant*, Columbia Records, 1973
- Herbie Hancock: *You'll Know When You Get There* from *Mwandishi*, Warner Bros, 1971
- Herbie Hancock, *Crossings*, Warner Bros, 1972
- Herbie Hancock, *Headhunters*, Columbia, 1973
- Herbie Hancock: *Nobu* from *Realization*, Columbia, 1974
- Jimi Hendrix: *And the Gods Made Love* from *Electric Ladyland*, Polydor, 1968
- George Russell, *Electronic Sonata for Souls Loved by Nature* (1980), Soul Note, 1980
- George Russell, *Electronic Sonata for Souls Loved by Nature* (1968), Soul Note, 1985a
- George Russell, *The African Game*, Blue Note, 1985b
- Lenny White, *Venusian Summer*, Nemperor Records, 1975
- Gunter Kaiser, *The Medusa Head*, Poster Art, 1969
- Mati Klarwein, Sleeve Art to *Bitches Brew*, CBS, 1970
- Robert Springett, Sleeve Art to *Sextant*, Columbia, 1973; to *Crossings*, Warner Bros, 1972; to *Thrust*, CBS, 1974
- Tadanoori Yokoo, Sleeve Art to *Agharta*, CBS, 1975
- *Il Deserto Russo*, Michaelangelo Antonioni, 1964, NCA
- *The Terminator*, James Cameron, 1984, 4 Front Video

Thoughtware: Transmaterializing the Breakbeat

[013] 'The discovery of...', Karlheinz Stockhausen in Cott, 1974, p37; 'After I took...', Grandmaster Flash in Toop, 1982, p128

[014] 'Turntable Terranova', The Mighty Upsetter, Sleevenote Manifesto to The Mighty Upsetter, 1975; 'omnigenre: I understood that HipHop was an amalgamation of all forms of music...', DJ Shadow in Matt Chicone, *Rap Pages*, Oct 1996; 'The Incredible Bongo Band...', Grandmaster Flash, Toop, 1982, p72; 'in a mythical battle', ibid, p128; 'the fantasy level', ibid, p128

[015] 'skratchadelia', from track title *Skratchadelikizm*, Sonz of A Loop da Loop Era, 1993

[017] 'Grandmaster cuts faster...', George, 1992, p73; 'I was like...', Grandmaster Flash in Dan Keeling, *Melody Maker*, June 29, 1996; 'My mind ain't...', New Kingdom, 1996; 'The record does what...', Ice T in Mike Barnes, *The Wire*, July 1996; 'Leave that shit...', Grandmaster Flash, Toop, 1982, p130

[018] 'Doing *Bring the*...', Chuck D, Sleevenotes to Terminator X, 1991

[019] 'Given four film...', John Cage, *The Future of Music: Credo* in Kostelanetz, 1970, p54; 'I could take...', Marley Marl in Rose, 1994, p79; 'I wanted to...', Marley Marl, ibid, p79

[020] 'sudden multiplication of...', Virilio, 1991, p72

[021] 'turntabilization', from album title *Strictly Turntabilized*, DJ Krush, 1995

[023] 'Mars needs', Double Dee & Steinski, 1984

- John Cage, *Imaginary Landscape No 1* (1937), Hat Art
- Chic, *Good Times*, Atlantic, 1979
- DJ Krush, *Strictly Turntabilized*, Mo Wax, 1995
- DJ Zinc, *Supersharp Shooter Remix*, Ganja Records, 1996
- Double Dee & Steinski, *Lesson 3*, Tommy Boy, 1984
- Eric B & Rakim: *I Know You Got Soul* from *Paid in Full*, 4th & Broadway, 1986
- Grandmaster Flash & the Furious Five: *The Amazing Adventures of Grandmaster Flash on the Wheels of Steel*, Sugarhill, 1981
- Grand Wizard Theodore: *Can I get a Soul Clap* from *Old School Butter*, Tuff City Records, 1997
- The Hellers, *Singers, Talkers, Players, Swingers and Doers*, 1968, label unknown
- The Incredible Bongo Band: *Bongo Rock* from *Return to Bongo Mania*, 1973, MGM
- Bob James: *Take Me to the Mardi Gras* from *Bob James Two*, Columbia, 1975
- The Knights of the Turntable, *Fresh Mess [... Jam your Radio]*, JDC Records, 1985
- Kraftwerk, *Trans-Europe Express*, Capitol, 1985
- Mantronix: *Electronic Energy Of...* from *Music Madness*, Virgin, 1986
- Mantronix: *Loop 2; Loop 3; Loop 7* from *King of the Beats*, EMI, 1988
- Marley Marl, *Marley Marl Scratch*, Nia Records, 1985
- The Mighty Upsetter, *Kung Fu Meets the Dragon*, Justice League, 1975
- New Kingdom: *Animal* from *Paradise Don't Come Cheap*, Gee Street, 1996
- Phuture, *Acid Tracks*, Trax, 1987
- Public Enemy, *Bring the Noise*, Def Jam, 1989
- Queen, *Another One Bites the Dust*, EMI, 1981
- Sonz of A Loop da Loop Era: *Skratchadelikizm* from *Flowers in My Garden*, Suburban Base, 1993
- Spoonie Gee & The Sequence, *Monster Jam*, Sugarhill, 1981
- Terminator X, *Terminator X and the Valley of the Jeep Beats*, Def Jam, 1991
- Thin Lizzy: *Johnny the Fox meets Jimmy the Weed* from *Johnny the Fox*, Vertigo, 1976

- 3D/Robert Del Naja, Sleeve Art to *Headz 2*, Mo Wax, 1996
- The Winstons: *Amen Brother* from *Ultimate Breaks and Beats, Volume 2*, Street Beat Records, 1986

- *Flash Gordon*, Michael Hodges, 1980, BMG Video

Thoughtware: Sampladelia of the Breakbeat

[025] 'building molecules on...', Ultramagnetic MCs, 1996

[026] 'We're opening the magnetic field', Critical Beatdown, 1987; 'the auditory canals are...', Ultramagnetic MCs, 1987; 'elevating a physical...', ibid; 'ultrapower flowing', Four Horsemen of the Apocalypse, 1993; 'All elements converge...', Ultramagnetic MCs, 1996; 'inhabitants disappear through...', Ultramagnetic MCs, 1996 (*Smoking Dust*); 'wires leaking with...', Four Horsemen of the Apocalypse, 1993 (*Bring it*)

[027] 'hypothetical basic mechanisms', Ultramagnetic MCs, 1987; 'like a Commodore...', ibid; 'rhymes in my...', Critical Beatdown, 1987 (*Ain't it*); 'combinating elements', Ultramagnetic MCs, 1996 (*Brainiac*); 'On vocab, connect...', Critical Beatdown, 1987 (*When I Burn*); 'fuel ignite blood', Ultramagnetic MCs, 1996 (*Brainiac*)

[028] 'power ignites the...', Four Horsemen of the Apocalypse, 1993 (*Bring it*); 'Artemis Level 4', ibid; 'I Get a Warp...', Ultramagnetic MCs, 1996 (*Smoking Dust*); 'I'lltakeyourbraintoanotherdimension...', Ultramagnetic MCs, Critical Breakdown, 1987 (*Critical Beatdown*)‹›The Prodigy, 1992; 'truly confuse as..., Ultramagnetic MCs, 1987; 'advancing technical', ibid

[029] 'charging energy at...', Ultramagnetic MCs, 1996 (*Brainiac*); 'boosting crystalloids ...'as, ibid; 'cybotron, completely on...' ibid; 'To survive we must...', Cybotron, Sleevenote Manifesto to Cybotron, 1985; 'What is an...', Rammellzee in Malu Halaza, *Soul Underground*, Summer 1988; 'your common and...', Sunz of Man, 1995b; 'Science and technology...', Virilio, 1983a, p62; '*Astro Black* is...', Sun Ra in Lock, 1994, p148

[030] 'Turntable Terranova', The Mighty Upsetter, Sleevenote Manifesto to The Mighty Upsetter, 1975; 'I'm here to...', Eric B & Rakim, 1988; 'Graffiti is not...', Bando in Chalfont & Prigoff, 1987, p72; 'Graffiti is a...', Rammellzee, Malu Halaza, 1988

[031] 'Wildstyle is totally..., Fab 5 Freddy in Gablik, 1982, p72; 'ballet of postures...', McLuhan, 1962, p61; 'I make letters...', Bando, Chalfont & Prigoff, 1987, p 71; 'You have the...', Rammellzee, *Ikonoklast Panzerism Manifesto* in Beat Culture, Artforum, 1985, quoted in Tate, 1992, p155; 'Their sound is...', Rammellzee, ibid, p155; 'a constellation of...', Mailer, 1970, p149

[032] 'a mathematician and...', Rammellzee, 1987; 'builds weapons for...', ibid; 'The Romans stole...', Rammellzee, *The Movement of the Letter: The Polishing of the Equation Rammellzee* in Dery, 1993, p739; 'means symbol destroyer...', Rammellzee, Tate, 1992, p155

[033] 'on Aerodynamics and...', Rammellzee & Shock Dell, 1987; 'But we want...', ibid; 'All formation and...', ibid; 'As the Interrogator...', ibid; 'In a war...', Rammellzee, 1992, p145/155

[034] 'Wrath of the...', from track title *Wrath of the Math*, Jeru the Damajaa, 1996; 'The infinity sign...', Rammellzee, Tate, 1992, p155; 'The 4 integers...', Rammellzee & Shock Dell, 1987; 'The effective mathematician...', Wiener, 1989, p xi

[035] 'Mental Machine', Electrifying Mojo, from title of *The Mental Machine: a Book Opera*, Electrifying Mojo, 1993, J Stone Audio Books, 1993; 'You must talk...', Rammellzee & Shock

Dell, 1987; 'Only he has...', ibid; 'You hold the...', ibid; 'You have just gotten...', ibid
[036] 'We want you...', ibid; 'Sometimes I don't...', Kool Keith in Andre Daniel, *True Magazine*, July 1996; 'Space is my...', Dr Octagon, 1996 (*Earth People*)
[038] 'I study and...', Kool Keith‹›Dr Octagon in Dave Tompkins, *Rap Pages*, July 1996; 'When he says...', Dr Octagon, Tompkins, July, 1996; 'The forms of...', Felix Guattari, *Chaosmosis*, Power Publications, 1995, p36; 'elevation', Dr Octagon, July, Tompkins, 1996; 'new terms...', ibid; 'advance technical' Kool Keith‹›Dr Octagon, Tompkins, July 1996; 'program one and...', Dr Octagon, 1996 (*3000*)
[039] 'I'll take a...', ibid (*Blue Flowers*); 'It's like if...', Dr Octagon, Tompkins, July, 1996; 'Dr Octagon was...', ibid; 'Haloes were found...', ibid; 'I see it...' Keith‹›Daniel, July 1996
[040] 'Vanishing victims kept...', Dr Octagon, 1996 (*Dr Octagon*); 'Megatron, Rejuvenate...', ibid (*No Awareness*); 'Galaxy Rays powerful!', ibid (*Raise It Up*); 'Controlled by gamma lights...', ibid (*Earth People*); 'Octagon, oxygen...', ibid; 'walking through a...', ibid (*Technical Difficulties*); 'My first impression...', ibid
[041] 'this sense of...', DuBois, 1969, p45; 'talking in everyone's...', Sir Menelik from Dr Octagon, 1996
[042] 'What of the others...', Sir Menelik in James Tai, *Urb 50*, Aug/Sept 96; 'the time when...', Chris Marker, *Sans soleil*, 1983; 'Does science reach...', Dr Octagon, 1996 (*On Production*); 'All mankind must...' Sir Menelik, from ibid
[043] 'Acoustic death by...', ibid; 'increase magnetic fields...', Dr Octagon, 1996 (*On Production*); 'We think as...', Mixmaster Mike in Bucky Fukumoto & Jamandru Reynolds, *Grand Royale*, Issue 4; 'It's the only...', Disk in Kevin Marques Moo, *URB 50*, Aug/Sept, 1996
[044] 'Identification Code unidentified...', Dr Octagon, 1996 (*Dr Octagon*); 'skin is green...', ibid; 'paramedic fetus of...', ibid (*Blue Flowers*); 'cybernetic microscopes, ibid; '2 telescopes that...' ibid; 'Church of the...', Dr Octagon, 1996 (*Blue Flowers*); 'a future pathological...', David Cronenberg in Chris Rodley, *Sight and Sound*, June 1996; 'out the skull,' Dr Octagon, 1996 (*Earth People*); 'necks for the...', ibid; 'I study and...', Kool Keith‹›Dr Octagon, Tompkins, 1996; 'macroscope', from track title *Macroscope*, Cyclops 4000‹›Sir Menelik, 1997; 'operate on patients...', Kool Keith‹›Dr Octagon, Tompkins, 1996; 'intestinal surgery', Dr Octagon, 1996 (*I Got to Tell You*); 'saliva', ibid; 'basic human design', from track title *Basic Human Design* from Jeff Mills, 1994
[045] 'I would just...', Kool Keith‹›Dr Octagon, Tompkins, July, 1996; 'bees around your...', Dr Octagon, 1996 (*On Production*); 'naked pictures of,' ibid (*Dr Octagon*); 'the cartoon Donald', ibid; 'Sometime I don't...', Kool Keith‹›Dr Octagon, Tompkins, July, 1996; 'half shark, half...', Dr Octagon, 1996 (*Mr Gerbik*); 'masturbating with humans...', ibid (*Dr Octagon*); 'leading humans with...', ibid; 'all Earth people...', ibid (*Earth People*); 'you there like...', Kool Keith‹›Dr Octagon, Tompkins, July, 1996
[046] 'Doctor Ludicrous into...', Dr Octagon, 1996 (*Dr Octagon*); 'The perfect enzyme's...', ibid (*Technical Difficulties*); 'Oh man homey...', The Geto Boys, 1992
[047] 'I'm having illusions...', Cypress Hill, 1995 (*Illusions*); 'Looking at the...', Sly Stone, 1972; 'schizophony', R. Murray Schafer, *Radical Radio* in Strauss, 1993, p292; 'They took a sonogram...', Gravediggaz, 1994 (*Diary of*)
[048] 'It's a form of psychosis...', Tricky in Gavin Martin, *NME*, 28 Oct 1995; 'I believe you're...', Redman in Adario Strange, *The Source*, Nov 1994
[049] 'Now I dwell...', Gravediggaz, 1994; 'Holycore', Scientific Shabazz‹›Shabazz the Disciple in Joyce, *URB*, 40; 'Heaven and Hell is...', The RZA, Everett True, *Melody Maker*, Sept 17, 1994; 'learning the torture...', The RZA, Everett True, 1994

[050] 'I contain the...', Sunz of Man, 1995b; 'Visions of me...', Sunz of Man, 1995a; 'the depths of', ibid; 'I was shown...', Genius, 1995

[051] 'All this seems...', Antonin Artaud, *On the Balinese Theater* in Rothenberg & Rothenberg, 1983, p239; 'soldiers of idolatry...', Sunz of Man, 1995a; 'the universal warlord...', ibid; 'came together for...', ibid; 'Hearken as the...', ibid; 'be done away...', ibid; 'side effects...', ibid; 'insanity enters humanity...', ibid; 'this technique is...', ibid; 'the 4 run...', Sunz of Man, 1995b; 'a light beam...', Killah Priest, Genius, 1995; 'bring the wicked...', Sunz of Man, 1995a

[052] 'Something outside had...', Dick, 1992, p209; 'We relinquished the..., ibid, p209-10

[053] 'The brain is...', Deleuze & Guattari, 1987, p64; 'When you trip...', Manuel De Landa in Erik Davis, *Mondo 2000*, Nov 1992; 'I could get...', George Clinton in Lloyd Bradley, *Mojo*, Sept 1996; 'Descriptions of it...', Stevens, 1987, p343

[054] 'The catastrophe represents...', J. G. Ballard, *Cataclysms and Dooms*, in Ballard, 1996, p209-10; 'We can't clean...', Clinton, Bradley, Sept 1996; 'We took the...', ibid; 'Thought is biological...', Rene Menil in Richardson & Fisalkowski, 1996, p150; 'Behold, I Am Funkadelic...', Funkadelic, 1970a

[055] 'the eating of...', Sontag, 1994, p99; 'If you will...', Funkadelic, 1970a; 'I have tasted...', Funkadelic, 1971; 'could scare you..., Roy Haynes, Sleevenotes to Funkadelic, 1993

[056] 'into the service...', Salvador Dali in Sartre, 1988, p153; 'my brain C3...', Jeru the Damajaa, 1994; 'Equipped with contradictory...', Delany, 1976, p26; 'Can you fly...', Tricky, 1995 (*Abbaon Fat*); 'Sampling allows...', Greg Tate in *The Last Angel of History*, 1995

[057] 'Yesternow', from track title *Yesternow*, Davis, 1970; 'A mixture of...', Ishmael Reed, *Neo HooDoo Manifesto* in Rothenberg & Rothenberg, 1983, p420

[058] 'Headspace is the...', Schafer, 1973, p31

[059] 'I feel alien...', Tricky in Simon Reynolds, *Melody Maker*, June 24, 1995; 'everything happens at...', Tricky, David Bennun, *Melody Maker*, Jan 21, 1995; 'My brain thinks...', Tricky, 1995 (*Hell is*)

[060] 'The first sign...', Job in *The Lawnmower Man*; 'So it seems...', Tricky & Gravediggaz, 1996; 'I smoke a...', Tricky, Martin, Oct 1995; 'Space race the...', Tricky & Gravediggaz, 1996

[061] 'I escape with...', Organized Konfusion, 1991; 'There is no...', Tricky & Gravediggaz, 1996; 'You have been...', ibid

· James Brown: *Mind Power* from *The Payback*, Polydor, 1973
· James Brown, *Revolution of the Mind*, Polydor, 1973
· Critical Beatdown: *Ain't It Good to You*; *When I Burn*; *Critical Beatdown* from *Critical Beatdown*, Next Plateau, 1987
· Cybotron, *Enter*, Fantasy Records, 1985
· Cyclops 4000‹›Sir Menelik, *Macroscope*, Ultimate Dilemma, 1997
· Cypress Hill: *Ultraviolet Dreams* from *Cypress Hill*, Ruffhouse/ Columbia, 1992
· Cypress Hill: *Illusions*; *Temple of Boom* from *Temple of Boom*, Ruffhouse/Columbia, 1995
· Miles Davis: *Yesternow* from *A Tribute to Jack Johnson*, Columbia, 1970
· Dr Octagon: *I Got to Tell You*; *Earth People*; *No Awareness*; *Technical Difficulties*; *Blue Flowers*; *Dr Octagon*; *Wild and Crazy*; *On Production* from *Dr Octagon*, Bulk/Mo Wax, 1996
· Electrifying Mojo, *The Mental Machine: a Book Opera*, J Stone Audio Books, 1993
· Eric B & Rakim, *Follow the Leader Dub*, MCA, 1988
· Four Horsemen of the Apocalypse: *Bring It Down to Earth*; *We Are the Horsemen*; *Raise it Up* from *Four Horsemen of the Apocalypse*, Mercury, 1993

- Funkadelic: *What Is Soul*; *Mommy What's A Funkadelic* from *Funkadelic*, Westbound, 1970a
- Funkadelic: *Eulogy and Light* from *Free Your Mind And Your Ass Will Follow*, Westbound, 1970b
- Funkadelic: *Maggot Brain*; *Wars of Armageddon* from *Maggot Brain*, Westbound, 1971
- Funkadelic: *America Eats Its Young* from *America Eats Its Young*, Westbound, 1972
- Funkadelic, *Cosmic Slop*, Westbound, 1973
- Funkadelic, *Standing on the Verge of Getting It On*, Westbound, 1974
- Funkadelic, *Let's Take It to the Stage*, Westbound, 1975
- Funkadelic, *Tales of Kidd Funkadelic*, Westbound, 1976
- Funkadelic, *Hardcore Jollies*, Westbound, 1976
- Funkadelic, *Music For Your Mother*, Westbound, 1993
- Genius: *Greyhound Part 2 Remix* from *Experimental Remixes*, Jon Spencer Blues Explosion, Matador, 1995
- The Geto Boys, *Mind Playing Tricks on Me*, Rap-a-Lot, 1992
- Jerry Goldsmith, *Planet of the Apes OST*, Project 3 Records, 1967
- Gravediggaz: *Diary of a Madman*; *Mommy What's a Gravedigga?*; *Dial 1-800 Suicide* from *Niggamortis*, Island, 1994
- Japan: *Ghost* from *Tin Drum*, Virgin, 1981
- Jeru the Damajaa: *Mental Stamina* from *The Sun Rises in the East*, ffrr, 1994
- Jeru the Damajaa, *Wrath of the Math*, Payday, 1996
- Led Zeppelin: *Friends* from *Led Zeppelin 3*, Atlantic, 1972
- Massive Attack, *Blue Lines*, Virgin, 1991
- Method Man: *Sub Crazy* from *Tical*, Def Jam, 1994
- The Mighty Upsetter, *Kung Fu Meets the Dragon*, Justice League, 1975
- Jeff Mills: *Basic Human Design* from *Waveform Transmissions Volume 3*, Tresor, 1994
- Organized Konfusion: *Releasing Hypnotical Gases* from *Organized Konfusion*, Hollywood Basic, 1991
- The Prodigy, *Outta Space*, XL, 1992
- Public Enemy: *Black Steel in the Hour of Chaos* from *It Takes a Nation of Millions to Hold Us Back*, Def Jam, 1988
- Rammellzee & Shock Dell, *The Lecture*, GeeStreet/Island Records, 1987
- Rammellzee vs K-Rob, *Beat Bop*, Profile Records, 1983
- Sly Stone: *Thank You Falletin Me Be Mice Elf Agin* from *There's A Riot Going On*, Edsel, 1972
- Sunz of Man, *Soldiers of Darkness*, Wu Tang Records, 1995a
- Sunz of Man, *Five Arch Angels*, Wu Tang Records, 1995b
- Tricky, *Aftermath*, Island, 1994
- Tricky: *Abbaon Fat Tracks*; *Hell Is Round the Corner* from *Maxinquaye*, Island, 1995
- Tricky & Gravediggaz, *Psychosis*, Island, 1996
- Ultramagnetic MCs: *Brainiac*; *Smoking Dust* from *The Basement Tapes*, Tuff City Records, 1996
- Ultramagnetic MCs: *MCs' Ultra [Part II]*, City Beat, 1987
- Stevie Wonder, *Innervisions*, Motown, 1973

- Jean-Michel Basquiat, *Pegasus*, painting, 1987
- Pedro Bell, Sleeve Art for *Cosmic Slop*, Westbound, 1973; *Standing on the Verge of Getting It On*, Westbound, 1974; *Let's Take It to the Stage*, Westbound, 1975; *Tales of Kidd Funkadelic*, Westbound, 1976; *Hardcore Jollies*, Westbound, 1976
- Don Brautigan, Sleeve Art for James Brown, *The Payback*, Polydor, 1973
- Effram Wolf, Sleeve Art to *Innervisions*, Motown, 1973

- *Atomic Cafe*, Kevin Rafferty/Jayne Loader/Pierce Rafferty, 1982, Academy Video
- *Beneath the Planet of the Apes*, Ted Post, 1970, NCA
- *Coma*, Michael Crichton, 1978, NCA
- *Dead Ringers*, David Cronenberg, 1988, 20th Century Fox Home Entertainment
- *Jacob's Ladder*, Adrian Lyne, 1990, 4 Front Video
- *The Last Angel of History*, John Akomfrah/Black Audio Film Collective, 1995, NCA
- *The Lawnmower Man*, Brett Leonard, 1992, First Independent Video
- *The Man Who Fell to Earth*, Nic Roeg, 1976, NCA
- *Sans soleil*, Chris Marker, 1983, Academy Video
- *The Terminator*, James Cameron, 1984, 4 Front Video

Thoughtware: Inner Spatializing the Song

[062] 'I put my...', Lee Perry in Toop, 1995, p113
[063] 'I introduce myself...', Indelible MCs, 1997; 'I see the...', Lee Perry in Toop, 1995, p113; 'You are listening...', Lee Perry in Kevin Martin, *The Wire*, May 1995; 'We're taking over...', The Mighty Upsetter, Sleevenote Manifesto to The Mighty Upsetter, 1975; 'Well, the drums...', Lee Perry in Thomas Markett, *Grand Royale 2*, 1995-1996; 'The drum controls...', Lee Perry in Toop, 1995, p114
[064] 'We are here..., The Mighty Upsetter, Sleevenote Manifesto to The Mighty Upsetter, 1975
[065] 'So me join...', Lee Perry, Martin, 1995
[066] 'His method of...', Steve Barrow in *Dubcatcher*, April/May 1994

- 4 Hero: *The Paranormal in Four Forms* from *Various Artists, Macro Dub Infection*, Virgin, 1995
- Indelible MCs, *The Fire in Which You Burn*, Rawkus, 1997
- The Mighty Upsetter, *Kung Fu Meets the Dragon*, Justice League, 1975
- The Mighty Upsetter: *The Tackro* from *Shocks of the Mighty*, Attack, 1988
- The Upsetter: *Bird in Hand*; *The Lion* from *Return of the Super Ape*, Trojan, 1978
- The Upsetter: *Revolution Dub*; *Woman's Dub*; *Kojak*; *Bush Weed*; *Rain Drops* from *Revolution Dub*, Esoldun, 1975

- *Farewell my Concubine*, Chen Kaige, 1993, Artificial Eye
- *Persona*, Ingmar Bergman, 1966, NCA

Thoughtware: Virtualizing the Breakbeat

[068] 'Technology has made...', Goldie in *The Last Angel of History*, 1995; 'Our drummers don't...', Kraftwerk, Andy Gill, *Mojo*, April 1997; 'thinking and hearing...', ibid; 'we've lost the...', Goldie in *Musik*, 1995; 'you're reading the...', ibid; 'You end up with...', Dego McFarlane in Tim Barr, *The Mix*, Aug 1996
[069] 'used to talk...', Dego McFarlane in Bethan Cole, *Mixmag*, Feb 1995; 'audiomaze', from track title *Audiomaze*, Gachet, 1995; 'subcraziness', from track title *SubCrazy*, Method Man, 1994; 'kids coming up...', Dego McFarlane in *Musik*, 1995
[070] 'Science today has...', Paul Virilio, *Block 14*, Autumn 1988; 'phantasmaphysics', Foucault, 1977, p172; 'speculative fantasy of...', Ballard, 1996, p198

[071] 'Phizical', from track title *Phyzical*, Roni Size, 1994; 'limb by limb...', from track title *Limb by Limb*, Marvellous Cain, 1994; 'We are obliged...', Norman Mailer, *The White Negro*, in Feldman & Gartenberg, 1960, p295

[072] 'temporal resolving powers', Chion, 1994, p134; 'flava in the...', track title *Flava in your Ear*, Mack, 1994; 'When kinetic sensations...', Chion, 1994, p137; 'we used to...', Mark Clair in Tim Barr, *The Mix*, Aug 1996; 'needlepoint magick', track title of *Needlepoint Magick*, Magick, 1995

[073] 'The graffiti artist', Goldie in *Musik*, 1995; 'Wildstyle was the...', Kaze 2 in Chalfont & Palmer, 1984, p71; 'three gravitional forces...' J. J. Wagener in Escher, 1989, p99; 'background and foreground', ibid

[074] 'Across the horizontal', Goldie, Sleevenotes to Goldie, 1995a; 'I can conceive...', Escher, 1989, p121; 'The graffiti artist...', Goldie in *Musik*, 1995; 'The loops, they've...', Goldie in Simon Reynolds, *The Wire*, Sept 1994

[075] 'On *Timeless*, there...', Rob Playford in Tim Barr, *The Mix*, Aug 1996; 'different steps of...', Escher, 1989, p121; 'We'd go round...', Playford, Barr, 1996; 'snaking out a...', Goldie, Reynolds, 1994; 'the zord, the blade...', ibid

[076] 'With a sample...', A Guy Called Gerald in Peter Shapiro, *The Wire*, Oct 1996; 'Does time work...', A Guy Called Gerald, Sleevenote Manifesto to A Guy Called Gerald, 1995; 'You could create', Gerald, Shapiro, 1996; 'We have advanced...', A Guy Called Gerald, Sleevenote Manifesto to A Guy Called Gerald, 1995; 'Say someone has...', Gerald, Shapiro, 1996

- Brian Eno, *Apollo Atmospheres & Soundtracks*, EG Records, 1983
- 4 Hero: *Solar Emissions*; *Shadow Run*; *Sunspots*; *Wrinkles in Time* from *Parallel Universe*, Reinforced Records, 1994
- 4 Hero: *The Paranormal in 4 Forms* from *Various Artists, Macro Dub Infection*, Virgin, 1995
- 4 Hero, *Inner City Life Part 1 Remix*, ffrr, 1995
- Dr S. Gachet, *Audiomaze*, Labello Blanco, 1995
- Goldie: *Jah the Seventh Seal* from *Timeless*, London, 1995a
- Goldie, *Timeless, i. Inner City Life ii. Pressure iii. Jah*, ffrr Records, 1995b
- Goldie, *Inner City Life*, ffrr, 1995c
- Goldie, *T3*, Metalheadz, 1997
- A Guy Called Gerald: *Finley's Rainbow*; *The Glok Track* from *Black Secret Technology*, Juice Box, 1995
- A Guy Called Gerald, *Nazinji Zaka*, Juicebox, 1995
- Gustav Holst, *Planets Suite*, Deutsche Gramophon, date unknown
- Craig Mack, *Flava in Your Ear*, RCA, 1994
- Jay Magick, *Needlepoint Magick*, Metalheadz, 1995
- Metalheadz, *Terminator*, Synthetic Hardcore Phonography, 1992
- Method Man: *SubCrazy* from *Tical*, Def Jam, 1994
- Marvellous Cain, *Limb by Limb*, Suburban Base, 1994
- Nookie, *Inner City Life Remix*, ffrr, 1995
- Peshay, *Inner City Life Mix*, ffrr, 1995
- Peshay, *Jah Remix*, Razors Edge, 1996
- Roni Size, *Phyzical*, Full Cycle Records, 1994
- Roni Size, *Inner City Life Instant Remix*, ffrr, 1995
- Rufige Kru, *Terminator II Remix*, Reinforced, 1993

- Ryuichi Sakamoto, *Riot in Lagos*, Island, 1980
- Vangelis, *Blade Runner OST*, East West, 1994

- M.C. Escher, *Relativity*, lithograph, 1953
- M.C. Escher, *Tetrahedral Planetoid*, lithograph, 1953
- Goldie, *Future World Machine*, aeroglyph, reproduced in Chalfont & Prigoff, 1987, p65

- *2001: A Space Odyssey*, Stanley Kubrick, 1968, MGM Home Entertainment
- *The Last Angel of History*, John Akomfrah/Black Audio Film Collective, 1995, NCA

Thoughtware: Programming Rhythmatic Frequencies

[078] 'It is the rationalizing...', Georges Canguilhem, *Machine and Organism* in Crary & Kwinzer, 1992, p63
[079] 'I need an...', Edgard Varèse in Ouellette, 1973, p147
[080] 'Sonotron', Xenakis, 1974, p 237; 'Imagine somewhere in...', Man Parrish, 1983
[081] 'power in the...', Darth Vader in *The Empire Strikes Back*; 'Clear are these...', Cybotron, 1985 *(Clear)*; 'Electronic Music affects...', Merce Cunningham in Virilio, 1995, p124; 'Boogalooin', rollin'...', Shrimp in Ben Higa, *Rap Pages*, Sept 1996
[082] 'Trains themselves are...', Kraftwerk in Mark Sinker, *Music Technology*, 1991 [see also Webtalk: Synthsite/Roland Discussion Group http://neural 13.cs.york.ac.uk/cgi-bis/Roland(33K)]; 'our synthesizers to...', Kraftwerk in Mark Sinker in Kempster, 1996, p96
[083] 'dreaded Drexciyan stingray...', The Unknown Writer, Label Fiction from Drexciya, 1993a; 'pregnant America-bound...', Drexciya, Sleevenote Manifesto to Drexciya, 1997
[084] 'water breathing, aquatically...', ibid; 'The ships landed...', Mark Sinker, *The Wire*, Sept 1992; 'Did they migrate...', Drexciya, Sleevenote Manifesto to Drexciya, 1997; 'The border between...', Donna Haraway, *A Manifesto for Cyborgs* in Haraway, 1991, p149; 'This is Drexciyan...', Drexciya, 1993b *(Bubble Metropolis)*
[085] 'When the first...', Clarke, 1992, p157; 'magnetron which puts...', Killah Priest from Sunz of Man, 1995; 'Video games are...', Chris Marker in *Sans soleil*
[086] 'the factories that...', Kraftwerk in Bussy, 1993, p63; 'automatic machines are...', Wiener, 1989, p162
[087] '*More Bounce to*...', Shrimp in Ben Higa, *Rap Pages*, Sept 1996; 'a square rollout...', JoJo in Ben Higa, *Rap Pages*, Sept 1996
[088] 'When you pop...', Shrimp, Higa, 1996; 'android doowop', Simon Reynolds in Weisbard, 1995, p216; 'We are beginning...', Manuel De Landa in Erik Davis, *Mondo 2000*, Nov 1992; 'EssR'ays', from track title *EssR'ay [Reece Mix]*, Reece, 1994
[089] 'For a very...', Gertrude Stein, *Composition as Explanation* in Kostelanetz, 1993; 'It wasn't looping...', The Jungle Brothers, Toure, *The Source*, July 1993; 'Arhythmic, asymmetrical, alinear...', ibid
[090] 'the wind of...', Christopher Walken in *The Addiction*
[091] 'You must learn...', The Jungle Brothers, Toure, July 1993; 'No... We must...', The Jungle Brothers, 1993 *(Manmade Material)*
[092] 'Brainstorms, Brainstorms, mass...', The Jungle Brothers, 1993 *(Spittin' Wicked)*; 'The paradox I...', Organized Konfusion, 1991; 'I'm gone... I'm', Af Next Man Flip in David Davies, *i-D*, Nov 1991; 'scientific people...', ibid

- Art of Noise, *Close [To the Edit]*, Zang Tuum Tumb, 1984
- Cybotron: *Clear* from *Enter*, Fantasy Records, 1985
- Drexciya: *Sea Snake* from *Deep Sea Dweller*, Shockwave Records, 1992
- Drexciya, *Aquatic Invasion EP*, UR, 1993a
- Drexciya: *Danger Bay*; *Positron Island*; *Bubble Metropolis* from *Bubble Metropolis* EP, UR 1993b
- Drexciya: *Intensified Magnetron* from *Molecular Enhancement EP*, Rephlex, 1993c
- Drexciya: *The Red Hills of Lardossa*; *The Basalt Zone 4.97Z* from *The Unknown Aquazone Aquapak*, UR, 1994 ibid
- Drexciya: *Darthouven Fish Men* from *The Journey Home EP*, Warp, 1995
- Drexciya, *The Return of Drexciya*, UR, 1996
- Drexciya, *Uncharted*, Sold In Detroit, 1996
- Drexciya, *The Quest*, Submerge, 1997
- Haashim, *Primrose Path*, Cutting Records, 1986
- The JBs: *[It's not the Express] It's the JBs' Monaurail* from *Hustle with Speed*, Polydor, 1975
- Jonzun Crew, *Space Is the Place*, Tommy Boy, 1983
- The Jungle Brothers: *Blahbludify*; *Manmade Material*; *Spittin' Wicked Randomness*; *For the Headz at Company Z* from *J Beez Wit the Remedy*, WEA, 1993
- The Jungle Brothers, *Crazy Wisdom*, WEA, unreleased
- Kraftwerk, *Autobahn*, EMI, 1975
- Kraftwerk, *Radioactivity*, Capitol, 1976
- Kraftwerk: *Showroom Dummies* from *Trans-Europe Express*, EMI, 1977
- Kraftwerk, *Tour de France [Francois Kervorkian Remix]*, EMI, 1984
- Man Parrish: *In the Beginning* from *Man Parrish*, Importe/12, 1983
- Organized Konfusion: *Releasing Hypnotical Gases* from *Organized Konfusion*, Hollywood Basic, 1991
- Reece: *EssR'ay [Reece Mix]* from *Forces*, Network/KMS 1994
- Soul Sonic Force, *Planet Rock*, Tommy Boy, 1982
- Sunz of Man, *Soldiers of Darkness*, Wu Tang Records, 1995
- The Velvet Underground, *White Light White Heat*, Verve, 1968
- Zapp: *More Bounce to the Ounce* from *Zapp*, Warner Brothers, 1980
- Zapp, *Computer Love* from *Zapp IV U*, Warner Brothers, 1986
- Zapp: *I Play the Talkbox* from *Zapp 5*, Warner Brothers, 1987

- *The Addiction*, Abel Ferrara, 1997, Pathe Distribution
- *The Empire Strikes Back*, George Lucas, 1980, 20th Century Fox Home Entertainment
- *Sans soleil*, Chris Marker, 1983, Academy Video

Thoughtware: Synthetic Fiction/Electronic Thought

[093] 'The world of...', Marshall McLuhan & G. E. Stearn, *A Dialogue* in Stearn, 1968, p333
[094] 'For the white...', Brown, 1972; 'This is Cocaine...', Phuture, 1987; 'You have been...', ibid; 'Take a shot...', ibid
[096] 'Some Gods will...', Reed, 1976, p11; 'Parents, Don't let...', Bam Bam, 1994; 'Where's your child?...', ibid
[097] 'Nobody likes to...', ibid

[098] 'In the beginning...', Fingers Inc featuring Chuck Roberts, 1988; 'Once you enter...,
Fingers Inc, 1988; 'the automatic community', Walter Hughes, *In the Empire of the Beat*, in
Ross & Rose, 1994, p152

[099] 'The way to', Pat Cadigan in Trilling & Swezey, 1993, p110; 'emotions electric', track
title *Emotions Electric*, A Guy Called Gerald, 1988

[100] '[Kraftwerk] sounded straight...', Model 500 in Mark E.G, *Eternity 29*, May 1995

[101] 'the music is...', Rhythim is Rhythim, Sleevenotes to Various Artists, 1991; 'a continual
telescoping...', Rene Menil in Richardson & Fisalkowski, 1996, p73; 'We are misled...',
Samuel Butler, *The Book of the Machines*, in Butler, 1969, p239; 'Geography is replaced...',
Virilio, 1983a, p 61

[102] 'Techno City was...', 3070 in Jon Savage, Sleevenotes to Cybotron, 1994

[103] 'We dedicate this...', Cybotron, Sleevenote Manifesto to Cybotron, 1985

[105] 'thinking and hearing...', Kraftwerk, Gill, April 1997; 'drum sounds on...', Model 500
in Tim Barr, *Generator*, May 1995; 'Science fiction doesn't...', William Gibson in James Flint,
UK Wired, May 1996; 'It was so...', Model 500, Barr, May 1995; 'If you listen...', Model 500,
E.G., May 1995; 'Then I heard...', Model 500, Barr, May 1995

[106] 'medium which processes...', Marshall McLuhan in Molinaro, McLuhan & Toye, 1987,
p 427; 'The machine is...', Donna Haraway, *A Manifesto for Cyborgs* in Haraway, 1991, p180; 'takes
the immediate...', Norman Mailer, *The White Negro*, in Feldman & Gartenberg, 1960, p 298

[107] 'Berry Gordy built..., Model 500 in Sleevenotes to Various Artists, 1987; 'Today the
plants...', ibid; 'I'm probably more...', ibid; 'automanikk', album title *Automanikk*, A Guy
Called Gerald, 1991

[108] 'My concept has...', Rhythim is Rhythim in Kempster, 1996, p53; 'My string sounds...',
ibid

[109] 'UFOs, they're drawn...', Fox Mulder in *The X Files*; 'When the synthesizer...', Model
500, Barr, May 1995; 'I was into...', ibid; 'a story about...', Eddie 'Flashin' Fowlkes in Tim
Barr, *Musik*, Aug 1996; 'I wanted to...', Model 500 in *The Last Angel in History*, 1995; 'Tell
me if...', Model 500, 1985b

[110] 'They say there...', ibid; 'Things you haven't...', ibid; 'ufonic', album title *Ufonic*,
Sabalon Glitz, 1996; 'I'm driving through...', Model 500, 1985a

[111] 'It's like somebody...', Hank Shocklee in Rose, 1994, p80; 'technical assault
squadron...', from Sleevenotes to Public Enemy, 1989

[112] 'launched, fuelled, planted..., ibid; 'It started in..., Public Enemy, 1992c; 'Slaveships.
There are...', ibid; 'already been in...', Public Enemy, 1989

[113] 'robot', Karel Capek from *Opilec*, 1917, from Capek, 1923 (from the Czech term *robota*,
meaning compulsory labour or servitude, from *robotnik* meaning workman); 'the automatic
machine...', Wiener, 1989, p162; 'Not only physical...', Jones, 1963, p7; 'At the eve...', Public
Enemy, 1994; 'There is something...', Public Enemy, 1990 (*Contract on*)

[114] 'alarm for the World', Public Enemy, 1987 (*Rightstarter*); 'That noise came..., Chuck D
in Simon Reynolds, from Jones, 1996, p26; 'The drone on..., ibid

[115] 'Related to schizophrenia...', Schafer, 1977, p 91; 'the overkill of...', ibid; 'Turn it all...'
Eric 'Vietnam' Sadler in Rose, 1994, p74; 'functions of eyesight...', Virilio, 1991, p 27

[116] 'Final transmission...', Mad Mike, Run-Out Groove Communication, Galaxy 2 Galaxy,
1993 (*Hi-Tech Jazz*); 'Technology is not...', Virilio, 1983a, p138

[117] 'a project devised..., Mike Banks in Dow Jones, *Touch*, June 1991

[118] 'hard music from...', Underground Resistance, 1991e; 'you just want...', Joey Beltram
in Vaughan Allen, *Mixmag*, Jan 1992

[119] 'No hope, no...', Underground Resistance, several Communications, 1991/2; 'We could have...', Jon Hassell in Toop, 1995, p167; 'Undetectible', track title of Scan 7, 1995; 'you can hear...', Doyle Foreman in Reed, 1989, p193

[120] 'Techno is like..., Mike Banks in Peter Walsh, *Jockey Slut*, July/Aug 1994; 'There are definite...', ibid; 'We're silent and...', ibid; 'a sort of...', Baudrillard, 1995, p 43; 'Spectral Nomad', track title of The Vision‹›Robert Hood, 1995; '6 dark energy...', Label Communique, Suburban Knight, 1994

[121] 'the deprogramming of...', Banks, Walsh, July/Aug 1994

[122] 'The World Power...', World Power Alliance, 1992; 'Disappearance is our...', Virilio, 1983a, p148; 'Every visible power...', ibid, p148

[123] 'is a CPU...', Label Fiction from Scan 7, 1995; 'induce viruses and...', ibid; 'designed to destroy...', ibid; 'digitized and returned...', ibid; 'Technology takes the...', Goldie in *NME*, 1995

[124] 'repudiated any ethnic...', Juan Atkins‹›Model 500, Kempster, 1996, p44; 'It becomes increasingly informative to simulate the thought of the cops', Nick Land in o[rphan]d[rift›], 1995, p356

[125] 'Inventions, the creations...', Virilio, 1983a, p 63; 'An electronic instrument...', Robert Moog, *Historical & Prophetic Writings* in Vale & Juno, 1994, p134; 'personal electronic...', Banks, Walsh, July/Aug 1994

[126] 'The synthesiser is ...', Kraftwerk, Gill, April 1997; 'Techno will be...', Banks, Walsh, July/Aug 1994; 'Thought forms in...', Tristan Tzara in Leiris, 1989, p87

[127] 'Techno to me...', Banks, Walsh, July/Aug 1994

[128] 'so that if...', ibid

[130] 'Electric circuitry confers...', McLuhan & Fiore, 1967, p114

[131] 'mythic worlds of...', ibid, p100

[132] 'materialize an idea...', Jeff Mills in Paul Benney, *Jockey Slut*, June/July, 1996; 'Everything you press...', Mouse on Mars in Rob Young, *The Wire*, Dec 1994; 'the needle spirals', Catalogue Notes, Axis Catalogue, 1995

[133] 'showed us a...', Banks, Dow Jones, June 1991; 'a sudden multiplication', Virilio, 1991, p 72; 'You have to...', Mills, Benney, June/July 1996

[134] 'Imagine being in...', Sleevenote Manifesto from X-102, 1992; 'Saturn's rings were...', ibid

[135] 'How long a...', Mills, Benney, June/July 1996; 'What he sets...', Antonin Artaud, *On the Balinese Theater*, Rothenberg & Rothenberg, 1983, p239; 'Theories and subjects...', Axis Manifesto from Axis Catalogue, 1995

[136] 'When the needle...', Mills, Benney, June/July 1996; 'I recall a NASA...', Sleevenotes to Mills, 1997

• Bam Bam: *Where's Your Child* from *Bam Bam, Best of Westbrook Classics*, Tresor, 1994
• James Brown, *Revolution of the Mind*, Polydor, 1968
• James Brown, *King Heroin*, Polydor, 1972
• Alice Coltrane with Strings, *World Galaxy*, Impulse!, 1971
• John Coltrane, *Interstellar Space*, Impulse!, 1967
• Cybotron, *Techno City*, Fantasy, 1984
• Cybotron, *Enter*, Fantasy, 1985
• Cybotron, *Interface: The Roots of Techno*, Fantasy Records, 1994
• Fingers Inc, *Can You Feel It*, Jack Trax, 1988
• Fingers Inc featuring Chuck Roberts, *Can You Feel It*, Desire, 1988

- 4 Hero, *Mr Kirk's Nightmare*, Reinforced, 1991
- Galaxy 2 Galaxy: *Astral Apache [Star Stories]*; *Hi-Tech Jazz [The Science]*; *Hi-Tech Jazz [The Elements]* from *Galaxy 2 Galaxy EP*, UR, 1993
- A Guy Called Gerald, *Automanikk*, CBS, 1991
- A Guy Called Gerald: *Emotions Electric* from *Peel Sessions*, BBC Records, 1988
- Herbie Hancock, *Quasar*, CBS, 1972
- Grace Jones, *She's Lost Control*, Island, 1982
- Joy Division: *She's Lost Control* from *Unknown Pleasures*, Factory, 1979
- Roland Kirk, *Volunteer Slavery*, Atlantic, 1969
- Kraftwerk, *Die Mensch Maschine/The Man Machine*, EMI, 1978
- Kraftwerk, *The Model*, EMI, 1981
- Mandrill: *Two Sisters of Mercy* from *Solid*, Polydor, 1971
- A Martian from Detroit: *Stardancer* from *Red Planet 2*, Red Planet, 1993
- The Martian: *808˚ [Surface Temperature mix]* from *Red Planet 3*, Red Planet, 1994
- The Martian: *Journey to the Martian Polar Cap*, from *Red Planet 4*, Red Planet, 1994
- The Martian: *The Long Winter of Mars: Renegades on the Red Planet*; *Season of the Solar Wind*; *Base Station 303*; *Skypainter* from *Red Planet 5*, Red Planet, 1995
- The Martian: *Marisian Probes over Montana*; *Ghostdancer*, *Starchild* (as by The Martians and Starchild on the Mothership LMNO-Funk); *Windwalker* (as by The Martians, Additional Production by The Suburban Knight) from *Red Planet 6*, Red Planet, 1995
- The Martian: *Firekeeper* from *Red Planet 7*, Red Planet, 1997
- The Meters, *Just Kissed My Baby*, Epic, 1973
- Jeff Mills, *Inner Sanctum*, Axis, 1993
- Jeff Mills: *Utopia*; *Man from Tomorrow* from *Cycle 30 EP*, Axis, 1994
- Jeff Mills: *i9* from *The Other Day*, Axis, 1997
- Model 500, *Night Drive [thru Babylon]*, Metroplex, 1985a
- Model 500, *No UFOs [Original Vocal Mix]*, Metroplex, 1985b
- Phuture, *Your Only Friend*, Trax, 1987
- Public Enemy: *Rightstarter [Message to A Black Man]*; *Terminator X Speaks with his Hands*, *Megablast*; *Timebomb* from *Yo! Bum Rush the Show*, Def Jam, 1987
- Public Enemy: *Countdown to Armageddon*; *Mind Terrorist*; *Show 'em Whatcha Got*; *Rebel Without a Pause*; *Terminator X to the Edge of Panic*; *Louder than a Bomb* from *It Takes a Nation of Millions to Hold Us Back*, Def Jam, 1988
- Public Enemy, *Welcome to the Terrordome*, Def Jam, 1989
- Public Enemy: *Contract on the Love World Jam*, *War at 33.3*, *Incident at 66.6FM*, *Final Count of the Collision Between Us and the Damned*, *Welcome to the Terrordome* from *Fear of a Black Planet*, Def Jam, 1990
- Public Enemy, *Arizona Assassination Attempt Acca Double Dub*, Def Jam, 1992a
- Public Enemy, *By the Time I Get to Arizona*, Def Jam, 1992b
- Public Enemy: *Can't Truss It [Almighty Raw 125th Street Bootleg Mix]*, Def Jam 1992c
- Public Enemy: *Whole Lotta Love Goin' On in the Middle of Hell* from *Muse Sick N'Hour Message*, Def Jam, 1994
- Reece, *Just Another Chance*, KMS, 1988
- Rhythim is Rhythim, *Ikon*, Buzz/Transmat, 1992
- Rhythim is Rhythim, *Kao-tic Harmony*, Buzz/Transmat, 1992
- Sabalon Glitz, *Ufonic*, Organico, 1996
- Scan 7, *Undetectible EP*, UR, 1995

- Scientist: *Laser Attack*; *Space Invaders*; *Beam Down*; *Red Shift*; *Time Warp*; *Pulsar*; *De Materialise* from *Scientist Meets the Space Invaders*, Greensleeves, 1978
- Second Phase, *Mentasm [Joey Beltram Remix]*, R&S Records, 1991
- K. Alexi Shelby, *All for Lee·Sah*, Transmat, 1989
- Sleezy D, *I've Lost Control*, Trax, 1986
- Suburban Knight, *The Art of Stalking [Stalker Mix]*, Transmat, 1990
- Suburban Knight: *Mind of a Panther* from *Dark Energy EP*, UR, 1994
- Underground Resistance, *Cyberwolf EP*, UR, 1991a
- Underground Resistance, *Death Star EP*, UR, 1991b
- Underground Resistance, *Piranha EP*, 1991c
- Underground Resistance, *The Punisher EP*, UR, 1991d
- Underground Resistance, *Riot EP*, UR, 1991e
- Underground Resistance, *Revolution for Change*, Network, 1992
- Underground Resistance, *Seawolf EP*, UR, 1992
- Underground Resistance: *Biosensors in Tunnel Complex Africa* from *Electronic Warfare: Designs for Sonic Revolutions double EP*, UR, 1996
- Various Artists, *Electro 1-12*, Streetsounds, 1983-1988
- Various Artists, *Techno The New Dance Sound of Detroit*, 10 Records, 1987
- Various Artists, *Retro Techno*, Network, 1991
- Various Artists, *The Joint*, Suburban Base/Moving Shadow, 1994
- Various Artists, *The Deepest Shade of Techno*, Reinforced, 1994
- Various Artists, *Macro Dub Infection*, Virgin, 1995
- Various Artists, Deep Concentration, Om Records, 1997
- The Vision, *Spectral Nomad EP*, Metroplex, 1995
- John Williams, *OST Title Theme from Star Wars*, 1977, label unknown
- World Power Alliance: *WPA Backing Plate #1* from *Kamikaze EP*, UR, 1992
- World 2 World: *Jupiter Jazz* from *World 2 World EP*, UR, 1992
- X-101: *Rave New World*; *Mindpower* from *X-101 EP*, Tresor, 1991
- X-102: *Phoebe*; *Titan*; *Rhea*; *Tethys*; *Hyperion*; *C-Ring*; *B- Ring*; *Enceladus*; *A-Ring*; *Ground Zero [The Planet]* from *X-102 Discovers 'The Rings of Saturn'*, UR, 1992

- Jean-Michel Basquiat, *Pegasus*, painting, 1987
- Gunther Frohling, Sleeve Art for *Die Mensch Maschine*, EMI, 1978

- *Alien*, Ridley Scott, 1979, 20th Century Fox Home Entertainment
- *Alien Resurrection*, Philippe Jeunet, 1997, 20th Century Fox Home Entertainment
- *Alien³*, David Fincher, 1992, 20th Century Fox Home Entertainment
- *Aliens*, James Cameron, 1986, 20th Century Fox Home Entertainment
- *The Empire Strikes Back*, George Lucas, 1980, 20th Century Fox Home Entertainment
- *Ghost in the Shell*, Masamune Shirow, 1996, Manga Entertainment
- *The Man Who Fell to Earth*, Nic Roeg, 1976, NCA
- *The Last Angel of History*, John Akomfrah/Black Audio Film Collective, 1995, NCA
- *Metropolis*, Fritz Lang, 1927, Eureka Video
- *Predator 2*, Stephen Hopkins, 1990, 20th Century Fox Home Entertainment
- *2001: A Space Odyssey*, Stanley Kubrick, 1968, MGM Home Entertainment
- *Tron*, Stephen Lisberger, 1982, NCA
- *The X Files*, Chris Carter, 1993, 20th Century Fox Home Entertainment

Thoughtware: Mixadelic Universe

[138] 'Good Evening. Do...', Parliament, 1975a (*P Funk*); 'an invisible excitement...', R. Murray Schafer, *Radical Radio* in Strauss, 1993, p292

[139] 'We have taken...', Parliament, 1975a (*P Funk*); 'Welcome to the...', ibid; 'Coming to you...', ibid; 'Draw a spaceman...', Overton Lloyd in Lloyd Bradley, *Mojo*, Sept 1996

[140] 'ego tripping and...', Parliament, 1975b (*Dr Funkenstein*); 'And funk is...', Parliament, 1975b (*Prelude*); 'Like a trick...', Parliament, 1975a (*Unfunky UFO*); 'I was merely...', Bootsy Collins in Michael Gonzalez, *The Source*, Dec 1994; 'in which a...', Reed, 1989, p259; 'I've got a...', Collins, 1978 (*Hollywood Squares*)

[141] 'the mind to...', Stuart Cosgrove, *Collusion*, Sept 1983; 'When you meet...', Sly and the Family Stone, 1973 ibid; 'swings low', Parliament, 1975a (*Mothership Connection*); 'Light years in...', ibid; 'have returned to...', ibid; 'has been hidden...' Parliament, 1975b (*Prelude*); 'citizens of the...', Parliament, 1975a

[142] 'In the days...', Parliament, 1975b (*Prelude*); 'There in these...', ibid; 'super cool oh...', Overton Lloyd from Booklet to Parliament, 1977; 'And in a...', Lloyd, ibid; 'the active repression...', Sidran, 1995, p110; 'Picture within a...', Parliament, 1977 (*Sir Nose*)

[143] 'I am Sir...', ibid; 'the sub lim...', ibid; 'doing it to...', Parliament, 1975a (*P Funk*)

[144] 'Threee blind mice...', Parliament, 1977 (*Sir Nose*); 'I wanna be...', Collins, 1978 (*Roto-Rooter*); 'Have you ever...; Parliament, 1977 (*Funkentelechy*)

[145] 'you are a...', Burroughs, 1987, p156; 'a part of...', Ray Davis, Sleevenotes from Funkadelic, 1993; 'gaming on ya', track title *Gaming on Ya*, Parliament, 1975a; 'Pay attention because...', Parliament, 1977 (*Funkentelechy*); 'operative signals directing...' Schafer, 1977; 'overburden with logic', Slogan from Gatefold Inner Sleeve, Parliament, 1979; 'a positive force...', Parliament, 1979 (*Theme*); 'you're destined to...', Slogan from Gatefold Inner Sleeve, Parliament, 1979

[146] 'metaprogramming is an operation in which a central control system controls hundreds of thousands of programs operating in parallel simultaneously... metaprogramming is done outside the big solid state computers by the human programmers', Lily, 1974, p ix; 'Look at you...', Sly and the Family Stone, 1972; 'How do Yeaw...', Funkadelic, 1976a; 'really dog you', Prince Paul, *Vibe*, 1995; 'burning, churning and...' Parliament, 1975b (*Dr Funkenstein*); 'burning you on...', ibid

[147] 'urge overkill', Parliament, 1977; 'This is Mood...', ibid; 'Fasten your seat...', ibid; 'Do thoughts of...', Funkadelic, 1976a (*How do Yeaw*); 'Mood Mood, Someone...', Parliament, 1977; 'whole cultures could...', McLuhan, 1994, p28; 'Someone's talking, funking...', Parliament, 1977

[148] 'A funk a...', ibid; 'The secret to...', ibid; 'There's nothing that...', ibid

[149] 'You deserve a...', ibid; 'Everything was stacked...', Clinton, Bradley, Sept 1996

[150] 'Funk not only...' Parliament, 1977 (*Funkentelechy*); '"I'm gonna add..."', Larry Graham in *Dancing in the Streets*, BBC2, 1996; 'Whatcha gonna do...', Sun Ra, 1982

[151] 'We are the...', Parliament, 1978b; 'Now I lay...', ibid

[152] 'just Me, Myself...', De la Soul, 1989; 'A motion picture...', Parliament, 1978a (*Aqua Boogie*); 'We are a...', Karlheinz Stockhausen in Björk, *Dazed and Confused*, Aug 1996; 'raise to the...', Parliament, 1978a (*Deep*); 'a mystical meeting...', ibid (*The Motor*), 'on the same...', ibid (*Water Sign*)

[153] 'With the rhythm...', ibid (*Aqua Boogie*); 'Technology automatically causes...', Pedro Bell in James, 1995, p141; 'the primal act...', William Gibson, *Academy Leader* in Benedikt, 1991, p27

- Bootsy Collins: *Hollywood Squares*; *Roto-Rooter* from *Player of the Year*, Warner Brothers, 1978
- De la Soul, *Me Myself and I*, Big Life, 1989
- Funkadelic: *How do Yeaw view You?* from *Tales of Kidd Funkadelic*, Westbound, 1976a
- Funkadelic: *Undisco Kidd* from *Hardcore Jollies*, Westbound, 1976b
- Funkadelic: *One Nation Under a Groove*; *Who says a Funk Band Can't Play Rock Music* from *One Nation Under a Groove*, Warner Brothers, 1978
- Funkadelic, *Music for Your Mother*, Westbound, 1993
- Parliament: *P Funk [Wants to Get Funked Up]*; *Mothership Connection (Star Child)*; *Unfunky UFO*; from *Mothership Connection*, Casablanca, 1975a
- Parliament: *Prelude to Dr Funkenstein*; *The Clones of Dr Funkenstein*; *Gaming on Ya* from *The Clones of Dr Funkenstein*, Casablanca, 1975b
- Parliament: *Funkentelechy*; *Sir Nose D'Voidofunk*; *The Placebo Syndrome* from *Funkentelechy vs. The Placebo Syndrome*, Casablanca, 1977
- Parliament: *The Motor-Booty Affair*; *Aqua Boogie [A Psychoalphadiscobeta-bioaquadoloop]*; *[You're a Fish and I'm a] Water Sign*; *Deep* from *Motor-Booty Affair*, Casablanca, 1978a
- Parliament, *Flashlight 12" mix*, Casablanca, 1978b
- Parliament: *Gloryhallastoopid [Pin the Tale on the Funky]*; *Theme from the Black Hole* from *Gloryhallastoopid*, Casablanca, 1979
- Parliament: *Funkencyclo-p-dia* from *Tear the Roof Off 1974-1980*, Casablanca, 1993
- Sly and the Family Stone: *Running Away* from *There's a Riot Goin' On*, Edsel, 1972
- Sly and the Family Stone: *If You Want Me to Stay* from *Fresh*, Edsel, 1973
- Sun Ra, *Nuclear War*, Y Records, 1982

- *Dancing in the Streets*, BBC2, 1996
- *Dune*, David Lynch, 1984, Electric Pictures
- *The Man Who Fell to Earth*, Nic Roeg, 1976, NCA
- *Twin Peaks*, David Lynch, 1989, Warner Home Video

Thoughtware: Synthesizing the Omniverse

[154] 'The Impossible attracts...', Sun Ra in Lock, 1988, p15; 'I ain't part...', Sun Ra in Lock, 1994, p150
[155] 'The people have...', Sun Ra in *Space Is the Place*; 'It's after the...', June Tyson, ibid
[156] 'New Philosophy of...', James, 1992, pp153-160; 'even the dead...', Walter Benjamin, *Theses on the Philosophy of History* in Benjamin, 1992, p 247; 'turns to the...', Fanon, 1967, p169; 'very beautiful and..., ibid, p169
[157] 'If you launch...', Rammellzee, Peter Shapiro, *The Wire*, April 1997; 'a reasonable citizen...', Ellison, 1984, p355; 'I'm not a...', Sun Ra, *Fallen Angel* in *Oasis Semiotext[e] Volume IV, Number 3*, 1984, p115; 'It's an inner...', Stockhausen in Nevill, 1989, p18; 'The Impossible is...', Sun Ra, Sleevenote Manifesto from Sun Ra and his Solar Arkestra, 1992
[158] 'The Mothership and...', Ol' Dirty Bastard in Emma Forest, *The Independent*, 5 July, 1996; 'How do you...', *Space Is the Place*; '*Chronicle of Post Soul Black Culture*' in George, 1992, pp1-40; 'a spacite picture...', Sun Ra, Sleevenotes to Sun Ra, 1956
[159] 'In *Brainville*, I...', ibid; 'Earth is already...', Killah Priest from Genius/GZA, 1995;

'INSTRUCTION TO THE...', Sun Ra, Sleevenotes to *Sun Song*, quoted in Lock, 1988, pp14-15; 'We didn't have...', Phil Cohran, Sleevenotes, Sun Ra and his Solar Arkestra, 1992; 'With the aid...', Xenakis, 1974, p144

[160] 'Sonotron: an accelerator of sonorous particles, a disintegrator of sonorous masses, a synthesiser', ibid, p237; 'EssR'ays', from track title *EssR'ay [Reece Mix]*, Reece, 1994; 'Are there any...', *Space is the Place*; 'Multiplicity Adjustment, Readjustment...', ibid; 'Any sufficiently advanced...', Clarke in Haldeman, 1979, p1; 'At the material...', Delany in Dery, 1993, p748

[161] 'In fact, I've...', Sun Ra in Steve Dollar, *Eight Rock Vol 2 No 3*, 1993 p168. 'I am an...', from Sun Ra, Poem, Sun Ra, 1994; 'When the army...', Sun Ra in Wilmer, 1977, p 77

[162] 'Only one thing...', Lewis Mumford, *The Myth of the Machine* in Brockman & Rosenfeld, 1973, p104; 'kao-tic harmony', track title *Kao-Tic Harmony [Relic of Relics]*, Rhythim is Rhythim, 1992

[163] 'Space is a...', Phil Cohran, Sleevenotes, Sun Ra and his Solar Arkestra, 1992; 'I was using...', Tab Hunter, Sleevenotes to Sun Ra and his Myth Science Arkestra, 1992; 'What is the...', *Space is the Place*; 'This music is...', ibid

· Earth Wind and Fire, *I Am*, CBS, 1979
· Genius/GZA: *Basic Instructions Before Leaving Earth* from *Liquid Swords*, Geffen, 1995
· Herbie Hancock, *Thrust*, Warner Brothers, 1974
· Reece: *EssR'ay [Reece Mix]* from *Forces*, Network/KMS 1994
· Rhythim is Rhythim, *Kao-Tic Harmony [Relic of Relics]*, Transmat/Buzz, 1992
· Sun Ra: *Brainville* from *Jazz by Sun Ra/Sun Song*, Delmark, 1956
· Sun Ra, *The Heliocentric World of Sun Ra Vol 2*, ESP, 1965
· Sun Ra: *Astro Black Mythology* from *Astro Black*, Impulse, 1972
· Sun Ra and his Myth Science Arkestra, *Cosmic Tones for Mental Therapy*, Evidence, 1992
· Sun Ra and his Solar Arkestra, *Interstellar Low Ways* (1960), Evidence, 1992
· Sun Ra and his Astro Infinity Arkestra, *My Brother The Wind Volume II*, Evidence, 1992
· Sun Ra and his Myth Science Arkestra, *Fate in a Pleasant Mood/When Sun Comes Out*, Evidence, 1993
· Sun Ra, *I Am an Instrument*, Blast First/Wire Editions, 1994

· Shuzei Nagaoka, Sleeve Art for Earth Wind and Fire, *I Am*, CBS, 1979

· *Alien Nation*, Graham Baker, 1988, 20th Century Fox Home Entertainment
· *Blade Runner*, Ridley Scott, 1982, Warner Home Video
· *Brother from Another Planet*, John Sayles, 1984, Arrow Film Distributors
· *Intolerance*, D. W. Griffiths, 1916, Vision
· *La Jetee*, Chris Marker, 1962, Nouveau Entertainment
· *Night of the Living Dead*, George Romero, 1968, Tartan Video
· *Planet of the Apes*, Franklin J. Shaffner, 1968, 20th Century Fox Home Entertainment
· *The Terminator*, James Cameron, 1984, 4 Front Video
· *Space Is the Place*, Sun Ra and his Intergalactic Solar Arkestra, 1994, Blast First Video

Thoughtware: Cosmology of Volume

[164] 'The audience for...', Julian Schnabel, *Basquiat*; 'It's like rewriting...', Rashied Ali in Wilmer, 1977, p234

[165] 'Ohnedaruth [John Coltrane]...', Alice Coltrane, Sleevenotes to Alice Coltrane, 1971; 'Electric channels of...', Marshall McLuhan in Molinaro, McLuhan & Toye, 1987, p443

[166] 'Cosmic energy – atomic...', Alice Coltrane, Sleevenotes to John Coltrane/Alice Coltrane, 1968; 'Before Ohnedaruth's initiation...', Alice Coltrane, Sleevenote Manifesto to Alice Coltrane, 1972; 'embrace is so...', ibid; 'Andromeda is a...', ibid

[167] 'extraordinary transonic and...', Alice Coltrane, Sleevenotes to Alice Coltrane, 1971; 'embraces cosmic thought...', ibid; 'is reminiscent of...', ibid

[168] 'She is a...', Ameer Baraka‹›Leroi Jones, Sleevenotes to Alice Coltrane, 1968

[169] 'He always felt...', Alice Coltrane, ibid; 'He was doing...' Alice Coltrane, Sleevenotes to Alice Coltrane, 1978; 'I am looking...', John Coltrane in Alice Coltrane, Sleevenotes to Alice Coltrane, 1968; 'I do wish...', Alice Coltrane, 1978

[070] 'Nuclear death gives...', Sylvere Lotringer in Virilio, 1983a, p158; 'plexus of voices...', A. B. Spellman, Sleevenotes to John Coltrane, 1965a; 'Most of the..., Archie Shepp in ibid; 'what the action...', ibid; 'textures rather than...', ibid; 'Coltrane's stress on...,' Sidran, 1995, p148; 'a complex theory...', ibid, p148; 'We're taking them...', ibid, p141

[071] 'We are getting...', ibid, p141; 'an energy field...', ibid, p148; 'Kiyoshi Koyama: What...', Thomas, 1994, p 210; 'When John Coltrane..., Sidran, 1995, p147; 'an instrument which...', ibid, p140; '"I perceived the..."', Coltrane in Thomas, 1994, p215; 'When you trip...', Manuel De Landa in Erik Davis, *Mondo 2000*, Nov 1992

[172] 'And the offerings...', John Coltrane from John Coltrane, 1965c; 'It is the...', Pharaoh Sanders, Sleevenotes to Sanders, 1967; 'The time feeling..., Sidran, 1995, p139

[173] 'So we sang...', Juno Lewis from John Coltrane, 1965b; 'I always thought...', Art Davis in Thomas, 1994, p215; 'a musical one...', Alice Coltrane, Sleevenotes to Alice Coltrane, 1978

[174] 'In all ritual...', Wilmer, 1977, p33; 'AaaHaa, The Case of...', Kirk, 1968 (*Black Mystery*)

- Ornette Coleman, *Free Jazz*, Atlantic, 1960
- Alice Coltrane: *Oceanic Beloved*; *Atomic Peace* from *A Monastic Trio*, Impulse!, 1968
- Alice Coltrane: *Hare Krishna*; *Wars of Armageddon*; *The Ankh of Amen Ra*; *Om Allah*; *Sita Ram* from *Universal Consciousness*, Impulse!, 1971
- Alice Coltrane with Strings: *Galaxy around Olodumare*; *Galaxy in Turiya* and *Galaxy in Satchidananda* from *World Galaxy*, Impulse!, 1971
- Alice Coltrane: *Andromeda's Suffering* from *Lord of Lords*, Impulse!, 1972
- Alice Coltrane, *Transfiguration*, Warner Bros, 1978
- John Coltrane/Alice Coltrane: *The Sun* from *Cosmic Music*, Impulse!, 1968
- John Coltrane, *A Love Supreme*, Impulse!, 1963
- John Coltrane, *Ascension*, Impulse!, 1965a
- John Coltrane, *Kulé Sé Mama*, Impulse!, 1965b
- John Coltrane, *Om*, Impulse!, 1965c
- John Coltrane, *Out of this World* from *Live in Seattle*, Impulse! 1966
- John Coltrane: *Saturn*; *Mars*; *Venus*; *Jupiter* from *Interstellar Space*, Impulse!, 1967
- John Coltrane with String Orchestra arranged and conducted by Alice Coltrane: *Living Space [Alice Coltrane Remix]* from *Infinity*, Impulse!, 1972
- Egyptian Empire, *The Horn*, ffrr, 1992

- Roland Kirk, *Blacknuss*, Atlantic, 1972
- Roland Kirk, *Black Mystery Has Been Revealed* from *Left and Right*, Atlantic, 1968
- Pharoah Sanders: *Capricorn Rising* from *Tauhid*, Impulse!, 1967
- Pharoah Sanders: *The Creator Has a Master Plan*, from *Karma*, Impulse!, 1969
- Pharoah Sanders: *Let Us Go into the House of the Lord*, from *Deaf, Dumb and Blind*, Impulse!/Probe, 1970
- Pharoah Sanders, *Black Unity*, Impulse!, 1971
- Pharoah Sanders, *Hum Allah – Hum Allah, Hum Allah*, Impulse!, 1972
- Pharoah Sanders: *Sun in Aquarius [Part 1 & Part 2]* from *Jewels of Thought*, Impulse! 1973
- Sun Ra, *Astro Black*, Impulse!, 1972
- Bridget Riley, *Phase*, painting, 1962
- *Basquiat*, Julian Schnabel, 1997, Pathe Distribution

DATAMINING THE INFOVERSE

Jerome Agel (ed), *The Making of Kubrick's 2001*, Signet, 1970
Umbrio Appollonio, (ed), *Futurist Manifestos*, Thames and Hudson, 1973
Archigram, *A Guide to Archigram 1961-1974*, Academy Editions
J. G. Ballard, *The Atrocity Exhibition*, Pan, 1970
J. G. Ballard, *Myths of the Near Future*, Vintage, 1994
J. G. Ballard, *A User's Guide to the Millennium*, HarperCollins, 1996
Roland Barthes, *Sade, Fourier, Loyola*, Jonathan Cape, 1977
Jean Baudrillard, *The Gulf War Did Not Take Place*, Power Publications, 1995
Paul Beatty, *The White Boy Shuffle*, Minerva, 1996
Michael Benedikt (ed), *Cyberspace: First Steps*, MIT Press, 1991
Walter Benjamin, *Illuminations*, Fontana Press, 1992
Adrian Boot & Chris Salewicz, *Jimi Hendrix: The Ultimate Experience*, Boxtree, 1995
John Brockman & Ed Rosenfeld (eds), *Real Time*, Picador, 1973
Scott Bukatman, *Terminal Identity*, Duke University Press, 1993
William Burroughs, *The Ticket that Exploded*, Paladin, 1987
Pascal Bussy, *Kraftwerk*, SAF Publishing, 1993
Samuel Butler, *Erewhon*, Heron Books, 1969
Pat Cadigan, *Synners*, HarperCollins, 1991
Karel Capek, *RUR, Rossum's Universal Robots*, Vydalo Aventinium, 1923
Ian Carr, *Miles Davis*, Quartet Books, 1992
Henry Chalfont & Martha Palmer, *Subway Art*, Thames & Hudson, 1984
Henry Chalfont & James Prigoff, *Spray Can Art*, Thames & Hudson, 1987
Michel Chion, *AudioVision*, Columbia University Press, 1994

Arthur C. Clarke, *How the World was One*, Victor Gollancz, 1992

Peter Cook (ed), *Archigram*, Studio Vista, 1972

John Corbett, *Extended Play*, Duke University Press, 1994

Jonathan Cott, *Stockhausen, Conversations with the Composer*, Robson Books, 1974

Jonathan Crary & Sanford Kwinzer (eds), *Zone 6: Incorporations*, Zone Books, 1992

Dennis Crompton (ed), *Concerning Archigram*, Archigram Archives, 1998

Critical Art Ensemble, *The Electronic Disturbance*, Autonomedia, 1994

Salvador Dali, *The Secret Life of Salvador Dali*, Vision Press, 1968

Salvador Dali, *Diary of a Genius*, Creation Books, 1994

Les Daniels, *Marvel: Five Fabulous Decades of the World's Greatest Comics*, Virgin Books, 1991

Les Daniels, *DC Comics: Sixty Years of the Worlds Favorite Comic Book Heroes*, Virgin Books, 1995

Manuel De Landa, *War in the Age of Intelligent Machines*, Zone Books, 1991

Samuel R. Delany, *Dhalgren*, Bantam, 1976

Gilles Deleuze & Felix Guattari, *Anti Oedipus*, Athlone Press, 1984

Gilles Deleuze & Felix Guattari, *A Thousand Plateaux*, University of Minnesota Press, 1987

Gilles Deleuze, *Negotiations*, Columbia University Press, 1990

Mark Dery (ed), *Flame Wars*, Duke University Press, 1993

Mark Dery, *Escape Velocity*, Hodder & Stoughton, 1996

Philip K. Dick, *Valis*, Grafton, 1992

W. E. B. DuBois, *The Souls of Black Folk*, Signet Classic, 1969

Ralph Ellison, *The Invisible Man*, Penguin Books, 1984

Brian Eno, *A Year with Swollen Appendices*, Faber & Faber, 1996

M. C. Escher, *Exploring the Infinite: Escher on Escher* (trans Karin Ford), Harry N. Abrams Inc, 1989

Frantz Fanon, *The Wretched of the Earth*, Penguin, 1967

Gene Feldman & Max Gartenberg (eds), *Protest: The Beat Generation and the Angry Young Men*, Panther, 1960

Michel Foucault, *Language, Counter-Memory, Practice*, Cornell University, 1977

Suzy Gablik, *Brand New York*, ICA Editions, 1982

Hartmut Geerken & Bernhard Hefele, *Omniverse Sun Ra*, Waitawhile, 1994

Nelson George, *The Death of Rhythm and Blues*, Pantheon Books, 1988

Nelson George, *Buppies, B-Boys, Baps & Bohos*, HarperCollins, 1992

William Gibson, *Neuromancer*, Victor Gollancz, 1984

William Gibson, *Virtual Light*, Viking, 1993

Paul Gilroy, *The Black Atlantic*, Verso, 1993

Jean-Luc Godard, *Pierrot le Fou*, Lorimer Publishing, 1969

Felix Guattari, *Chaosmosis*, Power Publications, 1995

Joe Haldeman, *The Forever War*, Futura, 1977

Joe Haldeman, *Star Trek: World Without End*, Bantam, 1979

Donna Haraway, *Simians, Cyborgs and Women*, Routledge, 1991

David Henderson, *'Scuse Me While I Kiss the Sky*, Bantam, 1981

Arthur Jafa, *69* in Michele Wallace (ed), *Black Popular Culture*, Bay Press, 1992

Darius James, *That's Blaxploitation*, St Martins Press, 1995

George M. James, *Stolen Legacy*, Africa World Press, 1992

Allan Jones (ed), *First Among Sequels*, BPC Paperbacks, 1996

Leroi Jones, *Blues People*, Morrow Quill, 1963

Leroi Jones, *Black Music*, Quill, 1967

Charles Keil & Steven Feld, *Music Grooves*, University of Chicago Press, 1994

Kevin Kelly, *Out of Control*, Fourth Estate, 1994

Chris Kempster (ed), *History of House*, Castle Communications, 1996

Richard Kostelanetz (ed), *John Cage*, Allen Lane, 1970

Richard Kostelanetz, *Dictionary of the Avant Garde*, accapella books, 1993

Donna Kurtz, *Kooks*, Feral House, 1995

Michael Kurtz, *Stockhausen* (trans. Richard Toop), Faber & Faber, 1992

Michel Leiris, *Brises: Broken Branches*, North Point Press, 1989

John C. Lily, *Programming and Metaprogramming in the Human Biocomputer*, Bantam
  Books, 1974

Graham Lock, *Forces in Motion*, Quartet Books, 1988

Graham Lock, *Chasing the Vibration*, Stride Publications, 1994

Robin Maconie, *Stockhausen*, OUP, 1976

Larry McCaffery (ed), *Across the Wounded Galaxies*, University of Illinois Press, 1990

Marshall McLuhan, *The Gutenberg Galaxy*, Signet, 1962/1969

Marshall McLuhan, *The Mechanical Bride*, Beacon Press, 1967a

Marshall McLuhan, *Understanding Media*, Sphere Books, 1967b

Marshall McLuhan & Quentin Fiore, *The Medium is the Massage*, Penguin Books, 1967

Marshall McLuhan & Quentin Fiore, *War and Peace in the Global Village*, Bantam Books, 1968

Norman Mailer, *A Fire on the Moon*, Weidenfeld & Nicholson, 1970

Philip Marchand, *Marshall McLuhan*, Ticknor & Fields, 1989

Richard Marshall, *Jean-Michel Basquiat*, Whitney Museum of American Art, 1994

Stephen Metcalf (trans and ed), Friedrich Nietzsche, *Hammer of the Gods*, Creation Books, 1995

Walter Miller, *A Canticle for Leibowitz*, Lippincott, 1960

Matie Molinaro, Corinne McLuhan & William Toye (selec and ed), *Letters of Marshall
  McLuhan*, OUP, 1987

Tim Nevill (ed), *Karlheinz Stockhausen, Towards a Cosmic Music*, Element Books, 1989

Friedrich Nietzsche, *Untimely Meditations*, Cambridge University Press, 1983

o[rphan] d[rift›], *o[rphan] d[rift›]*, Cabinet Editions, 1995

Fernand Ouellette, *Edgard Varèse*, Calder & Boyars, 1973

Yambo Ouologuem, *Bound to Violence*, Heinemann, 1986

Robert Pepperall, *The Post Human Condition*, Intellect Books, 1996

Sadie Plant, *The Virtual Complexity of Culture* in *Future Natural*, Robertson, Mash, Tickner,
  Bird, Curtis & Putnam, (eds), Routledge, 1996

Ishmael Reed, *Flight to Canada*, Atheneum, 1976

Ishmael Reed, *Mumbo Jumbo*, Alison & Busby, 1978

Ishmael Reed, *Neo Hoodoo Manifesto* in Jerome & Diane Rothenberg (eds), *Symposium of
  the Whole*, University of Chicago Press, 1983

Ishmael Reed, *Shrovetide in Old New Orleans*, Atheneum, 1989

Wilhelm Reich, *The Function of the Orgasm*, Bantam Books, 1967

Simon Reynolds, *Blissed Out*, Serpents Tail, 1990

Simon Reynolds & Joy Press, *The Sex Revolts*, Serpents Tail, 1995

Michael Richardson & Kryzystof Fisalkowski (eds and trans), *Refusal of the Shadow*, Verso, 1996

Robertson, Mash, Tickner, Bird, Curtis & Putnam, (eds), *Future Natural*, Routledge, 1996

Cynthia Rose, *Living in America*, Serpents Tail, 1990

Tricia Rose, *Black Noise*, Wesleyan University Press, 1994

Andrew Ross & Tricia Rose, (eds), *Microphone Fiends*, Routledge, 1994
Jerome & Diane Rothenberg (eds), *Symposium of the Whole*, University of California, Press, 1983
Ross Russell, *Bird*, Quartet Books, 1994
Dorion Sagan, *Biospheres*, Arkana, 1990
Jean Paul Sartre, *What Is Literature? and Other Essays*, Harvard University Press, 1988
Susan Sontag, *Against Interpretation*, Vintage, 1994
R. Murray Schafer, *The Tuning of the World*, Alfred A. Knopf, 1977
R. Murray Schafer, *The Music of the Environment* in *Cultures Volume 1 No 1*, UNESCO, 1973
Ben Sidran, *Black Talk*, Payback Press, 1995
Gerald Emanuel Stearn (ed), *McLuhan: Hot and Cool*, Penguin Books, 1968
Bruce Sterling, *Spook* in *Crystal Express*, Legend, 1990
Bruce Sterling, *Schizmatrix*, Penguin, 1995
Bruce Sterling, *Schizmatrix Plus*, Ace Books, 1996
Jay Stevens, *Storming Heaven*, Heinemann, 1987
Julian Stallabrass, *Gargantua*, Verso, 1996
Neil Strauss (ed), *Radiotext(e)*, Semiotext(e), 1993
Roger Sutherland, *New Perspectives in Music*, Sun Tavern Fields, 1994
Greg Tate, *Flyboy in the Buttermilk*, Simon & Shuster, 1992
Greg Tate, *Altered Spade: Readings in Race Mutation Theory* in Andrew Ross & Tricia Rose, (eds), *Microphone Fiends*, Routledge, 1994
Eric Tamm, *Brian Eno, his Music and the Vertical Colour of Sound*, Faber & Faber, 1989
J. C. Thomas, *Chasin' the Trane*, Da Capo, 1994
Caroline Tisdall & Angelo Bozzola, *Futurism*, Thames & Hudson, 1977
Stephen Todd & William Latham, *Evolutionary Art and Computers*, Acadamic Press, 1992
Alvin Toffler, *The Third Wave*, Pan Books, 1980
David Toop, The *Rap Attack*, Pluto Press, 1982/1994
David Toop, *Rap Attack 2*, Serpents Tail, 1991
David Toop, *Ocean of Sound*, Serpents Tail, 1995
Roger Trilling & Stuart Swezey (eds), *The Wild Palms Reader*, St Martins Press, 1993
Amos Tuotola, *My Life in the Bush of Ghosts*, Faber & Faber, 1990
V. Vale & Andrea Juno (eds), *Re/Search 8/9: J. G. Ballard*, Re/Search, 1984
V. Vale & Andrea Juno (eds), *Re/Search 15: Incredibly Strange Music Volume II*, Re/Search, 1994
Rickey Vincent, *Funk*, St Martins Griffin, 1996
Paul Virilio, *Pure War*, Semiotext(e), 1983a
Paul Virilio, *Speed and Politics*, Semiotext(e), 1983b
Paul Virilio, *War and Cinema*, Verso, 1989
Paul Virilio, *The Lost Dimension*, Semiotext(e), 1991
Paul Virilio, *The Vision Machine*, BFI, 1994
Paul Virilio, *The Art of the Motor*, University of Minnesota, 1995
Eric Weisbard with Craig Marks (eds), *Spin Alternative Record Guide*, Vintage Books, 1995
Norbert Wiener, *The Human Use of Human Beings*, Free Association Books, 1989
Valerie Wilmer, *As Serious as Your Life*, Quartet Books, 1977
Jack Womack, *Terraplane*, Grafton Books, 1991
Jack Womack, *Elvissey*, HarperCollins, 1993
Jack Womack, *Random Acts of Senseless Violence*, HarperCollins, 1993
Iannis Xenakis, *Formalised Music*, University of Indiana Press, 1974

Co Pilots: Steve Beard, Edward George, Mark Sinker.

Optimizers: Grandpa, Adelaide Eshun, Joe Eshun, Esi Eshun, Araba Eshun, Ekow Eshun, Helen Boateng, Tony Boateng, Angela Ackun, Sam Mensah, Kwesi Eshun, Thomas Eshun, Janet Karikari, Josephine Eshun.

Accelerators: Sadie Plant, J. G. Ballard, Marshall McLuhan, Simon Reynolds, Greg Tate, Fred Vermorel, Paul Beatty, Archigram (Ron Herron, Warren Chalk, Dennis Crompton, David Greene, Peter Cook, Michael Webb), David Toop, Ian Penman, Chris Marker, Jack Womack, Filipo Marinetti, Giacommo Balla, Umberto Boccioni, Maya Deren, William Gibson, Samuel R. Delany, Yambo Ouologuem, Manuel De Landa, Pat Cadigan, Ben Sidran, Masumune Shirow, Lynn Margulis, Rene Menil, Ilya Prigogine, Arthur Jafa, Isabelle Stengers, Rodney Brooks, O[rphan] D[rift], Neil Kulkarni, Peter Shapiro, Dave Tompkins, Suzanne Cesaire, Samuel Butler, Vera Chytilova, Nic Roeg, Daniel Dennett, Ishmael Reed, Jean-Luc Godard, Michel Chion, Tom Wilson, David Henderson, Geert Lovink, Aime Cesaire, Erik Davis, Bruce Sterling, Jean Michel Basquiat, Robert Rauschenberg, Gilles Deleuze, Frantz Fanon, Felix Guattari, William S. Burroughs, Paul D. Miller, Paul Virilio, Matthew Barney, Colson Whitehead, Bridget Riley, Christof Steinegger, Brian Eno, Nick Land, Francis Bacon, Wong Kar-Wai, Oswald dé Andrade, Leslie Fiedler, The Wire, Wyndham Lewis, Katsuhiro Otomo.

Intensifiers: Ian Sen, Deirdre Crowley, Duke Odiachi, Stella Kane, Jim McClellan, Travis, Jeni Glasgow, Tony Marcus, Matthew Collin, Bethan Cole, Rupert Howe, AnnMarie Davy, Matt ffytche, Melanie Beer, Pippa Moreau, Nadja Abdelkader, Dego McFarlane, John O'Reilly, Sharon Bowes, Black Audio Film Collective (David Lawson, John Akomfrah, Reece Auguiste, Avril Johnson, Lina Gopaul), Orly Klein, Simon Hopkins, Raymond Oaka, Stephen J. Metcalfe, Joy Press, Heiko Hoffmann, Thaddie Hermann, Michael Cornelius, Peter Kruder, Ulf Poschardt, Robert Jelinek, Hans Kulisch, Richard Sen, Lynn Leaver, Dympna Sherry, Mark Fisher, Anne Greenspan, Cybernetic Culture Research Unit, Richard Thompson, Viv Boyd, Elaine O'Donoghue, Olywn Doran, Helen Leary, Helen Mills, Martin Takawira, Gideon Hollis, Adele Yaron, Kevin Martin, Rob Bulman, Sean 'P-Ski' Pennycook, Howard Hageman, Adrian 'Blunt' Hughes, Hector Heathcote, Mick Kirkman.

In Memoriam: Michelle Stavrino

C[222]